1691

A Novel

Joe Joyce

First published by Cove Books in 2020
7 Ballygihen Avenue
Sandycove
County Dublin

ISBN (paperback): 978-1-9162951-1-7
ISBN (ebook): 978-1-9162951-2-4

Cover design and maps by Karen Vaughan

Joe Joyce grew up in Aughrim, County Galway where his father, the local headmaster, collected artefacts from the nearby battlefield in a museum in his school. He is the author of five thrillers including *Echoland*, a historical spy thriller which was the choice of Dublin city library's annual One City One Book festival in 2017. He is also the author and co-author of three non-fiction books and a play. He worked previously for *The Irish Times*, *The Guardian* and Reuters news agency.

Also by Joe Joyce

Novels

Echowave
Echobeat
Echoland
The Trigger Man
Off The Record

Non-Fiction

The Guinnesses
Blind Justice
(with Peter Murtagh)
The Boss: Charles J Haughey in Government
(with Peter Murtagh)

Plays

The Tower

www.joe joyce.ie

The place where this Battle was fought [Aughrim] will make a noise in
History for the future

--Reverend George Story
A Continuation of the Impartial History of the Wars of Ireland (1693)

Chance, skill and treachery all hit the mark
Just when the sun's rod tipped the altar hill

--Richard Murphy
The Battle of Aughrim (1966)

Contents

1691

It is the third year of the war, the war to control Ireland, Scotland, England and Wales; the war to control western Europe; the war between rival versions of Christianity. The war that will cast a shadow over Ireland for centuries to come.

This war has come towards the end of a turbulent century in Ireland as elsewhere. There have been plantations, rebellions, massacres, seizures of property, civil wars and switching allegiances. Keeping your head has, literally, not been easy and securing your family fortunes -- if you are fortunate enough to have enough land to constitute one -- even more difficult. Faith and righteousness stalk the land: everyone believes they have them on their side.

King James II, latest head of the Stuart dynasty, is trying to win back the kingdoms he lost when his nephew and son-in-law, Prince William III of Orange, *stadtholder* of the Dutch Republic, seized his throne in 1688 in a near bloodless invasion of England encouraged by Protestant parliamentarians. Fearing a Catholic revival after the birth of James's first official son they invited William and his wife Mary, James's eldest daughter, to jointly rule them.

In the fervid English atmosphere of the time -- a time of Popish plots and lurid stories that the new-born prince was really the son of a Jesuit smuggled into the queen's bed in a warming pan -- the Protestant plotters have presented James's decision to flee the country as an abdication. And the legitimate successor in their eyes is not his infant son but his Protestant daughter Mary whom they have jointly crowned monarch with her husband William.

James has found refuge with his cousin, Louis XIV, the 'sun king' of France and the most powerful monarch in Europe. Louis is at war with all his neighbours -- led by William – in an attempt to push out his kingdom's boundaries. Two years ago, in the spring of 1689, James landed in loyal Ireland as a first step to seizing back Scotland and then England with Louis' encouragement and assistance.

With its Catholic population of 'old Irish' and 'old English' (Norman families who have been in the country for up to 500 years), Ireland sees James as the legitimate king and William as the usurper. Under James's rule, Catholics have taken back power from Protestants in Ireland and an offer of self-determination as well as religious freedom is before a new Irish, Catholic, parliament.

But the English and Scottish Protestant settlers of Ulster, notably of Londonderry and Enniskillen, held out against James, stymieing his efforts to take total control of the country and creating the space for William to land at Carrickfergus last year and lead his expeditionary army to victory at the River Boyne. However, William subsequently failed to deliver the *coup de grâce* at Limerick, leaving James's army in control of the lands west of the River Shannon.

The two kings have now left Ireland, James to France after the battle of the Boyne, William to England en route to the Netherlands after his failure to take Limerick. Their armies are designated as Jacobites and Williamites, more loosely and less accurately as Irish and English, and are now facing into a new campaign.

Both armies can put similar-sized forces into action although the Williamites are more numerous, more experienced and better supplied. Both include officers and men, Irish, Scottish and English, who had served together in James's forces and divided over William's invasion of England, and mostly, although not always, over religion. The Jacobites are predominantly Irish but have English and Scottish officers and men in their ranks. French reinforcements active in the previous year have returned home. A French general and more supplies promised by King Louis are now awaited for this, the third year of the war.

The Williamites are a polyglot force: perhaps half are English recruits and the remainder include Irish Protestants and experienced troops from the Netherlands and Denmark, as well as Huguenots, the Calvinists exiled from their French homeland. They are led mainly by continental officers from Holland, Germany and France, as well as England and Scotland. They now control, to a greater or lesser extent, most of Ireland, except for Connacht and the western parts of Munster. An area of perhaps ten miles to the east of the River Shannon is a no-man's land, roamed by patrols from both sides, and denuded of its population.

This war is not just the headline events that will go down in history: the siege of Londonderry, the battle of the Boyne, the siege of Limerick. It has also been fought in hundreds of small engagements, ambushes, raids, running battles, all leaving a few dead and maimed on a weekly and sometimes daily basis. Bands of rapparees -- made up of the dispossessed, deserters, bandits -- also roam the countryside, living off their wits and what they can seize.

The Williamites are led by **Godard van Reede, Baron de Ginckel**, a Dutch cavalry officer, now approaching his 47th birthday. He has been in the Dutch army since he was twelve, was with William during the invasion of England, and came to Ireland with his expeditionary force. He commanded a section of Dutch cavalry during the battle of the Boyne. His elevation to general and commander last autumn was widely seen as a stop-gap appointment until a more experienced and inspirational general could be selected for this year's campaign. But William has left him in command.

Hugh Mackay is a native of Scourie in the Scottish Highlands where he inherited his father's estate after his two elder brothers were murdered in separate incidents. He has had a varied military career in King James's army, seconded at times to the French, Venetian, and Dutch forces. While billeted in Holland, he married a daughter of the family, Clara de Bie, and because of that and his devout Protestantism transferred his allegiance from James to William. He led the English and Scots divisions ashore during William's invasion of England. Then sent to pacify Scotland he was defeated at the battle of Killiecrankie two years ago but successfully ground down the Jacobite resistance in Scotland last year. Now aged 50 or so, he is sent to join William's army in Ireland.

Thomas Talmash (also known as Tollemache) has also just arrived in Ireland. Aged about 40, he has served in the English army on the Continent and in Tangier against the Moors. He has twice lost his commissions, once for duelling, and, secondly, in voluntary protest at the admission of Catholics into the army after James became king. A member of the Treason Club, which conspired to have William seize the English throne, he accompanied him during the invasion of England and fought in Flanders last year against Louis' French forces. His mother, Lady Elizabeth Murray, although a royalist conspirator, was rumoured to be Cromwell's mistress. He himself never married but he has a son, Tom, who is also in the army.

Henri de Massue, Marquis de Ruvigny, is another new arrival in Ireland. A French nobleman, he had gone from the French army into diplomacy and become the representative of the Huguenots at the court of Louis XIV. However, he moved to England after Louis revoked the Edict of Nantes six years ago, removing the rights of Protestants in France and forcing them to convert to Catholicism or flee the country. Now aged 43, Ruvigny has gone back to soldiering and has accepted a position as major-general in William's forces in Ireland this year. He commands a cavalry regiment.

Ferdinand Willem, the Duke of Württemberg-Neuenstadt, is a German nobleman in his early thirties who has spent more than half his life in the Danish army and commands its forces in Ireland since last year. He has fought against the Swedes and in Austria and Hungary against the Turks, suffering a serious head wound six years ago that will eventually kill him. His younger brother, Carl Rudolf, eight years his junior, is also with the Danish contingent, which is itself a polyglot force that includes Danes, Germans, French, Poles and even a few Irish and Scots.

On the Jacobite side the dominant figure is **Richard Talbot, Duke of Tyrconnell**, King James's viceroy in Ireland. Known as 'Fighting Dick', he has had a highly eventful career though now slowed by age and illness; he is in his early sixties. The youngest son of a large family of Norman descent, he was a cavalry officer during the siege of Drogheda in 1649 and so badly wounded he was left for dead. He escaped to Spain, volunteered to assassinate Cromwell in London, was captured there and interrogated by Cromwell himself. Facing torture and probable execution, he got his guards drunk, escaped, and made his way to Flanders where the Stuart monarch, Charles II, was in exile. He became a close friend of Charles' brother, James, fought a duel to secure

13

command of his regiment and returned to England with James when the monarchy was restored in 1660.

He quickly became a controversial courtier, accused of bribery and corruption for helping Irish families secure the return of lands seized by Cromwell, and of being a pimp for arranging James's many extra-marital affairs. Outrage at his activities -- which made him very rich -- led to his arrest and imprisonment in the Tower of London for two brief periods. Accused by Titus Oates, author of the Popish plot, of planning a military uprising, he was later jailed in Dublin Castle but was allowed to go into exile in France.

James's accession to the throne in 1685 brought him back to command the army in Ireland and earned him even greater political power. He set about removing Protestants from the army, ensuring that Catholic judges controlled the courts, and preparing the ground for a Catholic parliament. At the Boyne last year he commanded the force facing the main Williamite attack at Oldbridge, fought bravely but favoured negotiations after the defeat.

His second wife, the English Frances Jennings, is sister of Sarah Churchill, wife of John Churchill, the military commander whose defection to William of Orange helped his invasion of England to succeed. Talbot has two daughters from his first marriage and several illegitimate children, including a son Mark who is in the army.

Patrick Sarsfield has just been appointed a major general and given the title Earl of Lucan by James. He straddles the often uneasy alliance between the 'old Irish' and 'old English', of Norman descent on his father's side and Irish descent on his mother's. In his mid-thirties, he has been a soldier for most of his life, apart from a period when he was expelled from the army in England for being a Catholic, before he was reinstated under King James. In between, he led a dissolute life in London and spent time in the French army. Back in the English army he served under John Churchill and was clubbed from his horse and presumed dead during the abortive Monmouth rebellion against James's reign six years ago. He led the only significant (and unsuccessful) military resistance to William's invasion of England at Wincanton in Somerset. Exiled to France, he returned to Ireland with James two years ago and has been actively involved in the war since then, seizing Sligo and, notably, destroying the enemy's supplies last year at Ballyneety which forced William to call off the siege at Limerick. Since his return to Ireland, he has married 15-year-old Honor Burke, daughter of Lord Clanricarde and sister and half-sister of several officers.

Henry Luttrell is a cavalry colonel and close friend and adviser to Sarsfield. A few years older than him, he too has been a career soldier, serving at first with the French army and then with the English army after James's accession to the throne. He was at Wincanton, exiled to Paris, and came back to Ireland with James and Sarsfield where they were both involved in seizing Sligo. Luttrell became governor of the town for a time. An outspoken opponent of Tyrconnell, he was one of a delegation that went to Paris last autumn to persuade James to remove him but was outwitted by Tyrconnell. His older brother Simon was governor of Dublin during the period of Catholic hegemony and accompanied Henry to Paris on his mission to have Tyrconnell removed, although he is married to Tyrconnell's (Protestant) niece, Katherine Newcomen.

Charles O'Kelly is one of the 'old Irish' aristocracy. He was educated in St Omer in the Spanish Netherlands and became a proficient linguist. Returning to Ireland in his early twenties in time for the mid-century wars he fought against Cromwell and went into exile with Charles II to France and subsequently Spain. With the restoration of the Stuarts, he travelled to England and succeeded his father, who had successfully reclaimed the family lands in Galway and Roscommon. When this war started, he volunteered, at the age of 68, for James's army and was given the rank of colonel but mainly in a staff rather than a command role.

He was active in the Sligo area and seized the town along with Sarsfield and Luttrell and was thereafter high sheriff of County Roscommon.

John Wauchope is a relative of a landed Scottish royalist family who was in the English army in Holland where he was wounded and subsequently succeeded Hugh Mackay as colonel of a regiment. While there, he had an affair with Betty Villiers, William's mistress, and killed a fellow officer in unclear circumstances, presumably in a duel. The killing required a pardon from King James before he could return to Scotland, where he raised a regiment but fled to France after William's invasion. In Ireland, he commanded the artillery during the siege of Derry and was among those at the Boyne who were successfully diverted away from the main Williamite attack. He is now a brigadier in charge of infantry and an ally of Sarsfield's.

Charles Chalmont, Marquis de Saint-Ruhe, is a French general on his way to Ireland to take command of the Jacobite forces. He has earned a reputation at home for his determined persecutions of Protestants during the *dragonnades*, the policy of billeting unruly troops on their homes which preceded the formal removal of their rights some six years ago. He has fought against Savoy in northern Italy after it joined in the Grand Alliance against France, leading Irish troops who had gone there in return for the French troops who came to Ireland. In his early forties, he is married to a widowed duchess, Maire de Cossé, who is more than 25 years his senior.

With him on his way to Ireland are two lieutenant generals, **Jean de Bonnac, Marquis d'Usson**, and **Philibert-Emmanuel de Froulay**, *le chevalier de* **Tessé**. D'Usson is a career soldier and convert to Catholicism from Protestantism and has been colonel of an infantry regiment. Tessé comes from a military family and has fought as a commander of dragoons in Germany and Flanders during the current war against the Grand Alliance along France's borders.

16

It is now early summer in this the third year of the war. It has been another harsh winter -- northern Europe is still suffering the 'little Ice Age' -- although Ireland has been less affected than the neighbouring island and the Continent. Growth has returned to the land, which means there is grass for the thousands and thousands of horses required to move an army. And that large-scale military actions can resume on the front lines left over from last year.

WILLIAMITE
CAMPAIGN
1691

Derry

Antrim

Donegal

Belfast

Enniskillen

Armagh

Sligo

Newry

Cavan

Dundalk

Lanesborough

Navan

LOUGH REE

Ballymore

Ballinasloe

Mullingar

Athenry

Athlone

Galway

Tullamore

Dublin

Aughrim

Banagher

LOUGH DERG

Nenagh

Clare

Ennis

Killaloe

Kilrush

Limerick

Cashel

Kilkenny

RIVER SHANNON

Clonmel

Tralee

Mallow

Killarney

Cork

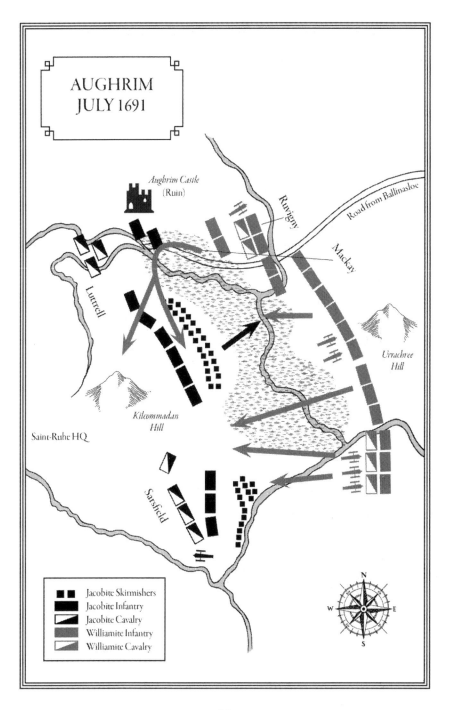

AUGHRIM
JULY 1691

Aughrim Castle
(Ruin)

Ravigny

Road from Ballinasloe

Mackay

Luttrell

Urrachree
Hill

Kilcommadan
Hill

Saint-Ruhe HQ

Sarsfield

N
W   E
S

Jacobite Skirmishers
Jacobite Infantry
Jacobite Cavalry
Williamite Infantry
Williamite Cavalry

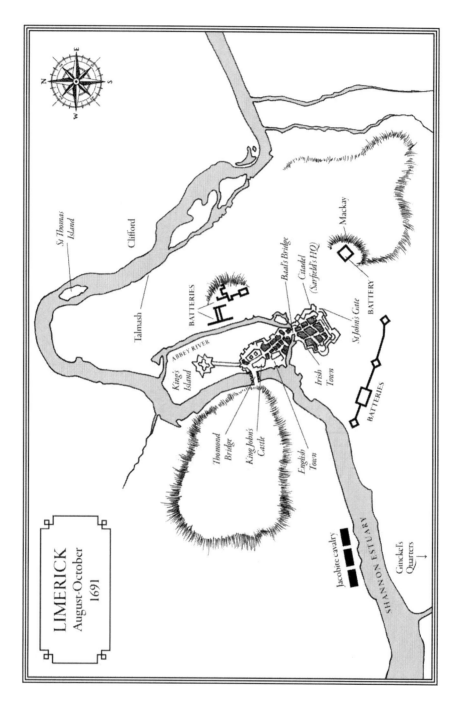

LIMERICK
August-October
1691

N E S W

St Thomas Island

Clifford

Talmash

BATTERIES

King's Island

ABBEY RIVER

Thomond Bridge

King John's Castle

English Town

Baal's Bridge

Citadel (Sarsfield's HQ)

Irish Town

St John's Gate

BATTERY

Mackay

BATTERY

BATTERIES

Jacobite cavalry

SHANNON ESTUARY

Ginckel's Quarters

MAY

Sarsfield

A scatter of scared crows squawked in the sky, upset by the boom of the welcoming cannon. They began to settle back on the towers of the castle as Major General Patrick Sarsfield strode down Great Street towards the harbour at the head of his entourage. A group of small boys raced out of a lane to catch up with him, their dirty faces pale and pinched after the winter. They fell into step alongside, stretching their bare-footed strides to try and match his cavalry-booted ones.

'*Tá siad annseo*,' one of the cheekier boys said.

Sarsfield gave him a 'tell me something I don't know' glance.

'We'll beat the rebels now,' the boy continued in Irish.

'Of course we will,' Sarsfield said.

They wheeled right by St Mary's cathedral, down to the harbour. A fresh breeze blew up the river from the estuary, bringing with it the promise of summer's warmth as well as the new beginning of the French fleet's arrival. A frigate flying the white ensign of the kingdom of France was moored at the quay, its crew lined up on deck above the cannon portholes on either side of a gangway sloping ashore.

A second frigate was coming in between the harbour's pincer

mouth, its crew on the yardarms beginning to roll up its sails as its momentum carried it towards its berth. A cannon at one side of the pincer fired another welcoming blank and the breeze blew away the cloud of grey smoke with casual ease. Away to the right the crows rose into the sky again with raucous complaints.

Sarsfield and his entourage stopped twenty yards short of the gangway and waited. He stood a head taller than most of his subordinates, his wide-brimmed hat exaggerating his height. The dark ringlets of his wig hung down to his shoulders, framing his narrow face and dark, searching eyes. A shoulder belt held a sword on his left hip and he wore a three-quarter-length red tunic with a white band around his neck creating a loose cravat.

One of his followers shooed away the boys with a swish of his scabbard and they retreated to stand in front of a group of the townspeople silently watching the second frigate coast up to the quayside. Two more ships approached the mouth of the harbour and the tops of the masts of more were visible, like a flight of falling stairs, over the flat land where the river turned towards the Atlantic.

'Where's Lying Dick?' one of the officers behind Sarsfield muttered.

'Trying to find four men strong enough to carry his sedan chair down the hill,' another sniggered.

A chuckle of derision rippled behind him like a physical movement.

'Or to carry it back up again,' the first officer shot back, adding momentum to the derision.

'Not now,' Sarsfield ordered from the side of his mouth and the ripple died away.

He wasn't in the mood for their banter. Today was a critical day but not the kind of critical day he relished. Not a fighting day. A political day. A lot of questions would be answered, uncertainties cleared up. For good or ill.

The absence of Richard Talbot from the quayside would

24

confirm to the French general what he should already know. That he, Sarsfield, was the true leader of King James's forces in Ireland, not the viceroy, Talbot, the Duke of Tyrconnell. First blood to me, he thought. But this stage in the long duel was just beginning.

The French were well aware of the differences between Sarsfield and Talbot. Both sides had sent their emissaries to King James's emigrant court in Saint-Germain-en-Laye over the winter to lobby him and King Louis. In Sarsfield's and the army's case, to make sure James and the French supported a continuation of the war: in Talbot's, case, to suggest they do a deal with the prince of Orange while they remained undefeated.

As usual, James had dithered, leaving Talbot as viceroy in charge of Jacobite Ireland and trying to appease Sarsfield with promotion and an earldom. The French, too, had offered a compromise: a new general to lead the Jacobite forces in Ireland and more supplies. But no more troops to replace those that General Lauzun had taken back to France at the end of the previous year's disastrous campaign.

The arrogant and impatient Lauzun was no loss, Sarsfield thought. Couldn't wait for the war to end and get back to France. Wanted to surrender Limerick without a fight. But they'd shown him. The only thing in Lauzun's favour was that he did not get on with Talbot, although their policies were much the same.

Sarsfield knew nothing about this new general, had never come across him in person or by reputation during his own service on the Continent. Which suggested that he was probably a second ranker or an ambitious newcomer, out to make his name at the expense of the Irish.

A group of French officers came down the gangway of the first frigate and formed a passageway. Then Charles Chalmont, the Marquis de Saint-Ruhe, appeared, in the blue uniform of France and the regalia of a general. He paused when he stepped onto the quay, a tall, well-built figure, and looked from right to left at the people standing around. Then he fixed his attention on Sarsfield.

25

'God save us,' an officer said in Irish behind Sarsfield, not bothering to lower his voice, 'that's the ugliest looking general I've ever seen.'

It's true, Sarsfield thought as he stepped forward. Saint-Ruhe had a lopsided face, its features at odds with one another. The face seemed to be undecided whether it was round or oval, creating a misshapen effect, with small eyes over an outsize nose and a thin mouth pushed into a pout by protruding upper teeth. He was in his early forties, some five or six years older than Sarsfield, and beginning to put on weight.

'*Mon général*,' Sarsfield doffed his hat and bowed his head. '*Maréchal de camp Sarsfield. Bienvenue à Limerick. Bienvenue en Irlande.*'

Saint-Ruhe acknowledged the welcome with a nod. '*Où est le vice-roi? Le duc de Tyrconnell?*'

'Waiting to greet you in the city, General.'

Over Saint-Ruhe's shoulder Sarsfield saw Henry Luttrell and Nicholas Purcell, his emissaries to the kings, coming down the gangplank from the second frigate, and part of him relaxed. It had not been at all certain that they would be allowed back to Ireland: Tyrconnell had wanted them kept in Paris, locked up in the Bastille. Luttrell caught Sarsfield's eye and gave him a broad wink.

Saint-Ruhe indicated with a short hand gesture that Sarsfield should lead on. Sarsfield turned and they went up the incline to Great Street and began to climb the hill. The French group followed, led by two more generals, one thin, the other portly, and then Sarsfield's entourage. Townspeople bowed their heads as they passed, as though it was a royal procession.

'How was the voyage, *mon général*?'

'Long,' Saint-Ruhe said, noting the houses, most of stone, some of timber-framed cagework, the slate roofs, the trickle of urine running down the hill. He glanced down a side street, taking in the muck, the wattle walls, the thatched roofs, the holes for chimneys. And the people standing silently at the corners in ragged clothes and barefooted.

Sarsfield's first impression of Saint-Ruhe was not what he had expected. He didn't appear to have the usual manners of French generals, the arrogance perhaps but none of the foppishness that usually went with it. He seemed to be curt to the point of rudeness, interested only in business. Which was all right with him.

'How is the army?' Saint-Ruhe asked, confirming Sarsfield's assessment of him.

'In need of everything,' Sarsfield said truthfully: there was no point pretending otherwise. 'Arms, ammunition, training. Supplies of all kinds. But the feeling is positive.'

'How many men?'

'Thirty thousand.'

'Armed?'

'Half of them.'

'Horse?'

'Seven thousand, including dragoons.' Dragoons were the troops who moved on horseback but fought on foot.

'How soon can we move?'

Sarsfield hesitated. There was no point in giving false encouragement. 'That depends,' he said, 'on what you have brought us.'

'Tessé will give you the details.'

The groups of onlookers were replaced by a line of infantry on either side of the street as they neared the top of the hill, their red uniforms neat and spotless, their flintlocks the most up to date. As if to contradict what I've just said, Sarsfield thought. But these men were the exceptions, Tyrconnell putting on a display.

Tyrconnell himself waited on the brow of the hill, an obese figure dressed in his formal robes, a red cloak fringed with ermine overall, a blue riband crossing his huge body from his left shoulder to his right hip. His left hand rested on the hilt of his

27

sword, his right hung down by his side, half hidden by the draped lace cuff of his shirt. Behind him were the civil administration, the attorney general, Sir Richard Nagle, the lord chancellor, Lord Gawsworth, the commissioner of revenue, Francis Plowden, and a plethora of lesser officials.

Saint-Ruhe halted before Tyrconnell and gave a small bow. Sarsfield introduced them, watching their reactions closely. They haven't met before, he decided as they exchanged formalities in French, each weighing up the other. But that didn't tell him what he really wanted to know: which of these two men was in ultimate command of the army.

They moved back towards the French officers' quarters and Tyrconnell's men closed around the party, cutting off Sarsfield and his entourage.

'A good day's work,' Major General Thomas Maxwell said in his Scot's burr as he moved ahead of Sarsfield.

Sarsfield didn't respond, not sure what Maxwell meant but knowing that whatever he meant was not complimentary to him. Maxwell was one of Tyrconnell's men.

'What did he say?' Colonel Henry Luttrell appeared at Sarsfield's shoulder, ready to take offence.

'Nothing.' Sarsfield turned to him, putting his hands on his shoulders. 'You got back safely.'

But Luttrell was still looking after Maxwell, a scowl on his broad face. 'We should have thrown him overboard when we had the chance,' he said. Maxwell had gone to France on the same ship the previous year but on a different mission: to make Tyrconnell's case to the kings. And he had managed to get from Brest to Paris ahead of Luttrell and Sarsfield's emissaries and to present his case to the kings before them. 'I wanted to drown him before we cleared the coast but the bishop and my soft-hearted brother wouldn't let me. Damned prelates,' he added as if his older brother, Simon, the governor of Dublin before the loss at the Boyne, was a bishop too.

'He didn't come back with you?' Sarsfield looked over his shoulder as if he expected to see Simon Luttrell trudging up the hill.

Luttrell shook his head. 'I think he prefers the life at court to the life of action. Not like us.'

'You'd prefer the life at court too. All those conspiracies.'

Luttrell stepped back as if shocked at the thought. 'Me? Conspiracies?' His broad face tried and failed to express surprise and he broke into a knowing laugh. 'You misunderstand me, my lord Lucan.'

Sarsfield caught the hint of something – was it sarcasm? – in Luttrell's use of his new title.

'My lord Lucan,' Luttrell repeated, holding his head to one side, as if he was trying out the sound of it, testing a note on a violin. 'Yes,' he nodded with satisfaction. 'It suits you.'

Sarsfield clapped him on both shoulders. 'It's good to see you.'

'I trust you haven't done anything foolish in my absence.' Luttrell narrowed his eyes, converting the statement into a question. 'That your title hasn't turned your head?'

'Mind your manners, Colonel,' Sarsfield snapped back, stiffening his posture. 'That's no way to talk to a *maréchal de camp*.'

'You jest, of course,' Luttrell said with more assurance than the flicker of doubt on his face indicated. He liked to think that he was inscrutable but, like many who delighted in intrigue, his face often signalled his true feelings ahead of his words.

'Of course.' Sarsfield relaxed. 'He's been acting as if we are comrades in arms now. As if we are the best of friends.' There was no need to spell out who 'he' was. Tyrconnell.

'But you've not been fooled.'

'I've not been fooled,' Sarsfield agreed. 'I know he hasn't changed his mind. That he wants to seek negotiations with the rebels.'

'But the fight's not yet over,' Luttrell prompted, making sure that Sarsfield's resolve hadn't weakened in his absence.

'It's far from over,' Sarsfield agreed, moving after the departing crowd. 'We'll talk later. You can tell me all about our new general.'

'Ah, the gossip.' Luttrell laughed.

'All of it.'

Luttrell stayed where he was, watching Sarsfield go. Colonel Nicholas Purcell, his fellow emissary and traveller from France, joined him. 'All well?' he asked.

'All is well,' Luttrell confirmed. Their man hadn't lost his resolve in their absence.

The banquet for the French went on for hours, course after course of soup, salmon, lamb and beef, bottle after bottle of Madeira wine and then Tyrconnell's current favourite tipple, ratafia, brandy mixed wth crushed apricot stones. The conversation was in French; courteous, formal, cautious, getting to know each other. Tyrconnell and Saint-Ruhe sat at the head of the table, Tyrconnell doing most of the talking.

Sarsfield was beside *le chevalier de* Tessé, Saint-Ruhe's lieutenant-general and second in command: he was also a *maréchal de camp* but the French bumped their officers up a rank when they served in Ireland. On the other side of Tessé was the English cavalry officer, Major-General Dominic Sheldon. Across the table from them the Scottish major-general, Thomas Maxwell, engaged in conversation with the other French lieutenant-general, the Marquis d'Usson.

Earlier, the general staff had toured the town, showing the Frenchmen the layout of Englishtown on King's Island and crossing into Irishtown by Baal's bridge over the channel of the river that created the island. Sarsfield had pointed out where the enemy forces had breached the wall during the previous year's siege but had been driven back and eventually forced to withdraw after he had blown up their powder and cannons at Ballyneety.

'It was a great achievement,' d'Usson said, examining with a practised eye the walls that had been built for the era of arrows and ladders rather than siege guns. A short barrel of a man, his job in Ireland was primarily defensive, to protect the main towns still in Jacobite hands: Limerick, Athlone, Galway and Sligo.

'One of your engineers has been making improvements,' Sarsfield said, pointing along the wall to where some workmen were tipping earth over it to build up the sloping glacis outside, designed to absorb cannon fire and make attackers easier targets for the defenders. 'If the prince of Orange tries again, he won't succeed.'

D'Usson nodded his approval.

Back in Englishtown, they passed by the harbour where the first of the supply ships was being unloaded, barrels and crates beginning to pile up on the quay.

'The general has asked that all available wagons be provided to distribute the supplies,' Tessé said, reaching into an inside pocket to withdraw a sheaf of paper.

Sarsfield took it and glanced down at the list: 51 supply ships along with the 34 men-of-war; thousands of *justaucorps*, the grey, three-quarter-length French infantry coats, and other uniforms; thousands of barrels of gunpowder and boxes of musket and cannonballs; tons of wheat and biscuits; barrels of wine and crates of brandy; hundreds of saddles and tents.

'How do you supply Athlone?' Tessé was asking.

'By land and river.'

'How many boats?'

'Six.'

'Six?' Tessé gave him an incredulous look. 'Does the enemy control the east bank of the river?'

Sarsfield shook his head. 'He drew well back after last year's siege. And we've patrolled the land since. There's nothing there but a couple of our outposts.'

Both sides had raided and foraged the area so frequently over the winter that the land was laid waste, the animals rounded up and taken away, the country people left to fend for themselves as best they could. The young and fit men joined bands of rapparees in the hills, raiding the areas to the east and south controlled by the Williamites. Most of the rest of the population had fled wherever they could but refuge from the winter's cold and wet was not easily found. They were not welcome in Williamite areas and the Jacobites turned them back from the Shannon crossings: neither army wanted more mouths to feed.

The dismal cold and wet of the winter seemed far away now at a banquet table cluttered with food and drink. They had finished eating, pipes were out and the tobacco smoke was beginning to cloud the chandeliers.

'The modern army,' Tessé was saying, concluding a lecture on the military prowess of France, 'will be a fully professional army. No more so-called colonels raising a company of their peasants to pretend they are soldiers.'

'And claiming payment for them even after they've gone again,' Sheldon chipped in.

'Exactly,' Tessé nodded.

'Or not bothering to pay the soldiers what the king is paying them per man,' Sarsfield added. Like some I know, he thought, but didn't say.

'A full-time, professional army. No amateurs. No militias. No mercenaries.' Tessé said. 'Fully trained. Like the Irishmen who have joined the army in France under my lord Mountcashel.'

Sarsfield nodded. As a lifelong professional soldier, he agreed fully with the pattern the French had set. The proof was there to be seen: France was by far the most powerful military force in Europe. And the thousands of raw recruits who had gone to France the year before in return for the trained French troops who had been sent to Ireland had performed wonders there. Or so their commander and his friend Justin McCarthy, Lord Mountcashel, had written to him.

'And the army should be able to do its duty without the interference of court intrigues,' he said.

'*Évidemment*,' Tessé said, casting him a suspicious look which belied his agreement. Tessé was more like what Sarsfield had expected in a French general: well-bred, haughty, secure in his own superiority. And from a world where criticism of the court and its intrigues could mark one out as suspect.

'I hope that will be the case with General Saint-Ruhe,' Sarsfield added. 'That he will be able to make all the military decisions.'

Tessé gave him a questioning look, not sure now whether he was questioning the general's competence.

'I mean that I hope he will be the commander in chief,' Sarsfield indicated Tyrconnell with a backward movement of his head. 'And not have to answer to anyone else.'

Tessé gave him a small smile, catching his meaning. 'You can rest assured that that is so. It has been clarified in Paris. The general will make all military decisions. Another will deal only with civilian matters.'

'I am very pleased to hear that,' Sarsfield said, noting the concentration on Maxwell's face across the table as he strove to hear the exchange. He was aware, unlike Tessé, of the nuances behind it and all the internal disputes since the Boyne disaster. He'll be reporting back to Tyrconnell, Sarsfield thought. But Tyrconnell will surely have learned already that command of the army had been taken from him and given to the ugly Frenchman. Sarsfield resisted the temptation to give Maxwell a victorious smile.

A sound from the top table took their attention and they watched Tyrconnell struggle to his feet, leaning heavily on the table. He had to wait a moment to catch his breath and then lifted his glass. 'A toast, gentlemen.' Everybody stood and took their glasses.

'*Le roi Louis*,' Tyrconnell raised his glass and drank. Everyone followed suit.

'*Le roi Jacques*,' he added, and they toasted again.

Tyrconnell lowered himself into his outsize chair and the buzz of conversation resumed. Sarsfield glanced at him and the viceroy caught his eye. He had his glass halfway to his lips and tipped it towards Sarsfield in a gesture of recognition. Sarsfield gave him a small nod in return. He knows his place now, he thought with satisfaction. As long as he stays in it.

Sarsfield walked down Great Street in the dark to the lord mayor's old tower house, feeling mellow from the warmth of the brandy. One of the pikemen at the gate told him Colonels Luttrell and Purcell were inside, waiting for him. He climbed the spiral stone stairs to the first floor, hearing laughter coming from the room ahead of him.

Henry Luttrell and Nicholas Purcell were seated across from each other at the heavy oak table, an empty port bottle between two candlesticks, half-full glasses in front of them. They both looked up with grins wide and lopsided enough to suggest that the bottle had not been their first.

'Who let in you reprobates?' Sarsfield said, softening the words with a smile.

'The lovely Lady Honor.' Luttrell slurred a little, pulling out the chair beside him as if he was the host. He reached under the table and took a fresh bottle from a bag. 'Get yourself a glass.'

Sarsfield took a glass from a cabinet and sat down. 'I hope you weren't drunk then,' he said, holding out his glass for Luttrell to pour the port. Honor Burke was Sarsfield's young wife, still in her mid-teens and more than half his age. 'And that you didn't upset her.'

'Upset   her?'   Purcell   bristled   with   a   drunk's argumentativeness. 'How would we upset her?'

'With rough talk or the like.'

'Of course not,' Purcell said. 'She's looking forward to going to

Saint-Germain.'

'She said that?' Sarsfield glanced at him. Honor had mentioned something in passing about life at King James's court but he had thought nothing of it. A passing curiosity.

Purcell nodded. 'She's going back with the French convoy.'

'What?' Sarsfield said, an exclamation of surprise rather than a question. He didn't know that was what Honor wanted to do and certainly hadn't approved her imminent departure for France.

Luttrell looked from one to the other. 'You don't think it's a good idea?'

Sarsfield shook his head: it was certainly not a good idea. He knew all too well what a beautiful young woman like Honor would face in Paris: the flattery of rival suitors, the competition to be the first to seduce her. 'Saint-Germain is a long way from Portumna Castle,' he said drily.

'She'll be there in two or three weeks,' Purcell said, adrift in his own world, taking Sarsfield's words literally. 'Even quicker with favourable winds.'

'She'd settle in easily there,' Luttrell offered, wondering if Sarsfield was being protective or jealous. Was he concerned about her lack of experience of the intrigues of court life? Or worried that she might fall for the wiles of the many pursuers of young ladies? 'Be a lady-in-waiting to the Queen.'

'I don't think she should go there on her own,' Sarsfield said.

'There are lots of ladies to look after her,' Luttrell said. Most of the wives of the Jacobite leaders were already at Saint-Germain-en-Laye, outside Paris, in the royal palace lent to his cousin by King Louis. 'We could ask the Duchess of Tyrconnell to take her under her wing.' Tyrconnell's wife Frances was a formidable woman and more than a match for any man who overrated his charms.

Sarsfield agreed with a half-nod.

'My lord Berwick will look after her,' Purcell interjected,

oblivious of the import of what he was saying. 'We just passed on his compliments to her.'

'Which he sends to you as well,' Luttrell added quickly, glowering at Purcell to shut up. Berwick, the 20-year old illegitimate son of the king, had shown an interest in Honor the previous year before Sarsfield had married her. 'Tell Notorious he is ever in my thoughts, he said.'

'Notorious,' Purcell echoed with a laugh, oblivious to Luttrell's warning but inadvertently falling for his diversion. 'Why does he call you that?'

'Impudent pup,' Sarsfield said with no hint of humour, offering no explanation, although he suspected the reason. He had arrested the Protestant civilians of Sligo after he captured the town in order to have someone to trade for the Jacobite soldiers held by the Protestants of Enniskillen: the move worked but the king disapproved of it.

'But the King's pup,' Purcell waved a warning finger at him. Berwick, an army commander, had been deeply involved in the Irish campaign the previous year and had been left in charge of the Jacobites' territory when Tyrconnell had gone off to France to seek the king's permission to make peace with the prince of Orange.

'He's still talking about Ballyneety,' Luttrell added, seizing the opportunity to steer the conversation away from Honor. 'How he wished he had led that raid. Telling everybody how you saved Limerick and kept the King's cause alive.'

'He had his chance to make sure it got even stronger,' Sarsfield said, referring to Berwick's refusal to go along with a plot by Sarsfield and Luttrell to oust Tyrconnell in his absence, set Berwick up as lord lieutenant of Ireland, and continue the military campaign in 1691. Even though he agreed with the plotters about continuing the war, Berwick wouldn't go against his father's representative. The disagreement had brought some frost into what had been a warm relationship between him and Sarsfield.

'He helped us to come back,' Luttrell said, pointing to Purcell and himself. Berwick could be a very useful ally and, in his eyes, there was no point antagonising potential allies.

'He did?'

'Yes,' Luttrell added with more certainty than his actual knowledge warranted. 'You-know-who and his minions were pouring their usual poison into the King's ear, trying to persuade him and the French to keep us in Paris. Even to throw us in jail.'

Sarsfield nodded, aware that Tyrconnell believed Luttrell and Purcell were his manipulators and that Tyrconnell's attempts to befriend him in their absence was designed to neutralise his opposition to the viceroy. 'And Berwick persuaded the King otherwise?'

Luttrell nodded. 'We reminded him of the consequences if we weren't allowed back. That you'd be upset and the army could even revolt. He knows all too well that the army will follow you, not Tyrconnell.'

Sarsfield rubbed his eyes, feeling tired. He was not in the mood for a recitation of their political disputes. Luttrell, he knew, could talk about these all night, indeed would love to rehash, analyse and reinterpret them all night. 'Tell me the news from Paris,' he said.

'About Henry's swiving?' Purcell laughed and started giggling as a memory struck him. 'He put his eye on the comely wife, the very comely wife of *le comte* --.'

'You want to know about our new commanders?' Luttrell cut him off, filling up their glasses again. 'Yes?'

'Yes.'

'My lord Mountcashel talks highly of Saint-Ruhe and he of Mountcashel's men. They served under him in Savoy at the siege of Annecy and won a great victory against the Grand Alliance at Staffarde.'

'Mountcashel told me about that battle but I didn't realise Saint-Ruhe was the commander.'

'A no-quarter man,' Luttrell nodded. 'Learned his trade against the French heretics.'

'Not likely to want to make peace with them here then,' Sarsfield said.

'Definitely not. He has no time for them. Besides, this is his first overall command, so he wants to impress his king. But the real gossip,' he paused to add relish to the information he was about to impart, 'is about his marriage to *la Marechale* de la Meilleraye, the widow of the marshal who had some mad idea about colonising Madagascar in the manner of the *Compagnie des Indes* back in the 'sixties. Saint-Ruhe was her page and they married after she was widowed although she was much older than him. She kept the marriage secret, not so much because of the age difference but because he was beneath her station and it might upset her position at court. She was quite a beauty in her day but she seems to like ugly men. The marshal was nothing much to look at either, it's said.'

'Like the King,' Purcell said of King James whose attraction to ugly women, like Berwick's mother, Annabelle Churchill, was a source of much gossip. That her brother, John Churchill, had deserted to the prince of Orange and was now one of his leading commanders was also a factor in the complex of relations among the leading players in the war. Churchill had captured Cork and Kinsale for the Williamites the previous winter while his sister's son, Berwick, was leading Jacobite raids to burn local Protestant-controlled towns like Mallow. And, to add to the family complications, the Duchess of Tyrconnell was the elder sister of Churchill's wife Sarah.

'Mind your manners,' Sarsfield snapped at him.

'There's no accounting for taste in matters of the heart,' Luttrell intervened, playing the peacemaker again. He was well aware of Sarsfield's devotion to the King in whose army he had spent most of his life. 'As I know myself.'

'As you should,' Purcell nodded several times in drunken

agreement. His attention was caught suddenly by one of the candles which was listing to one side. He put a hand to it to straighten it and a blob of hot wax fell on his wrist. He let out a string of curses.

'Saint-Ruhe,' Luttrell continued, 'is said to have brought his rough ways home and to have taken a cudgel to *la Marechale* on occasions. So much so that she revealed her married state and appealed to Louis. The king made his displeasure known but Saint-Ruhe didn't mend his ways and was dispatched to Guyenne to cool his ardour.'

Sarsfield looked at him with a sinking feeling. 'That's why he's here?'

Luttrell shrugged, his hands raised, and then took a drink. 'I don't think so. He gets on well with Irish soldiers and has no time for heretics. And if his unfortunate wife has a little peace and stops complaining to Louis isn't everybody happy?'

Sarsfield sighed inwardly: that was the kind of court politics that always disrupted the true business at hand. 'And Tessé?'

'A younger brother.' Luttrell gave a dismissive shrug.

'You're a younger brother,' Purcell muttered, folding his arms on the table and lowering his head.

Luttrell ignored him. 'In the shadow of his older brother, René, the *comte de Tessé*. Another noted Huguenot hunter. The *chevalier* wants to make his mark here, impress his brother and his masters. I got the feeling they don't expect to be impressed.'

'And d'Usson?'

'Formerly one of the hunted, a Huguenot who saw the error of his ways. Switched to the true faith when Louis decided to rid his kingdom of heretics.'

'How is he as a general?'

Luttrell shrugged, as if that didn't interest him much. So, Sarsfield thought, a motley group of Frenchmen. A wife-beater, a commander in whom no one had much confidence, and a turncoat. But he would suspend judgement: what the Parisian gossips thought of them was of no importance compared to what they do on the battlefield in Ireland.

Purcell let out a loud snore which jerked him awake for a moment and then he settled back to sleep on his arms. Luttrell went to top up their glasses but Sarsfield waved him away. He had had enough. Luttrell, a creature of the night, filled up his own glass: he gave little sign of being drunk.

'So, Notorious,' he raised his glass to Sarsfield. 'To victory in 1691.'

'Victory in 1691,' Sarsfield clinked his empty glass against Luttrell's full one.

Mackay

The fleet anchored off a spit of land that stretched out into the centre of the bay, surrounded by wet sand as the tide receded. Major General Hugh Mackay stepped ashore from a tender, relieved to be back on solid ground and took his first look at Ireland. To his left and right were hills while ahead of him the sun was going down like a great light shining from the interior, dazzling and inviting at the same time. It obliterated any sight of Dublin beyond the scatter of stone houses in front of him. A cross between the hills and valleys of his native Scotland and the flat land of his adopted Holland, he thought.

Soldiers were coming ashore from the ships, forming into groups and being led at a quick pace across the sands. Shallow barges were being hauled into place to take their cargoes into the city's quays.

Out of the sun came what appeared at first to be a chariot, a horse driven at speed by a man standing wide-legged on some kind of crossbar. It came closer and Mackay could see that there was a bench behind the driver on which another figure was sitting. The vehicle came off the sand and pulled up on the grass in front of Mackay with a stopping swerve.

The passenger jumped off and Mackay recognised a Dutch officer on General Ginckel's staff who hurried over to him. *'Mijn excuses voor het te laat,'* the officer said with a slight bow. *'Welkom bij Ierland.'*

Mackay acknowledged the apology and welcome with a slight inclination of his head and the Dutch officer snapped an order in English at two of the red-coated soldiers standing nearby. They picked up Mackay's trunk and brought it to the carriage.

'What is that?' Mackay asked the officer, pointing to the car. The driver was still standing upright with the reins held tight as if he was straining to hold back the small horse.

'They call it a Ringsend car,' the officer said. 'After this place. They're the only cars that travel across the sand here. You're unlucky the tide is out and the ships can't come in further.'

This whole journey had been unlucky for Mackay. It had taken a long time from Holland, through England, and, worst of all, worse even than the North Sea, the long stomach-churning crossing of the Irish Sea. The harsh northerly winds which slowed down the convoy had died away at last as they came into Dublin Bay in a sunny calm which came too late to help Mackay's mood.

He should have arrived weeks ago, should have had plenty of time to acquaint himself fully with the situation but there had been one delay after another. Actually, he felt he shouldn't be in Ireland at all, having to take orders from a man like Ginckel, whom everyone knew had been but a stopgap commander for King William's forces in Ireland. If he had to be in the country at all, that he should be second in command rather in the third line of generals after a couple of other continentals.

'General Ginckel wishes you to come immediately to a council of war,' the officer said, as if to remind Mackay who was in charge.

'Right now?' Mackay replied in English, his Scottish accent underlining his irritation.

'It's about to begin.' The officer switched to English, a note of apology in his voice. 'The general expected you earlier.'

Mackay got up beside him on the heavily patched seat and the driver released the horse, taking off with a jolt that almost threw them off. They were shaken from side to side as the horse galloped across the ribbed sand, passed the marching men and splashed through a shallow river without breaking a stride. Mackay felt his nausea rise again.

The officer paid off the Ringsend car man with three pence at Lazy Hill where his own carriage was waiting and they got on board. The city gradually took shape and they passed by Trinity College and went along a rutted road of big houses to the Dam gate and into the narrow streets of the city itself. It was still busy with many people about, the streets narrowed even more by hucksters selling rabbits, chickens, sheepskins and tin utensils.

The carriage made its way slowly up the hill to Dublin castle. The wheels resounded on the wooden drawbridge at the entrance and they halted at the iron gates until the sentry waved them through into the courtyard.

The interior still bore the marks of the fire that had devastated it some years earlier, and of the controlled explosions required to stop it from spreading to the magazine in the tower. Some of the buildings were still ruined, the long gallery on their left only partly repaired, the reconstruction interrupted by the momentous political and military events shaking the three kingdoms in recent years which had led to the rapid changes in control of the city from Protestants to Catholics and back to Protestants again after the Boyne battle the previous year.

The carriage turned to the right and pulled up between what had been the parliament building and a line of old wooden houses untouched by the fire. The Dutch officer led Mackay at a brisk pace up a stairway and announced him into a room of uniformed men standing around a large table.

Mackay hid his disdain for his new commander in a bow to Godard van Reede, Baron de Ginckel. Those who played

43

preferment games and indulged in intrigues had little time for him, seeing him as solid and dependable but lacking in imagination. Certainly not another John Churchill. But King William preferred to put his trust in his Dutch and Danish commanders, even in the French Huguenots, above most of his English and Scottish officers. Devoted as they might be to the reformed church, they had all forsworn their allegiance to the former king, James, his father-in-law and uncle.

A quick glance around the table underlined Mackay's sense of injustice: the only other Briton there was the Englishman, Thomas Talmash, who, like Mackay himself, had remained on in Holland with the Anglo-Dutch brigade when given a choice of returning to serve King James or staying with William's forces. The others were all from the continent including the commander of the Danish mercenaries, the Duke of Württemberg, Ginckel's lieutenant general, a position that Mackay believed should, at the very least, have been his. He also recognised Henri de Massue, the Marquis of Ruvigny, leader of the French Huguenots. Some of the others were new to him, notably the leaders of the Irish Protestants who had kept the island safe for the new king with their heroic action at Londonderry. They stared back at him with unconcealed interest, taking in his baby face, which, with the black curls of his wig, created the impression of a child dressing up as an adult.

'Je suis désolé que je suis en retard,' Mackay apologised, lapsing into French, the language of the councils of war. 'The winds were unfavourable.'

'We have just begun,' Ginckel replied. 'We will leave any introductions necessary until we have finished.' He turned back to the map of Ireland laid out on the table and Ruvigny edged to one side to make room for Mackay.

'The French have landed here at Limerick' -- Ginckel pointed to the city -- 'and we don't yet know their strength or intentions. The papists hold everything beyond the river Shannon' -- he ran his finger down the 200 plus miles of the river -- 'with two outposts to the east here and here' – his finger stabbed at Ballymore and Nenagh -- 'and the south bank of the Shannon estuary' -- he circled an area taking in most of counties Kerry and Limerick. 'The rest of this area' -- he drew a line down the east of the river with two outspread fingers -- 'is desolate. The natives have taken to the bogs and mountains, the land has been laid waste. Their strong points are at Sligo, Athlone, Galway and Limerick.' His index finger hopped from one to the other, north to south, and then he straightened up.

A beam of sunlight from the west suddenly shone through the distorting glass of a small window, picking out flecks of dust and angling into the eyes of some of those on the other side of the table. They sidled away from it.

'Is it certain the Marquis de Saint-Ruhe is leading the French?' Ruvigny asked.

'That's our information,' Ginckel said.

'*Le missionaire botté.*' Ruvigny turned Saint-Ruhe's soubriquet, the booted missionary, into an angry snort. 'He is well known for his savagery against our people.'

'Yes, we know,' Ginckel quickly cut him off. The rights and wrongs of the religious disputes in France were not his immediate concern.

'The worst form of papist,' Ruvigny muttered.

'The French are declaring their intentions then,' Mackay noted, 'by their choice of general.'

'To exterminate all Protestants,' one of the Irish commanders said with a satisfied tone.

'Their intention is to take over Ireland with as little trouble to themselves and as much trouble to us as possible,' Talmash said. Though he had spent most of his military career on the continent there was no doubt he thought of 'us' as England. 'Louis cares little for his cousin and less for the Irish and their cause.'

'Be that as it may,' Ginckel intervened, asserting his authority.

'We're not concerned now with their political intentions but with their military strategy. And how we secure a decisive victory.'

They were all conscious of the failure the previous year to maintain the momentum of their victory at the Boyne and bring the war in Ireland to a quick conclusion. Mackay had heard the reasons already in briefings in London on his way from Holland: lack of siege guns caused the failure to take Athlone when the Irish had withdrawn beyond the Shannon; atrocious weather was to blame for the failure to capture Limerick. As well as the loss of materials at Ballyneety, of course. They had run out of time: winter had set in and the war had gone into another year and had to be ended now as quickly as possible to secure England and Scotland against further French threats from the west and to free up this army to change the balance of forces in the wider war on the Continent.

'They have spent the winter improving their defences at Limerick and Athlone,' Ginckel continued. 'Some French officers stayed behind to oversee the works when their main force left at the end of last year. Which means it will be more difficult to reduce them this year. On the other hand, we will also be better prepared this time. We have already considered several approaches,' he added for Mackay's benefit, drawing an oval around the centre of the Shannon's course. 'To strike in this area, push west to Galway, divide their territory in two and split their forces. The question is where to cross the river. Here or here or here' -- he put his finger on Lanesborough, north of Athlone, and Banagher and Portumna south of it -- 'or at Athlone itself.'

He paused and looked around. Everybody's eyes remained on the map. The stray beam of sunlight had gone out like someone snuffing a candle and left the room in a sudden gloom.

'Banagher looks to meet our requirements. Defended but not as strongly as Athlone. And a success there will allow us to circle around and besiege Athlone from the west as well as the east.'

Mackay saw more than a shadow of scepticism on some faces.

46

All he had heard of the war in Ireland suggested that the papist forces there were not that well trained, organised, or led. They tended to scatter easily when faced with a determined force, or so all the reports to London said. And the proof had been at the Boyne and even before it, when the enemy missed an opportunity to destroy the king's forces as they lay debilitated by the flux at Dundalk.

'We have asked the navy to besiege Galway at the same time,' Ginckel said. There was a snort from someone at the other side of the table. The general looked up but was met with a line of blank stares. 'It is questionable if they will get there in time,' he admitted, half-expecting another expression of scepticism, a scepticism that he shared but could not admit. The English navy's loyalty was still somewhat suspect and, besides, it was wary of being caught too far abroad by the superior French fleet. 'Late will serve our purpose almost as well, drawing off some of the enemy's forces to defend Galway, dividing and weakening them.'

'Perhaps we could alert the enemy to the naval plan anyway,' Talmash suggested. 'Let one of their spies know about it. It could have the same effect.'

Ginckel nodded.

Spies and deserters were constantly moving from side to side, bringing with them the perennial problem that such people always did. How credible was their information? Were they exaggerating or distorting it, telling you what they thought you wanted to hear? Were they double agents, deliberately sowing false information?

The Jacobites had most of the population on their side, so civilians couldn't be trusted. But you couldn't trust all your own side either, as Marshall Schomberg had discovered the previous year when French papists were found among the Huguenot regiments at Dundalk secretly corresponding and plotting with the enemy. He'd had ten of them hanged and ordered a search for any others in the ranks, ordering a check on whether all officers had received communion since receiving their commissions.

Ginckel looked from person to person, offering each of them an opportunity to question his plan. Nobody said anything. Mackay had some opinions on it but remained silent. Immediately after he had arrived was not the time to question it. He might not have a high opinion of Ginckel but he did believe in the command structure and in avoiding unnecessary divisions.

Later, after dinner, they sat with brandy and pipes in Ginckel's quarters -- Mackay, Talmash and the general, newcomers to their current positions or to the country. The meeting was Ginckel's idea, an informal opportunity to size up one another. He was particularly conscious of the private instruction from King William that he should overcome his normal mildness of manner and maintain control, particularly over the Englishmen in his command.

A small fire burned in the grate: the temperature had dropped; and the evening verged on the chilly, a reminder that summer had not quite arrived. 'I hear the Os and Macs have been very excited about some O'Donnell who has come back from Spain and is raising an army,' Talmash was saying. 'Apparently there's an old Irish prophesy that an O'Donnell with a red mark on his forehead will lead the Irish to victory somewhere in Galway.'

'Hugh Balldearg O'Donnell.' Ginckel gave a weary nod. 'Which means red spot in their language. He arrived last year after the Boyne with some men and started recruiting among the papists in Donegal where his family comes from. Got a large rabble together, mostly rapparees.'

'Rapparees.' Talmash rolled the word on his tongue as though savouring it: it was a new one to him, a peculiarly Irish one from the word for their favourite weapon, a half-length pike. 'O'Donnell is the one behind them, is he?'

'No,' Ginckel said. 'They're mostly small groups of bandits

48

controlled by no one person. Many of them are deserters from their army, some even from ours. Raiding supply lines, pillaging and murdering everywhere, especially the homes and persons of the reformed faith. They're a nuisance.'

'So we're not worried about this papist superstition of the man with the red mark,' Talmash said with a chuckle.

'I worry about everything,' Ginckel admitted with a feeble smile. 'But he seems to be at odds with everyone on their side, particularly with my Lord Tyrconnell whom he thinks has stolen his title. We hear that he doesn't trust any of the Old English, as they call them. Claims to represent the real Irish.'

'Where is he now?' Talmash leaned forward to take a taper from beside the fire to relight his pipe. He had something of the rapparee about him, Mackay thought: a desire for action above all else and a lack of discipline at times. Prone to get carried away in the heat of the moment and to do something ill-advised.

As a deeply religious man, Mackay also disapproved of Talmash's willingness, even eagerness, to let it be known that he was the bastard son of Oliver Cromwell. Whether it was true or not -- and it probably was not, which made it even worse -- it was a disreputable claim in which to take pride, an insult to his own father as much as to the great puritan.

'Somewhere in Connacht, probably Mayo.' Ginckel reached for the brandy bottle on a small table by his chair. 'He could cause a lot of trouble yet.'

'The strengths we discussed earlier,' Mackay asked, 'did they include Balldearg O'Donnell?'

Ginckel shook his head. Their estimates had put their own and the enemy's forces at roughly the same, 25,000 each, about 20,000 infantry and 5,000 mounted troops. But the figures were fluid. They had more on the island but needed to garrison many towns. And they did not know how many more French might be on the way to Limerick or Galway.

'So he could make a difference to their strength,' Mackay said.

'Yes,' Ginckel concurred, leaning over to top up Talmash's glass. 'He is a factor we need to keep in mind. So far he has not been involved in any significant action.'

'What about the rapparees?' Mackay asked as he held out his almost empty glass to the proffered bottle. 'How do we deal with them?'

'Send the Danes after them,' Talmash said with a laugh. 'They say the Irish are terrified of them. Think they're like the Vikings of old whose brutality has gone down in their legends.'

Ginckel ignored him and gave the weary sigh of a man bothered by a minor problem that refused to go away. 'The Ulstermen and the local militias will keep them in check while we go about our main business.' The militias were made up of Protestants, many of whom had been victims of rapparees or Catholic forces in the past. More and more rapparees were created as the militias took revenge for past wrongs. Neither side took any prisoners, neither in the literal nor figurative sense of the phrase.

Keep them in check, Mackay noted as Ginckel filled his pipe, not defeat them. But perhaps they were the kind of infestation that it was impossible to be rid of, an irritation that one had to live with. Like lice in wigs.

They lapsed into silence, watching a pale flicker of flame rise and die in fits and starts from a lump of coal in the grate. Talmash inhaled heavily from his pipe and held the smoke for a long moment before exhaling with an air of satisfaction.

'The outposts they have on our side of the river,' Mackay began and paused, trying to remember their names.

'Ballymore and Nenagh,' Ginckel prompted.

'How will we handle them?'

Ginckel gave another dismissive shake of his head. 'I don't foresee any need to. They'll abandon them as soon as they see the full army approach and fall back to their defensive positions across the river.'

'We know their strengths?'

'We know everything about Ballymore,' Talmash interjected before Ginckel could answer. 'One of their officers sent to inspect it has come over to our side.'

'Reliable?' Mackay asked.

'Probably,' Ginckel replied. 'His information tallies with what we know from others. There are about a thousand men and as many camp followers. They're well supplied but it would be folly for them to try and withstand a full siege.'

'That's what we need,' Mackay said. 'Good information. And the best way to get it, I found in Scotland, was to pay for it. The papists will do anything for money.'

Ginckel gave him a sceptical glance. 'Even tell you lies,' he said.

One of the candles on a candle-tree sputtered and flickered and died, sending a thin spiral of grey smoke towards the ceiling.

'Tell me some more about this man Sarsfield,' Ginckel said to Mackay. 'He seems to be the real commander of the papist army.'

Mackay took a sip of his brandy. 'A bit of a hothead. Came to attention at the battle of Sedgemoor when Monmouth's rebellion was put down. He was one of a few cavalrymen who continued a charge into a group of pikemen when most of the cavalry turned back. He was dragged from his horse and clubbed with a musket butt and left for dead but he was rescued when the rebels were routed later. The late king gave him a commission afterwards and he became quite well known in London.'

'A lucky man,' Ginckel offered.

Mackay nodded. 'Survived a few duels too. He was run through in at least one of them. We think he was slashed as well at Wincanton when he came across some of my men who were leading the new king to London.' He gave a small smile of satisfaction. 'It turned out to be the only real skirmish in the Glorious Revolution and he was fooled by one of the locals shouting that the Dutch are here, away with you quick. He withdrew although there were only a few of my men there, outnumbered by at least four to one.'

'You knew him well?'

Mackay shook his head. 'No. I've seen him, of course, but I don't remember ever speaking to him before we went to Holland. Haven't seen him since then.'

'He's someone to be reckoned with now,' Ginckel said. 'After he took back Sligo and then ambushed our wagon train on the way to Limerick last year.'

Ginckel sank into his own thoughts but they weren't about Sarsfield. There was one way to bring this campaign to a quick conclusion, he knew, to best serve the King's interests and to avoid a lot of effort and bloodshed. Offer the Irish what they wanted. They would quickly abandon the Stuarts and switch their allegiance to King William and Queen Mary if they were allowed to keep their lands and practice their religion unhindered.

The King was willing to be generous but the parliament in London and the lords justices, all Protestants who now ruled Ireland, were not. They were willing to offer amnesties to all the junior officers and foot soldiers and even to allow Romish priests some freedom to continue their idolatrous practices. But they would not countenance any offer to allow their leaders to keep the lands they had recovered during the Restoration. The land settlement had to be final. And those who had kept their lands during all the seizures and restorations of the century must be made pay for their opposition to the new order. Besides, the parliamentarians and lord justices needed lands to seize and sell to pay for this campaign to put down the opponents of progress. This war had to pay for itself.

Another candle burned down and went out in a thin line of grey smoke.

'What's the news from the Low Countries?' Ginckel asked Mackay, shifting in his chair as if to dislodge the subject which occupied most of his waking thoughts and turn to something more congenial.

Sarsfield

The wagon train stretched the length of the causeway across the high bog and back the mile or so from Limerick and on along the road towards Killaloe. Companies of soldiers walked between the overloaded supply wagons, led by drumbeats that matched the slow pace of the garrons straining to pull the heavy loads. Regimental flags were held aloft, half-furled, showing slashes of red, green and white and bits of Latin, and the first words of the motto on the white flag of the Grand Prior's regiment which said 'The Fruits of Rebellion' under a burning building.

Most of the men wore their usual uniforms, now in various shades of faded and muddied red, but some were outfitted in the newly arrived grey French *trucoats*, occasionally with the sleeves cut off. Typical, Colonel Charles O'Kelly fumed to Sarsfield when he saw them filing across Thomond Bridge out of Limerick: the French have sent us their rejects, reject uniforms with the sleeves so short and narrow that the men could not put their arms through them. Look at the wagons, Sarsfield had replied, as a heavily laden cart of barrels of gun powder went by: we need that more than uniforms.

The long line of soldiers was followed by the sutlers' wagons and then the camp followers, women, children and a few old men, barefooted and mostly in rags.

Around them the countryside was bleak, a succession of bogs and commons with no signs of life, neither human nor animal. The only habitation was an occasional *creagh,* one of last summer's temporary cabins now in a state of collapse after the winter. After the army had gone, the few people still living in the area might come up again from the lowlands with their cattle to graze the available grass. They knew well to avoid all armies, friend or foe, and their insatiable need for food of every kind, grain, vegetable or animal.

The day was airless under an unbroken cloud the colour of fine wood ash. The sounds of the wooden cartwheels on the hard-packed earthen and stone road, the jingle of the horses' harnesses and the rustle of the cargoes and the people were all smothered in the expanse of the bleak land and sky. From behind the sound of raised voices slowly gathered strength as a couple of horsemen appeared in single file shouting in Irish '*Fág an bealach*' as they cleared a narrow path at the edge of the road. The soldiers and the camp followers edged aside without a glance as the horsemen went by and were followed at a cautious canter by Major General Sarsfield and his senior officers.

They rode on alongside the wagons and men, mile after mile, having to slow now and then to make their way past when the track narrowed or a group of marchers was hesitant to give way. Sarsfield glanced behind him and signalled to Nicholas Purcell to move up and join him as they splashed through a shallow stream that crossed the road.

'The rebels have brought in some new commanders,' he told Purcell. 'Including Mackay. You came across him in Scotland at the start of the war.'

'Ah,' Purcell said with a touch of nostalgia. 'Bonnie Dundee and Killiecrankie.'

'Tell me about him.'

'Bonnie Dundee?' Purcell said in surprise. The Viscount of Dundee had been dead two years, killed at the battle of Killiecrankie at which his Highlanders, loyal to King James, had defeated the prince of Orange's forces under Mackay. Purcell had been with a party of 300 Irish dragoons fighting with the Highlanders during the brief uprising.

'No.' Sarsfield glanced at him to see if he was being deliberately obtuse. 'Mackay. The man we're going to be dealing with.'

'Didn't you know him yourself in your English days?' Purcell shot back as they entered a small wood of skeletal trees beginning to sprout their summer sheen of green.

'Just knew that he was a dour Scot. A colonel of foot.'

'We caught him by surprise at Killiecrankie,' Purcell said. 'At a pass through the hills and charged their line and put them to the sword. It was a massacre really.'

'Why? What were their mistakes?'

'They formed up in a single line along the valley floor while we were on the hillside. There were many more of them than us but we concentrated our charge on the centre of their line. They hadn't time to plug their bayonets into their musket barrels after firing their first volley before we were on them and scattered them. I don't know how many thousand we killed that day.'

They cleared the wood in silence, emerging from the gloom into the dull daylight. 'He didn't make that mistake again,' Purcell said. 'He invented the socket bayonet afterwards so you can have it fixed in position before firing.'

Sarsfield couldn't see any advantage to be gained from what Purcell had told him. It was unlikely, as Purcell said, that Mackay would make the same mistake twice. But the thing to do with him, and with Ginckel, was to surprise them. All the intelligence indicated they were not imaginative men. Not daring men.

'You should ask Brigadier Wauchope about him,' Purcell

suggested. 'Wasn't he in the Dutch brigade with him before the usurper arrived?'

Sarsfield came across John Wauchope as they reached Killaloe where the expanse of Lough Derg finally narrowed back into the Shannon. He was leading a party of horsemen out of the town and Sarsfield pulled up his horse and called to him. 'I thought you had taken command of Athlone castle,' he said when Wauchope wheeled his mount and came over to him.

'I have,' Wauchope said in his Scottish accent. 'On my way there now.'

'I wanted to ask you about Mackay. We hear he's arrived as one of Ginckel's deputies.'

'Aye, they won't do anything surprising,' Wauchope gave a short laugh, confirming what they all believed. 'They'll go by the book. I've told the Frenchmen all about them.'

Wauchope had served under Mackay in Holland when an English regiment had been lent to the Dutch by King James some years earlier. And while James was still playing his difficult game of trying to appease the Catholics in his kingdoms without alarming the Protestants. As it began to fall apart in the late 1680s, the regiment in Holland was recalled but those who wished to stay on were allowed to. Many of the Protestants did and formed part of the prince of Orange's force which subsequently landed in England and forced James to seek asylum in France.

'Mackay is more concerned with the heretics' immortal souls than with their fighting ability,' Wauchope said. 'Gets upset by their gambling, swearing and thieving. He's even drawn up a special prayer for them to say as they go into battle.'

'They're all going to hell anyway,' Sarsfield muttered.

'And we're going to speed them on their way.' Wauchope tipped his hat and rode off towards Loughrea where Saint-Ruhe and his French generals were already camped.

Loughrea was the obvious place for them to position themselves for the coming campaign. It was clear that the prince of Orange's forces wouldn't attack Limerick first but would opt for some of the mid-river crossings and Loughrea was well suited as a mustering point, able to cover all likely crossings. Besides, it was the only route with a road suitable to take the heavy supplies needed for Athlone or the defence of any other river positions: the infantry could slog through the bogs and hillside alongside the river but the cavalry and supply wagons could not.

Killaloe was overwhelmed by the army. The few stone houses had been taken over for the senior officers and Sarsfield was assigned to the ground floor of one. Most of the mud cabins had been occupied by other officers and another town of tents had grown up to its south as battalions of infantry arrived from Limerick and others departed on their way to Athlone. There was little sign of the native population.

Sarsfield found the house where he had been billeted and was just unbuckling his sword when there was a curt knock on his door and Henry Luttrell put his head around it without waiting for a reply. 'Your old friend Clifford is looking for you,' he said.

Sarsfield gave a dismissive grunt. It was a long time since Robert Clifford had been a friend of his, not since they were both Irish captains in the King's army in London. And especially not in the last year when Clifford, now a colonel, had sided with the Tyrconnell faction. 'What does he want?'

'Don't worry,' Luttrell smirked. 'Not another widow.'

Sarsfield threw his hat at him but it floated in the air and fell short. Luttrell gave a whooping laugh from the other side of the door as he pulled it shut behind him. Sarsfield took off his tunic and loosened his neck band. He poured an inch of water into the bowl on the table beside the settle bed and, scooping some up with his joined hands, lowered his face into them. He stopped, his hands against his wet face, letting the water drop back into the bowl, thinking how much simpler things had been then, when he and Clifford had been young men about London.

Though it hadn't seemed so at the time. It was touch and go

57

for his future after he had helped Clifford to kidnap a rich young widow. They had taken her to France, to Dunkirk, while Clifford tried to persuade her to marry him. Unfortunately, she was well-connected. The King was lobbied and he asked his cousin King Louis for help. Louis sent a troop of soldiers to Dunkirk to rescue the widow. Sarsfield had escaped by the skin of his teeth but Clifford had been sent back to England and thrown in jail. Sarsfield had signed up with the French army until the scandal blew over and he could go back quietly to James's army in England.

He dried his face with his shirt sleeves, put his tunic and sword back on and picked his hat from the floor as he went looking for Clifford. He found him outside the surgeon's tent from which screams of agony were coming.

'What happened?' Sarsfield asked.

Clifford had lost some of his usual swagger. His face was grey with tiredness and streaked with dirt and dried blood. His normally impeccable uniform was also patched with brown stains. 'We were on a foray into Tipperary when we were ambushed by five or more squadrons of horse. We were lucky to get away with only five men lost. And some more wounded.' Another screech of pain from inside the tent made him wince.

Sarsfield gave him an impatient look and resisted a temptation to remind him he should not have allowed himself to be ambushed in the first place. Forays and ambushes by both sides were almost daily occurrences in the largely no-man's-land across the river as they went foraging and testing each other's positions and defences.

'That's not what I wanted to tell you,' Clifford went on. 'They were Danes. And they weren't on a foray. They were an advance guard of the Danes coming from Clonmel.'

'How do you know?' Sarsfield gave him his full attention now. 'Did you take some captives?'

'Some rapparees told us,' Clifford said. 'After the engagement, when we had put some distance between us.'

'Maybe they were just after the rapparees?'

'That's what I thought. And that's what the rapparees thought but they'd been watching them for a couple of days and saw the main body of their army coming behind.'

'Was it Galloping Hogan?' Sarsfield asked, naming the best-known rapparee in the area, the man who had led him to Ballyneety.

'No. Someone called O'Connell.'

'He might have warned you.'

'He didn't see us. We met up only afterwards when we got into the hills. He was keeping out of their way.'

Sarsfield wasn't listening. Was Portumna their target after all? All their informants and a few deserters had told them that the prince of Orange's army was mustering in Mullingar for a straight assault on Athlone. But could that be a feint? Hardly, with almost the whole army heading there. No, it was probably a different ploy. The Danes would try to cross at Portumna or Banagher and encircle Athlone while Ginckel attacked it head on.

He nodded to himself and walked off, slotting this information into his own favourite plan. It would still work, he thought as he walked around the camp. All the better if they were only pretending to attack Athlone while their real target was farther downstream.

Around him the latest arrivals were lighting their fires and pitching their few tents. Those without a place in a tent were claiming the best spots to sleep by the ditches, arguing over those that had protective branches left in place by the previous night's occupants. Many had already settled into their interminable games of four cards, gambling their brass pennies. They had little regard for the money anyway: it was worth less by the day, especially when the French still had gold and silver to buy whatever was available. The King's coins, made from melted-down cannons and whatever brass they could find in heretics' churches and homes, was supposed to be of equal value but it now took nearly ten times the amount of brass money to buy the same as one gold or silver coin.

One of the card players glanced up at Sarsfield as he passed and nudged his companion when he saw a faint smile cross Sarsfield's face. His presence always boosted the mood of the men and seeing him happy was a bonus, a good omen.

Immersed in his thoughts, Sarsfield didn't notice them. He was smiling at the prospect of his plan working, of the rebels falling into his trap. If they were targeting Banagher or, even better, Portumna, to cross the Shannon, he could lead a major raid behind their lines into Leinster, spearheaded by the men at Ballymore, their outpost to the east of the river. Even raid Dublin itself. That would give their generals an unpleasant surprise that would shake their confidence --Ballyneety writ large -- and justify his insistence on keeping Ballymore despite Tyrconnell's defeatist argument that they should pull all their forces behind the Shannon.

JUNE

Mackay

Mullingar was alive with purpose. Energy coursed through its narrow streets after the long winter of cold and hunger and of small-scale activity; the raids and forays into no-man's land, the inconclusive clashes with papist patrols, the false alarms of the frontier, and the frustrations of pursuing will-o-the-wisp rapparees who disappeared into woods and bogs. The waiting was over at last. The army was going to war.

Major General Mackay straightened his uniform, picked his hat off the table, and took a last look around his room. A hurrah in the street below accompanied by a loud rumble made him pause and go to the window. A 24-pounder cannon drawn by two horses was passing by, the first of the heavy siege guns to arrive from Dublin after four days on the road. The sight of it alone raised spirits, another sign that the army now meant business.

He felt it, too, the sense of anticipation, the relief of action after all the talking, thinking and planning. The outcome of the campaign was now in the hands of Providence. And he was certain what that outcome would be.

In the yard behind the house a trooper was holding Mackay's

horse, already saddled, and he mounted up and rode out to where his men were camped on the edge of the town. Nearby, the town's Irish inhabitants, who had been expelled by its governor, lived in the ditches under the haphazard cover of scraws on top of leaning branches. A few had built more substantial mud cabins roofed with rushes: smoke filtered through the rushes covering one, giving the impression that it was on fire. Dirty-faced children with big hungry eyes peered from the openings of the makeshift homes but the adults stayed out of sight.

The day was both dull and bright. Dirty white cloud covered the sky but the light was bright enough to make Mackay tip his hat forward to shade his eyes. The land was wet after a couple of days of storms, a mix of sodden bogs, woods and hilly farmland. An optimistic farmer tended a few short potato beds beside his cabin, the plants' leaves beginning to break the soil: he ignored the passing parade, more than 10,000 men, scores of wagons, dozens of cannons and field guns, and then a long straggle of camp followers, women, children and sutlers.

Mackay pulled off to one side to a slight rise and halted his horse to watch the infantry go by in squads of grenadiers, musketeers and pikemen, their 14-foot long weapons visible long before their holders arrived and long after they had disappeared into the distance. They looked to Mackay to be in good shape in spite of all the usual grumbling about the lack of food, the sporadic pay, and the harsh discipline. A deserter had been hanged the previous day after being caught by a patrol, trying to make his way across the Shannon. His body had been left hanging on the road out of the town but few soldiers even looked at it as they passed: all but the new recruits from England were inured to the sight of dead bodies.

A drumbeat in the distance came closer and he could hear someone singing. As they approached he recognised the tune of Lilliburlero, the satirical song about the papists' brief takeover of Ireland before their king had abdicated. A strong-voiced singer in the middle of a detachment was belting out the words:

There was an old prophecy found in a bog
Lilliburlero bullen a la
The country'd be ruled by an ass and a dog
Lilliburlero bullen a la

His comrades in the English regiment took up the pidgin-Irish refrain as they passed Mackay.

Lero Lero Lilliburlero
Lilliburlero bullen a la
Lero Lero Lilliburlero
Lilliburlero bullen a la

The singer went on to the next verse, the drumbeat insistent.

Now this prophecy is all come to pass
Lilliburlero bullen a la
For Talbot's the dog and Tyrconnell's the ass
Lilliburlero bullen a la

The marchers again took up the refrain, repeating it twice at the end of the song as they faded around a bend by a wood. A distant cheer came to him on the westerly wind as they finished.

Major General Talmash rode over to Mackay and brought his horse around to face the passing parade as if they were on a reviewing stand. 'You still think we've made the wrong decision?' he asked after a few moments, referring to the latest council of war the previous day. 'On second thoughts?'

'Yes,' Mackay said without hesitation. He hadn't changed his mind, hadn't had any second thoughts. They had had a lengthy discussion after General Ginckel had announced his new plan: they were no longer going to try and cross the Shannon at Banagher or nearby Meelick but would make a direct assault on Athlone. Ginckel was nervous, afraid of what might be happening in the west beyond their knowledge, especially the possibility that French troops might be arriving there.

'Surely our spies will tell us if that happens,' Mackay had suggested.

'Perhaps not quickly enough,' Ginckel had countered. It could take days for news to travel from the west coast, days during which the French could move their men to the Shannon almost as fast as the news could get to Mullingar. The most straightforward action was the best, he had said. A direct challenge to the papists who were known to shy away from large-scale confrontations. A breach in their Shannon defences would not be as decisive as the seizure of one of their strongholds at the same time. Besides, although he did not say it, he also wanted a major victory and an opportunity to present the enemy with reasonable surrender terms. The combination of the demoralisation of a defeat and the offer of a fair way out should end the campaign quickly.

'He knows nothing about sieges or how to cross a river under fire,' Mackay said now, personalising his main objections to Ginckel's plan. He had argued strenuously against attacking Athlone because of the difficulty of taking a strongly walled town across a wide and deep river. Either task was difficult enough: both at the same time compounded the difficulty and made success more unlikely. He thought he had been careful not to reveal his lack of confidence in Ginckel's leadership qualities but his views were not lost on his fellow-generals. Mackay was not a subtle man. They could read between the lines, as could Ginckel.

'Maybe he's right,' Talmash said.

'It's the general's decision,' Mackay shrugged. His fellow-generals were wrong to assume he was merely bitter at being passed over. Yes, he was disappointed, but it was the will of God and God's will was not a matter for bitterness or even personal disappointments. 'We have to make it work.'

As the first of the camp followers came into sight, they galloped away, rounding the bend in the road by the wood. Four rapparees were hanging from branches, their broken bodies as limp as their rags. Maybe that's what the singers were cheering at earlier when they had finished their song, Mackay thought.

They camped that night more than halfway to Ballymore, knowing they would come face to face with the enemy the next day.

They moved out in light rain shortly after dawn the next morning, a Sunday, and were at the village of Ballymore by noon. The defenders had made no effort to withdraw to Athlone during the night, as Ginckel half-expected: neither had there been an attempt to reinforce them. There was a quick exchange of musket fire with some Jacobites but they withdrew quickly into the fort which stood on a spit of land stretching into a lake to the north of the village.

The first formalities of the theatrics of a siege were conducted with speed, everybody knowing their lines. Ginckel sent a messenger with a drummer beating a parley to the fort to call on them to surrender. The fort's commander, Colonel Milo Burke, refused and Ginckel ordered the next move, the placing of cannons to batter down the walls and of mortars to rain down explosives and rocks on its inhabitants.

Mackay rode through the village, a string of a hundred or so mud cabins lining the road, seeing for himself the lie of the land, taking care to remain beyond musket range of the fortifications. Dragoons and infantry were moving quickly to isolate the castle. It was protected by the lake water to the north and north-east. To the west and east lay boggy land, leaving the only clear approach

67

by the road over dry fields from the south.

Ahead of him and to his left, musket fire was being exchanged between a party of dragoons now reinforced by infantry around an old stone tower house. Mackay halted and watched the exchange, marvelling at the pointlessness of the defenders. They had seen the large force arrive, knew that they were surrounded without hope of relief, and had but two options: to surrender without putting their besiegers to unnecessary trouble and probably be allowed to retire to the fort, or to fight on and at best suffer immediate captivity or at worst death.

He watched the puffs of grey gun smoke hanging in the damp air from the top of the tower and heard the explosive sound of the shots a moment later. A dragoon officer among the besiegers ran back to his horse, jumped on its back and rode quickly towards him.

Mackay halted him with a hand. 'Haven't they been called upon to surrender?'

'Yes, general,' the officer said. 'They said they'd consider it but then they began shooting again.'

The officer continued on his way and Mackay watched some field guns being pulled into position and prepared beside the track into the fort. He wheeled his horse around and made his way back to the main camp on high ground to the east. At the headquarters tent, an engineer had finished sketching a map of the area and was pinning it down to the trestle table. Ginckel waited impatiently for him to finish and waved his staff forward as the engineer left.

'How many cannons have arrived?' he asked an artillery officer.

'Only twelve.'

Mackay gave an audible sigh, designed to be heard. He had already made plain his criticism of the lack of preparations for this campaign. The fact that they had a shortage of horses to pull wagons and cannons was no excuse. Neither was the winter weather which made the roads difficult. There had been plenty of time to move supplies into forward positions like Mullingar, but Ginckel had been too cautious to do that, fearing that those positions might be overrun while doing nothing much to strengthen their defences.

'Arrange the batteries here, here and here,' Ginckel ordered the artillery officer, pointing to spots on the high ground closer to the castle and ignoring Mackay's insubordination. 'And the mortars here.' He indicated a position to the south of the castle and closer to it.

'Do we have any reports from the scouts to the west?' he asked.

'We've patrolled towards Athlone, my lord,' one of Ruvigny's Huguenot cavalry officers replied. 'There's no sign of the enemy moving out of the town.'

Ginckel nodded with a limited satisfaction. It was good that there was no indication that they would try to relieve Ballymore but did it suggest that they believed the outpost was well enough fortified and supplied to resist a long siege? It was essential that it not be prolonged. He needed quick victories and momentum but he reassured himself that the fort couldn't hold out against their heavy artillery.

He turned to another officer. 'Despatch a rider to Mullingar to bring forward more pontoon boats as soon as possible.'

Mackay resisted the temptation to sigh again. All the pontoons should have been with them when they left Mullingar. They knew they were going to have to cross water at some point, if not here then at the Shannon. But they were still waiting for more pontoons to arrive from England, although that was probably not Ginckel's fault.

The first salvo from the field guns sounded, drowning out the distant popping of the muskets and sending an echo rolling along the low hills. Waterhens skittered across the lake, ducks took flight and the crows in the trees behind their camp rose into the air.

Mackay stepped out of the tent to watch. The balls from the field pieces were bouncing off the thick stone walls of the fort, making no impression. A mortar tossed its explosive ball over the wall of the inner castle, aiming to intimidate the occupants. In front of the fort the infantry were beginning to dig the saps, deep narrow trenches that would take them close enough to the walls to storm a breach once the siege cannons had blasted a hole.

Away to the left he could see their men moving in on the tower house. A white flag fluttered from a high window and a group of less than a dozen enemy emerged. One of them was detached from the others and hurried along at a run to the camp. 'Their sergeant,' one of his captors said as he presented the captive to Ginckel outside his tent.

The general studied him for a moment. He was hatless, with reddish hair, and his tunic, once red, was a muddy brown, dirty and torn at the cuffs. It looked as if it had belonged to someone else, probably more than one person. His trousers were of coarse wool, grey and patched. He wore no shoes.

'You're a rapparee,' Ginckel said with disdain.

'I'm a sergeant in the lawful King's army,' the sergeant said.

'Then tell me, sergeant, how many of your army are in the fort?' Ginckel's tone was almost playful, as if going along with a child's fanciful story.

The sergeant stared back at him in silence.

'You don't know?'

The sergeant said nothing.

'You don't know who's in your army?'

The sergeant held his stare.

Ginckel's tone hardened. 'I'm told you offered to surrender and then killed one of my men who moved forward to accept it.'

The sergeant shook his head but said nothing.

Ginckel said to the prisoner's escort: 'Hang him. On the top of the hill. So that those inside the fort can see him and know the price of their recalcitrance.'

He turned and went back into his tent.

The cannonade began in earnest at dawn, another murky morning with the sunlight trying to seep through cloud that lay like blotting paper over the land, soaking up its energy. The batteries had been completed as darkness descended the night before and all twelve cannons announced the new day and the start of the siege proper. They targeted two spots on the fort's walls, one on its outer ring, the second on its inner wall. Bits of the walls could be seen falling after the first salvos and then the mortars opened up, tossing bombs and rocks into the fort. Soon a cloud of grey smoke hung over the area, replenished as quickly as the westerly breeze dispersed it. The noise was incessant, blast after blast merging into a continuous thunder. The smell of gunpowder was thick on the air, its taste on everyone's tongue.

Those not involved sat on the hillside, well back from musket range, enjoying the spectacle. It was a one-sided siege; they were in no danger from the defenders, and it was only a matter of time before they succeeded, with or without the need to storm the fortifications.

After a couple of hours Ginckel ordered a ceasefire and waited for the silence to reassert itself, broken only by the frightened neighing of horses and lowing of cattle within the fort. Gaps had appeared on two of the walls and were being widened inexorably. He ordered a drummer to sound the chamade, the signal for a parlay, and sent a messenger to the castle demanding its surrender within two hours or its commander, Colonel Burke, would meet the same fate as the sergeant whose body was hanging from the rough gallows on the hill.

The general officers stood around waiting for the reply, watching the messenger make his way back on horseback from the fort, confident of a positive response. It was pointless for the garrison to hold out.

71

'Colonel Burke says he does not understand the message and would like to receive it in writing,' the messenger reported.

Talmash gave a loud laugh, tinged with respect. Someone else muttered something about the man's insolence. Ginckel did not appear amused, neither at Talmash's reaction nor the fact that Burke was treating him as a fool. Nevertheless, he went into his tent and sat at the trestle table that served as his desk and wrote out a message:

'Since the Governor desires to see in Writing the Message which I just now sent him, by word of mouth, he may know, That if he surrenders the Fort of Ballymore to me within two hours, I will give him and his Garrison their Lives, and make them Prisoners of War; if not, neither he nor they shall have any Quarter, nor another opportunity of saving themselves: However, if in that time their Women and Children will go out, they have my leave.

'Given at the Camp, this 8th, day of June, 1691, at 8 a Clock in the Morning.'

He signed it with a flourish, Baron de Ginckel, folded it and emerged from the tent to hand it to the messenger.

It took another half hour for the messenger to return with a counter proposal. 'Colonel Burke wishes to quit the fort with his bags and baggage, drums and standards and repair to Athlone,' he said.

There was a grim silence for a moment, most of the general staff setting their faces against any more time-wasting. Ginckel gave the order to resume the bombardment.

It continued throughout the morning, the gaps in the walls widening and deepening as the cannons breathed tongues of flame and blasted their heavy balls into the stone walls, sending splinters of rock flying, demolishing them piece by piece. Smoke rose from within the fort as the mortar bombs set fire to its wooden structures, an occasional flame soaring above the walls as something explosive went up.

The besieged garrison fired back with their two small field guns and kept up their musket fire at the trenches which were progressing with stealthy intent towards the growing gap in the outer wall. In the early afternoon a white flag was raised over the fort. Mackay brought it to Ginckel's attention but Ginckel gave a curt shake of his head: he had no time for a further exchange with Colonel Burke. The bombardment went on.

Mackay was returning to his tent to rest and read his bible when he saw a detachment of horse arriving from Mullingar with a cart loaded with bodies. He went over to look when the party drew up. In the cart were four bodies, all stripped naked and decapitated. The heads were lined up beside one another, lying at different angles, at the top of the cart. The torsos were bloodied, numerous stab marks from pikes and a few bullet wounds visible.

'Rapparees,' the officer in charge said. 'They ambushed a supply wagon.'

'Didn't it have a proper escort?' Mackay asked with a touch of anger. This was more incompetence.

'Apparently it broke down and these soldiers were left behind to defend it until it was repaired.'

Mackay shook his head with dismay. 'What was it carrying?'

'Bread,' the officer said.

'Did you find them?'

'They had gone back into the bogs when we arrived. With the bread.'

Later Ginckel called a council of war to prepare for the assault on the castle the following morning when the breaches in the walls would be wide enough.

'What about the pontoons?' Mackay asked. 'Can we send a force across the water at the same time? Force them to defend from two directions.'

Ginckel nodded. There were no defensive walls to breach or to scale on the lake side of the fort. 'We'll have more boats by the morning.'

73

'More boats? How many do we have now?' Talmash asked.

Ginckel looked to one of his staff for an answer. 'Four,' the officer said.

'Can't we send a party over now?' Talmash suggested.

'That's not enough to ensure success,' Ginckel said.

The same thought struck several of them at the same time. Instead of planning a surprise attack across the water, what about making their intentions plain? The enemy knew they were vulnerable from that side, they were heavily outnumbered anyway, and they couldn't resist a two-pronged assault once the walls were breached.

'Yes,' Ginckel said, seeing the possibilities as well as anyone. 'Bring the boats down to the shore one by one and move a large body of troops into the area. All within sight of the enemy.'

The boats and men were gathered slowly by the lakeshore, far enough away to be beyond musket range. The fort's defenders quickly saw what was happening and fired one of their field guns towards the concentration of men but the shot fell short, splashing into the water. Meanwhile, the siege guns kept up their barrage as the evening began to draw in. The breach in the outer wall was now low and wide enough to allow an assault group to clamber in. And the saps were zig-zagging their way closer and closer to the opening.

The white flag went up over the fort again shortly afterwards, in the early evening. This time Ginckel ordered a ceasefire and, in the silence, they heard a drummer beat a parley from the walls. A couple of horsemen emerged from the fort's entrance and were brought to the headquarters camp to deliver their message: Colonel Burke wished to surrender the fort on discretion, without conditions.

It was over.

Sarsfield

Major General Sarsfield led his horse down to the edge of the grey lake that gave Loughrea its name and dropped the reins while it stepped into the shallows and drank, scooping up the water with a thirsty tongue. Nearby, the camp was breaking up once more, about to move closer to Athlone now that the usurpers had made clear their intentions. Wagons were arriving from Limerick where more French supplies were still piled up on the quayside waiting to be moved. They had to be shuttled onwards but everything was taking longer than it should have.

The army was still on the move too, most of the infantry now directed straight towards Athlone over the hills nearer the Shannon but that route was impassable for the supply wagons, heavy guns and cavalry. Sarsfield could see the French general moving back and forth on his horse on a hillside, watching several squads of new recruits being put through drills by an Irish sergeant who had learned his trade in France. The westerly wind carried his shouts away in the opposite direction but Sarsfield could imagine the abuse he was giving them as he got them to form into hollow and full squares and rows.

He had to admit that Saint-Ruhe was a soldiers' general, not at all the usual haughty French aristocratic type of commander. He paid a lot of attention to his foot soldiers, especially to their training, and you could feel the enthusiasm rising in the ranks as they sensed the purpose and determination behind all the routines. It was especially true among the new recruits, including the rapparees who had joined them, and even among the seasoned soldiers who had slipped into slovenly ways during the long winter. Saint-Ruhe's interest and visible presence was giving them new heart.

Sarsfield stepped into the edge of the water to retrieve the reins when his horse had finished slaking its thirst and rode back around the lake to where his cavalry was waiting on the edge of the town, all mounted and ready to go. Henry Luttrell's dragoons were still striking camp nearby and Sarsfield rode over to where Luttrell was slumped on his horse watching the work.

'Come on, Luttrell,' Sarsfield ordered in a mock serious tone. 'Don't you know we've places to be.'

Luttrell gave him a bleary look and a snort, careful not to move his throbbing head.

'The fat man has gone already,' Sarsfield said of Tyrconnell. 'Left at first light.'

'And *le général*?'

'Still here, watching the drilling.'

'Thinks he's in Saint-Germain.' Luttrell did not sound impressed. 'Training the sentries to change the guard against a non-existent enemy.' He had a tankard of ale in one hand and put his other hand into a leather bag hanging from his saddle. He extracted a hard French biscuit and took a tentative bite followed by a draught of ale. He winced as if the breakfast was medicinal.

'You can't fault his energy,' Sarsfield said.

Saint-Ruhe had been up and down the Shannon several times since his arrival, examining the crossings and their defences, making suggestions, and addressing garrisons. He was a model of an engaged commander.

'Not pretty but he gets the job done,' Luttrell said, almost to himself, as if that was a criticism.

'We'd better get to Athlone quickly.' Sarsfield wheeled his horse around to give his words urgency. 'Or his grace will be making trouble there.'

Luttrell took another bite of the biscuit and threw the remainder over his shoulder. 'Trying to seize control of the army,' he grunted.

'I doubt he would go that far.'

'Why doubt it?' Luttrell drained the tankard and tossed it to his trumpeter. 'It's what he always does, isn't it? Goes after what he wants and gets it. And he wants command of the army again.'

It was true, Sarsfield thought. Tyrconnell had appeared to accept that Saint-Ruhe was in charge of military matters, not him. But that only meant that he was out manoeuvred for the moment by the King's orders, not that he had given up. Fighting Dick never gave up, at least not until he had exhausted all avenues, even the most unlikely ones.

'Why is he even in Athlone?' Luttrell demanded in an angry tone, the thought of Tyrconnell's scheming waking him up properly. 'It's not for him to conduct the war. He should be still in Limerick, looking after civil matters.'

'Maybe it's better that he is there,' Sarsfield offered. 'Not conspiring to do a deal with the King's enemies behind our backs.'

Luttrell gave him a glance that suggested he was ridiculously naïve: you couldn't trust Tyrconnell, even if he was at St Peter's right hand. He kicked his horse into action and called to one of his subordinates to get a move on.

Sarsfield smiled to himself at having galvanised Luttrell. The jolting ride to Athlone might teach him not to drink so much every night.

Another officer rode over and told him all the cavalry detachments were ready to move. Sarsfield signalled to his trumpeter, a boy in the golden uniform of his trade, and told him to sound the 'fall in'. When they were all in position, the trumpeter blew the forward trot and they set off across the open countryside, avoiding the roadway with its lumbering wagons and cannons.

It was another day of dullness and brightness, the unbroken cloud like a covering that would never lift. Most of the land was open but there were enclosures of sticks and some of stones around crops of corn and potatoes in places, usually near the more substantial cabins. Behind Sarsfield's back a few riders diverted from the column to jump them for sport, one raising a derisive laugh from his colleagues when his horse simply went through a flimsy wattle fence, flattening it and the young corn beyond.

The inhabitants kept out of sight and the land might have been deserted but for the smoke seeping through some roofs. They rode up a high hill and the land spread out all around them. Sarsfield halted and stood up in the saddle to look back at where they had come from. He felt that he was on top of the world, close to the pressing sky.

The land was green with the fresh grass of early summer. Clumps of furze bushes dotted the landscape with their early blossoms and, in the distance, some men were driving a herd of small black cattle away from them, no doubt hoping to save them from seizure. He could see a couple of old tower houses, remnants of battles and struggles long ago. The western horizon was a curving white line drawn before him, as definitive as if it truly was the world's end.

He had been around here before, in Galway the previous year to arrest some of Tyrconnell's supporters who had been talking to the enemy. And in Portumna before that, where he had met Honor.

The column passed him by and Sarsfield turned after it and cantered back to his position at its head, his trumpeter following in his wake.

It was evening by the time they reached the camp near Athlone. It stretched over a patch of raised ground between two bogs west of the town and was spreading by the hour as more and more columns and wagons arrived. Men were uprooting bushes and clearing stones to make way for their tents. Card games were underway among those who cared less about where they would sleep. Fires burned under the bread ovens. Artillery men carefully mixed the barrels of gunpowder that had broken down into its inert constituent parts during the rattling journey from Limerick. Camp followers sought out dry stretches on the bogs. Two prostitutes kneaded a mixture of urine and ash from a bowl into each other's hair to turn it yellow.

Sarsfield stood outside his tent, taking in all the activity, and didn't notice Colonel Clifford approach from the side until he coughed. 'My lord Tyrconnell would like you to dine with him this evening,' Clifford said when he had got Sarsfield's attention.

Sarsfield almost laughed at the transparency of the invitation. Tyrconnell wanted to try and get him on his side before Saint-Ruhe arrived. He knew that the army, especially the cavalry, would follow Sarsfield, and he needed his support if he had any hope of influencing the military campaign. There was no prospect of that happening, Sarsfield knew, but he couldn't refuse the invitation to dinner.

'Who else will be there?' Sarsfield asked.

'Lieutenant General d'Usson,' Clifford said. 'And me.'

Sarsfield looked at him in surprise: he knew that Clifford had been taken in by Tyrconnell's weaselly words but he hadn't realised that Clifford had become close enough to him to be invited to a dinner with generals.

'He wants to discuss the defence of Athlone,' Clifford said by way of explanation. He had been in command of the town's defences earlier in the year and d'Usson was now in charge.

That made sense, Sarsfield thought. They were the men who knew most about its defences – he himself had spent a lot of time there in the spring -- but was that any of Tyrconnell's business? On the other hand, he was the King's representative in Ireland, so he had a right to know what was happening. As long as he kept his distance and behaved like someone in his position should, leaving military matters to the military men. But Tyrconnell was also a military man as well as a courtier and politician, and he was never a person to give up any of his roles and cede any control.

If only I could send Luttrell, Sarsfield thought. He'd be at home there, playing verbal games and trading barbed politenesses.

In the event, Tyrconnell was at his most benign and charming, reminiscing about his days at the Duke of York's exile court on the Continent and then in Restoration London before the duke became King James and didn't have the cares of the crown upon his own head, or on Tyrconnell's. 'The days,' he pointed his fork at Sarsfield as they finished their first course and then at Clifford with a fond laugh, as if they were two favourite sons, 'when you two were sowing your wild oats. The scourge of the city's fashionable young widows.'

He went on to tell d'Usson in detail about Clifford's kidnapping of a widow and then about Sarsfield's later attempt to force another young widow to marry him by kidnapping her. 'But Captain Sarsfield had learned from Captain Clifford's rash ardour and he wisely persuaded the lady to sign a waiver promising not to prosecute him when he released her.'

D'Usson gave Sarsfield a small appreciative bow. 'Very wise,' he murmured.

Sarsfield returned a modest grin and took another sip of his wine. Clifford seemed embarrassed by the stories. Or, Sarsfield thought, by Tyrconnell's efforts to present them as good friends, comrades in the pursuit of love.

'He has now found himself a young wife,' Tyrconnell assured d'Usson, 'without the need of either a sword or a fast horse.'

D'Usson laughed dutifully.

'I seem to remember there were other escapades in those days, too. More than one duel. I can't remember about what?' Tyrconnell gave Sarsfield a questioning look.

'I can scarcely remember myself,' Sarsfield said.

'But you were lucky to survive one.'

Sarsfield confirmed the accuracy of his statement with a nod. Was that a pointed remark? he wondered. That he had been bested in a duel and almost died?

'Over a lady again?' d'Usson asked.

'I think I would remember if that had been the case,' Sarsfield said with a smile.

'*Évidemment*,' d'Usson nodded.

It was only when they had finished their main course of boiled mutton and arrived at the brandy that Tyrconnell got to the point. 'I must compliment you gentlemen on the work you have done preparing the town's defences.'

'I hope to see the latest improvements for myself in the morning,' Sarsfield said, 'but I'm confident that we are even better prepared than we were last year.'

D'Usson demurred. 'Unfortunately we have not had time to build up the defences of the English town. The work during the winter was very slow.'

The French engineers charged with improving the defences since the previous year's siege had wanted to concentrate on the English town on the eastern bank of the river which had been burned and abandoned when the Williamites had unsuccessfully besieged the Irish town on the western side. It was on higher ground than the Irish town, giving its occupiers clear views into the western town and dominating it. But the western town was more easily defended, thanks to the wide river between them.

The works on improving the English town had gone slowly because of the near famine conditions during the winter. There were periods of a week and more when the small garrison had no bread or meat and the work to build up earthen banks by the relatively low walls had been halted by hunger and weakness.

The defences had still not been improved to the point where specialists like d'Usson were happy.

'There is one suggestion I would make for your consideration, if I may,' Tyrconnell said in his most reasonable tone. 'That you take down the ramparts built on this side of the Irish town last winter. They will impede us if the enemy cross the river and breach the walls and we need to send in reinforcements quickly to repel them.'

'Hmm,' d'Usson said. 'But what if they cross the Shannon elsewhere and attack from the west?'

Tyrconnell gave a dismissive shrug. 'It appears that they intend to attack Athlone directly.'

'That's very foolish of them,' d'Usson ventured.

'There are signs that they are moving towards Portumna or Banagher.' Sarsfield wanted to seize the opportunity to put forward his own favourite plan. Perhaps Tyrconnell would support it. 'In which case we may be able to raid across the river from here or Lanesborough.'

'Raid?' Tyrconnell queried.

'Attack their supply lines. Threaten Dublin. Force them to pull back.'

Tyrconnell appeared to give the suggestion a moment's consideration. 'You've heard the news from Ballymore?' He switched topic as suddenly as a swordsman changing the point of attack. 'It appears it will soon be lost.'

Nothing has changed, Sarsfield realised. Tyrconnell would not support him. He had been foolish to imagine so, even for a moment. He braced himself mentally for the expected attack.

Tyrconnell had opposed leaving the garrison at Ballymore. It had been Sarsfield's decision and his alone. On the basis that it was a strong and useful outpost for foraging and for forays into Leinster and even, possibly, to Dublin, and that it denied the rebels a swath of territory east of the Shannon. Tyrconnell had thought it pointless, ultimately undefendable, and potentially a waste of a garrison. And Clifford, sharing Tyrconnell's views, had abandoned one of its outposts closer to Mullingar the previous winter.

'Do we know what stage the siege is at?' Sarsfield asked in a neutral tone, not conceding that anything had been lost yet. There was every possibility Colonel Burke's men could hold out for quite a while. They were good men, well-equipped and well-supplied. They could resist long enough for a counterattack which would relieve them.

'Their heavy guns have been playing on the fort all day,' d'Usson said. 'Our scouts haven't been able to get close enough to see the state of the fortifications.'

'Well,' Tyrconnell said in his most reasonable voice, smoothing over the disagreements between the Irishmen before they became obvious to the Frenchman, 'they've delayed the enemy's approach for several days. Days that have been crucial to building up our forces here.'

Sarsfield and Clifford walked back to the cavalry camp in silence afterwards, each keeping his own counsel. It was late but there was a faint light in the western sky where the cloud cover had softened into gauze.

The infantry camp was quiet but for the snores of men exhausted by days of marching on often hungry stomachs. Many lay in the open, some awake, staring without expression at the cavalry officers passing by. Those lucky enough to have received one of the new French uniforms that fitted kept them wrapped tight around their bodies to prevent them from being stolen while they slept. A group of inveterate gamblers played in near silence, throwing down their cards with fatalistic determination on the top of an empty powder barrel.

As often after a conversation with Tyrconnell, Sarsfield felt a vague unease mixed with irritation. He always assumed that he had been manipulated, even if he did not know exactly how and to what end. Someone had told him once that Tyrconnell was a follower of an Italian who had written a book a century and a half ago on when to flatter and when to be ruthless, how to befriend your enemies and how to deceive your friends. He was exasperated by all that. He only knew one way of dealing with an enemy or a friend: straightforward enmity or friendship. No pretences.

He thought of Colonel Burke, a good man, and hoped he would survive the siege at Ballymore. And all the others, too, but he didn't think too much about them. That was the way with war. Soldiers died. He had killed some in his time. Nearly been killed, too, several times. Like at Sedgemoor, when he really thought he was done for. And that duel that Tyrconnell had alluded to. Unconsciously, he ran his fingers down his side over the scar from the sword thrust that had almost been fatal.

A dog barked in the distance and the frantic choking cries of a baby among the camp followers on the edge of the bog to the south cut through the snores and rustles around them. There were no sounds of war.

He reached his tent and turned into it without a word to Clifford.

News of Ballymore's surrender came overnight and Lieutenant General d'Usson gathered all the senior officers together shortly after dawn to discuss the situation. Brigadier Wauchope, tall and lanky in almost comical contrast to the short and round d'Usson, summarised what they knew: the fort had surrendered although its walls appeared from a distance to be largely intact; the fate of the garrison wasn't yet clear. One man had been hanged on a nearby hill.

'When can we expect them here?' d'Usson asked.

'Two or three days,' Wauchope suggested.

'Pointless waste of good men,' Major General Maxwell muttered as if to himself but loud enough to be heard.

His comment was clear to everybody. He was speaking for Tyrconnell, criticising Sarsfield's insistence on garrisoning and defending Ballymore. Luttrell looked as if he was about to reply but he changed his mind. Sarsfield did not respond either, disappointed that Ballymore had not held out for longer but aware that no one else at the meeting was likely to criticise him. Almost all the commanders present were on his side. Thankfully, there was no sign of Tyrconnell himself.

D'Usson, learning more daily of the fault lines among the Irish and the underlying import of their comments, moved quickly on. 'We don't have much time,' he said. 'I've sent a messenger to the general. We need to get all our men and supplies here as quickly as possible. It's clear now that they are coming to Athlone and we're far from ready.'

'The fortifications are ready,' someone interjected.

'On this side of the river,' d'Usson nodded, 'but we are still short of men and supplies if we are to withstand their whole army.'

'What about the English town?' Maxwell asked. 'Are we going to defend it this time?'

D'Usson invited responses with a silent look around the assembled group.

'Yes,' Wauchope said. He was now in command of the garrison in the ruins of the English town.

There was a murmur of approval and d'Usson fixed his questioning stare on Sarsfield.

'Yes,' Sarsfield agreed. 'We should defend it this time. And we should think about taking the battle to the enemy.'

'How?' d'Usson asked for the benefit of the others: he knew the answer from the previous night's dinner.

'By raiding across the river into Leinster.'

'You told me the Dutch and English have sent a detachment to

Lanesborough,' d'Usson said to Wauchope. 'And,' he turned back to Sarsfield, 'the Danish regiments are approaching the other crossings at Portumna and Meelick. So how are we to attack them without losing all our raiders and weakening our position here?'

'We could persuade Balldearg O'Donnell to cross the upper reaches of the river and attack southwards,' Sarsfield said.

'Ah,' d'Usson sighed at the mention of the name. 'Your Jeanne d'Arc. I keep hearing of this saviour from Spain but --,' he raised his hands in a shrug which seemed to inflate his whole body as he paused for effect, 'where is he?'

'In Mayo,' Sarsfield said. 'We should send an emissary to him. Coordinate his activities with ours. Invite him to bring his men into the army. He has six or seven thousand of them.'

'Trained?'

'Good fighting men,' Sarsfield deflected the question. 'We could use them.'

Luttrell caught Sarsfield's eye and gave him a hint of a wink that was little more than a blink to anyone watching. 'Could I propose that Colonel O'Kelly be the emissary to Balldearg?' he suggested. 'He's more likely to listen to him.'

O'Kelly looked at Luttrell in surprise. There was no love lost between them: O'Kelly thought him an unscrupulous opportunist; Luttrell saw O'Kelly as an old bore inhabiting a fantasy world of old Celtic myths. O'Kelly nodded his agreement, knowing that Luttrell was right: Balldearg was more likely to listen to a representative of one of the old native Irish families like his own.

'I will seek the general's approval when he gets here,' d'Usson said, detecting some of the tension between Luttrell and O'Kelly but not understanding its source. 'And,' he turned to Wauchope, 'he will decide whether or not we defend the English town.'

Seeing the meeting conclude an aide came forward with a plate of cheese, a freshly baked cake of bread, and a cup of coffee and placed them on d'Usson's desk, filling the tent with a hunger-inducing aroma.

'Well done, my lord Lucan,' Luttrell said as the officers filtered out into the fresh morning air and he fell into step beside Sarsfield.

'What?'

'What?' Luttrell repeated, his tone heavy with delighted sarcasm. 'And you say you don't play politics. I am impressed.'

'What are you talking about?' Sarsfield shot a sideways glance at him. He was thinking about Colonel Burke and his men at Ballymore, wondering what relationship Burke was to Honor. Distant, he hoped, but he wasn't *au fait* with the extensive Burke family tree.

'Balldearg,' Luttrell said. 'Getting the Frenchmen to seek his help. Which will only provoke O'Donnell into his rant about Lying Dick stealing his family's title while they were in Spain.'

'I wasn't thinking of that,' Sarsfield admitted.

'Of course you weren't.' Luttrell's tone made it clear that he didn't believe him. 'And giving the Frenchmen another argument to get rid of Tyrconnell. We need him out of here to get Balldearg's men into our ranks and boost the army's strength.'

Sarsfield stopped and looked at Luttrell as if he was seeing him for the first time. 'I was only thinking of the extra men. And of a way to attack the rebels, harry them from the rear.'

Luttrell studied his eyes for a moment and then nodded to himself: Sarsfield was serious. 'Still,' Luttrell said, clapping him on the shoulder, 'it was neatly done. Whether you realized it or not.'

Mackay

At first light Major General Mackay followed a group of soldiers down the hill and went into the fort through the gap their guns had made, picking his way with care over the loose stones that had been dislodged and broken.

Dead horses, cattle and sheep lay around the enclosure, some of them already cut up by the defenders' butchers the night before. Live animals were corralled by ropes in one corner, protected by men with muskets. Some of the soldiers were sent over to relieve them. Others were despatched to replace those who had kept a rough corral around the hundreds of women and children cornered at the other side of the enclosure. Most carried pikes to keep them in place and stop them from descending on the dead animals. A low wailing noise came from the women.

Mackay went on into the inner fort, entering by its main entrance over the deep ditch that protected its walls from assault. Farther along the wall, the guns had created a breach but it would have been difficult enough to fight their way in, he thought. He stopped, casting his professional eye over the layout of the ground to see if there was anything to be learned from it. Had they targeted the right part of the walls for the infantry to go through?

Probably, he decided, and continued into the inner fort.

A party of Irish soldiers was carrying corpses from among the rubble of broken buildings and placing them in a line on the ground just inside the entrance. The first was headless, probably Colonel Burke's second-in-command, an engineering officer whom, Burke had told them after the surrender, had been beheaded by a cannonball. Others were missing limbs; some had explosive burns; one's skull had been crushed by a mortar-fired rock.

A pile of muskets lay beside a building, their stocks broken by the garrison while the surrender arrangements were being made. Mackay noted that they were all old matchlocks, less reliable and slower to load and fire than the new flintlocks.

The garrison itself was sitting on the ground on the edge of the mound at the centre of the fort. Most of them wore some semblance of red uniform but others had little more than torn bits of clothing. They were quiet, subdued and sullen. The look of defeat, Mackay thought.

'Here comes the paymaster-general,' Major General Talmash said in his ear. 'Looking for his pound of flesh.'

Mackay turned to see Thomas Coningsby stepping with Ginckel onto the mound where the enemy's two small field pieces were, now with their mouths stuck in the ground in an attempt to destroy them before the surrender. Coningsby, one of the three lord justices who ruled Ireland on behalf of the King, had arrived at the camp the previous day in time to witness the end of the siege and to question Ginckel's decision not to implement his threat to give the garrison no quarter. Instead, Ginckel ordered, they were to be taken to Dublin as prisoners of war.

'Dublin doesn't want them,' Coningsby had declared. 'It doesn't want a horde of papist prisoners in its midst.'

'I can't keep them here,' Ginckel had replied.

The discussion had ended with the general, as commander in chief, insisting that the prisoners would be sent to Dublin, the officers to the castle and the men to wherever the city authorities decided. They eventually shipped them to Lambay Island off the coast.

'Look at them,' Coningsby was saying now as Mackay and Talmash joined their group; 'most of them are rapparees.'

Ginckel said nothing. They all knew, or suspected, that some of the garrison were rapparees, probably including those who had been raiding their outposts and ambushing their convoys in recent weeks and who had sought refuge in the fort when the army approached.

'They should be treated as rapparees,' Coningsby said. 'All hanged.'

'They're all part of the garrison that surrendered,' Ginckel replied.

'Surrendered on discretion.'

'Yes, and I have exercised my discretion.' Ginckel turned to face him. 'You may consult their Majesties if you disagree.'

Coningsby gave him a sour look, knowing what everyone knew -- that the Dutchman was close to the King and that the King was unlikely to rule against his fellow countryman and commander in favour of an Englishman. Even less likely in Coningsby's case because he was half-Irish thanks to his mother. Although his devotion to the revolution and the reformed church's cause was conceded even by those who complained of his well-known greed and corruption.

The burial party was now carrying the bodies of the dead defenders out of the fort to a pit already dug in the land beyond. The moaning among the women turned into a wail when they saw the bodies go past. Mackay ordered an infantry officer to strengthen the guard around the camp followers before they marched the prisoners off to Dublin.

'I trust you're not allowing their priests to attend them with their superstitious Romish cant,' Coningsby added as they waited for the funeral party to leave the outer compound.

'No,' Ginckel said. Two priests had been discovered among the garrison and would be hanged.

Coningsby stopped to look again at the large flock of sheep and the herd of small, black cattle in the enclosure. The men had already been promised the sheep and cattle, a guarantee of plentiful food for days to come. The better horses would be given to the dragoons and the garrons put to work hauling supply wagons.

Talmash nudged Mackay and pointed to Coningsby with a jerk of his other elbow. 'He's trying to count them,' he whispered.

Mackay glanced at Coningsby and realized Talmash was right. Coningsby's lips were moving and his eyes were narrowed as he concentrated on the shifting flock of sheep but it was a difficult, if not impossible, task as the sheep nudged and moved uneasily in their restricted area.

'He'll deduct those from our supplies,' Talmash added, 'and pocket the difference.'

Mackay did not reply, not wanting to believe it of such a strong supporter of the reformed religion but he was already aware of the stories of Coningsby's greed. He was the King's paymaster general in Ireland and known to pocket a little of everything that passed through his hands.

'Should we ask to see the handkerchief?' Talmash sniggered as they made their way back to the headquarters tent. As well as his greed Coningsby was noted for having staunched the blood from King William's shoulder where a cannonball had grazed it at the Boyne the previous July. Rumour had it that he carried the bloodied handkerchief on him at all times, perhaps as a protection against prosecution.

Mackay held his tongue, resisting the temptation to lecture Talmash on the ways of Providence which had protected the King from death at a critical time despite the venality of some of his supporters. Two men passed by bearing the body of the sergeant from the hill to the makeshift burial pit. A drum roll sounded as the bodies were buried with military honours but without religious rites.

In the tent, Ginckel asked for opinions about what needed to be done to make the fort more secure and turn it into a useful post to protect their supply lines from Dublin. 'Build some defences on the lake side,' Talmash suggested to general nods of agreement. Other suggestions followed: a proper platform for cannon on the mount; a shielding wall to screen and protect the inhabitants from the hill where the army was camped; better communication trenches within the enclosure.

A great wailing broke through their deliberations and they stepped outside to see what was happening. The prisoners were being marched out of the fort, past the crowd of women and children who were being held back by a line of soldiers with lowered pikes. Some of the prisoners tried to dally and shout to women in the crowd but were prodded onwards by bayonets. The noise rose to a climax of crying and screaming and shouting and wailing as the column shuffled by. It slowly tapered away to a keening moan when the prisoners had gone.

'Give them a cartload of bread,' Ginckel ordered, pointing to the women and children. 'And send them on their way.'

They were herded out of the fort's main gate, each group given loaves of the bread as they passed and pushed away from the village into the inhospitable land to fend for themselves.

The glow of success faded quickly as the saps were filled in, the siege batteries dismantled, and work began on repairing the breaches in the walls and then building the new defences. Days of dreary mist slowed progress, turned the camp into mud, and added to a growing sense of lethargy.

'When are we moving on Athlone?' Mackay asked Ginckel, his frustration growing at the inactivity.

'When we are ready,' Ginckel replied with a steely stare.

'And when will that be?'

'You know when that will be,' Ginckel said in his stolid Dutch fashion. 'When we have done here and when we have everything we need.'

'We are losing the advantage by delaying,' Mackay argued. 'We must push forward, keep pushing the enemy back.'

Ginckel looked like a man holding on to his patience. 'And we will lose all our advantages if we move forward too quickly. Before we are ready.'

'Maybe we should reconsider our next move,' Mackay suggested. He had not given up his opposition to a direct attack on Athlone which required the supplies that Ginckel was waiting for. 'It is not too late to change direction and attack at Meelick.'

Ginckel shook his head. 'My lord Württemberg is on his way here,' he said. Württemberg's Danes were due in a couple of days from Roscrea.

The steady stream of deserters from across the Shannon seemed to underline Mackay's argument. One had confirmed that the Irish were gathering at Athlone, expecting the attack to come there. A Frenchman who had worked on Athlone's defences the previous winter gave them detailed descriptions of what they were up against but he also told them that the French believed the defence of the English town was critical to holding the Shannon crossing. A Captain Taylor and two of his soldiers said the Irish were fed up with the French and the little help they had brought and were desperately trying to get all the rapparees in Connacht into their army to build up their numbers.

Ginckel had sent a strong force of 2,000 infantry and 500 horsemen northwards towards Lanesborough as a diversion but it was only that. He would not review his plans.

The supplies kept coming, as a relentless convoy of wagons arrived day after day, slowed by the wet weather, but bringing more heavy guns, more powder, more cannon and musket balls and the long-awaited pontoon boats.

Walking around the camp, Mackay was appalled at the degenerating behaviour of the troops. They were well fed for the moment, had nothing to complain about, but their language was foul, and gambling, drinking and whoring -- and thieving to support all the vices -- were rife. Some were known to sell anything they could get their hands on, even muskets and ammunition, to the sutlers who swarmed around the army and supplied drink, tobacco and extra food for a price.

'Something must be done about all this misbehaviour,' Mackay told Ginckel another day, arriving in his tent after a tour of inspection which had left him in a state of outrage at what he had seen and heard. 'It's not good for our cause that our men take the Lord's name with such casual disregard and indulge in all these other vices.'

'What do you suggest?' Ginckel looked up from writing his daily report to the King.

'Issue orders against them.'

Ginckel looked sceptical.

'At least an admonishment,' Mackay said, enough of a realist to know that an order against swearing would not clean up soldiers' language.

'Draw up something appropriate,' Ginckel said, turning back to his desk. 'Actually,' he halted Mackay as he was leaving, 'this problem with selling the army's goods to the sutlers is getting out of hand. I hear some men sold their shoes to buy ale and whiskey.'

'Yes,' Mackay agreed. 'It's disgraceful.'

'Issue a warning to the sutlers that they are not, under pain of death, to buy any of the army's goods from anyone.'

Mackay nodded his approval.

'And,' Ginckel added, warming to the task, 'find the most outrageous example of thievery and make an example of the culprit.'

'Might I suggest, as well,' Mackay added, seizing his opportunity, 'that the chaplains be asked to say prayers at the head of their regiments twice a day, perhaps at ten in the morning and seven in the evening.'

Ginckel nodded. That would keep the chaplains happy, he thought, and give Mackay something else to do other than turning his disappointments into continuous arguments.

They finally left Ballymore almost two weeks after they had arrived, joined now by Württemberg's Danish contingent of 7,000 men, and marched towards Athlone, some 20,000 strong. The wagon train of supplies and followers was strung out for miles.

They camped within a couple of miles of Athlone, where the land flattened out into boggy terrain broken by low hills. Ginckel and his general staff were led by scouts to a vantage-point from where they could see the town in the distance. Or, more accurately, the two towns, the closer English town on the east bank of the Shannon and the Irish town on the west bank. The wall around the English town was still intact but they knew that it enclosed only ruins left from the previous year's unsuccessful siege of the Irish town. A bridge with nine arches spanned the river and joined the two towns. On the far side was a high fortification, seven or eight storeys, overlooking the bridge and its approaches.

A patrol of enemy cavalry drew up on another hillside, close enough to watch them observing the lie of the land, but far enough away to avoid an engagement. A troop of cavalry cantered towards them and the enemy disappeared behind their hill. The cavalry circled back again, another minor feint in the endless succession of daily feints and forays.

Mackay's first sight to the town and its defences did not ease his doubts about the wisdom of attacking it. The English town appeared to pose no great difficulty: its walls were not much more than ten feet high but the Irish town on the far bank was another matter. The bridge was a hundred yards long and maybe three yards wide and the river was even wider on both sides of it, running fast from the lake above the town down to the flatlands below it where the water broadened and meandered southwards towards Portumna.

The information from the French deserter seemed to be accurate: there were hills on the eastern side which overlooked the fortifications on the western side, providing perfect firing points for their cannons. The enemy might be well protected by their walls and the river but there would not be too many hiding places in the Irish town when the heavy guns and mortars began to play upon it.

'Why didn't we destroy the walls around the town on this side when we took it last year?' Mackay asked.

'The Irish didn't defend it then,' someone replied. 'Just scuttled across the river into the other town.'

God willing, Mackay thought, they'll do the same again and we'll be spared the trouble of having to fight our way into the English town first.

The move on Athlone began early the next morning with a Prussian commander leading some Dutch dragoons and cavalry towards the town. Their orders were to skirt the path of the main infantry force, making sure the hills and wooded passes were free of ambushes. Desultory volleys of musket fire could be heard as they carried out their mission.

Close to the town, the main force was met with more sustained fire from ditches and hedgerows but the enemy withdrew quickly behind the town's walls when faced with horsemen. Work began immediately on building a battery of eight 24-pounder siege guns within 300 yards of the wall. At first light the next morning, they opened up on a bastion near Dublin Gate. By early afternoon, they had demolished a stretch of the walls running from the gate towards the river. As far as they could see, there were no defences inside the breached wall. Ginckel ordered the assault.

Mackay, as the general of the day in charge, took command and selected an English brigadier, Stuart, and a Danish one, Vitkimhof, to carry out the attack. Two hundred grenadiers from across the army were picked to lead the assault and Mackay gathered them near the battery. It was still firing, to deter the defenders from trying to throw up any barriers in the breach.

The land between the guns and the breach was open, apart from a slightly raised road that ran at an angle towards the Dublin gate. But there was no time to start digging saps: they hadn't expected any significant resistance on this side of the river. 'Use whatever cover you can with the road,' Mackay instructed the vanguard, a young French lieutenant from among the Huguenot regiments and 30 grenadiers.

He watched them go, crouching as low as they could, running alongside the road. But then he realized they were going too far to the right and getting too close to the breach but in such a way that made them an easy target. The defenders were firing from the walls and more of them appeared in the breach as the squad came within effective musket range of sixty yards or so. The squad faltered and was quickly pinned down.

Mackay grabbed a captain in the third line of the attack and ordered him to take his men straight for the breach. And then told the formations behind to follow him.

They did so, lighting their grenades as they ran and hurling them through the gap as they got close enough. They forced the defenders back and disappeared through the breach. Brigadier Stuart's infantry followed behind them and appeared on the walls moments later and fanned out along the perimeter.

The defenders pulled back in a fighting retreat through the ruins of the town towards the bridge, puffs of gun smoke marking their movements, swords clashing as the attackers closed on them. The English town's two gates were opened and the cavalry swept in but they were hampered by the ruined streets within. More infantry reinforcements piled in after them, shouting their war cries, eager for a share of the victory.

The retreating defenders bunched up at the bottleneck of the narrow bridge, becoming easy targets for their pursuers. Some fell under musket shots; others were stabbed with long pikes. A few jumped into the river to escape. Others avoided the bridge and ran into the river below it and waded as quickly as they could beyond the range of the muskets on the walls.

The bottleneck became worse as the last two of the bridge's nine arches were destroyed and those who had not got across in time were trapped. Most jumped into the fast current below and tried to swim towards safety as they were swept downstream. Musketeers tried to pick them off but those who could stay afloat were moving too fast.

Mackay was in the town and running towards the bridge. He passed by dead and dying bodies, paying little attention to them. Most wore shades of red, making it difficult to distinguish friend from foe without a closer look. But he had no time for that. It was imperative to keep the momentum going, to get across the bridge.

He ordered up the men with fascines to screen the soldiers who were pushing their way onto the bridge, clambering over the dying and dead. But the momentum was already faltering and came to a halt three-quarters of the way across where the retreating enemy had broken the last two arches in a planned defensive move. He sighed as he stopped in the shelter of the fascines. Musket balls from the castle on the other side thudded into the thickly woven sticks. Around him, a few papists who had been trapped by the destruction of the arches and had not jumped into the river tried to surrender but were run through with swords and bayonets. One was hauled back from the parapet by a bayonet in his back as he tried, too late, to dive into the water.

Mackay ignored the shouting and slowly receding mayhem as the temper of the action eased. It was as well, he thought, that the troops couldn't keep going. There weren't enough men here to push through the other side. And it might have given the papists an opportunity to counterattack. Besides, the general's orders were to take only the English town.

The fighting eased as both sides settled into the new situation. Musket fire was exchanged across the broken arches of the bridge. An occasional cannonball from the west flew overhead and crashed into the captured town. Mackay walked back through the narrow streets, paying more attention now to the casualties: only the direction in which the dead lay gave an immediate indication of which army they belonged to. Here and there were bodies in grey uniforms and he gave them a closer look, wondering if they were French or Irish. They didn't appear to be well fed so he assumed they were Irish, which confirmed their information, that the French had sent only uniforms, not men. 'Pouring brandy into a dying man's mouth,' as Talmash had put it recently when the general was agonising about King Louis's intentions.

Mackay caught up with Brigadier Stuart being helped back towards the camp, holding a bloodied handkerchief against his neck and wincing with pain as two men half-carried him.

'You knew Wauchope before the abdication,' Stuart said before Mackay could open his mouth.

Mackay nodded. He remembered Wauchope well, a fellow Scot, pleasant and convivial, but an irredeemable papist by temperament. It was no surprise that Wauchope had opted to go back to James from Holland while he himself had stayed with William.

'He's dead,' Stuart added. 'I saw his body picked up. Carried across the bridge.'

A tragedy, Mackay thought. That people like Wauchope just couldn't see the obvious error of their beliefs. He looked at Stuart's right arm, hanging down as if it was lifeless.

'Took a ball in the arm and another grazed my neck,' Stuart answered his unasked question.

'God's blessing on you,' Mackay said. 'You did His work

today.'

He went back through the breach in the wall and saw the body of the young French lieutenant who had led the first attack party lying alongside some of his grenadiers. The wounded among them shifted and moaned in pain. How long ago was that, he wondered, how long since I gave him orders? Half an hour? He had no idea. He had lost all sense of time.

He retrieved his horse from beside the battery, mounted and rode back to the camp.

Sarsfield

Luttrell dismounted at the foot of the earthworks and scrambled up the side of it to lie beside the men manning it. They were upriver, some distance from the castle and the bridge. There was still some shooting from both sides around the bridge and castle but it was quiet here. The red coats of the enemy were visible across the river. They were lying prone, like the men around him, or hunkered down beneath small hillocks by the water's edge, even though both sides knew the river was too wide for effective musket fire.

One of the enemy stood up and a soldier beside Luttrell blew on the cord of his smouldering match and angled his musket upwards, careful to stop before the powder in the pan slipped out. He touched the burning match to the pan. The gun went off with a roar and a huge belch of grey smoke. The musket ball curved upwards and fell into the river short of the opposite bank.

His ears rang for a moment and then Luttrell said to the man who had fired, 'Stop wasting your powder.'

A faint shout came from across the river from someone who had seen the smoke and the splash. 'Go frig yourself, you popish cully.'

The man who had fired slid down from sight to reload his musket but the one next to him roared back across the river, also in an English accent: 'Get back in your shit hole.'

'And wipe your arse with your English bible,' an Irish voice beside him bellowed.

A cacophony of abuse came from the far side of the river but the individual comments were indecipherable. Much the same was delivered from Luttrell's side, equally unintelligible as several men roared at the same time in Irish and English.

The shouting subsided after a few minutes and the shooting at the bridge reasserted itself and was then drowned out by the boom of a cannon firing from the castle, sending up a cloud of dust from the ruins in the centre of the English town.

Luttrell watched the movements across the river. They were still deploying along the bank, settling in for a formal siege. They would start preparing their batteries under cover of darkness but wouldn't have many hours to do it because the nights were now so short.

'Tadgh,' a Scottish or Ulster voice roared across to them, sounding like 'taig', 'would you like a side of Ballymore beef?'

The man with the English accent near Luttrell muttered a curse.

Luttrell looked at him. 'What?'

'Nothing,' the man, a captain in the Grand Prior's regiment, replied.

Luttrell continued to stare at him, effectively repeating the question.

'They say we shouldn't have wasted all those men at Ballymore,' the captain said.

'Who says?' Luttrell asked, trying to keep his tone curious without being demanding.

The captain shrugged.

'What do they mean?' Luttrell demanded, although he knew the answer. And who 'they' were. Tyrconnell's men.

The captain gave him a look that suggested he was very naive. 'What was the point?' he asked.

There was no easy answer to that, Luttrell knew but he would find one if it was needed.

Meanwhile someone was shouting back across the river: 'That beef's poisoned. That's why we left it for you.'

'Did your priests put a curse on it?' the voice on the other side retorted. Even at a distance they could make out the derision in it.

'The sooner you eat it up, the sooner you'll roast in hell.'

'It's delicious. He must've mixed up his curses.'

'That's the right one. Get you to eat more. Till your belly blows up.'

In the distance a flash of light caught Luttrell's attention and he saw the heads of a couple of riders appear briefly above the crown of a hill a little inland on the far side. Heading north, he thought, looking for the ford above the town. Someone would have told them about it.

'How many indulgences will a brass penny buy you now?' the shouter switched his attack.

'More than a heretic prince's ballocks.'

'And where's your tinker king? Whoring in Paris while you're in the shit.'

A cacophony of abuse was roared back at the Williamites but behind the words there was almost a good-natured quality to the abuse: both sides were enjoying it. An officer appeared on horseback on the far bank and rode up and down behind the line. The shouting from that side stopped and was replaced by a volley of shots which dropped into the river short of their bank.

A few fired back in response and Luttrell shouted: 'Don't waste your ammunition. Keep shouting at them and let them waste theirs.'

He slid back down to his horse and smiled to himself as he rode away and the sound of gunfire was replaced with another round of raucous shouts.

Men and supplies were still arriving at the main camp as the army finally began to approach its full strength of about 20,000. Recent arrivals were spread out on the bogs on either side of the raised ground, some of them asleep on the heather after two weeks on the march from Limerick through bogs, mountains, abandoned villages and rain and wind, with little food and only river water or rainwater to drink, flavoured with a little milk when there was some available.

General Saint-Ruhe had arrived and taken command and there was a stir of activity around his tent. Luttrell, curious as always, headed in that direction and asked a cavalry officer what was happening.

'Council of war.'

'What's he doing at it?' Luttrell said, almost to himself, as he caught sight of Tyrconnell's large bulk moving slowly towards the tent from the other side. 'He has no business being there.'

The cavalry officer smirked, knowing what he meant.

'Where's my lord Lucan?' Luttrell asked.

'Inside already. It's general staff only.'

Luttrell turned his horse and rode back towards his own quarters, hoping that Sarsfield would have his answers ready if he had to defend himself over Ballymore and not let Tyrconnell away with anything.

Major General Maxwell was giving an account of the loss of the English town when Tyrconnell entered, breathing heavily. He was met with a range of looks from surprise to anger. General Saint-Ruhe narrowed his eyes and raised himself to his full height to ask in French, 'Has something happened, my lord?'

Tyrconnell took a moment to catch his breath and savour the discomfort his arrival had caused. '*Non, mon général,*' he replied. 'May I be permitted to observe your council. To keep their Majesties informed of the military situation.'

'*Entrez, je vous en prie,*' Saint-Ruhe gave a short bow that hid the grudging welcome behind the formal words.

Sarsfield sighed with irritation as he watched one of Tyrconnell's men carry a chair close to the table around which they were standing. Tyrconnell settled into it as if it was a throne and everyone waited for him to get comfortable. He was wearing the full robes of the viceroy's office and, Sarsfield noted with disgust, his *Riband Bleu*, reminding the French generals that he stood higher up the social order in France, never mind the ruling order in Ireland, than any of them.

Saint-Ruhe motioned to Maxwell to continue and the major general wrapped it up with a report of the casualties, some fifty killed or wounded. 'Brigadier Wauchope is recovering from the blow to the head that left him senseless,' he added.

'What do we think the enemy will do now?' Saint-Ruhe asked around the table. The question was largely rhetorical: the enemy could do nothing other than try to cross the river and seize the Irish town. 'Is the Dutchman out of his mind?' he added in response to the obvious answer. 'Why does he think he can succeed?'

Nobody had an answer to that. Whatever about the arguments in favour of holding the English town, the Irish town was a strong, naturally defensive position and everything possible had been done to make it stronger. The enemy had failed to make any impression on it the previous year: even if they were now better prepared with siege guns, the underlying facts remained. Anyone trying to storm the fortifications had to do so under the worst possible conditions, crossing a wide river by a narrow bridge or by limited fords or exposed pontoons, which could easily be blown out of the water.

Saint-Ruhe turned to his deputy. 'Have the other garrisons been reinforced?'

'Yes, my lord,' Tessé said. Extra troops had been sent to all the nearby river crossings in case the Williamites tried to encircle them, although that appeared unlikely. There was no sign that the main Williamite army was moving away from the English town. In any event, the entire Jacobite army was on hand to deal with any minor incursions elsewhere.

'And our cavalry is ready to go to their aid if the heretics attack them?' Saint-Ruhe asked Sarsfield.

'Yes, my lord,' Sarsfield replied and added, 'We could also use the cavalry to bring the fight to them.'

'What do you mean?'

'Ballyneety again,' someone said.

Tyrconnell made a noise but it wasn't clear whether it was a grunting comment or a hiccup.

Saint-Ruhe looked confused for a moment, then understood the reference: Sarsfield's supporters were making sure he knew all about the successful raid on the Williamite wagons heading for Limerick the previous year. 'It's too late for that,' he said. 'Everything we're told by people from their side indicates that they have already brought all they need to Athlone.'

'We could upset their calculations, draw away some of their forces from Athlone,' Sarsfield said.

'To what end?' Saint-Ruhe said. He had little enthusiasm for that kind of foray as a method of warfare. It would merely cause the enemy annoyance when he wanted to deal him a decisive blow. 'We are not yet at the stage where we can contemplate an attempt to recapture Leinster. Are we?' He looked around the table. Nobody indicated that they thought that was a serious prospect in the near future.

'No,' he continued. 'Our purpose is to defend the territory we hold. Every day the enemy tries and fails to take any of it is a defeat for him and a victory for us. And allows us to continue training and improving the army so that we can best the prince of Orange's mercenaries when the right opportunity presents itself.'

This Frenchman was certainly different to all his predecessors here, Sarsfield thought. Not only did he lack their scorn for the

Irish, he wanted to build the army into an effective unit, not one that was divided by the reciprocal dislike of the French and the Irish which had marked the previous French expeditions. Probably a mark of his ambition: this was his chance to impress the French war minister and his king by his command of a significant army. But, whatever the reason, it was a welcome change.

Tyrconnell had a fit of coughing which interrupted the discussion and he muttered an apology through his handkerchief.

Saint-Ruhe stood to dismiss the council.

'May I ask,' Tyrconnell, red-faced from his coughing fit, intervened, 'if we have any prisoners of war we might exchange for Colonel Burke?'

Sarsfield felt his hackles rise, instantly detecting criticism of his decision to maintain the fort at Ballymore and now the loss of so many men.

Saint-Ruhe looked around for someone to answer that question.

'We don't have any prisoner of similar rank at present, my lord,' one of his staff officers ventured.

'A pity,' Tyrconnell said. 'A good man left in an impossible position. But he did delay the enemy long enough to allow us to get all of our forces here.'

Sarsfield clenched his jaw. That was typical of Lying Dick, what he disliked most about him, attacking and praising at the same time so that the target would be met with a surprised denial if he protested and the uninitiated would not see the dagger in the sleeve.

'True, your grace,' Saint-Ruhe said, adding ambiguously to show that he could hold his own at court too: 'I can't fathom what the Dutchman is thinking.'

'He is looking for a quick victory,' Tyrconnell said. 'But he won't have it.'

'He moves slowly for a man seeking a quick victory,' Saint-

Ruhe said.

'All the better for us. As you said, every day's delay deprives him of victory. All we have to do is be steadfast, hold our positions and our nerves. My compliments to you all on your excellent preparations.'

Saint-Ruhe bowed his thanks.

'I would make one observation, if I may,' Tyrconnell continued in a pleasant tone.

'Yes, I am aware of that,' Saint-Ruhe cut him off, nodding towards d'Usson to indicate that his other deputy had already informed him of Tyrconnell's suggestion that they level the earthen defences on the western side of the Irish town. 'But it would be strange to remove any of the town's defences when we cannot be certain of the enemy's intentions.'

'Just a precaution.' Tyrconnell backed away, realising that d'Usson had argued against the move. 'Probably unnecessary but it is well to be prepared for all eventualities.'

'Indeed,' Saint-Ruhe agreed. 'But I cannot foresee any eventuality in which the heretics can take this town.'

Sarsfield was in a fury when he left. Luttrell, waiting outside, could see it in his face. 'What happened?' he asked, falling into step with his superior's angry strides.

'The usual,' Sarsfield retorted.

'He's managed to take back control of the army?' Luttrell's voice rose in a mixture of incredulity and anger.

'Not yet. But he's still trying to give orders, wheedle his way back in. And criticising me over Ballymore.'

'What did he say?'

Sarsfield told him.

'Classic Dick,' Luttrell said, almost in admiration. 'I never heard him express any concern for Colonel Burke before.'

'Neither did I. He might have held out longer,' Sarsfield added of Burke. 'Didn't have to capitulate so easily.'

Luttrell said nothing, aware that that wouldn't have made much difference since the enemy had sat in Ballymore for almost two weeks after taking the fortifications anyway. And those two weeks had allowed the movement of thousands of men and supplies from Limerick.

'I shouldn't let him irritate me so easily,' Sarsfield continued.

'It's difficult to avoid.'

'But I can't stomach his pretence that we're all united now. That he has changed his mind and wants to fight when we know he was ready to surrender less than a year ago. All he really wants is to get back into a position where he's in control and can do an underhand deal with the prince of Orange to secure his own future.'

'Don't worry. The army won't let him.'

'I don't know.' Sarsfield shook his head.

'What?' Luttrell demanded in a worried tone. 'You think the Frenchman is going to give in to him?'

'I don't know,' Sarsfield said again. 'How long can anyone stand up against that endless conniving?'

'Forever,' Luttrell relaxed, knowing that politics never ended, even if its shape and aims changed. 'We can play the game as long as he can.'

The bombardment began at six o'clock the following morning, the 24-pound iron balls from a battery of five guns smashing into the north-east side of the castle, knocking splinters off its stones and dislodging mortar into plumes of dust. Then a stand of six mortars began to cough up their bombs interspersed with rocks, tossing them into the Irish town and over the castle walls into its enclosure. Incendiary carcasses set fire to wooden walls and thatched roofs, and smoke drifted through the narrow streets. The noise was all-consuming, drowning out the screams of the injured and dying and the shouts of orders as the defenders hunkered down to avoid the explosions, the splinters of stone, and the careering cannonballs.

It went on all day and through the night, slowly but inexorably demolishing the wall facing the river and exposing the castle's innards to the gunners. Movement became difficult as the gunners on the higher ground to the east could see into the town and target any activity. Trenches were dug and makeshift fortifications built up from rubble to provide cover. But the defenders had to wait until darkness to carry out the wounded, withdraw the dust-covered garrison, and send in new men to replace them. The rain of iron, rocks and explosives went on into the light of another day, systematically trying to lay waste all four acres of the town.

The hospital tents behind the town began to fill up - sick women and children who had been occupying them sent away to make more room. Surgeons amputated mangled arms and legs, used long forceps to extract musket balls from bodies, and applied salves to wounds. The noise here was different, screams as the knives cut into flesh and sawed at bones, groans from the treated and the untreated, and the cries of women who had found their dying or dead husbands, sons and fathers.

Some six-pounder field guns, which had arrived from Limerick, were set up in a battery on high ground behind the town, targeting the mortar positions on the other side. After some trial shots, they got the range and one of the mortars stopped firing for a little while but then started up again. The field pieces picked out any concentrations of heretics the gunners could see and watched them beat a hasty retreat beyond range as the shot began to fall among them.

The Williamite 24-pounders went on hammering the castle and all around it into a choking dust and then turned their attention to ploughing up the defensive earthworks on either side of it, gouging furrows and holes in them.

Sarsfield and Luttrell rode towards the town, left their horses at a safe distance, and made their way through the network of trenches to the river to see for themselves what was happening at the focal point of the siege, the bridge.

The Williamites were trying to repair its two broken arches, pushing forward behind their protective screen of fascines. They had already placed two rough planks from cut-down tree trunks across the first broken arch and were trying to push more into position to allow them advance. Continuous musket fire from the bridge's defences and from behind the ruined castle walls smashed into the sticks, weakening their protective strength. Some balls began to find their way through the fascines, hitting attackers.

Fire was returned non-stop across the river from infantry on the bridge. Cannonballs, fired low and flat, skittered over the stones of the ruined walls, damaging everything in their erratic path, walls and bodies, until their energy was expended.

The dust and smoke drifted eastwards on a warm and gentle breeze from the west and high above the noise and mayhem the sky was a soft and unmarked blue.

Mackay

The council of war ended with dissatisfaction all around. Mackay left in a foul mood. There had been almost as many opinions as there had been general officers present. Ginckel had shown himself unable to control the discussion or come to any clear-cut decisions. Everybody was talking at cross purposes; the cavalry officers as usual wanted an opportunity to prove their valour with a single glorious charge; the Ulstermen, as always, were seeking an opportunity for vengeance for a fifty-year-old war; and all the general did was expose his ignorance of siege warfare. It was impossible to have a proper discussion without being interrupted by somebody else with a half-baked idea. It was infuriating.

Mackay went for a brisk walk to ease his frustration and found himself on one of the hills that gave a view over both sides of the river. He could see the puffs of smoke from the muskets firing at each other across the broken bridge and the flash of the papist field pieces aimed at random into the already ruined English town. Its ruins were as nothing now compared to the ruin of the Irish town.

The cannonade was all very well but what did it achieve?

Flattening the town and making it very hot, a foretaste of hell, for the papists. But it didn't make it all that much easier to get across the narrow bridge. A handful of well-armed men could hold up a whole army there indefinitely. But Ginckel didn't seem to understand that there was only one way to succeed in a situation like this: to pretend to do one thing and to do something else.

Instead, he seemed to have no idea other than to smash the enemy position into dust and rely on an infantry charge across the repaired bridge.

'But that could cost us thousands of soldiers,' Mackay had pointed out at the council.

Ginckel had looked at him in surprise.

'I mean we could lose two or three thousand men. And still fail to take the enemy position. They have a whole army over there to defend a single passage,' Mackay said.

'Nonsense,' someone else rowed in behind the silent general. 'The papists will run away in the face of a determined attack. They always do.'

'And if they don't?' Mackay asked, conscious of how the late king's forces in Scotland had fought the previous year and loath to put all his faith in the belief of their own superiority. Even if Providence was on their side. 'Then it will be a defeat.'

Nobody seemed ready to contemplate that.

'A hundred wagons are on their way from Dublin,' Ginckel said after a brief pause, returning to the subject with which he seemed most comfortable - his supply lines. 'With more powder and more cannonballs.'

Mackay had given up then, suppressing a sigh of impatience. They didn't seem to understand that in the context of this campaign it would be a major defeat to lose two thousand dead and fail to achieve a crucial objective. That they could then be forced on the defensive in the face of a resurgent papist army, their confidence buoyed up. France would probably send more help if she saw a real chance of rolling back the previous year's victory at the Boyne and seriously embarrassing the King, regardless of the Stuart king whose real interest in Ireland was as a stepping stone to Scotland and thence to reclaim his English throne as well.

This has all the makings of a disaster, Mackay thought, brushing off the coating of fine dust that had settled on his shoulders from the grey cloud drifting overhead. I must talk to the general alone.

It was late at night before he got an opportunity. Ginckel was in his tent, writing at his desk, a candle by his elbow. Mackay asked his aide-de-camp if he could talk privately to the general. As he waited outside for a response, the flash of cannons interrupted the half-light of the summer night and he could see the pinpricks of the enemy muskets firing across the broken arches of the bridge.

The aide-de-camp showed him into the tent as Ginckel put down his quill and dabbed a piece of blotting paper over what he had been writing. He did not seem happy to see Mackay.

'My apologies, my lord,' Mackay said, speaking Dutch rather than French to make his approach less formal. 'But I feel I must speak to you about the situation.'

Ginckel invited him to take a seat with a silent gesture, a half-wave of an open palm. It was darker inside the tent than outside, the wavering candlelight casting a gloom into the areas where its yellow light did not penetrate.

'My lord, I believe we are at a dangerous impasse here.' Mackay took a breath and launched into his prepared speech. 'Failure to maintain our momentum will have a very deleterious effect on our cause and the cause of freedom in these three kingdoms, as well as on the continent. Protestant Ireland is very concerned at the lack of progress and Lord Justice Coningsby says that even in Dublin they fear the worst and have ordered the avenues to be barricaded lest the papists break out and attack the city.'

A flicker of his eyelids might or might not have indicated Ginckel's reaction to the mention of Coningsby. Ginckel, Mackay knew, did not consider Coningsby to be a helpful presence in the camp.

'Concentrating all our efforts on a single crossing of the river, especially an easily defended crossing like this bridge, is a mistake in my opinion,' Mackay continued, 'even if we were to succeed, the cost would be such ---'

'We are not concentrating all our efforts on a single crossing,' Ginckel interrupted. 'You forget the pontoon bridge.'

Mackay curbed a sudden rush of impatience. This was not Ballymore, where a heavily out-numbered and out-gunned garrison was easily intimidated by the prospect of a boat-borne assault.

'But we don't have the pontoons we need,' he said instead. Fewer pontoons than expected had arrived from Dublin and they were now trying to repair some left over from the unsuccessful siege of Limerick the previous year.

'All the laws of siege warfare say that the only way to capture a town like this one is to pretend to do one thing and to do another,' Mackay said. 'That is the only method that has worked in practice. There are many precedents for it. As there are for the failure of a single-pronged attack on a defended town across a wide and fast-flowing river.'

'What do you suggest?' Ginckel inquired in a tone that suggested politeness rather than interest. None of Mackay's analysis was news to him.

'I have looked at all the maps and all the information from spies,' Mackay said. 'It appears to me that we should broaden the front, cross the river at Lanesborough and march on Athlone from the north. If I could have the Iniskilling and Londonderry regiments, who are eager to get to grips with the enemy and are adept at travelling light with, say, four days' worth of bread and fodder, I believe we could cross the river and move to Athlone before the enemy could act to stop us.'

Ginckel gave a sceptical sigh.

'That area around Lanesborough, if the intelligence is accurate, is not suitable for cavalry, so they will not be in a position to react quickly to our arrival,' Mackay added, his counter-arguments ready for the opposition that had not yet been voiced. 'And, if we should attack at Meelick, to the south, at the same time, we shall divide their response. Meelick is a succession of islands in the river and their only fort on one of them can be easily ignored, made irrelevant by a small body of men besieging it while the main group bypass it. The enemy won't know which is a diversion and which the real attack.'

'And which will be the real attack?'

'Through Lanesborough.' Mackay settled back in his chair, his case made.

'And what if the enemy goes on the offensive? Attacks across the bridge here while we are committed there or in Meelick?'

'It's unlikely,' Mackay said. 'Their attitude is defensive but we can build up the English town's defences just in case.'

'That would all take time,' Ginckel pointed out. 'And you say we don't have time.'

Mackay conceded the point with a nod. 'Better to make time for a workable plan than to waste it on an impossible effort.'

Ginckel did not react to the implied criticism.

They fell silent, listening to another cannon boom. The warm night air filtered through the open flap of the tent, its balm tainted by the smell of the candlewax and the whiff of gunpowder from the cannon fire.

'Another important point,' Mackay said. 'The success of this plan would depend on secrecy. That nobody knows the true point of the attack except yourself.'

'And yourself,' Ginckel pointed out.

'There are spies everywhere and there is too much talk

spreading out from the councils of war.'

'I wasn't aware of that.'

'Yes,' Mackay said. 'I have heard men debating the minutiae of the latest council discussion within hours of it taking place.'

'That cannot be allowed,' Ginckel said irritably.

'I fear there is only one way of stopping it. There are too many people involved in the councils to stop information seeping out because everybody tells their confidants what is planned. The only solution is to keep the true plan secret.'

Ginckel nodded several times, as if he accepted all of what Mackay had said.

Mackay looked up from reading his Bible outside his tent the following day to see Talmash coming back from the town. The wind had moved a few degrees farther to the west and was now blowing the smoke and dust from the siege directly eastwards. The sky was otherwise clear except for white puffs of high clouds moving in convoy along the horizon.

'Reading the good book,' Talmash noted aloud. 'Is that what has you looking so happy today?'

'It always raises the spirits,' Mackay said, closing the Bible on his finger to keep his place. He had told no one of his midnight talk with the general and of his belief that he had persuaded him to change his plan of attack. Secrecy had to be absolute.

'We're getting to close quarters,' Talmash said. He, too, seemed invigorated today, no longer weighed down by the interminable siege. 'We've crossed the first broken span.'

'Good,' Mackay said. Good in the sense that it would convince the enemy that the attack was coming there, he thought. They would not be expecting it to come from somewhere else after so much effort had gone into this one place.

'It's getting hot and heavy down there.'

'I can imagine.'

'We're within grenade distance of them now.'

As if to underline Talmash's words, a sudden burst of intense cannon fire and the cough of mortars broke what had become the steady rhythm of their days and nights. They listened to it, wondering what had prompted it, whether it was in response to some movement by the enemy or merely an artillery officer's whim.

'We could be across tonight,' Talmash added.

Mackay shook his head as he realised that repairing the arch was actually bad news, his worst fear about to be realised. 'It shouldn't be rushed.'

'We've wasted too much time here already,' Talmash said. 'Ruvigny is complaining that the cavalry is running out of fodder. They're having to go farther and farther afield to find grass for their horses. If we don't get across soon, we may have to withdraw.'

'That kind of worry can cause dangerous haste,' Mackay said, rubbing the cover of his Bible with his thumb as if it was a talisman. 'And lead to disaster.'

Talmash gave him a despairing look: this was the kind of caution that could turn this campaign into a disaster. Mackay was as bad as the general, happier to sit around reading his Bible and hoping God would do what needed to be done without any assistance from his army. Every peelgarlick in the place had an opinion, so that they spent their time talking a lot and doing little.

A messenger was running towards them, waving an arm. He came to a stop and paused for a moment while he gulped in air. 'Their fascines on the bridge are on fire,' he said. 'Fired with grenades.'

'Excellent,' Talmash replied, casting an I-told-you-so look at Mackay. That would give them a chance to finish the work on the broken span.

Sarsfield

The rumour spread among the officers, passed from one to the other with the certainty of fact among those who were ready to believe it, ignored by those who heard it as another unwarranted attack on Tyrconnell. Part of the war of words that was the constant background to the real war.

'Is it true?' Sarsfield asked Luttrell.

They were lounging on chairs outside Sarsfield's tent, enjoying the sunshine. In the distance the cannons were exploding regularly, the deep boom of the enemy siege guns and the lighter boom of the friendly field pieces but the noise seemed to be subdued by the glorious weather. The smoke and stench of the battle were absent here, replaced with the smells of cooking, dirty bodies, animals, and the stink from the bog holes which had turned into latrines around the overcrowded camp.

'It's believable,' Luttrell offered as an affirmative, adding a non-sequitur. 'He moved his money to France last year, didn't he?'

Sarsfield nodded with an absent air. 'But where has this information come from?'

Luttrell shrugged as if that was an insignificant detail. 'Do you doubt that he's capable of it?'

No, Sarsfield thought. He didn't doubt that Tyrconnell was capable of such underhand behaviour. He had certainly enriched himself in the past, helping people recover their estates, and securing favours from the King for those who needed them. Always at a price.

He was said now to have made an arrangement with the French to provide men for their army on the continent and was to be paid personally for every one supplied. And that was why General Saint-Ruhe was showing such an interest in the new recruits and spending so much time training them: they were to fight for France, not for Ireland.

'I'll ask the Frenchman,' Sarsfield said.

Luttrell gave a pained look, as if the suggestion caused him some discomfort.

'Why not?' Sarsfield challenged him. 'You think he's part of the plot?'

'If he is, he will deny it. If he isn't, he will deny it too.'

Sarsfield sighed. Court talk worthy of Lying Dick himself.

He doubted if Saint-Ruhe was part of the plot. The Frenchman was undoubtedly ambitious but he appeared to be ambitious in a proper military sense: he wanted to make his name with a victory in Ireland. But Sarsfield knew that wouldn't count for anything if he was under instruction from his all-powerful war minister Louvois to recruit and train more Irishmen for the war in the Low Countries. Or had been brought into his own scheme by Tyrconnell.

'What we need to do,' Luttrell was saying about Tyrconnell, 'is to get him out of here. Everything is poisoned when he's around. We have to stop him from interfering, walking into councils of war at will, spreading dissension.'

That much I can agree with, Sarsfield thought. But it was intolerable that Tyrconnell could be profiting personally from selling to France men badly needed for the defence of Connacht.

120

There had been a trade the previous year; six thousand untrained Irish recruits had gone to France in exchange for the few thousand trained French troops who had come to Ireland. It was an honourable arrangement, a way of ensuring that the French help to the King would not deplete Louis's strength against the prince of Orange on the Continent.

Or was it? Sarsfield decided to talk to Saint-Ruhe but he kept his decision to himself.

Colonel Nicholas Purcell rode up, looking tired and dusty, two paniers hanging behind his saddle, stuffed with loaves of bread. He had led a cavalry troop to Loughrea to bring back supplies because of the shortage of garrons to haul enough wagons to keep the army fed now that it was camped at Athlone. He dismounted, tossed the reins to an aide and told him to bring the paniers to the commissary.

'How's the bakers' boy,' Luttrell laughed at him.

'Very funny,' Purcell snapped back. 'It's ridiculous, using chargers for this work.'

'There's no choice,' Sarsfield said.

'And sending cavalry out to cut down bushes and trees for fascines,' Purcell continued.

'We wouldn't have to do things like that if the civilian authority did its job properly,' Luttrell said, not wasting an opportunity to criticise Tyrconnell.

Purcell reached inside his tunic, extracted a letter and handed it to Sarsfield. 'Another letter from Limerick,' he said.

Sarsfield looked at the wax seal and slid a finger between the pages and was about to prise them open but changed his mind and slipped the letter into his pocket. Another missive from Honor. More of the same, he assumed. Protestations of devotion and mild complaints about the boredom of Limerick. Nothing to do, no society life worth talking about. Most of the other ladies in Paris, at the King and Queen's court in Saint-Germain, the few left in Limerick old and uninterested, even uninteresting.

121

Purcell glanced at Luttrell and raised an eyebrow.

'Have you decided?' Luttrell asked, offering Sarsfield an opportunity to discuss what they knew the letter was about.

Sarsfield shook his head. He didn't want Honor to go into the hothouse atmosphere at Saint-Germain. A court-in-exile was even worse than a normal court: lots of people with little to do other than conspire with and against one another. And seduce one another. Just for entertainment.

'If you want my advice …' Luttrell paused to give Sarsfield the opportunity to reject his offer. Sarsfield said nothing.

'You should let her go,' Luttrell continued. 'Then you won't have to worry about her safety here.'

'Her safety here is not at risk.'

'No,' Luttrell agreed. 'Not at the moment.'

'Why do you think it will be?' Sarsfield demanded.

'I don't.' Luttrell tried to order his thoughts. 'But you shouldn't have to be worrying about that as well as everything else.'

'I'm not worried about her safety here. I'd be more worried about it there.'

Purcell filled his pipe and they lapsed into silence. It was broken by a group of new recruits, young countrymen, bright-faced and eager, marching into the camp, pikes aloft, belting out their marching song:

> Babóg na Bealtaine, maighdean an tsamhraidh,
> Suas gach cnoc is sios gach gleann,
> Cailiní maiseacha bán-gheala glégeal,
> Thugamar féin an samradh linn.
>
> Samhradh, samhradh, bainne na ngamhna
> Thugamar féin an samhradh linn.
> Samhradh buí na nóinín glégeal,
> Thugamar féin an samhradh linn.

Purcell chugged on his pipe, blowing out quick puffs of smoke to get it going as they watched a sergeant direct the group to a narrow spot on the edge of the bog. A few young women with yellow hair hurried over to applaud as they ended their song with a second round of the chorus.

'More business for the *cailíní glégeal*,' Luttrell muttered.

Purcell laughed through a cloud of smoke. 'Anything happening?' he nodded towards the town.

'They fired our fascines at the bridge,' Luttrell told him in a tone that suggested that was scarcely worthy of mention. He added with more enthusiasm: 'Have you signed the petition?'

'What petition?' Purcell asked.

Off to the side of the camp men with burns and wounds from musket balls and cannon splinters had been arriving at the surgeons' tents in ones and twos during the day. They would come in large groups once darkness descended when they could be evacuated from the town in greater safety.

The fire at the fascines had spread quickly, consuming the remains of wooden houses and other protective barriers on either side of the bridge. Several detachments were sent in to try to prevent its spread by creating firebreaks. Working in intense heat and under musket fire through burning barricades, dozens had been killed and scores injured. It took four hours to contain the fire. Out of one detachment of forty men only 14 emerged unscathed.

Sarsfield was shaken awake by the shoulder. He sat up with a start, still half in a dream where he was on a ship and looked up at Luttrell.

'They've bridged the last span,' Luttrell said and disappeared from the tent.

He got dressed quickly, still half in the dream, wondering if the ship had been going to France or coming from there. He couldn't remember but the image of the heavy sea was so vivid, he sensed the ground moving beneath his feet when he stood up.

His horse was waiting outside and he caught up with Luttrell along the causeway into the town. The night was still and not too dark, sometime in the few hours between the long-drawn-out dusk and the early glow of dawn at this time of year. Gunpowder flashes ahead of them made the time even more uncertain.

'Have they crossed?' Sarsfield demanded.

'I don't know.'

'Who's manning the defences?'

'Maxwell's regiment,' Luttrell replied, aware of the concern behind the question. Saint-Ruhe had made it a policy of regularly rotating the infantry at the front line in order to give the new recruits experience of being under fire. 'They'll be all right. Mostly from Ulster.'

They veered off to the left as they approached the town, heading for the trenches upriver of the bridge, from where they could see what was happening without getting in the way.

The musket fire across the gap in the bridge was intense, the flashes almost continuous, turning the grey smoke overhanging it a murky red. Explosions from grenades hurled by both sides lit the scene in momentary black and white silhouettes that were reflected on the water racing through the unbridged channel.

It was difficult to see exactly what had happened but it was clear that some planks had been pushed across the remaining gap in the bridge. From where they were, they couldn't tell how many.

The critical point of the siege had arrived.

'The general knows about this?' Sarsfield asked Luttrell.

'He's been informed.'

Some of the musketeers around them were now firing as well, trying to pick out targets on the bridge and the riverbank opposite, although they were beyond effective range. Responding

124

fire came from all along the opposite bank as everybody joined in, aware that the stand-off was finally over. The cannons and mortars speeded up the drumbeat they had been beating without cease for more than a week.

The trench became more crowded as infantry reinforcements moved in. The noise grew deafening and the still night air thickened with the smoke from hundreds of guns. All attention remained focused on the bridge and the tenuous line across its last gap.

The Williamites were edging their fascines forward onto the planks they had laid across the span, trying to cover it over enough to rush the defences on the other side.

'God's troth,' Luttrell breathed as Sarsfield gave a sharp intake of breath and the firing around them died away for a moment. Everybody saw it at the same time.

In the flashing light and dense smoke a couple of figures were moving forward from the Irish side of the bridge towards the gap. It was hard to tell how many. Half a dozen, maybe ten. Some seemed to stumble and fall, then rise again. Or maybe that was someone else. A few reached the gap and a thin shadow in the grey smoke showed a plank fall diagonally into the river and splash in the reflected gunfire. Then another. Followed by a figure flailing into the water. Then there was no more movement on the bridge. The thin line bridging the gap remained.

It seemed as if everybody around them had been holding their breath at the dream-like scene before them. The firing began again with greater intensity, the musketeers reloading as quickly as possible, ramming the powder and ball down the barrels and bringing the guns up and firing in one movement and then reloading and firing again. As though a fierce rate of fire could undo what they had seen.

Then more figures emerged from the defences and ran to the gap. Again some stumbled and fell. A thin shadow fell diagonally into the river, followed by another. A couple of figures scrambled back towards the defences.

The thin line bridging the gap had disappeared: the span was unpassable again.

A faint cheer from the defenders could be heard in the split-second gaps between the sounds of gunfire. The pops of muskets began to die away slowly. The attempted crossing had been thwarted but the cannons continued firing, reasserting the rhythm of the siege as the sky lightened on another day.

The mood in the camp was euphoric. Saint-Ruhe ordered extra food and drink to be distributed to everyone and presented gold *pistole* coins to the few survivors of the party who had demolished the bridge. He toasted their success with brandy at the next council of war, all raising their glasses to Major General Maxwell, the hero of the hour. Maxwell proposed his own toast, to Sergeant Custume and the men who had died breaking the bridge. He appeared exhausted and far from happy after the night's efforts.

'We should go on the attack now,' Sarsfield suggested. 'Foray across the river at Portumna or Banagher and harry their flank or rear.'

Saint-Ruhe nodded. 'We could hasten their departure. They can't stay here for much longer.'

'Cut their supply line from Dublin,' Sarsfield agreed, seeing the general's point. The latest deserters from the other side said that the Williamites were running out of forage around their camp and having to go farther and farther afield to sustain their horses and men. 'That would force them to withdraw. And then we can move the army across the river and march on Dublin.'

Saint-Ruhe puffed out his cheeks as if to say that was a step too far. 'We're not ready yet to go on the offensive,' he said, 'but it would be useful to force the Dutchman to withdraw and accept his failure. His defeat.'

He's still more concerned about training than about anything else, Sarsfield thought with a touch of impatience. And wondered again about the rumour that Tyrconnell was planning to ship more men to France once they were trained. He hadn't had an opportunity yet to ask Saint-Ruhe about it but it seemed like a minor matter at the moment. Besides, moves were afoot to force Tyrconnell to leave the army alone.

The formal council ended but they stood around talking, nobody in a hurry to break up what had been a celebration. Maxwell made his way over to Sarsfield and pulled a sheet of paper from inside his jacket. 'Is this your idea?' he demanded with a thunderous look.

'No,' Sarsfield said truthfully. It wasn't his idea to get up the petition from the army telling Tyrconnell to quit the camp and return to Limerick.

'But your men are behind it.'

'It's for the best,' Sarsfield said calmly, not denying the accusation. He hadn't asked Luttrell if it was his idea because he didn't want to know.

'And one of them, Lieutenant Colonel O'Connor, has had the audacity to tell the viceroy to his face that he will cut the guy ropes and collapse his tent unless he has left by this evening.' Maxwell's voice rose in anger. All around were now listening to the exchange but Maxwell didn't care. He knew, as they all knew, that most of them had signed the petition in the few hours that it had gone around. And, to the surprise of his supporters, that Tyrconnell had given in to the demand and agreed to leave the camp.

There was a moment of awkward silence and Sarsfield tried to change the subject. 'How many of your men died throwing down the bridge?'

'They died for their King,' Maxwell retorted.

'Brave men.' Sarsfield adopted a calming tone.

'They died for their King,' Maxwell repeated, brandishing the sheet of paper. 'While you were doing this to his representative.'

He scrunched up the paper and threw it down with futile force as he marched out of the tent. Someone tittered but the laugh wasn't taken up. Maxwell's support for Tyrconnell was known to all and no one was surprised by his anger. But his men were also the ones who had beaten back the enemy at the cost of their own lives. This was no time to rub salt in his wounds.

Saint-Ruhe summoned d'Usson, in command of the garrison today, with a raised finger and told him in a quiet voice to break down the ramparts on this side of the town. D'Usson appeared taken aback and there was a quiet exchange between the two men in rapid French.

Sarsfield overheard the order but couldn't hear the angry words. That's unnecessary now, he thought -- just a sop to Tyrconnell, to make him think that his concerns had been taken into account. Removing the western defences was no longer necessary since the enemy had lost the initiative.

Colonel Charles O'Kelly came towards Sarsfield and shook his hand without a word, a public gesture of support and congratulations at his victory over Tyrconnell.

The Tyrconnell faction took their lead from Maxwell, complaining with bitterness to any of Sarsfield's supporters who would listen as the viceroy's entourage began to pack up and prepare to move back to Limerick. Sarsfield kept his distance, having no desire for a confrontation with Tyrconnell. Lying Dick did not accept defeat graciously. Or easily for that matter. And he appeared to have given in easily on this occasion.

'What do you think he'll do?' Sarsfield asked Luttrell.

'Try to get revenge,' Luttrell responded. 'Naturally.'

'How?'

Luttrell pursed his lips. 'Complain to the King . . . about the Frenchman. You notice he didn't stand up for him. He'll try to have the general recalled.'

Sarsfield told him about Saint-Ruhe's order to d'Usson and what appeared to be the latter's disagreement.

'Exactly,' Luttrell said, as if that confirmed what he had just said. 'Lying Dick wouldn't be leaving so easily if the Frenchman supported him, would he? He's bound to have sought the general's opinion about the petition and the Frenchman must have told him it was best for the army that he leave.'

Sarsfield thought about that. 'So they're not conspiring together to send our recruits to France.'

'That doesn't follow.'

Sarsfield shook his head to express his impatience. This was why he hated the devious politics. Why he preferred a good straight-forward fight any day.

Mackay

Mackay tried to get a private word with Ginckel before the council of war but the general was deep in conversation with Lieutenant General Württemberg. Or, more accurately, Mackay noted, being lectured by the German, who was obviously trying to convince him of something.

Ginckel detached himself and called the council to order. The mood was sombre: everyone knew that they were at a critical juncture. The failure of the bridge assault had narrowed their options and increased the possibility that they would have to lift the siege.

'Gentlemen,' Ginckel said. 'I have received all your opinions and have decided that we will continue with our original plan.'

There was a shuffle of impatience around the table; Mackay felt his irritation rise. Perhaps Ginckel was taking his advice to keep their real plan secret but he feared he wasn't: contrary to what they had agreed, Ginckel had made no arrangements to send the Ulster regiments to Lanesborough for a surprise crossing of the river. Mackay had made discreet inquiries of their officers and they were expecting to be part of the assault on the bridge or the ford.

'We shall have a three-pronged attack,' Ginckel continued, pointing out the positions on the map although they knew them all too well by now: the bridge, the ford downriver of it, and the pontoons a little farther downriver again. 'We'll construct a gallery to protect the men repairing the bridge. But we'll focus on one point,' he ran his finger across the ford, 'in the hopes of surprising the enemy.'

Mackay shook his head with such vehemence that Ginckel stopped and looked at him. 'That is much too risky' Mackay said, noting the nods from some others. 'We cannot allow all the hopes of our King and our religion to rest on that.'

'You exaggerate,' Ginckel sighed.

'Do I?' Mackay asked. 'We want to cross a river at a ford of uncertain depth that is well-known to the enemy. And where they have strengthened their defences since we arrived here. The prospect of success is very small. And failure will set back our cause for months, if not years.'

'We'll have the element of surprise,' Württemberg said.

'The enemy's only surprise will be that we are desperate enough to try to force a passage there,' Mackay retorted, surmising that Württemberg was the one behind this idea; he had persuaded the general.

'Do you have a better plan?' Württemberg asked.

'We'll test the depth of the ford,' Ginckel interrupted the exchange. 'Before the final decision.'

Mackay shook his head, rejecting that sop to his objections. 'My lord, there are other possibilities.'

'Time is of importance,' Ginckel said. 'We cannot afford to remain here indefinitely. Or plan more indirect operations at this stage.'

'We can afford another failure even less,' Mackay said.

No one disputed his words: they all knew he was right. Another failure would force them to lift the siege and withdraw, probably back to Mullingar. Which was not a strong defensive position against an enemy who scented victory. Mackay might be exaggerating the dangers for the cause of Protestantism and the King but he was not exaggerating the dangers for Ireland. The papists and the Stuart king could recover the country, aligning Ireland with France and encouraging the French king to support an invasion of Scotland. This would open up a new front against the Grand Alliance with unpredictable consequences.

'We must make a supreme effort,' Ginckel said. 'to take this ford and follow it immediately with more men across the pontoons and the bridge. As my lord Württemberg says, surprise is our best weapon.'

'Then secrecy must be maintained above all else,' Mackay said, admitting that he had lost the argument.

'Yes,' Ginckel looked around the table. 'There is to be no talk about this plan.' He turned to Talmash, the major general in command the next day. 'The regiments necessary are to be given minimal information. We will cross the ford at six o'clock in the morning when the church bell rings the start of the day.'

Mackay closed his eyes. There was nothing to do, he thought, but pray.

'Why such pessimism?' Talmash asked as they went outside.

'As I said, it's too risky.'

'They'll run away when we surprise them.' Talmash was in high good humour, looking forward to the assault.

'They didn't run away at the bridge last night.'

'That wasn't a surprise.'

Mackay gave a grunt, not wishing to respond to such a fatuous comment.

'You'll see,' Talmash smiled. 'They think they've beaten us. They're relaxing, already dreaming of marching back into Dublin.'

'You believe the deserters?' Mackay asked.

'You worry too much.'

And you don't realize what is at stake here, Mackay thought, but he said nothing. Nothing less than the future of humanity, whether it advance to freedom with the reformed faith or be forever mired in priest-ridden superstition. But people like Talmash cared less for the cause than for the combat.

Mackay watched him go, a spring in his step, as happy as a boy with a new bow and quiver.

Mackay found a spot on a hillside with a good view of the ford, aware that it was also visible to the papist gunners on the other side and that one officer had already been killed here by a cannon shot. But he wanted to see for himself the testing of the ford. Four young officers from Danish regiments who were in disgrace had been offered an opportunity to redeem themselves by scouting the ford to check its depth and width.

He watched them go into the Shannon where they thought the extent of the ford lay, spread out in a wide line, with long pikes in their hands to steady them and help them measure the depth. They wore helmets and had cavalrymen's half-chest armour concealed under their coats. As they moved towards the centre, their comrades on the bank began to shout and wave at them and then pretended to fire at them, trying to indicate that they were deserters.

Mackay ignored the shouting and firing, watching their progress carefully. They moved slowly, slipping and stumbling on the stony riverbed, and leaned against the strong current. The water rose above their knees and up to the waist of the tallest one as they neared the centre of the river. The one on the extreme left was up to his chest in water, on the edge of the ford and struggled back to his right to the shallower path.

The defenders on the other side watched them come, uncertain about what was happening, and holding their fire. When the Danes were close to the other side and the water began to fall away, they turned and hurried back. A line of muskets opened fire and a couple of grenadiers rose up behind the defences and hurled their bombs. One of the Danes pitched forward and floated downriver, twisting in the current.

Three of them made it back safely, slowing down once they were more than halfway across and beyond the killing range of the muskets. A cannon shot from a field piece, hurriedly directed towards them, threw up a plume of water but they made it to the bank and were helped out of the water with cheers.

Mackay went back to Ginckel's headquarters where he found the three still dripping wet and exhausted. One, a Norseman, was having a musket wound in his calf bandaged; a second had a cut on his jaw and had been punched three times in the body armour by musket balls; the third had emerged unscathed and was giving Württemberg a rapid account in Danish of what they had found.

'We can get at least fifteen or sixteen men abreast across there,' Württemberg translated into Dutch for Ginckel. 'It's much wider than the bridge.'

Ginckel gave a nod of satisfaction and opened a small chest on his desk. He handed ten gold guineas each to the wounded Norseman and Dane and twelve to the Dane who was unscathed. 'Take your places back in your regiments,' he said and turned to Mackay while Württemberg translated the order. 'Does that satisfy your concerns?'

'I will abide by your decision, my lord,' Mackay gave a small bow. It was a help, he thought, but still a high-risk strategy. A determined defence could certainly stop a sixteen-man-wide assault struggling through a fast-flowing ford.

Ginckel, in a generous mood, turned to an aide and ordered him to distribute another barrel of beer among the over-worked gunners.

Eight hundred grenadiers were selected from different regiments for the assault across the ford. The front-line men were given a shot of brandy and a guinea each as encouragement. Green sprigs were distributed for their hats, to identify friend from foe in the expected melee where most on both sides wore similar red uniforms. The password, an added identifier, for the operation was 'Kilkenny'.

Mackay moved among them as they gathered close to the riverbank, handing out copies of the prayer he had written for soldiers about to go into battle. He did not approve of the gold and alcohol inducements, believing that it undermined their higher purpose: one shouldn't need such incentives to do God's work but he accepted that it was standard military practice. Talmash passed by, a fleeting smile on his face when he saw what Mackay was doing.

They were all ready, the leading group of Colonel Gustavus Hamilton's grenadiers weighed down by heavy body armour, looking more like medieval knights than modern soldiers. The cannons, field guns and mortars fired overhead, upping their pace as the minutes ticked by to six o'clock and ratcheting up the tension and anticipation.

Mackay withdrew to the vantage point from which he had watched the previous day: it was now becoming crowded with onlookers not involved in the initial assault. But the hour came and went and the signal for the assault, the bells of St Mary's church, did not sound. 'What's the delay?' Mackay asked one of the officers who had arrived from the riverbank.

'The pontoons aren't ready yet,' the officer said.

Mackay shook his head in disbelief. The saga of the pontoons that either came too late, never came at all, had to be repaired when they did, was symptomatic of the general's inability to properly lead a campaign. Nothing was where it should be. Nothing had been thought through. Plans were chopped and changed, the normal rules of warfare ignored.

It took four hours for the pontoons to be readied for the launch downriver but still the signal did not ring out. Instead, they could see enemy reinforcements moving into position downriver from the bridge and castle. Cannon shot and mortars rained down on them but did not deter them. It was obvious that the papists had spotted their preparations and correctly divined their intentions. The assault was called off.

'They weren't relaxing after all,' Mackay couldn't resist pointing out when he found Talmash later.

Talmash looked dejected but refused to admit defeat. 'We can still do it,' he insisted.

'Our only real weapon - surprise - has gone.'

Talmash kicked at a stone and sent it skittering into the river and muttered a curse, keeping it under his breath to avoid a lecture about giving bad example to the troops.

A cloud of smoke from the bridge caught their attention. It grew quickly in volume, blowing back towards them with the dust and smoke from the mortars exploding on the other side.

'They've fired our fascines,' someone shouted unnecessarily.

Talmash swore loudly and Mackay didn't bother to give him a dirty look.

A papist grenade had finally succeeded in setting fire to the tightly packed bundles of sticks at the front of their advance across the bridge and had turned it into a wall of flame. The westerly wind fanned the flames into a fury, sending them into the wooden roof they had been building overhead. In a pause in the renewed cannonade, they could hear the crackling of the fire, as it consumed the dry wood. The men at the front were being forced back by flames, smoke and volleys from the other side of the river as the Irish fired through the flames. Mackay saw several stumble as they hurried back to safety.

Muskets and a couple of flags were waved in the air with delight on the other bank. A crash of angry cannons responded.

They watched until the fire had almost burned itself out and the smoke dwindled away. New fascines were being pushed forward but were short of where the embers were still burning.

There was no immediate prospect now of an assault across the bridge.

'So much for the Protestant wind that's supposed to favour us,' Talmash snorted with derision.

Another council of war decided to go ahead with the assault on the ford the next day, although with more apprehension than enthusiasm.

'The element of surprise will be all the greater,' Talmash argued with a burst of zeal that no one else shared.

A mark of desperation, Mackay thought, because nobody has any idea of what else to do now, other than withdraw. And that was unthinkable.

'We'll use the same men,' Ginckel said. 'We'll go in the early evening, at the hour we normally rotate men in and out of the front line to avoid alerting the enemy this time to anything out of the ordinary. And,' he wagged a warning finger, 'nobody is to crowd onto hills to watch the assault. That gave the plan away this morning.'

He signalled to Mackay to remain after the others had left. 'I know you're due to take command tomorrow,' he said, 'but I think it would be best if Major General Talmash remained in charge of this operation.'

Mackay was taken aback. 'I –

'He knows all the details. Has briefed the grenadiers and the others.'

'I also know all the details,' Mackay said stiffly.

'But you don't agree with this plan.'

'I will carry out my duty to my utmost,' Mackay said, pulling himself up to his full height. 'I did disagree with the plan but once it is adopted and ordered by you, I will implement it with all my being and with the help of God.'

They stared at each other in silence for a moment, then Ginckel backed off. 'Very well,' he said. 'Convey that decision to the major general.'

'Certainly, my lord.' Mackay gave him a departing bow.

Once outside, he could no longer contain his anger. It was outrageous to be relieved of command in such a manner. And it was clear that Ginckel had already promised command to Talmash. It was an insult that justified a duel, if he believed in duelling, which he didn't.

He found Talmash in his tent and told him without any preliminaries that he would be in command on the morrow.

Talmash took in the determined set of Mackay's baby face and thought better of arguing with him.

'It's intolerable if the arrangement for our commands is to be changed at the general's whim,' Mackay continued.

'Perhaps,' Talmash said 'you'll allow me accompany the party as an ordinary infantryman.'

'That's not a good idea. We would soon run out of general officers if they were all to come along on every action as mere onlookers.'

'I know,' Talmash gave him a half-smile. 'But you could make an exception this one time.'

Mackay sighed and nodded his agreement.

The grenadiers again moved into position on the riverbank in the late afternoon at the same hour as the men there were replaced every day. A couple of desultory cannon shots from the other side marked what the gunners saw as a routine handover. Some workmen who were due to follow the assault party to help break down defences and rebuild new ones were injured but the few shots were seen as a welcome sign of normality, part of the daily pattern into which the siege had settled.

The sky had clouded over and a drizzle was blowing from the west into their faces, dulling the sounds of the cannons and mortars still firing into the town opposite and reducing distant objects to indistinct shadows.

Mackay came down to the lead unit and their Irish commander Colonel Hamilton. 'You all know what you are fighting for,' he said to those around him. 'Your freedom, your homes, your religion. You've shown your fidelity to King and religion time after time in this war. And you will do it again today. Stay close together. Do not hesitate, do not falter. Keep pushing forward. Don't throw your grenades until you are close enough for them to have effect. Don't draw your swords until you have fired your muskets. Those of you without sword or bayonet, use your musket as a club. Remember: do not falter, do not hesitate. We have but one chance to succeed. We must push forward without hesitation. And we shall succeed because Providence is with us. God bless you all.'

The heavy siege guns and the light field pieces had slowly switched their aim to the defences around the ford on the far side of the river. Cannon shot gouged craters in the earthworks, cutting gaps in the defensive ridge overlooking it. Others continued to pound the remains of the castle nearby. Only its central tower remained standing, resistant to all that had been thrown at it.

Just after six o'clock the bell on St Mary's church rang out and Mackay nodded to Hamilton. The grenadiers slipped into the water in a line almost twenty abreast. Talmash was among them and Mackay grabbed his arm to hold him back. 'No,' he told him, 'not in the front line.' Talmash looked disappointed but didn't argue. Downriver, the first of the pontoons was eased into the water and the Danes began rowing across.

Mackay watched the line move forward, praying that they would stick close together and emerge as a determined force to punch their way through when they reached the other side. A couple of men stumbled on the uneven riverbed and were unbalanced by the heavy armour on their chests. One fell into the water and was helped up by two comrades. The line was in danger of becoming ragged but it held as another group entered the water, Talmash among them.

As a wave of fusiliers moved forward, Mackay told an aide to repeat his instructions to each detachment as it followed, and he slipped into the chilling water himself. The riverbed was dotted with rocks which threatened to undermine his footing. The current became stronger and rose to his waist as he moved towards the centre of the river. The rain blowing into his face made it difficult to see what was happening ahead. Cannonballs passed overhead and Mackay could make out spatters of dirt rising from the defensive earthworks where they struck. Flashes from musket shots glowed through the gloom amid the brighter flashes of exploding grenades but he couldn't tell at this distance whether they were the grenades of attackers or defenders.

A man on the left of the line fell and disappeared under the water, stumbled or shot. Another man ahead of him fell into the water and Mackay grabbed him and pulled him upright: he appeared to have been stunned by a musket ball near the end of its flight.

Mackay slipped on the side of an underwater stone which rolled under his weight and almost fell but he recovered and kept going, saying his own prayer for men going into battle under his breath. 'Take us and our cause into thine own hand and judge between us and our enemies. Stir up thy strength, O Lord, and come and help us.'

The cannon fire stopped and the shouting of the front line took over as they clambered up the soggy earthworks, men falling but rising again and then the second line was on the earthworks and the first line disappeared over the top. It's working, he thought. Thank the Lord, it's working. There were no more flashes of musket fire coming from the defences by the time he reached the earthworks of black and boggy soil. His boots sank into it, making it difficult to climb. A musketeer to one side, a squat man who seemed accustomed to walking on such earth, grabbed him by the arm and helped him scramble up the incline. Around him, more and more men were trying to rush up the bank, roaring with excitement and the scent of victory even as the sucking black clay slowed their progress.

Mackay went over the top and found a small group of papist prisoners huddled on the ground. Among them to his surprise, he recognised Major General Maxwell. He went over to him. Maxwell looked up at him, the shock of what had happened evident on his face, although his words were defiant. 'You can't hold it,' he said, shaking his head. 'You can't hold it against our whole army.'

Mackay was already thinking that. The priority was to get as many men as possible over the river before the papists counterattacked. He gave a curt order to a captain in charge of the prisoners that none of them was to be harmed, aware of the tendency of victorious soldiers to slaughter indiscriminately.

The Danes from the pontoons were now flooding into the area, too, and he picked out an English lieutenant colonel and ordered him to attack the tower in the middle of the castle. Fire was still coming from it. He looked back at the river and saw the wave of workmen coming over the embankment with their pickaxes and shovels to clear obstructions and create defences if necessary. Behind them, Württemberg was among the next wave of grenadiers, being carried on the shoulders of two men who were struggling to keep their footing as they neared the bank.

Mackay gathered more men and directed them to seize the bridge defences and fan out around the town. Attacked from the side, the defenders at the bridge had to pull back and it quickly turned from a disorderly retreat into a rout. The bridge was spanned with planks from the other side and the workmen cleared away the fascines and other defences as scores, then hundreds, then thousands of men came racing over, chasing the defenders through the rubble of the town, its narrow streets clogged with the debris of burned and demolished buildings and the tons of rocks fired from mortars. The stench of rotting corpses hovered over the piles of rubble and the newly dead and wounded were trampled underfoot in the narrow passageways.

Mackay came upon a group of infantrymen swearing as they clambered over loose stones, not waiting to reload their flintlocks as, their blood up, they chased a couple of Irish soldiers with fixed bayonets. 'You'd be better off falling on your knees to thank the Lord than taking his name in vain,' he said as they went by. One of them laughed at him.

He was trying to keep up with the action, conscious that the town was not yet secured, that the entire Jacobite army was only a mile or so beyond its perimeter and was certain to counterattack. He could scarcely believe it when he reached the edge of the town: its western defences were still intact. The only access was through a narrow entrance, easily sealed off.

Some of the King's soldiers were racing through it in pursuit of the fleeing papists and he saw Talmash among them. Mackay stopped others following them and sent a messenger after Talmash to order him and the others back immediately. He arranged the growing numbers into positions along the town's defences as more and more arrived.

Talmash, a spatter of blood on his tunic, joined him on the rampart as they waited for the counterattack, content now that they could not be easily forced back into the river. The rain had eased but the wind was rising, bringing darker grey clouds scudding from the west.

'Surprise is a great weapon,' Talmash couldn't resist reminding him. Aglow with excitement, he didn't appear to resent the fact that Mackay would now get the credit for seizing Athlone.

After two weeks before the town, it had been taken in little more than half an hour.

Sarsfield

The first they knew about it was a scatter of shouts that grew in strength and continuity as small groups of men and then more and more emerged from the town, running towards the refuge of the bogs. Panic spread like an avalanche gathering speed, width and depth. The shouting was taken up with shrieks among the camp followers as women gathered up their belongings and began to flee.

Most of the cavalry and dragoons were dismounted, their horses grazing some distance away. Purcell was one of the few whose unit was close by and Sarsfield ordered him to go and see what was happening. Infantrymen on standby to relieve the new recruits in the town were sent hurrying towards it.

Both quickly realized that the town had fallen. The cavalrymen charged the heretics emerging in pursuit of fleeing defenders and forced them into a quick retreat. The infantry lined up but failed to halt the panicked defenders, never mind counterattack. Both were faced with a solid line of new defenders on the town's ramparts. There was nothing they could do, locked out from what had been their own positions only minutes earlier.

Saint-Ruhe found it difficult to accept the news when he was told. 'How can that be?' he demanded of d'Usson but his face paled as he accepted the reality, showing that he knew all too well the consequences of what had happened. The question was one he was going to have to answer to Louvois, the war minister, and the King. And there was no good answer: from a strong defensive position he had handed the enemy a major victory at a time when things had looked positive for the Kings' cause.

D'Usson had been in the town when the attack came and had tried to rally the panicked defenders but had been knocked down in the rout. A large bruise on his right cheek was already turning an angry red. He looked stunned and gave a bewildered shrug.

The general staff stood around in shock as more reports came in. The infantry was deserting in large numbers. As usual, those in the rear were the first to melt away when things went wrong. Saint-Ruhe ordered all the colonels to rally their regiments, telling them they were going to take back the town.

But they all knew that was next to impossible. They didn't have the equipment to besiege it. And their camp was now exposed and open to attack.

Rumours of treachery spread quickly as explanations for the disaster were sought.

'Maxwell was seen greeting them at the ford,' Colonel Charles O'Kelly said, reporting what one of the fleeing defenders had told him.

That was hard to credit, Sarsfield thought, although the Scot had been clearly angry at the treatment of Tyrconnell. But angry enough to betray the cause he'd been fighting for since the usurper arrived in England? He didn't think so.

'He refused to give the men more ammunition today,' O'Kelly added. 'They were worried about movements across the river but he just laughed at them. Asked them if they wanted to shoot at birds.'

'Were they short of ammunition?' Saint-Ruhe demanded of d'Usson.

'*Non, mon général,*' d'Usson replied.

'Where's Colonel O'Gara?' Saint-Ruhe asked, as if he was suddenly aware of O'Gara's absence. Nobody knew where O'Gara was. Either dead or a prisoner, everyone assumed. His regiment had been defending the ford but they were new recruits with little experience of being under fire. And it was Saint-Ruhe's policy to put raw recruits in the front line as he said he wanted everyone blooded and ready for the decisive encounter when it came.

'More treachery,' someone muttered about O'Gara.

'We don't know that,' Sarsfield retorted. There was no point putting everything down to treachery unless there was reason to think so.

There was a sudden silence as Tyrconnell entered the tent. He had kept away from the councils during the previous days, ever since he had agreed to leave the camp. He was packed up and ready to go now. He looked around the room, his jowly face showing no emotion, and settled on Saint-Ruhe. 'What shall I tell the King?' he asked.

'We are trying to find out what happened.' Saint-Ruhe held his stare, aware that the king referred to included both Tyrconnell's and his own, James and Louis. 'There is talk of treachery,' he added. 'By Major General Maxwell.'

Tyrconnell gave no sign that he was aware of the barb that it was one of his supporters who might have sold out the kings' cause. 'And the ramparts?' he batted back, his face expressionless. 'Now preventing our counterattack?'

D'Usson shifted uneasily. He knew he was going to be blamed for the delay in carrying out the order to take down the town's western defences. Nobody said anything. Tyrconnell let the silence hang heavily in the tent.

Nobody mentioned what they all knew: there was more than enough blame to go around. They had all relaxed their guard to some extent, believing that the enemy had tried his best and failed and that the siege was effectively over.

The atmosphere was hot and close under the canvas. A sudden shower of rain spattered on its roof and beat against its western wall. Urgent voices could be heard from outside but their words were indistinct.

'What now?' Tyrconnell broke the silence.

'We are trying to decide that, your grace,' Saint-Ruhe said.

Tyrconnell held his inquiring gaze, not allowing Saint-Ruhe avoid what they all knew was inevitable.

'We shall withdraw,' Saint-Ruhe conceded at last, 'while we consider what has happened and what we should do next.' He nodded to his lieutenants general, not needing to spell out the order to strike camp. He pointed to his map and the next obvious defensive point. 'We will regroup here and assess the situation.' He pointed to the River Suck at Ballinasloe, some fourteen miles west. 'This is a setback, not a disaster.'

The council broke up. 'It is a disaster, not just a setback,' O'Kelly muttered to Sarsfield as they stepped out into the rain. 'You know,' he added in a knowing whisper, 'that d'Usson used to be a heretic?'

Sarsfield closed his eyes and didn't reply, feeling a weight on his shoulders, a weight that was heavy enough without having to look with suspicion on all his fellow generals. He looked around for Luttrell and headed towards him, summoning his trumpeter with a crooked finger as he went.

The work of moving the camp began as the wind strengthened and lashed the site with rain, turning the mud into muck. It was hampered, too, by the disappearances of thousands of men who had fled into the bogs and woods as panic had spread, and by the shortage of garrons and other horses to pull the wagons and guns.

The camp followers, with less possessions, were already on the move. Tyrconnell and his entourage, packed up and ready to leave, made their way through them, their wagons following closely behind the mounted riders.

Sarsfield and Luttrell rode back towards the town with a detachment of cavalry to make sure that the heretics stayed put. As they neared the ramparts musket shots rang out but they stopped before they came into range: the rebels hadn't had time yet to bring up their field guns or reposition the ones they had captured in the town.

'What do you think?' Sarsfield asked.

Luttrell shrugged and, unusually for him, said nothing.

'O'Kelly suspects d'Usson as well as Maxwell,' Sarsfield added.

'O'Kelly suspects everyone,' Luttrell retorted. 'Blames everyone for everything.'

Across the river a burst of fireworks exploded in the sky and was dampened quickly by the rain and wind. Three salvos of celebratory cannon fire sounded as their victory celebrations began, the thuds dulled by distance. The sound reinforced the emptiness of defeat that Sarsfield felt.

'It's not the end of the world,' Luttrell said after a while.

They watched more distant fireworks rise in a lazy arc and die out as they were blown away by the wind. The captured town was silent now after all the violence that had been rained down upon it. Thin wisps of smoke rose above the defences, barely discernible from the grey rain.

'A setback,' Sarsfield sighed. 'As the Frenchman said. That's all it is.'

He wheeled his horse and his trumpeter signalled a trot and they went back towards the camp and the straggling column of men, wagons and camp followers heading westwards with heads bowed against the wind and rain.

JULY

Mackay

The dawn seeped through the cloud, brightening into a dull day by four o'clock in the morning. Mackay made his way from his camp through the streets of the English Town, now almost silent after the previous night's raucous celebrations. Soldiers slept in corners, weapons lying casually nearby; others wandered about, too tired and too drunk to care where they were or what they were doing. A party of drinkers sat on the ground by a dying fire, passing around a bottle and talking across each other in slurred German. A card school had fallen asleep around their last hand, cards still displayed on a makeshift table of broken boards.

The generals had tried to keep control of the celebrations, forming up units for a parade, setting off fireworks and firing blank cannon salvos. But, to Mackay's disgust, things had then degenerated into an orgy of drunkenness, fornication, squabbling, and hunting out enemy survivors among the ruins and killing them with shouts of glee. Ginckel had ordered all units not on its western defences to withdraw from the Irish town but the order had gone largely unheeded in the midst of the bloody revelry.

The rain had stopped after midnight and the early morning air was still and cool. Mackay crossed the bridge, his steps sounding hollow on the rough planks that replaced the broken arches. He picked his way over the shattered walls of the enemy's defences, avoiding the bodies of attackers and defenders still intermingled among the detritus of the assault.

In the Irish town the streets were barely passable, clotted with rubble and half-burned timbers and enemy bodies stripped of everything reusable. Already tattered uniforms had been torn into bits of rags in the search for coins hidden in seams. Washed of blood and dirt by the rain, the wounds that had killed many of them looked oddly small and almost inconsequential. Two soldiers came towards Mackay, one aiming an unsteady kick at a severed head and only half-connecting. The other laughed as the head, wrapped in blood-matted hair, skittered away sideways. They passed Mackay with a sullen glare, daring him to criticise their drunkenness.

Talmash was standing on the rampart beside the western entrance to the town, his eyes squinting towards the horizon like an explorer on the prow of a ship trying to distinguish land from a haze. Mackay was about to remark that he was up very early when Talmash wavered as if hit by a strong gust of wind. Mackay realized that he had not slept and was still drunk.

'Have they all gone?' Mackay asked.

'It appears so,' Talmash said, pronouncing each word with exaggerated care. 'Scattered to the four winds.' He threw his right arm to one side, almost unbalancing himself.

'How far have they withdrawn?'

Talmash gave Mackay a look that suggested that he was asking a ridiculous question. 'They're gone,' he said. 'It's all over.'

'You should get some sleep,' Mackay muttered as he turned away in disapproval. How could the soldiery be expected to behave properly if their betters did not set a proper example?

Most of the men supposed to be on duty were asleep. Outside the ramparts, a couple of small parties were picking up weapons discarded by the fleeing papists and searching the bodies of the dead. Their arms were already full of booty.

On his way back to his tent, Mackay found Württemberg standing at the bridge, scowling at the ruins of the Irish town. 'We need to clear a way through here for the cavalry,' the German said. 'We can end this war now if we pursue them.'

Mackay nodded. 'We'll get the work battalions at it if we can find enough sober men.'

Württemberg gave him a mocking grin, well aware of Mackay's excessive sobriety and religious ardour. 'They're entitled to their victory too,' he said.

'If the enemy attacked now. they could undo that victory as swiftly as it was gained.'

'They're beaten,' Württemberg said. 'This campaign is nearly over. It needs only one more push.'

The day's council of war began with glasses of brandy for everyone, Ginckel proposing a toast to King William and Queen Mary, answered by a cry of 'Their Majesties'. The sense of relief in the tent was almost palpable, now overlaid with the satisfaction of a success that had been achieved against the odds. Ginckel was like a new man, decisive and full of energy. The strain of the last week was gone from his broad face and had been replaced with a contented tiredness.

Mackay sipped his brandy, happy that he had insisted on leading the crossing: if he hadn't, he knew, he would be out of favour now for having opposed an operation that had succeeded. Not that being out of favour worried him unduly. His sense of duty and devotion to the reforming revolution inured him to a large extent against the views of his peers. But it did not entirely extinguish his vanity.

'Your views now, gentlemen, on our next move.' Ginckel put down his empty glass, signalling that it was time to get down to business.

'Pursue the enemy quickly,' Württemberg said, 'while he is still in disarray.'

'Chase them into the western sea,' Talmash echoed drunkenly.

Ginckel gave him a disapproving look and turned his attention to Ruvigny whose Huguenot cavalry had crossed the river and was scouting the whereabouts of the Jacobite army. 'Where are they now?'

'We've run into their cavalry three to four miles to the west,' Ruvigny said. 'No sign of the infantry, so we assume they are moving westwards.'

'To Galway?'

'It appears so.'

Ginckel leaned over the table, resting his palms on the map. The Irish still held the three ports of Sligo, Galway and Limerick, of which the most dangerous was probably Galway. Its bay was too wide for the weak English navy to blockade against a French fleet and he had to assume that French reinforcements were a definite possibility, even a probability. Sligo was that much farther for the French and not a good option to land troops so near to the loyal areas of Ulster. Limerick was a possible landing place too but it was easier to blockade its long and narrow estuary.

Yet he couldn't rely on the English navy to prevent a landing anywhere: there was no sign that they had managed to even get to Galway Bay, as he had requested more than a month before. He tapped his index finger several times on Galway. There was silence for a moment as they all considered his choice. Mackay held his peace, glancing around at the others.

'Limerick,' Talmash shook his head in disagreement. 'Cut off the head.'

A couple of officers nodded approval.

'We can't leave Galway open to the French navy,' Ginckel explained. 'What would happen if the French landed an army there while we were besieging Limerick? We can't besiege both.'

They could all visualise that scenario: their army committed to surrounding Limerick; the French heading for Athlone and Dublin. They having to lift the siege, leaving them vulnerable to attack from Limerick in the rear as they were forced to pursue the French and stop them from taking Dublin. A nightmare that could overturn all that had been gained in the previous two years.

'Louis won't send any more troops to Ireland,' Ruvigny pronounced. 'Everything we've heard from spies and deserters tells us the French and the Irish don't get on. They hate each other.'

'That's not Louis' concern,' Ginckel pointed out. France's only interest in Ireland was to tie up King William's army in Ireland at worst and, at best, defeat it and use Ireland as a base for reinstating King James on the Scottish and English thrones.

'But we know he wants Irish recruits to replace any French ones he sends to Ireland,' Ruvigny persisted. 'And there was something we heard recently.' He looked around for one of his officers who whispered to him in rapid French. 'Something about a row among the papists about sending any men at all to France. In which case, Louis won't send any of his soldiers here.'

'That may be,' Ginckel conceded, 'but we can't divide our forces to besiege Galway and Limerick at the same time. Leaving Galway in their hands is a risk we shouldn't take.'

'If we pursue them vigorously now, we might not need to besiege either,' Württemberg suggested. 'We can destroy them while they're in disarray.'

'Hear, hear,' Talmash said.

'Are they in disarray?' Ginckel turned to Württemberg. 'Their cavalry is untouched. Few of their infantry were involved here. We're moving into their territory now with little firm information about what's ahead of us. We don't know where the Spaniard O'Donnell and his rapparee army is. We're short of munitions. We've no shot left for our field guns. Our supply lines will lengthen and more men will be needed to protect them, depleting our strength as we move forward.' He paused to let his words sink in. 'We have to consolidate our position here, secure this town and the other river crossings to the north and south, and build up our supplies to besiege Galway.'

Talmash looked as if he was going to argue but his shoulders slumped in exhaustion.

'Firstly,' Ginckel continued, 'we need more information about the enemy's location and intentions. They appear to be heading for Ballinasloe and the River Suck.' He pointed to the town and his finger sketched the line of the river looping around it. 'Do we follow their path? Or do we aim to cross this river up here' – he specified a spot some ten miles north of the town -- 'where we're told there's an easy ford?'

'Follow them directly,' Württemberg persisted. 'Maintain the pressure and they will collapse.'

'I'm not so sure,' Mackay offered. 'As the general said, their army is still largely intact.'

'They're just a rabble,' Württemberg snorted. 'A collection of rapparees, some horsemen and a few French officers who can't control them. They won't stand up against a determined attack by a disciplined army. You saw that yesterday.'

Mackay half-conceded the point with a slight nod. He still wasn't sure exactly why the attack on Athlone had succeeded. The initial defenders had capitulated too easily and luck was on the side of the righteous. But there was no guarantee that it would always be so. 'It can be dangerous to underestimate an enemy,' he said.

There were some smirks around the table at his comment, an unspoken commentary on the fact that he had underestimated Bonnie Dundee and his Scots at Killiecrankie and paid a heavy price. *Some of them think I've lost my nerve since then*, Mackay realized. *It wasn't true but there was nothing he could do about it. No point in trying to assert the fact that his objections to crossing the river at Athlone were based on established military* practices. There was no reason other than the will of God and the foolishness of the enemy why that crossing had succeeded.

'There are other factors,' Ginckel intervened. 'There's no fodder to be had here. The enemy cavalry consumed it all. There's probably more to be had if we follow a different route.'

'We can send the horses northwards for it and march the infantry after the enemy.' Württemberg said without thinking, his impatience at all this dithering getting the better of him.

'And who will defend your infantry if their cavalry attacks them?' Ginckel asked him mildly.

Württemberg's face settled into a glower, aware that he had made himself look foolish. 'This campaign should be brought to a quick end now that we've breached their defences and crossed into their territory,' he muttered.

Ginckel held his stare in silence for a long moment. 'Get me all the information I need on the enemy and the terrain we're entering.'

The council broke up in silence and the generals filtered out of the tent, Mackay taking up the rear. 'You're right,' Ginckel stopped him as he went by.

'Not to underestimate the enemy,' he went on. 'We can't afford any setbacks here. That would only encourage the French to send reinforcements.'

'And you were right to insist on crossing the ford here,' Mackay said.

Ginckel nodded, accepting the line drawn under their previous disagreements. 'I hope we can bring this campaign to a swift end but not by throwing caution to the winds.' He went over to his small writing desk, took some papers from it and handed them to Mackay. 'A proclamation that we can now issue,' he said. 'Offering terms to anyone who comes over to us and accepts their Majesties' rule.'

It had been prepared weeks earlier after rounds of discussion between the parliament in London and the lords justices, Thomas

Coningsby and Charles Porter, in Dublin but had been held back until a significant victory provided the most opportune moment for publication.

Mackay scanned through the document which offered pardons to all soldiers who surrendered, good prices for any horses and equipment they brought with them, and the restoration of any lands already seized from them. The same was available to officers who brought their units with them and to inhabitants of Galway and Limerick who helped the King's forces take over the cities. Soldiers who wanted to continue in arms would be admitted to William's army at the same pay rates. Nobody need have any apprehensions about being allowed to practise their religion, it said. They would be allowed the same freedoms as Roman Catholics in England. As soon as a parliament could be set up in Ireland, their Majesties would endeavour to preserve them from any disturbance on account of their religion.

Mackay skimmed over the last paragraph which admonished the Jacobites to think carefully over their present circumstances, to compare the benefits of benign English rule to French tyranny, and to contemplate the terrible consequences that would follow if they didn't accept this offer within three weeks. 'Will this do it?' he asked.

'The moment is propitious. But,' Ginckel paused to make sure everybody else had left, 'I fear the terms are not generous enough.'

'Not generous enough,' Mackay found himself spluttering. 'They look very generous to me.'

'The religious terms,' Ginckel prompted.

Mackay glanced at the terms relating to religion again. 'They are generous,' he asserted. 'Very generous. Why should we encourage popish intransigence? The very cause of all these troubles?'

Ginckel sighed. 'I had hoped for something more. But the lords justices said no. And the parliament in London also said no.'

'I can see why.'

'That's not their reasoning. It's not religious. Parliament wants to be able to seize enough lands from papists to pay for this entire campaign.'

Mackay nodded. The religious reason was enough for him but he could also see the practicalities involved. God and Mammon on the same side.

'But there's isn't enough land to seize in this country to pay for it,' Ginckel said. He had been hoping to get Mackay on his side in case some of the Irish Protestants in the army objected to the terms on offer, as their co-religionists in Dublin had done. 'Another month's fighting will probably cost more than all the lands seized are worth. They would save more by offering better terms and it would avoid more bloodshed.'

Mackay looked at him, taken aback at the exasperation in Ginckel's voice. 'I still think the terms are generous. In view of all the circumstances.'

'They would be more generous if the King had his way.'

'I find it difficult to believe that the King would put the revolution at risk,' Mackay said, surprised at the idea, but knowing, too, that Ginckel was much closer to William than anyone else in Ireland and more likely to know the state of his mind.

'Your Glorious Revolution will be over if we lose to the French.'

'Indeed. But this is not just a power struggle between kings.' Defeating Louis XIV was a means to an end in Mackay's mind, the end being the security and extension of the Reformation, the cause of freedom, and the destruction of popery. Maybe Ginckel sees it differently, he realized now; just a war between kings. 'Remember the revocation of the Edict of Nantes and Louis' persecution of the Protestants in his kingdom. That's what he has in mind for us all if he's victorious.'

Ginckel gave several weary nods, as though he had heard all

159

that before.

'Maybe my lord Württemberg is right,' Mackay added, suddenly seeing the urgency of bringing the war to an end before even more generous terms were offered to the Irish simply to save money. 'We should pursue the enemy as quickly as possible and destroy them.'

'But you were right, too. We shouldn't underestimate the enemy.' Patience, Ginckel thought. Everybody needs to be more patient. Including the lords justices, especially Coningsby, who was now quibbling that he, Ginckel, had used up 12,000 cannonballs and 50 tons of explosives during the siege of Athlone. Wasn't that an unnecessary waste of expensive material on such a small town?

Such was a general's life, Ginckel sighed to himself, always under pressure from above, every decision questioned from below.

'Don't mention the proclamation's terms to anyone yet,' he cautioned Mackay, hoping that he would not stir up opposition to it in the camp. It had been a mistake to show him the document at all.

The weather turned suddenly sultry, days of hot sunshine interspersed with heavy clouds which burst in showers of torrential rain, leaving the countryside steaming when the sun came back out again. Work on repairing the town of Athlone continued with the building of magazines and stores for supplies of ammunition and gunpowder which arrived in convoys under strong escort from Mullingar. Reinforcements came too -- more Dutch troops -- along with food and money to pay the army. In the other direction, sutlers were ordered to bring back the wounded to the Royal Hospital in Dublin as they replenished their own supplies of food and drink.

The camp moved to the west of Athlone, beyond the

160

devastated area where the enemy had gathered during the siege. Spirits were high, boosted by the victory and the arrival of more generous rations and promised payments. With money in their pockets and nothing much to do, the infantry was spending a lot of time gambling and drinking, much to Mackay's disgust. Meanwhile, the cavalry reconnoitred the countryside to find the enemy and to divine his intentions.

'I hope this lot is more successful than the previous one,' Talmash growled to Mackay as they watched a group of some twenty horsemen, cavalry and mounted dragoons, head westwards on another patrol.

The Jacobite cavalry had so far managed to keep prying eyes well away from their main camp. Deserters and locals seeking protection had provided some information but it was far from clear where exactly the papist camp was and what the French general intended to do now.

'They might have better luck,' Mackay said of the departing horsemen. 'They have a converted papist priest with them.'

'They trust him?' Talmash's tone suggested he certainly would not.

Mackay shrugged. 'He knows the area well and has given us a lot of information already.'

'Once a priest always a priest.'

'One should give the benefit of the doubt to anyone who has seen the error of his ways.'

Talmash tried to relight his pipe with a piece of smouldering match, sucking heavily on its stem until he got a mouthful of smoke. They were seated on a hillock in the sunshine outside Mackay's tent, keeping a wary eye on a heavy cloud. It was fringed with bright white but its centre was leaden and it was suspended in the windless air hundreds of feet high. It appeared to be unmoving but was making its slow way towards them at an angle from the west. With luck, Mackay thought, it will pass to the north.

Around them the countryside was a dark green, the grass cropped back by the thousands of horses that had been grazing it. A herd of small black cattle, seized in the latest foray northwards, lay on the ground, their tails twitching to frighten off flies. Men sat or lay about on the grass as well, some with women, others in circles playing cards. The heavy afternoon heat cast a lethargic blanket over everything beneath the enormous sky of blue.

'Is the general wavering again?' Talmash asked.

'Hmm.' Mackay felt his eyelids growing heavy in the heat. He didn't feel like discussing the latest council of war at which Ginckel had decided to circle around where they thought the enemy was at Ballinasloe.

'Are we going this way or that way?' Talmash waved his pipe to the south and then to the north.

'That way,' Mackay said, pointing northwards. The general had decided not to pursue the enemy directly but to cross the River Suck some ten miles north of Ballinasloe.

'Pity,' Talmash sighed. He was tired of long-drawn out sieges, the tit-for-tat forays, the irritation of rapparees, and inconclusive engagements.

Yes, Mackay thought, closing his eyes. It was a pity. It was Ginckel being cautious again. He would normally have supported such circumspection, especially against hotheads like Talmash and even the impatient Württemberg but he found himself now in favour of direct action, of provoking a battle that would conclude the war in Ireland. Part of the reason was the peace terms on offer which had, as Ginckel feared, raised some protest within the ranks. Mackay had done his best to quell them, as the general had hoped, in the interests of discipline and not because he thought the complaints were invalid.

They lapsed into silence and Mackay felt himself drifting off, succumbing to the afternoon torpor. The sun was bright on his closed eyelids and he could hear the muted murmur of conversations, the creak of wagon wheels, the occasional thud of

162

hooves on soft ground and, sometimes in between the other sounds, the buzzing of insects and bursts of birdsong.

He woke to a shout and opened his eyes to see men running. He shot up out of his chair, fearing that they were under attack, incredulous at the thought. But it was only a small group who were on their feet; most of the soldiers lying about were sitting up to stare towards the edge of the camp but making no other moves. The runners were congregating around a group of horsemen, their mounts rearing up and twisting in the shifting circle around them.

Mackay reached the edge of the group and was about to push his way through when Talmash emerged. 'The patrol,' he said in reply to Mackay's unasked question. 'Ambushed by papist cavalry a couple of miles west. Half of them gone, killed or captured.'

'The priest?' Mackay inquired, suspecting treachery, that he had led them into a trap.

Talmash nodded towards the horsemen. 'Wounded. Dying, I'd say.'

The onlookers cleared a path for Mackay. Three men were lying on the ground, two in obvious distress from bleeding sword slashes across their arms and shoulders. The third, the former priest, was lying still, blood seeping from the neck of his jacket, his eyes flickering in his paling face.

'Get these men to the surgeons,' Mackay ordered, wondering why Talmash hadn't already done so. 'And give the horses some space.'

He turned to a cavalry cornet whose unshaven beardless face suggested that he was only fifteen or sixteen. 'What happened?'

'We saw no sight of them, my lord,' he said, presuming Mackay's status was higher than it was, 'Until they fell upon us in a wood. There must have been four hundred of them.'

'Four hundred,' Mackay repeated, his tone not hiding his scepticism. It would be a miracle if anyone returned had four hundred enemy come upon them.

'Yes, my lord, I think so. They were everywhere.' The lad tried to steady his nervous horse with gentle pats on its neck. 'We managed to pull back to a bridge over a river and fight them off. But the dragoons ---'

Mackay nodded, knowing what he meant but didn't want to say. The dragoons had dismounted at the bridge and covered the retreat: they were probably all dead or captured by now. 'Did he lead you into the ambush?' Mackay asked, nodding towards the dying priest.

'I don't think so, my lord. The captain might know for certain but he hasn't come back. Yet,' he added in a hopeful tone.

'All right,' Mackay said, glancing at the other riders and noticing the bloodied state of some of them, unsure whether it was their own blood or that of comrades or enemies.

The crowd around them had dispersed, the badly wounded were taken away, and the survivors followed their young lieutenant in a slow line towards the surgeon's tents at the rear of the encampment. Mackay headed back to his own tent, passing Württemberg who was standing nearby with his arms folded, observing the scene.

'They can still do damage,' Mackay said as he went by.

Württemberg responded with a shrug and a short exhalation of breath that suggested the damage they could do was of little significance.

Sarsfield

S arsfield had grown angrier as the days had gone by after the initial task of securing their position following the fall of Athlone. Everyone but his closest associates knew better than to approach him unless they had to. It should never have happened, he told Luttrell repeatedly, and certainly not that easily.

'I know, I know,' Luttrell agreed. 'But what do we do now?'

They had drawn back to where the River Suck twisted in several channels at Ballinasloe, looping around an old stone fort that overlooked the main bridge there. It had taken them several days to arrive, days marked at first by a receding panic and then by the slow return of deserters drifting back into the camp. But the army's numbers were depleted; they were still less than they had been at Athlone.

'We have to keep the heretics as far away as possible,' Sarsfield said, repeating what he had told the latest council of war. 'Send out strong patrols, make sure they don't come near. And, above all, that they don't learn how weak we are.'

General Saint-Ruhe appeared to be in shock for the first couple of days after the defeat, paying no attention to what anyone said, unable to believe that he had let a very defensible position fall into the enemy's hands. 'Terrified of how he's going to explain it to his king,' Luttrell opined. 'I wouldn't like to be in his shoes.'

Sarsfield grunted, not concerned with Saint-Ruhe's career problems. They were riding slowly at the head of two squadrons of cavalry, a hundred men or so, in a wide sweep from south to north several miles to the east of their main camp. The countryside was hilly and scattered with woods and soggy hollows after the recent rain. There were no signs of local inhabitants, their rough cabins in the lea of the hills apparently abandoned. A few stone enclosures, most disused and overgrown, broke up the open country. Their horses trod carefully, avoiding the many stones on the ground. Scouts rode ahead and to their flanks, checking out the woods and passes for signs of ambushes. The day was cooling into evening, the western sun throwing long shadows to their right.

'You can imagine what Tyrconnell is writing to Paris,' Luttrell continued. 'You can be sure he hasn't wasted any time dispatching messengers to the kings.'

'A pox on all that,' Sarsfield snorted.

Luttrell went quiet, keeping his thoughts to himself. The kings would hardly withdraw Saint-Ruhe now in the middle of the campaign. Neither Tessé nor d'Usson seemed likely to be given the top job. But it wouldn't surprise him if Tyrconnell wrested control of the army back from Saint-Ruhe and tried to negotiate a deal with the Dutchman.

A shout from one of the scouts who had been investigating a wood ahead to their left brought them over in that direction. Half a dozen bowed figures were being herded out from the trees. Sarsfield and Luttrell looked at them. Their uniforms were tattered and dirty and their faces gaunt with hunger.

'Ce iad sibh?' Sarsfield shouted at them. Who are you?

The men said nothing, keeping their heads hanging, eyes on their filthy feet.

166

'Ah,' Sarsfield said in a loud voice, '*Sassanaigh.*'

A couple of the scouts drew their sabres and one of the men looked up, his eyes wild, and shouted, '*Ni ha. Eireannaigh.*'

'Deserters,' Sarsfield continued in Irish.

'No, my lord,' the man pleaded. 'We're lost. We're trying to find the camp.'

Sarsfield told the scouts to bring them back to the camp. 'We should hang them,' he muttered as they watched the men shamble away after the horses. But that would be bootless: they needed all the men they could find.

They resumed their slow patrol. 'We should send someone to talk to Balldearg again,' he said after a while. 'We need him now more than ever.'

'Who's the best person to persuade him?' Luttrell wondered aloud. 'That Tyrconnell has been isolated.'

'One of the O'Neills,' Sarsfield suggested.

'No,' Luttrell shook his head decisively, back on the ground he liked best. 'Nobody from Ulster. You'd never know what bad blood there might be there these days.'

Sarsfield shot him a glance. 'You know something I don't?'

'No. Just being careful. They say he's very touchy. Full of Spanish airs and graces.'

'O'Kelly's emissaries didn't achieve anything.'

'Did Balldearg reject their approach?'

'I don't know,' Sarsfield admitted. 'The colonel was vague about what happened. I'm not sure that whomever he sent even found Balldearg.'

'Maybe we could get him to go himself. Make a personal appeal to Balldearg. One of the old clans to another. Especially as we're now in O'Kelly territory.'

'Good idea,' Sarsfield agreed. 'See to it when we get back. And send out messengers to round up all rapparees who can be found.'

Luttrell gave a hollow laugh. 'You'd better see to O'Kelly yourself. The old curmudgeon practically spits when I cross his path.'

'He thinks you're a schemer,' Sarsfield said.

'What a strange thought,' Luttrell laughed, unconcerned.

They turned westwards, heading towards a fiery sunset and the camp spread out on the eastern side of the River Suck in a defensive pattern, lines of infantry in the centre and the cavalry on both wings. Cooking fires were beginning to flicker in the spreading shadows as many of the soldiers prepared to spend the night in the open. Even with their reduced numbers, there weren't enough tents for them all.

General Saint-Ruhe had recovered from the shock of losing Athlone. He opened the morning council of war with a determined thrust of his chin. 'We shall stand and fight them here,' he declared. 'This river will be our new front line. We will repulse their attacks, go on the offensive and seize back Athlone.'

Even before he finished speaking, many of his commanders were shaking their heads. Is he drunk? Sarsfield wondered, catching the eye of Wauchope who was staring at him as if he expected Sarsfield to do something about this madman. D'Usson, still unsure on his feet after being knocked unconscious during the rout, had his head lowered, eyes fixed on the ground. Tessé had his usual poker face, revealing nothing.

'My lord,' Sarsfield said, 'we are in no position to fight a pitched battle now.'

Saint-Ruhe turned on him. 'So what do you suggest? Surrender? That we let the heretics go wherever they please? That we confirm their view that we are merely a rabble?'

'Of course not.'

'What then?'

'That we move the army to Galway and Limerick. Strengthen both cities. And use the cavalry to attack them as they besiege either one or, if we're lucky, try to besiege both.'

'So you would give them free passage throughout Connacht, this land you say is so important to you?'

'No, my lord. Far from it. The farther they advance into Connacht, the more vulnerable they will be to our cavalry. We can easily cut their supply lines, isolate them. We can send cavalry squadrons back across the Shannon into Leinster and force them to withdraw. Turn Athlone into a pyrrhic victory.'

'No,' Saint-Ruhe exclaimed. 'We will not pretend to defeat them by allowing them to proceed.'

There was silence. Saint-Ruhe glanced around the tent but found few signs of encouragement. His fellow French generals looked neutral which, in the circumstances, was a negative. The expressions of the English generals, Sheldon and Dorrington, made it clear that they doubted the wisdom of making a stand here. A few of the Irish commanders gave him a nod of approval, encouraged by the aggressiveness of his tone more than by the detail of his plan.

Dorrington broke the silence. 'I don't think this is a good defensive position, my lord,' he offered, spreading his hands to indicate their surroundings as he enumerated their deficiencies. The old castle, encircled by cabins, its moat fed by cuttings from the river, was too low to resist a serious siege. Besides, it was on the east of the river, the wrong side for defensive purposes. 'And,' he added, 'this river is easily forded to the north and south of the bridge. And it's less than half the width of the Shannon.'

In other words, if they couldn't hold the fast-flowing, wide Shannon with much better defences in place, how could they stop the Williamites at this narrower, shallower, meandering river? Nobody thought it necessary to point out that the balance of forces had also changed.

'If I may speak, my lord,' Brigadier Mark Talbot, one of Tyrconnell's bastard sons, intervened. He had just returned from Limerick after escorting his father there.

Saint-Ruhe nodded with a heavy sigh.

'The viceroy sends his compliments and asked me to relay to you that his advice would be to withdraw to Galway and Limerick and let the cavalry roam the countryside to harry the enemy. He believes our best hope is to hold the cities and towns until next year's campaign when their Majesties in France will send more aid. He also instructed me to say that that is only his opinion and the decisions in relation to the army rest with your lordship.'

The message was received with small smiles by some of Sarsfield's supporters, amused that both he and Tyrconnell were on the same side for once.

Saint-Ruhe didn't look amused. 'So he would have us fight for time rather than victory,' he said, challenging them to rebut the defeatism of which most of them accused Tyrconnell. Nobody took the bait, realizing, as Saint Ruhe also knew, that holding out for more French aid for the 1692 campaign would probably mean the appointment of a new commander, unless he redeemed himself in the interim.

'I will take all your views into account,' he said in a tone that made it clear that he would also dismiss them. 'Meanwhile, we shall court martial the officers who failed in their duties in Athlone. And I want a muster of all the regiments, to see where we are deficient. And a tally of our supplies and equipment.'

'Well, well,' Luttrell said to Sarsfield afterwards as they walked away from the meeting. 'Who would have thought that Lying Dick would finally see eye to eye with us?'

'How can we fight a pitched battle?' Sarsfield said. 'I don't know how the Frenchman thinks he can do it.'

'He's only thinking of his own career. Trying to rub out the stain of Athlone. And blame someone else.'

'Yes,' Colonel Purcell said, catching the last comment as he joined them. 'I hear there's going to be courts martial. Who?'

Sarsfield shrugged, uninterested.

'Not any Frenchman who should be brought before one anyway,' Luttrell muttered. 'The rumour is that it will be some of the O'Neills.'

'Which O'Neills?' Sarsfield asked in surprise.

'From Cormac O'Neill's regiment,' Luttrell said. 'Lieutenant Colonel James O'Neill and some of his captains. They all ran away when the heretics crossed the Shannon.' He gave a short laugh and turned to Sarsfield. 'We should have sent one of them to find Balldearg since they're so quick on their feet.'

Sarsfield gave him a look that said that was not funny.

The sound of a trumpet signalling a parlay interrupted them and a small group of horsemen appeared, flying a white flag. 'Message for General Saint-Ruhe from General Ginckel,' one of them shouted in English.

'How did they get through to here without being stopped?' Sarsfield demanded as someone led them towards the general's tent. 'Make sure it doesn't happen again,' he ordered as he strode after the envoys.

Luttrell and Purcell shied back from his angry tone, letting him off on his own. 'Having Tyrconnell on his side hasn't improved his humour,' Luttrell said.

'Making him examine his conscience,' Purcell suggested.

In the general's tent, a Williamite lieutenant was relaying his commander's message in English which was being translated into French by one of Saint-Ruhe's aides. Ginckel was suggesting an exchange of prisoners and asking for General Maxwell's belongings to be sent to his camp. Saint-Ruhe handed the list of prisoners being offered for exchange to an aide and told him to check with the regiments concerned which men they wanted back. Another aide was sent to collect Maxwell's belongings, or what remained of them after the hurried departure from Athlone, while a third drew up a list of the few prisoners they held.

They had no one of Maxwell's status so he would not be

exchanged. But the request for his belongings would encourage the rumour that he had sold the pass, Sarsfield thought, although it didn't prove it.

More and more of the deserters filtered back into the camp during the following days, driven by hunger and the lack of choices, and reassured by finding the army intact and no sign of the enemy in immediate pursuit. The weather steadied down, too, into hot, airless days, the heat lying heavily on the land, calming nerves while dulling the senses, although a distant storm sent a nervous twitch through the camp until it became clear that it was the sound of thunder and not cannon fire. The storm eventually arrived, lighting up the night sky with forked flashes and rain that cascaded through tent roofs as if they were porous.

Saint-Ruhe threw himself into reorganising his depleted army, concentrating on training routines and lectures delivered from horseback in French and translated into Irish directly or sometimes via English. You are fighting for your land, your religion, your king, your families, your lives, he kept repeating. Stand by the rightness of your cause. You are not mercenaries doing the bidding of anyone who will pay you like the heretics who care nothing for you or for the one, true, holy, Catholic church. We will prevail because right and God are on our side.

He gathered together all the priests in the camp to tell them about his own experiences hunting out heretics in France and to urge them to carry the message to all his forces that the Lord Jesus was with them and would ensure the defeat of those who ridiculed and persecuted his church.

The mood improved as deserters returned and was helped by the punishments meted out to the officers who had run away at Athlone: Lieutenant Colonel O'Neill was stripped of his rank and five of his regiment's captains were broken. Word of the Frenchman's determination somehow spread out into the hills and bogs where deserters, rapparees and locals were hiding, encouraging them to return or sign up. Slowly but surely, the camp filled up again and a sense of purpose grew as Saint-Ruhe lectured and trained the troops, pressured his commissary Jean-François de Fumeron to release more money and food supplies, and trained and lectured some more.

His own mood became calmer as that of the rank and file turned more confident and resolute under his tutelage. And then he confounded his senior officers by revising his plans, abandoning the idea of an early battle and conceding that Sarsfield's and Tyrconnell's preference for withdrawing to Galway and Limerick and waging a cavalry campaign was best.

'What?' Luttrell scratched his head when Sarsfield briefed him after the latest council of war. 'What's he playing at?'

'He's seen sense,' Sarsfield said.

Luttrell shook his head in a spontaneous response, trying to guess why Saint-Ruhe had changed tack. It couldn't be as obvious as that.

'D'Usson is going ahead to Galway to review its defences and start improving them,' Sarsfield was saying. 'Wauchope is going to Limerick and I'm going to Loughrea to prepare the way for the army's moves to the cities.'

'I don't understand.'

'He's seen sense,' Sarsfield repeated as if speaking to a child. 'The entire army agrees this is the best thing to do. There's no sign of Balldearg joining us.'

Colonel O'Kelly had returned from visiting Balldearg O'Donnell in Mayo, shaking his head. He had received nothing more than vague promises and had had to listen to Balldearg's usual rant about Tyrconnell stealing his family's title. 'He doesn't appear willing to put himself and his men under the control of any French general, or anyone else for that matter,' O'Kelly reported. 'But some of his men will join us. They're fed up with all his talk and failure to do anything.'

173

Sarsfield gave Luttrell a light punch on the shoulder. 'We're going to have a busy time for the next few months once the cities are reinforced and we're free to conduct our own cavalry actions.'

Luttrell nodded, his mind still trying to work out why the general had changed his. Maybe it was as simple as Sarsfield said. He couldn't see any calculation in it other than an admission by Saint-Ruhe that his critics' strategy was better than his own. Whatever the reason, he noted, it had certainly made Sarsfield a happier man now that he saw the prospect of what he liked best. And what he was best at. 'We'll base ourselves in Limerick?' Luttrell asked.

Sarsfield nodded. 'Give us greater room to manoeuvre. To attack them on both sides of the Shannon.'

'And keep you out of Galway,' Luttrell added with a sly smile. Sarsfield had imprisoned some of Galway's leaders the previous year when they attempted to sound out surrender terms from the prince of Orange. Tyrconnell, in France at the time, had the men released on his return to Ireland.

'Let's hope they're more resolute this time,' Sarsfield shot back. The peace moves the previous year came as French troops had embarked from Galway for France after a lot of bad blood between them and the Irish following the battle of the Boyne and the siege at Limerick. Many of Galway's successful merchants were also tired of the war. The introduction of the useless brass money that had replaced gold and silver was losing its value steadily and destroying the foreign trade on which the town relied.

'Maybe we can persuade the general to show them some of his *pistoles*,' Luttrell suggested, referring to the French *louis d'or* gold coins that were now worth perhaps twenty-five times the equivalent brass coins which carried King James's head.

'Should show them the edge of our sabres,' Sarsfield grunted.

'Show them some real gun money,' Luttrell laughed, happy to see Sarsfield back in good humour at the prospect of seizing the

174

initiative in the coming months.

Sarsfield was happy, too, to see that the next Williamite trumpeter to arrive in the camp came with an escort of one of their own cavalry patrols. The trumpeter delivered several copies of the proclamation by the usurper's lords justices offering terms to anyone who surrendered. Groups of officers gathered around each of the copies to read them. Derisive laughs and curses soon broke the silence;

one officer ostentatiously tore up a copy and threw the fluttering pieces into the air.

'Stupid,' Luttrell said. 'That's not going to entice anybody.'

'A waste of paper,' Purcell added.

Sarsfield nodded, dismissing the initiative as irrelevant. Like most of the other Irish senior officers, he had already been attainted -- declared a traitor -- by the prince of Orange's courts in Dublin. His house in the city had been ransacked and his lands in nearby Lucan seized.

Still, he thought, it was well that the Dutchman had waited a week after the Athlone debacle to distribute it. There was no chance of it having any effect now that despair had given way to a clear strategy, with every prospect of success. This war was far from over.

Mackay

The thunderstorm passed overnight, leaving everywhere sodden. Waterlogged tents sagged and collapsed as fierce gusts of wind tore across the countryside while lightning zigzagged between angry clouds and earth and instantaneous claps of thunder rolled away in long rumbles. Two men and a boy were killed by the lightning. A half-dozen cattle and horses also died. Trees were split and burned. An upright stack of pikes, acting as a lightning conductor, was scattered, the long wooden shafts left smouldering.

The sun rose to cast a calm light from a cloudless sky over the devastated camp, as if it all had been a bad dream. Soldiers and camp followers began to emerge damp and wet from wherever they had tried to shelter, some still shaken by the ferocity of the storm.

'The wrath of God,' Talmash said, half-comment, half-question. He glanced up as if he feared another bolt from the virginal blue which was spreading from the east as the sun moved higher in the sky.

Mackay nodded, shivering in his damp uniform. The air was fresh and clean and fires were being lit around the camp where something dry enough to burn had been found.

'A punishment for our sins,' Talmash added. 'For all the drinking and gambling.'

Mackay didn't respond, aware that Talmash was teasing him. He was in no mood for early morning banter. 'Just as well we're moving today,' Mackay yawned. He had had only a couple of hours' sleep before being awoken by the flashes of lightning and distant thunder coming closer until the storm was upon them.

'I think the general's changed his mind again,' Talmash said with a bitter laugh.

Mackay gave him a sharp look, trying to discern if he was joking. They were supposed to be moving northwards to cross the River Suck a good distance above Ballinasloe now that the works on Athlone had been completed and there was a sufficient garrison left behind to protect the town.

'He's called another council for five o'clock,' Talmash said.

An air of misery pervaded the council of war, the atmosphere heavy with the damp clothes and irritable men. Ginckel's tent had withstood the storm but not the torrential rain and the ground was wet underfoot with puddles and occasional drips still falling from the roof as a rising breeze stirred the canvas.

'We've received new information,' Ginckel began. 'Confirmed by a patrol. The enemy has decamped from the river at Ballinasloe and I propose to follow him there.'

'Where's he gone?' Ruvigny asked.

'According to a deserter, they had a prolonged debate about what to do. It appears that they have decided to split their numbers between Galway and Limerick. To strengthen both against a siege.'

'Perhaps we should strike for Limerick and seize it before they have an opportunity to reinforce it,' Württemberg suggested. He didn't relish the prospect of more long-drawn out sieges.

177

Ginckel sighed. 'I am more concerned right now with Galway.'

'They're trying to stave off defeat until the winter,' Württemberg pointed out. 'Tie us up here for another year.'

Ginckel nodded. That was obvious, as was Württemberg's impatience at the thought of being left in Ireland for another year by his Danish masters. 'But we still have three months to make sure that doesn't happen.'

Württemberg grunted, not appeased. At the rate we're progressing they have every chance of succeeding, he thought.

'What about the state of their army?' Mackay inquired. 'Any further information on that?'

'Not good, according to the deserter. Spirits are low. They have little food. And their numbers are down. So low, they're afraid to count them.'

Somebody gave a sarcastic laugh and muttered 'Deserters!'

'True.' Ginckel agreed as he looked around to see who had spoken. It was one of the brigadiers but he couldn't tell which. 'Our returned prisoners say much the same. They heard many complaints about food and the French withholding money and bread. And,' he added, 'our patrol confirmed that they had moved westwards. They're not patrolling as they have been for the last week, which suggests that their cavalry has moved out too.'

There was silence for a moment, broken only by some sniffles. Then Mackay found himself asking, 'Could it be a trap?'

'A trap?' Ginckel looked at him in surprise.

'Trying to lure us forward. 'Stopping their patrols. Pretending they have withdrawn.'

Ginckel gave the idea some thought and looked around at his generals with a questioning eyebrow. Nobody took up the invitation to comment. 'I don't think so,' he said at last. 'I don't see much danger to us between here and Ballinasloe. Beyond that Suck is another matter. We have very little information about what lies there.'

Mackay nodded. He wasn't sure why he had asked the

question. He was wavering in his own mind between caution and urgency, between the need to be careful and the necessity of a speedy victory. Despite his low opinion of the general's military capabilities, he had not hitherto had any doubt about his desire for victory. But the business of the proclamation had raised doubts in his mind about Ginckel's willingness to compromise with the papists. Which was a bad idea, guaranteed to store up more trouble for the future.

'I have ordered some more regiments from Leinster to Roscrea,' Ginckel was saying, 'to protect against any attempts by their cavalry to foray back across the Shannon. Is there anything else?'

There was nothing else. 'Then we'll move at noon,' Ginckel said.

Everyone was glad to leave the campsite, which had turned into a quagmire, but progress was slow with the heavy guns and wagons sinking into the muddied road. A warm breeze from the south-west and the sunshine was drying out the countryside but the first wagons churned up the mud, creating deeper furrows and slower conditions for those behind. The infantry and camp followers soon left the wagon train behind, splashing through the hollows of the undulating landscape.

It was early evening but the sun was still high in the sky when they reached a hill overlooking the twisting course of the River Suck and the village of Ballinasloe, clustered around the square of its old castle. There was no life around the cabins, no smoke rising through their roofs, no humans or animals to be seen.

Ruvigny handed a spyglass to Mackay and he tried to steady his horse as he scanned the area. 'They haven't broken the bridge,' he said. 'It's still intact as far as I can see.'

'No,' Ruvigny agreed. 'But they haven't left anything either. Look at the land.'

Mackay swept the landscape ahead of them. There were no animals and no crops in the few rough enclosures. The grass was merely a green sheen on the ground, showing up the scattering of grey stones that stood like hunched hares everywhere. Even the clumps of bushes seemed to have lost much of their summer foliage.

'No forage,' Ruvigny said. 'We can't stay here long.'

'Maybe that's why they've left.' Mackay handed the spyglass back to him. 'Why didn't they break the bridge?'

'Perhaps they couldn't be bothered,' Ruvigny shrugged.

Or wanted to use it again for an attack, Mackay thought but he said nothing.

They rode downhill to where the Jacobite camp had been. It was similar to what they had left behind, a muddied area dotted with the grey ash of dead fires and rudimentary cesspits. The more optimistic foot soldiers were kicking through small piles of rubbish, exposing bits of broken pottery, the bones of rabbits and hares, and scraps of cloth but nothing of use or value.

Quick patrols along the river found fords above and below the bridge and infantry with pikes and muskets were placed at them to prevent crossings from the west. A larger patrol of Ruvigny's Huguenot cavalry crossed the bridge to scout the land rising away to the west and to try and locate the enemy. They didn't have far to go. They had reached only the first plateau on the rising land when they saw a Jacobite patrol on the next step upwards of the hill, less than half a mile away. Both patrols kept their positions, observing each other.

'How many?' Ginckel asked when Ruvigny reported to him.

'A squadron or so,' he replied. About fifty cavalrymen.

That didn't tell him anything much but more information came shortly afterwards with the arrival of a local landowner, Frederick Trench, and his brother, the Rev. John Trench, who had given the Williamites information about Dublin the previous year before the battle of the Boyne. 'That's a good omen,' Mackay noted as one of the general's aides invited him to join them in his tent.

He passed one of their own chaplains, George Story, talking to another clergyman whom he took to be the Rev. John Trench at the entrance to the tent. Inside, a civilian who had to be Frederick Trench, a portly man in his fifties, was leaning over the table sketching a map of the district. 'Here,' Trench tapped a curved line at the top of the sheet, 'that's where they're camped. On this hill - Kilcommodan.'

He dipped his pen in the inkwell and put an X to the right of the hill. 'An old castle in ruins but with a useful surround, at this place they call Aughrim.' He sketched a wavy line back to the bottom of the sheet. 'The road from Ballinasloe. And.' He pointed to the left of the road. 'There's another hill here, called Urrachree, facing Kilcommodan. In between it's all marshy, useless land, a little river running through it.'

He straightened up and looked at the general, awaiting questions. Ginckel put his hand up under his wig and scratched the back of his neck. 'A good camp site,' he said in his heavily accented English. 'But why did the Frenchman stop there? How far away is it, did you say?'

'Three or four miles. They say they're going to do battle there.'

'Who says?'

'That's what I've heard. That's what some of the local people are saying.'

'What do *you* think?'

'I'm not a military expert, my lord,' Trench said. 'And I haven't seen the camp myself. You'll appreciate that it's not advisable for me to go there.'

Ginckel rubbed his chin with the palm of his left hand: he seemed to have developed a sudden itch.

'Let's hope the local people are correct.' Württemberg said. 'A battle is just what we want.'

'What's over here?' Ginckel point to the left side of the

makeshift map.

'The hills run down to flatter land,' Trench said. 'Better land.'

'Not marshy?'

'No.'

'And this hill?' Ginckel pointed at Kilcommodan. 'How far is it from right to left?'

'About two miles.'

'Perfect,' Württemberg interjected. 'They can't hold a two-mile front. They don't have enough men.'

'How high is the hill?'

'Three to four hundred feet.'

Württemberg laughed.

'Steep?' Ginckel ignored Württemberg's amusement.

Trench thought for a moment, trying to remember: his interest in land was in its quality for farming, not its military uses. 'Not very. A long incline. Good land on the hillside.'

'Thank you very much, Mr Trench.' Ginckel shook his hand. 'I hope you and your brother will join us for dinner this evening.'

'Our pleasure.' Trench gave a small bow.

Württemberg wasted no time the moment Trench left. 'The opportunity we've been waiting for to finish them off,' he said, looking around for allies. A few of the others nodded.'

Ginckel pursed his lips, staring at Trench's map. 'The Frenchman's not a fool, is he?' he said to Ruvigny.

'He was a ruthless persecutor in France,' Ruvigny replied in a bitter tone. 'But that didn't require much skill. Armed men against civilians.'

'He did a foolish thing in Athlone,' Mackay observed. 'Leaving the town's western defences intact so we could use them against his forces.'

'True,' Ginckel nodded. 'But can we trust him to do something foolish again?'

Mackay found himself seated beside the Reverend John Trench at dinner, placed there in the expectation that he could have theological conversations with him. Across the table from them Frederick Trench was telling Ruvigny about his great-grandfather's departure from France for England more than a century earlier.

'Frederic de la Tranche was his name,' he said in French. 'From the Poitou region. You know it?'

'*Non.*' Ruvigny managed to inject the single syllable with a Parisian disdain.

'He was persecuted for his religion. Never thought of going back, even when the Edict of Nantes promised religious freedom. It won't last, he used to say.'

'A perceptive man,' Mackay remarked.

'Yes.' Frederick gave a little laugh. 'Otherwise, I might be one of your cavalry officers now.'

Ruvigny's stern look gave the idea no credence. *Les baudets du Poitou*, he was thinking. The only thing he knew about Poitou; the big, long-haired donkeys for which it was famous.

'I'd find that hard to imagine,' John Trench interjected.

Ginckel followed the exchanges from the head of the table, mildly amused at Ruvigny's rejection of Trench's attempt to establish some kinship. It was good to have newcomers to dinner, to divert everyone from the day-to-day differences of opinion and personalities that were so well established by now.

'You've never been a military man?' Mackay asked Frederick Trench. He had assumed that Trench had acquired his land in the aftermath of the Civil War, one of the soldiers in the Lord Protector's army or a funder of his campaign in Ireland.

Trench shook his head. 'Our grandfather was a man of the cloth. Came to this country to help spread the reformed faith. John has taken after him but I've followed in my father's footsteps. He made a few astute purchases of land.'

'Of mortgages,' John said in a low voice to Mackay.

More bottles of red wine appeared as the main course of beef and mutton and a stew of vegetables was put on the table. Frederick Trench launched into what was clearly meat and drink to him - who owned what in his area – as the others listened and ate in silence.

'The O'Kellys owned most it,' he said. 'And the Burkes. Then the Brabazons came in the time of Elizabeth to bring some English law to the area.'

Mackay nodded. He had seen the Brabazon name over the gateway to the castle and the date 1597. Trench took his nod as an interest in the Brabazons and continued: 'But his son went native, married a Dillon and brought up their son as a papist. Then he joined the rebels in 1641 and escaped with his life to Spain when the parliamentarians won. The O'Kellys lost most of the land, as did the Brabazons but the widow and daughter were given some more in Cromwell's settlement. And then Spenser came. You know *The Faerie Queen*?' he asked, turning to Ruvigny.

'The what?' the Frenchman asked in confusion.

'It's a poem,' Talmash said from Trench's other side.

'Yes,' Trench continued. 'The poet himself knew how to deal with the Irish in his day but his sons went to the bad here, too, married papists, and his grandson William was brought up a papist and lost the family estate in Cork. He appealed to Cromwell himself on the basis of his grandfather's policies in Ireland but the Protector was having none of it. He sent him to Connacht with all the other recusants and gave him a thousand acres here. That had been O'Kelly land and Brabazon land, you know.'

Frederick was in full flight, going deeper into the cat's cradle of family and land relationships, religions, allegiances, alliances, marriages and enmities, claims and counter-claims, and the Acts of Settlement and of Explanation that followed the Restoration as the Stuart kings tried to appease various constituencies. Ruvigny reached for the wine bottle with increasing frequency as Trench delved into the factions within families, into the O'Kellys, Kellys, Burkes, Dillons, Spensers, Tullys, Brabazons, the reformed planters from earlier times and the displaced papists from other parts of Ireland, on top of the Cromwellian soldiers and adventurers, and the 'new interest' men, like Trench himself, who had bought their land from grantees or the hard-up.

'You see it all ended up with the Connacht Certificates in the sixteen seventies,' he was saying, 'which was something special to the west and was bringing some order to the situation until –'.

'I think, Frederick,' his brother interrupted, 'you're boring our hosts.'

Frederick stopped and saw the glazed expressions around the table. 'Well,' he continued, defiantly addressing Ruvigny, 'it was all becoming clear until the late king gave Tyrconnell his head and he tried to follow the example of the French king and drive the Protestants out of the land altogether.'

It seemed like a suitable time for a toast to the new King and Queen and the dinner wound up with the brandy bottle doing the round of the table.

'Thank God,' Ginckel remarked to Mackay as they left later, 'that we only have to win the war, not administer the peace.'

Sarsfield

R epeat that,' Sarsfield demanded, thinking he had misunderstood the French of the young messenger who had come from General Saint-Ruhe.

'The general wishes you to bring all your cavalry back to Aughrim.'

'Why?' Sarsfield was confused. All the cavalry? Why was that necessary for a council of war? He had been in Loughrea only a couple of days, arranging for supplies to be turned back to Limerick or sent on to Galway and preparing for the division of the army between the two strongholds.

'He wishes to do battle there, my lord,' the messenger said as if it was a routine matter.

'Do battle? Are you sure?' That doesn't make any sense, he thought. The strategy had been decided: they were going to defend Galway and Limerick, free the cavalry to harry and disrupt the enemy, and create time for more aid to come from France next year.

'Yes, my lord. Those are the general's orders,' the messenger added pointedly.

Sarsfield dismissed him with a nod. He tried to visualise

Aughrim, a half-dozen or so cabins, on the way back towards Athlone. A place the cavalry normally circled around: the road through it was narrow and surrounded by bogs. It was easier go well south of it.

'Penny for your thoughts,' Luttrell interrupted his reverie.

Sarsfield told him of the general's order.

'Is he mad?' Luttrell protested. 'I thought it was agreed …'

'It seems he's changed his mind.'

'Because there's nobody there to stop him changing it,' Luttrell said with a hint of disgust. 'You have to go back. Get him to reconsider.'

'*We* have to go back. It's an order, not a request.'

'Now?'

'Now. Get everyone organised.'

Luttrell left but Sarsfield remained where he was looking out over the lake. A flat-bottomed skiff floated on its calm blue, breaking up the reflection of the few puffs of white cloud drifting high overhead and shifting their shadows across the countryside like an indecisive painter seeking the best balance between light and shade.

They saw the flags fluttering on the ridge long before they reached the camp on the western slope of the hill. It already had the look of a semi-permanent settlement: paths were worn between tents; fire pits had built up a spreading surround of grey ash; the sutlers' wagons seemed as if they had been there for an age; and the horses and cattle grazing the surrounding area were going farther afield in search of grass.

Sarsfield rode to the brow of the hill where the white flag of royal France was stretched out by the breeze. Tessé was writing at a table outside a tent by an old rath and looked up as Sarsfield dismounted in front of him, his pen poised in mid-sentence.

'We're going to fight here?' Sarsfield asked.

Tessé nodded. 'The general has decided.'

'Why has he changed his mind?'

Tessé gave him a French shrug, ignoring the question. 'It's a good position,' he said.

'Where is he?'

'Down there,' Tessé tipped the top of his pen towards the hillside below them.

Sarsfield strode over to the rath and went up its earthen bank at a run, followed by Luttrell. They stopped on the top and surveyed the landscape to the east, towards Ballinasloe. The land ran downhill at a steady slope, undulating here and there, for a half mile or so and then flattened before rising again about a mile away into another hill. Glints of sun on water suggested that the flat area was boggy but it was impossible to tell how boggy from up here. The hill fell away to their left as well, down to where they could see an old stone tower which appeared to be enclosed by a wall.

'Must be good land there,' Luttrell said, bringing his attention back to where men were working at the ditches which criss-crossed the slopes below them, dividing them into fields. 'Worth enclosing.'

Sarsfield nodded. Men with axes and shovels were cutting away bushes and digging gaps in the ditches running down the slope to allow easy access from one field to another. A volley of musket fire came from somewhere to their left and a cloud of grey smoke rose above a line of trees and was whisked away eastwards into insignificance.

New recruits, Sarsfield thought. Which reminded him of something else: rapparees. 'Anything more from Balldearg O'Donnell?' he asked Luttrell.

'Some of his followers have broken away and joined us,' Luttrell replied.

'How many?'

'Not very many,' Luttrell said, loath to give O'Kelly any credit for having persuaded them to defect.

The two men rode down the northern side of the hill towards the ruined castle and the half-dozen cabins nearby. All their inhabitants had fled and the cabins were now occupied by soldiers and their women who had set up a semblance of homes in them. A track weaved among them and past the castle and on to a raised causeway in the direction of Ballinasloe. They went along it at a trot, a bog on their left and a marsh on their right, while keeping an eye on a cavalry patrol that had appeared to the south on the hill ahead of them.

'Ours or theirs?' Luttrell asked. They were too far away to see clearly the standard flapping in the wind.

'Ours, I think,' Sarsfield said.

'Hope you're right.'

Sarsfield brought his horse to a halt and turned it around on the narrow causeway. 'We've seen enough,' he said.

They rode back side by side, practically occupying the width of the causeway. The sun was still high in the afternoon sky and it was quiet. Away from the camp and the work parties, the only sounds were those of their horses and their tackle and the twittering of small birds on the soggy land.

'It's a good position,' Sarsfield admitted. 'It will be impossible for their cavalry to attack along this road. And their infantry will have trouble crossing that marsh.' He indicated the soft ground to their left. Ahead, to their right, pioneers were at work on the walls around the old castle, replacing stones and piling up earth to fill in the gaps. Above the village, three of the nine field guns they had after losing the rest at Athlone were being hauled into position overlooking the causeway.

'Still,' Luttrell said. 'Is our infantry good enough for a pitched battle?'

'Not on the evidence of Athlone,' Sarsfield agreed. 'It would be better to stick to the agreed plan.'

'Maybe the heretics will decline battle when they see the

position,' Luttrell suggested but without conviction. They wouldn't really have that choice, he knew: to turn down the offer of battle would be tantamount to a defeat.

'Let's have a look at the other end of the hill,' Sarsfield said. He turned off the road and jumped a small river that fed the marsh as the land began to rise on the other side of it.

They rode along the lower slope of the hill, passing through some of the newly cut gaps in the ditches, and by a platoon practising musketry with an impatient instructor who cursed at them in relentless Irish as he tried to get loading and firing co-ordinated into a smooth, efficient movement. More groups of young men, cottiers by the look of them, were being trained in the uses of pikes, one lot practising a charge, the fourteen-foot long weapons held parallel to the ground. A second lot practised using the pikes against cavalry, bending down with the end of the pike resting against the right foot and held by the left hand at an angle to spear or deter a horse while keeping its rider's sword slashing at thin air.

They crossed into another field and General Saint-Ruhe was riding towards them with his aides. 'My lord,' Sarsfield and Luttrell doffed their hats as both groups came to a halt.

'You've brought your cavalry?' Saint-Ruhe asked. He looked like a new man since Sarsfield had last seen him, less than a week earlier. His eyes were bright, his misshapen face tanned, and his demeanour exuded a confidence that had deserted him in the immediate aftermath of Athlone. Indeed, he appeared more relaxed and confident now than at any time since his arrival in Ireland.

'Yes, my lord.'

'Good. You will be on the right wing,' Saint-Ruhe indicated towards the southern side of the hill, the direction in which Sarsfield and Luttrell had been riding. 'The most important area. Where they will attack first.'

Sarsfield was taken aback. He had intended questioning the

change of plan but it was clear that the general was not going to countenance any debate. Saint-Ruhe nudged his horse and rode off without another word.

Luttrell let out a long breath, looked at Sarsfield and laughed. 'You were going to change his mind,' he said.

Sarsfield gave a rueful shake of his head.

They rode on to examine the southern end of Kilcommodan where the hill sloped down to ground level. The land here was firm and they continued until they were on the slope of the opposite hill. Saint-Ruhe was right, Sarsfield thought, the enemy would have to attack here. It was the weak spot in their position, the only place where the enemy cavalry could attack in force to try and outflank the infantry on Kilcommodan itself. This is where the battle will be won or lost, he decided.

Mackay

They crossed the River Suck early on the Sunday morning, the infantry marching over the stone bridge with the field guns and the horsemen splashing through the fords on either side. The camp followers had been ordered to stay where they were and maintain the camp. Fog lay on the land, shrouding its contours and reducing visibility to a less than a hundred yards. The men were mostly silent, each trudging after the man in front, paying little or no attention to their surroundings. The officers concentrated on keeping their own units in position in the column. The generals were far from clear about what was to happen.

Ginckel had decided to move forward and confront the enemy. 'All indications suggest that they are preparing to give battle there,' he had told his last council of war the night before. 'But reports about their strength are contradictory.'

'All the deserters say they've lost more than ever,' Württemberg interjected. There had been a small stream of deserters and of local people, seeking the protection offered by the lords justices' proclamation but it had been a failure, as Ginckel knew it would be; it had not attracted a significant numbers of papists or any of their leaders.

'We have to assume they are as strong as they ever were. Maybe even stronger, if the Spaniard's army of rapparees has joined them.'

'You've heard what they had to say about him,' Württemberg said, a hint of the impatience he felt becoming apparent despite his prior determination not to let it show at this meeting. 'They have no time for the Spaniard.'

'We have no choice but to confront them,' Mackay said.

Ginckel looked from one to the other, inviting them to dispute Mackay's suggestion. No one did. They all knew they could not disengage, fall back on Athlone, and lose all momentum. Neither could they seek to go around the papists' army and head for Galway or Limerick since that would leave the way open for a counterattack on Athlone and, worse, a possible crossing by the enemy into the province of Leinster.

'They'll run away at the first volleys,' Württemberg said, eliciting some nods of agreement.

Mackay kept his opinion about the danger of overconfidence to himself, not wishing to provoke any more knowing grins about Killiecrankie. Ginckel caught his eye and Mackay knew the general shared his opinion but he, too, made no comment.

The fog swirled around them, thickening on the lower ground and thinning as they climbed the hills beyond the river. Ahead of them, unseen, the scouts and patrols criss-crossed their path to secure it from ambushes or other signs of the enemy. At the second height above the river, the fog eased, revealing a dull day under what appeared to be a grey sky. The Trench brothers were waiting for them and the Reverend John guided his horse alongside Mackay's.

'Any movements overnight?' Mackay asked him.

'No,' Trench said. 'They've been busy preparing for a battle.'

'How so?'

'They've got their cannons spread out across the hill, pointing back this way.'

That didn't mean much, Mackay thought. They rode in silence, dipping down into a shallow hollow, and then the land began rising again.

'Perhaps I can help out with the Sabbath services,' Trench said after a while.

'You're too late,' Mackay smiled. 'We've already had morning prayers.'

'Later then perhaps.'

'The Lord's help will always be welcome.'

'I hope you don't think ill of my brother,' Trench said after a moment. 'His interests are more of this world than the next.'

'Not at all,' Mackay replied in surprise. 'We need men to ensure our success in this world too, to carry the revolution forward. I'm sure his heart is in the right place.'

'Indeed, it is,' Trench said with an air of relief, as if this had been something that had been weighing on his mind.

Ahead of them, the column had slowed almost to a halt and they could see men moving to the left at the brow of the hill. When they got there, Mackay and Trench halted and looked across the shallow valley at the distant rise.

'There they are,' Trench said unnecessarily. It was just after eight o'clock in the morning. 'I don't know if I should mention this,' he added as Talmash came over to join them.

'What?' Mackay asked.

'You know the Irish are great believers in prophecies,' Trench said, casting a wary eye at Talmash. 'Some Ulster men passed through here last year, driving cattle, and they told us of an old Irish prophecy that a great battle would be fought in this place and that the English would find their coats too heavy as they climbed the hills.'

'What does that mean?' Talmash interjected.

'I don't know,' Trench said in a defensive tone. 'But they took it to mean the English would be running away. Defeated.'

'And did the man who was going to defeat us have a red spot on his forehead and speak Spanish?' Talmash asked with a smirk.

'I'm only telling you what we were told.'

'I fear, Reverend, you've been too long in Ireland. You're beginning to believe their superstitions.'

'I'm not a superstitious man,' Trench protested, turning his horse to leave. 'I'll pray for your success.'

'Thank you,' Mackay said. 'What do you think?' he asked Talmash as Trench rode away.

'Balderdash,' Talmash exploded. 'English men living in Ireland become pests. Most of them over there' -- he pointed to the hill opposite -- 'are degenerate Englishmen who have become Irish in a few generations, forgetting where they came from, ending up speaking their language, marrying their women and adopting their superstitions.'

'I meant, what do you think of the lie of the land?'

The fog had lightened on the higher ground, turning the scene into shades of grey. Tents and flags were visible in the distance as shapes on a dirty white canvas, the movement of men and horses passing shadows. Mackay visualised the landscape as described by Frederick Trench's map, seeing the narrow roadway ahead of them which would lead by the old castle, now obscured by the fog, the invisible marsh ahead, and the hills falling away to the left to merge into flat ground that was also now lost in the fog.

Orders were being given around them, deploying the army across the hillside to mirror what they assumed were the positions on the opposite hill, the standard order of battle with the infantry battalions in the centre and the cavalry and dragoons on both wings. Ginckel's headquarters was being set up at the centre of the hill and Mackay rode over there and dismounted. Riders were returning from the southern end of the hill, where the flat land was, reporting on the enemy's dispositions.

Ginckel absorbed all the information in silence, scanning Kilcommodan hill with his telescope. He offered it to Mackay as he arrived. It didn't provide much help, mainly making the fog appear more dense than it actually was. He passed it to Talmash as he joined the general party. A cavalry cornet reported to Ginckel that the enemy were in position close by on the flat ground to the south, on their side of one of the rivers running across the probable battlefield.

'Post some vedettes there,' Ginckel ordered. Württemberg passed the command in Danish to one of his officers who mounted up and rode off to see that the cavalry sentinels were put there to deter an incursion by the enemy.

Trench's makeshift map of the area was already spread out on the table in the tent. Ginckel pointed to the flat area to the south and told Württemberg and Ruvigny to position most of their cavalries and dragoons there. 'That's the critical area,' he said. 'The only point from which we can attack. or, for that matter, from which they can attack. And,' he looked at Mackay and Talmash, 'move the infantry down the hill as far as possible while the rest of the cavalry covers the right wing and the roadway to Galway.'

'We're going to attack when the fog lifts?' Talmash asked.

'We'll see.' Ginckel said.

Württemberg gave a pointed sigh. Ginckel ignored him. He wasn't prepared to do anything precipitate until the mist dissipated and the picture became clearer.

Mackay followed as the infantry moved down the hill into the fog and to the edge of the marshy land. Visibility was still poor here and sounds swirled about, seeming to come from ahead as well as behind them. Men, as they marched, had already gathered green sprigs off bushes, putting them in their caps to distinguish them from the enemies also in red uniforms when they came to close quarters: the watchword of the day was 'Dublin'. The first line pushed forward cautiously to where the land became wet and their feet began to squelch and sink a little into the rough grass. Artillery units and pioneers tried to push forward some of the field guns, putting planks under their wheels to prevent them from stalling and sinking into the marsh.

Three booms in quick succession signalled the papists' intentions as one of their field gun batteries opened fire. The noise was followed by splashes as the cannonballs fell short into the marsh somewhere ahead of them. Mackay ordered the first line to halt and retrace their steps to the dry ground at the foot of the hill and to await further instructions.

He returned to the general's tent. 'They're ready to fight,' he remarked of the Jacobites.

Ginckel nodded. 'But we'll decide when.'

Sarsfield

General Saint-Ruhe was in an expectant mood, as eager as a craftsman about to present his handiwork to an assembly he knew would be complimentary. 'Hah,' he said with satisfaction as he watched the Williamites spread out across the hill opposite. 'The Dutchman thinks he has nothing to do but wave his sword at us.'

He lowered his telescope, passed it back so it could be taken by an unseen aide behind him and clasped his hands together. 'All is in readiness, yes?' he said to his lieutenant general, Tessé, and his major generals, Sarsfield and Sheldon, from the cavalry, and Hamilton and Dorrington from the infantry. 'You know your positions.'

It was a statement, not a question, not even a rhetorical one. They all knew their positions: Tessé on the left, near the old castle, and Sarsfield on the right, the most dangerous part of the battlefield. Sheldon would command the cavalry on the left wing with Hamilton and Dorrington in charge of the two lines of infantry in the centre, behind the ditches facing the marsh.

'Remember what you are fighting for,' Saint-Ruhe reminded them, launching into a summary of the message he had been repeating at every opportunity for days now. 'Your families, your lands, your religion, your kings and your honour. Today we shall show the heretics what we are made of. Today we take the first step to retrieve all that is ours by right under God.' He paused. 'God is with you all.'

They dispersed in the directions of their commands as the battery of field guns near the castle fired a single salvo, the three quick crashes seeming to reverberate across the bank of fog lying on the marsh. The smoke disappeared among the wisps of vapour still wafting about the hill. But the morning was becoming brighter: the sun was now a bright ball behind the gauzy sky, bright enough to hurt eyes that looked at it directly.

Luttrell was waiting by Sarsfield's horse, holding his own by the reins. He and Purcell, with their cavalry and dragoons, had been assigned to the left wing, behind the castle and under Major General Sheldon's command. 'Be careful,' Luttrell said to Sarsfield, holding out his hand.

Sarsfield shook it. 'What do you mean?' he asked with a half-grin, even though he knew exactly what Luttrell meant.

'Don't do anything rash,' Luttrell said. 'You don't have to win this battle all by yourself.'

Sarsfield mounted his horse and looked down at them. 'I'm a general now,' he grinned. 'Generals don't do rash things.'

He kicked the horse with his heels, cutting off what Luttrell was beginning to say, and rode down the hill, followed closely by the grey mount of his young trumpeter in his gold uniform. He was happy now, a man in his element. Action was what Patrick Sarsfield lived for.

'You think he'll be careful?' Purcell asked as they watched him go.

Luttrell replied with a snort of derision. He put a foot in the stirrup and mounted his horse. Purcell followed his example and added as they moved off to the left, 'I mean now that he's married?'

'I doubt it,' Luttrell said, prodding his horse into a canter. 'Once the trumpets sound, he'll be in the thick of it.'

Groups of men were still on their knees behind priests saying Mass at makeshift altars. As Sarsfield rode past one group the priest turned to give his congregation a general absolution, his arm raised high as he recited the sonorous Latin words *ego te absolvo a peccatis tuis* and made the sign of the cross *in nomine patris, et filii, et spiritus sancti, amen.* The men rose, blessing themselves, and put on their hats and caps. A waiting sergeant was tearing up strips of white paper and was doling them out to those without grey French uniforms - the majority - for their caps.

Sarsfield continued to where the hill sloped down to the dry land and where preparations for the battle were most advanced. The enemy had already begun probing their positions but so far had pulled back from contact. Infantry lined the bottom row of ditches, muskets resting on the earthen banks, pikes protruding here and there. Behind them, a couple of squadrons of dragoons, backed by more squadrons of cavalry, waited for something to happen, circling their horses in impatience as adrenaline energised men and beasts. The atmosphere was expectant more than tense, confident rather than fearful, determined rather than fatalistic.

The general mood was palpable. Sarsfield felt it as well, admitting to himself that Saint-Ruhe was right after all. He had turned an army in disarray two weeks ago into this fighting force, restored its will and belief, and given it the best possible opportunity to redeem itself. Of course, Athlone should never have been lost. But this was no time for should-have-beens.

A messenger came riding up to him. 'They're pushing forward,' he said before turning his horse, riding back from where he had come.

Sarsfield galloped after him, to a rise on the lower slope which offered a vantage-point over the battlefield. Their forward positions were around a cabin on the far side of the small river running southwards, which was the dividing line between the two armies. Beyond them a small body of enemy horsemen was advancing slowly. The defenders at the cabin and the enclosure around it began firing at them and puffs of smoke came from the advancing dragoons.

'Send a squadron down to push them back,' Sarsfield ordered an aide, 'and allow the withdrawal from that cabin.'

The aide galloped away and minutes later a squadron of horse thundered down to the area, a few crossing a bridge, most jumping the river, swords in hand. They closed quickly on the advancing dragoons. Shouts, curses, neighs carried on the still air, broken by high-pitched rings of steel on steel as swords rose and fell and horses reared up and stumbled. The defenders around the cabin mounted up and came back across the river as the enemy dragoons began to disengage.

Then another body of horsemen appeared out of the rising fog to reinforce them, outnumbering the Jacobites. 'Send in more,' one of Sarsfield's aides said, expecting the order to do so.

Sarsfield shook his head. 'Sound the withdrawal,' he ordered a waiting trumpeter.

His aide looked at Sarsfield in surprise as the trumpeter rode off.

The horsemen began to disengage as the order percolated through the din of the engagement and men saw their comrades pulling back. Sarsfield watched them return across the river, pursued by the Williamite cavalry, leaving behind a score of men and horses lying on the ground. Some were moving, others still. The enemy kept coming, speeding up to try and catch the last of those fleeing up the sloping ground.

'Now,' Sarsfield ordered, and another trumpeter took off at speed, sounding the signal to attack. They converged at a canter from left and right on the attackers who quickly realized their mistake: they were outnumbered and trapped.

The battle was on.

Mackay

General Ginckel cursed under his breath in Dutch as he watched what was happening over to the south, on his left wing. 'What are they doing? Can't they follow orders?' he demanded. No one felt the need to answer him as they watched the horsemen pursue the papists across the river and begin to climb the hill.

He lowered his spyglass in exasperation. Worried about an attack on that wing by the Jacobites, he had ordered the Danish vedettes to push back the enemy outpost on this side of the river to the far side. That was all. But they had been attacked by a superior number and the reinforcements sent to help them were not meant to cross over in pursuit as they were now doing. It wasn't meant to be the start of a battle, just a small adjustment to the battlefield while the general decided what to do.

'Who are they?' he demanded of Württemberg.

Württemberg lowered his telescope. 'One of the Irish,' he said. 'Sir Albert Cunningham's dragoons.'

Ginckel shook his head in despair. The Irish had their uses but discipline wasn't their strong point: they were all too keen to kill papists at every opportunity, whether it was necessary or even wise to do so. 'Better send in some horse to extricate them,' he ordered an aide. 'And tell them to withdraw behind that river.'

Württemberg hesitated for a moment as if he would argue while a messenger rode off with instructions for the Dutch dragoons.

They watched for a while until the reinforcements crossed the river. The mass of fighting men on the other side expanded into a looser group. From the top of the hill where they stood a half mile away, the noise of the struggle was muted, the raised voices as easily mistaken for an enthusiastic crowd at a sporting event as the anger and fear of a life and death engagement. Unnoticed by anyone, the fog had cleared and the sky was now a bright blue, the sun spreading warmth over the whole scene, stirred by a gentle breeze from the west. The hills were a verdant green, the bushes and trees heavy with luxuriant foliage, the marsh in between reddish and level.

When they went back to what they had been discussing. Württemberg seized the initiative. 'We should commit more cavalry,' he said, raising an arm towards the engagement. 'A full-scale attack.'

Ginckel raised his telescope and scanned the top of Kilcommodan hill. It looked peaceful: pennants fluttering in the lazy breeze; men and horses moving about without haste; puffs of smoke coming from a field battery long before the distant boom arrived. What concerned him was what he couldn't see, what might be beyond the hill. More reserves. O'Donnell's rapparees? French reinforcements from Galway? But he would surely have heard if the French had landed in Galway.

'We'll wait and see how things develop,' he said.

Württemberg sighed and looked towards Talmash for support.

Talmash took up the argument. 'All that's required, my lord, is enough pressure. Then they will run, as always.'

'Exactly,' Württemberg nodded.

203

'We'll wait,' Ginckel repeated. 'Order up the baggage from Ballinasloe.'

'We're going to camp here, my lord?' Mackay asked, to make sure he had heard correctly.

Ginckel nodded. 'We'll consider an attack tomorrow.'

'And what if they attack us in the meantime?' Talmash asked, an edge of unbidden incredulity raising the pitch of his voice.

'Then they will face the same problems we face.' Ginckel gave him a wintry smile. 'Their infantry will have to cross that marsh and climb this hill. Their cavalry will have to traverse that narrow road between the bogs on this side.'

'That will give them the initiative,' Württemberg said.

'But you don't believe they are capable of taking the initiative.'

Württemberg raised his arms in a shrug of defeat; there was no point trying to have a rational discussion with this man.

'They might sneak away in the night if we don't attack now,' Talmash said.

'They might,' Ginckel conceded. But that might not be the worst outcome in the world, he thought. They might move away to a worse position.

Württemberg glanced at Talmash and shook his head in a gesture of despair. Mackay saw the look with a sense of satisfaction: it was clear that most of those present shared his view of Ginckel's limited leadership abilities.

A boom of cannons from their side was answered like an echo with a corresponding rumble from across the marsh but neither side was causing the other much distress in the artillery exchanges. The lighter Jacobite guns could barely reach the Williamite positions and the heavier Williamite guns did little damage to the Jacobites behind their ditches on Kilcommodan hill.

Meanwhile, the fighting had eased away to the left. The Dutch dragoons had withdrawn to their side of the river, bringing with them the bloodied remnants of the Enniskillen squadrons.

Sarsfield

There was a lull in the battle.

Sarsfield, on horseback, watched from his vantage-point as a couple of injured troopers were carried by comrades up the hill towards the surgeons' tents. Below him some of the infantry were going among the enemy dead and wounded, gathering up swords and carbines and searching bodies for booty. Around him the cavalry men who had been engaged in the action were jubilant, still fired up by adrenaline. He spurred his horse into movement and went among them, congratulating them and repeating in Irish and English, '*Choinneáil bhur phoist. Beid siad arais.* Keep your positions. They'll be back.'

'The sooner the better,' a young trooper, his face flushed with excitement, called back.

Sarsfield gave him a nod of encouragement as he saw General Saint-Ruhe approaching from the hilltop and turned to ride towards him.

'*Felicitations,*' Saint-Ruhe said in greeting. 'They thought they could just ride up the hill and we would let them.'

'Yes, they did.'

'How many did we kill?'

'Fifty or so. Maybe more. And as many wounded.'

'And our side?'

'Ten or twelve, I think.'

Saint-Ruhe nodded with satisfaction. It had been only a skirmish but it had given the heretics notice that they would not have another easy success. And it had raised confidence along the line as word spread that they had beaten back the first enemy thrust.

A cart came sideways down the hill, a couple of men holding it back to stop it from running too fast for the garron between its shafts. It was loaded with loaves of bread and containers of milk and water and a barrel of brandy. The men with it handed out bread and the watery milk to the troopers, followed by a tot of brandy. Similar carts were distributing the midday meal to the soldiers lining the first two rows of ditches facing the marsh.

Sarsfield accepted a small loaf of bread and a pewter cup of the tepid drink. 'We could counter-attack,' he suggested.

'It's too soon for that,' Saint-Ruhe said.

'It would surprise them.'

'Yes, but it would also be a relief to them and throw away our advantage. Let them waste their strength with unsuccessful attacks on us first.'

That made sense, Sarsfield thought.

'Come with me,' Saint-Ruhe said and set off to ride slowly along the line.

Sarsfield accompanied him in silence, aware that it was another spirit-building exercise, showing their presence. Saint-Ruhe stopped to exchange brief words with the infantry commanders, Major Generals Dorrington and Hamilton, who reported that all was well.

'The only action was a few of their scouts testing the marsh,' Dorrington said of his part of the battlefield. 'They were up to their knees in it but they didn't come anywhere near musket range. A few field gun shots sent them back again.'

Random cannon fire continued to come from across the marsh in a desultory fashion, throwing up spurts of dirt on the hill and injuring a few people with flying stones. The heavy heat of the early afternoon seemed to slow down everything, even the urgency of the cannons. Soldiers lay on the grass behind their ditches dozing in the sun.

Near the castle, the infantry was more alert, staying closer to their protective ditches as a battery on the far hill tried to target them. Likewise, around the castle itself the defenders stayed close to the parts of the old walls that had been reinforced with earthen ramparts. Others had pulled back to safer ground for the moment: there was no need to have it fully manned until an infantry or cavalry attack came.

'They sent some of their horse to test the edges of the causeway,' the castle commander, Ulick Burke, told Saint-Ruhe with a laugh. 'But they were quickly up to their hocks in the swamp and had trouble getting out again.'

'Excellent,' Saint-Ruhe replied. The more the enemy learned about the landscape, the more he would appreciate his predicament.

Behind the castle and out of range of the field guns some of its defenders lounged on the grass among Luttrell's dismounted dragoons. Apart from the occasional cannon shot, they could have been miles from a potential battlefield. Luttrell himself rode over as he saw them. 'They tried to force the other pass?' he asked.

'No. They were only testing our resolve.' Sarsfield told him the details.

Luttrell waited until Saint-Ruhe continued on his way to talk to his second in command, Tessé, and Major General Sheldon and his cavalry behind them. 'He was right after all.' Luttrell indicated the departing general. 'We can stop them here.'

'We can.'

Sarsfield rode after Saint-Ruhe, thinking we must stop them here now that we've made a stand. And we can do it. The skirmish showed how difficult it was for the enemy to achieve the standard cavalry objective of attacking the lines of infantry from the sides and rear. Our cavalry is at least a match for theirs and can keep them away from the infantry.

'The Dutchman must attack,' Saint-Ruhe said as they rode back towards the crown of the hill. 'But he can't launch a proper attack anywhere. He is handicapped.'

'But he has to try again,' Sarsfield said.

'He will try again,' Saint-Ruhe nodded. 'On your wing. Where the battle will be decided.'

The attack came four hours later as the sun was still high in the sky in the long summer afternoon. Sarsfield watched it develop, observing the preparations as more horsemen moved into position on the enemy's front line beyond the little river. Their infantry was also edging forward to the marsh in their area, clearly preparing for an assault.

The battle proper began with the Dutch and Danish cavalry crossing the river, pushing back the first defenders on the slopes of the hill. It soon intensified into a clash of hundreds, then thousands, of horsemen. Sarsfield led several squadrons into the fray, feeling the adrenaline rush as he fired his pistol and switched to sword without waiting to see whether his shot had hit his target. Then he was in the midst of the melee, slashing to right and left at anyone with a green sprig in his hat. There was no time for second thoughts about friend or foe, as he thrust his sword through the cuirass of an enemy hacking at someone else, feeling its tip push through the leather protection into the soft body organs until it hit a bone, and pulling it free before the man pitched forward and trapped his blade. The noise was terrifying: screams, curses, shouts, neighs mingled with steel on steel, pistol and carbine shots, and the thumps of hooves and thuds of bodies, of men and horses, hitting the ground. The smell was appalling -

of sweat and blood, of animals and men, of gunpowder and horse shit.

Sarsfield pulled away in a tight turn, his horse almost stumbling as it tried to avoid stepping on a body writhing on the ground, and he detached himself from the melee and rode back to his vantage-point, followed by his trumpeter. He dismounted and patted the sweat-soaked neck of the horse: its eyes still had a wild look and it shifted uneasily. An aide took the reins and handed him the reins of a fresh horse, glancing at the blood spattered on Sarsfield's thigh.

Sarsfield mounted the new horse and paced around in a tight circle to settle it while he examined the progress of the battle. Hundreds of enemy infantry were more than halfway across the marsh, most of them sinking up to their knees, some almost up to their waists, in the soggy ground. The column was maybe a hundred men wide, backed up by rank after rank to the far hill, the ranks becoming more ragged as men struggled with the uneven depths of the marsh. The front rank was coming within musket range of the lowest line of ditches on the hill but Sarsfield was pleased to note that few of the defenders were firing at them. They were waiting until the enemy came closer.

The cavalry battle was continuing, Sarsfield's men being pushed back slowly as more Dutch or Danish horsemen crossed the river and joined in. But the quality and contours of the land narrowed their options, preventing them from fanning out and attacking on a broad front. Still, they were committing more horsemen and Sarsfield instructed an aide to alert the general and request more cavalry from the other end of the hill where nothing appeared to be happening.

The line of enemy infantry was now emerging from the marsh and racing up the firm ground towards the first ditch. A volley of musket fire from the defenders halted half of them but they were quickly replaced by the second rank and then the third rank. A cloud of smoke hung over the ditch as both sides fired at each other at close quarters and pikemen jabbed and hacked at their opponents.

The defenders suddenly broke and raced uphill to the next line of ditches, followed more slowly by the flagging Williamites, tiring from their trudge through the marsh, then the climb. More and more came over the first ditch and chased after the defenders. The first of them reached the second line of ditches and tried to clamber over. The shooting gave way to hand-to-hand fighting, men on both sides using their fired muskets as clubs, stabbing with bayonets when they had them.

Sarsfield ordered a trumpeter to sound the attack. Two squadrons of cavalry cantered, swords in hand, through the gaps cut in the ditches running vertically up the hill. Roaring their war cries, they cut a swathe through the attackers. The Williamites realized too late they had been lured onto a killing ground. Their drummers beat a frantic retreat and they turned and ran as the horsemen criss-crossed among them, slashing at heads, necks and shoulders. More Jacobites appeared at the next vertical ditch, firing at them as they fled, dropping their muskets and pikes, for the safety of the marsh. Jacobite infantry splashed into the marsh after them, stabbing into backs with bayonets and pikes as officers tried to call them back.

The repulse and near rout of the Williamite infantry attack caused its cavalry onslaught to ease as well. A lull descended on the hill and the noise died down as the gentle breeze carried the cloud of gun smoke lazily eastwards over the heads of the retreating men.

Mackay

Most of the gun smoke had blown away, leaving a grainy tang on the tongue.

Württemberg greeted General Ginckel with bad news as he came down from his command position on the centre of the hill. 'Lieutenant Colonel Munchgaard is dead. Hit by a cannon shot.'

Ginckel accepted the information with a nod, noting that Württemberg no longer looked as confident of success as he had been before the battle began. His severe face was drawn and tense.

'We need to attack them again,' Württemberg insisted with the air of a man sticking to his assertions. 'And send in more horse to push them back.'

'We've already committed all the cavalry we should on this wing,' Ginckel replied. If they left the other end of the battlefield without any cavalry, the papists could send their horses across the causeway and attack his infantry.

Württemberg muttered a German curse under his breath. He was running out of options but the general was not offering him any help. As if to confirm his fears, Ginckel rode away towards the hilltop, trying to calculate their best move.

He had been drawn into a battle for which he was not properly prepared; he had not had enough time, nor enough knowledge of the enemy's numbers and positions, to satisfy himself about the terrain and all the possible factors involved. And it was now turning into something not previously experienced in Ireland. Far from being the easy task that Württemberg and Talmash had predicted, the enemy seemed unusually organised, disciplined and well positioned. But now the battle was joined there was no option but to see it through.

Mackay was coming towards him from the other end of the battlefield where all had been quiet so far. As they met, movement along Kilcommodan hill caught their attention and each raised his telescope in silence to see what was happening. Some enemy cavalry squadrons were cantering along the hillside from right to left, to reinforce Sarsfield's men. Ginckel gave a sigh that smacked of despair and raised his glass higher in a sort of nervous twitch to scan the brow of the hill opposite: he was still worried about what might be hidden on the other side of the hill, that the Frenchman had some secret up his sleeve in choosing to fight here, a secret that would explain the enemy's composure.

'We could send some of our cavalry from my wing over to Württemberg,' Mackay suggested with a nod towards the Jacobite cavalry reinforcing their side.

'They have made no moves on your wing?'

'Nothing much. Some of their cavalry have moved forward towards the causeway. That is all.'

'A counterattack?' Ginckel made no attempt to conceal the concern in his voice. Was that the Frenchman's plan? Tie up all the forces at the end of the battlefield which appeared most vulnerable and then counterattack from the other end?

'They may have that in mind,' Mackay said. 'I suggest we move some battalions and a few squadrons forward. Make sure they don't come any closer. And also stop them from sending even more cavalry to their other wing.'

212

Ginckel considered his proposals. The enemy was moving cavalry to where the fighting was: it made sense to concentrate as many of his cavalry there as well. And Mackay's suggestion of moving some men and horse towards the old castle would stop them from sending more reinforcements against Württemberg's cavalry and let the Frenchman know that he was alert to a counterattack.

'Do it,' he told Mackay.

'Excellent,' Talmash rubbed his hands when Mackay told him of the general's orders. He had been growing increasingly impatient at their inactivity.

Mackay, as the senior major general on this wing, sketched out his plan to Talmash and Ruvigny. They would move four battalions of infantry forward, backed by dragoons and some cavalry, testing the marsh's depth and seeing how wide a front they could establish. At the same time, twelve field guns were to advance as far as possible, firing three-gun salvos at the papists' positions around the old castle, the causeway, and the defensive ditches on the lower slopes of the hill near the castle.

The orders were issued down the line and the advance began. The day was still bright and warm, the sun high in the sky but beginning to slip slowly down towards the north-west. The noise of the battle a mile away was dulled by distance, a background rumble to the boom of cannons. As they advanced, the Jacobite three-gun battery opposite increased its rate of fire, most balls falling short and splashing into the marsh.

Soon, however, the cannon shot was falling among the men sloughing their way through the wet ground. A few fell, killed or wounded, but the soft ground also absorbed the shots, limiting the damage they did. They moved forward, more or less in a straight line, but on a narrow front alongside the causeway. The horsemen followed at a distance, picking their way carefully over the treacherous ground. Artillery men, with the help of sappers, cautiously pushed forward their guns on planks but it was slow work and their range wasn't as great as the Jacobite guns, which had the advantage of their hillside elevation.

Mackay stopped the front line close to the enemy at a point where the marsh eased and a ditch gave them some cover from musket fire at the limit of its effective range. As far as he could tell, the infantry away to his left, at the other end of the battlefield, was not moving forward.

Talmash came over to Mackay, demanding to know why he had halted the advance.

'Because the left wing is stopped,' Mackay said.

'That's no reason,' Talmash shot back. 'We should keep going.'

'Look ahead,' Mackay said with exasperation, pointing at the foothills of Kilcommodan where the muskets and pikes of the defenders were visible on the ditches. Behind them some squadrons of cavalry could also be seen, their horses prancing as they waited for an opportunity to attack.

'We can take the ditches,' Talmash insisted as a cannon shot dropped behind them, sending up a splatter of dirty water that rained down on them.

'No, we can't,' Mackay retorted. 'If we try, they can throw more men and horse against us. We'll be heavily outnumbered. We have to wait for an attack all along the front so they can't move more men against us.'

'The longer we delay, the more encouragement we give them.' Talmash looked to Ruvigny for support. 'We should attack now, shouldn't we?'

Ruvigny gave a Gallic shrug and glanced at Mackay. 'Whatever you wish to do.'

Talmash sighed in exasperation. 'If that's the case, I'll bring my men back to our positions. There's no point sitting here being cannonaded.'

'Send a messenger to the general,' Mackay said to Ruvigny.

'Ask him what he wants us to do. Tell him I want to wait for an attack all along the front before we move forward.'

One of Ruvigny's aides ran back to the horses, mounted and rode back along the causeway to their hill.

They waited in silence for his return. Cannon shot continued to fall around their position but caused little damage. Their own cannons were now within range of the hill and were returning fire almost four-fold, pushing back the waiting cavalry on the hillside but unable to make any impact on the infantry behind their ditches.

The messenger returned, asking the three major generals to come back for a discussion with Ginckel. They withdrew beyond cannon shot and Mackay explained his thinking to Ginckel. 'We have to attack all along the front,' he told him.

'We don't need to wait,' Talmash argued. 'We can attack here now, take over their positions and allow our cavalry across the causeway to outflank them.'

Ginckel looked to Ruvigny for his opinion. 'I await your orders,' Ruvigny told him unhelpfully.

'We're running out of time,' Mackay added with a nod of partial agreement to Talmash. 'We have to launch a full attack, make an all-out effort now or else we'll have to withdraw at dark.'

Ginckel looked hunted. This was what he feared. Withdrawal would effectively be a victory for the enemy, would greatly improve their confidence, and make his task even more difficult the next day. On the other hand, an all-out attack was a huge gamble: failure would be an effective defeat, whether or not the enemy was strong enough to counterattack. And if it was ... . That was not an option Ginckel wanted to contemplate.

Mackay watched the general agonise, aware of the pros and cons he was debating. We have to do it, he thought, closing his eyes in a silent prayer. Trust in providence.

'Yes,' Ginckel said at last. 'We will attack along the whole front.'

Sarsfield

The shadows were beginning to stretch out before the ditches, leaving the defenders in sunshine and darkening the other side of their protective lines. The cavalry and dragoon battle had waxed and waned for hours now, as horses and men threw themselves at one another, engaged and disengaged and engaged again in an exhausting and bloody struggle for supremacy. A hollow where the Dutch and Danes had been halted was now a no-man's land of dead and dying bodies of men and horses, avoided by both sides as no longer suitable for the living to fight over. Riderless horses dashed in panic to and fro along the hillside.

Sarsfield extracted himself from the line, breathing heavily, during another lull. Fresh blood ran down his high leather boots over the dried blood of earlier encounters. He changed horses again, cleaning the blade of his sword on the grass before remounting.

'Look,' an aide said to him, pointing across the marsh.

The infantry at the centre of the prince of Orange's army had left their positions on the opposite hill and were moving slowly towards them across the wet land. This was it, he thought. Their last effort to break through. A full-frontal assault.

He rode up the hillside to report to General Saint-Ruhe that they had pushed the enemy cavalry back to where they had begun the afternoon.

Saint-Ruhe accepted the news almost without interest, focused now on the infantry attack. He was in high good humour, like a man whose dream had seemed too much to hope for and who now saw it falling into place before his eyes. *'C'est parfait, non?'* he said, lowering his telescope.

'Yes, my lord,' Sarsfield agreed. Everything was going well. His men had shown their mettle against the rebels. The infantry, in full flight after Athlone, was standing its ground like a different army.

Below them, officers were moving back and forth behind the men manning the first line of ditches, ordering them to hold their fire and positions. The enemy's heaviest cannons increased their rate of fire, hurling their twelve-pound balls as near the ditches as their imperfect aim could achieve: few managed to break a gap in the first line.

The enemy lines of several thousand men kept coming, musketeers, pikemen and grenadiers ploughing their way through the marsh, up to their knees in the sucking mud. Those farther back sank and slipped even deeper into the ground as the mud was churned up by the ranks ahead of them. The sun was in their eyes, the ditches ahead of them a black line of shade.

The first of them emerged from the marsh, shouting their war cries in a cacophony of languages, and raced over the firm ground to the first ditch. The grenadiers tossed their grenades between the bushes on the ditch; the pikes of both sides jabbed at targets; and muskets were discharged at point-blank range and then turned into clubs or fixed with bayonets. A shroud of dirty grey smoke rose above the ditch and drifted back towards the marsh, into the faces of the next wave of attackers.

Sarsfield and Saint-Ruhe had a clear view from the hilltop,

watching as the Williamites fought their way over the ditch, men falling under the blades of bayonets, stabbed by pikes, clubbed by the butts of fired muskets. Some without weapons grappled with each other on the ground, hands seeking stones or other weapons. Then, the defenders began to run up the hill, the enemy clambering over the ditch and howling with blood lust as they pursued what seemed like frightened quarry.

'The fools.' Saint-Ruhe gave a short, mirthless laugh.

The defenders scattered to left and right, towards gaps in the vertical ditches. Once most of them were through, more Jacobites opened fire on the flanks of the pursuers and then two cavalry squadrons swooped through. The attackers' momentum disappeared like an onrushing tide sinking into soft sand and they turned tail, back the way they had come, running into their own comrades who were still coming over the first ditch. The horsemen bore down on them, swords swinging left and right as if they were cantering through a field, topping thistles.

The second line of Jacobites then came over their ditches and followed the cavalry. The Williamites ran back towards their own lines, stumbling in their haste through the marsh. The Jacobites followed, their momentum catching the slower runners, hacking them down, leaving some to drown in the marsh.

The cannon on both sides had gone silent, unable to fire at the intermingled forces. The Jacobites overran one of the enemy batteries as its gunners fled. Some tried to haul the guns back to their side but they quickly sank into the marsh and became immovable. A couple of others overtook a colonel trying to rally his fleeing man, disarmed him and dragged him back towards their own lines.

'Enough, enough,' Saint-Ruhe muttered as he watched his men pursue the enemy almost as far as the other hillside.

As if they had heard him, the pursuers slowed and turned back through the muddied marsh, now puddled with blood as well as water, to their own lines.

Bodies lay on both sides of the ditch, most in various shades of red uniforms, disguising their allegiances in common suffering and death. Wounded Jacobites struggled up the hill, its long slope now a stiff climb as they nursed injured limbs and tried to staunch bleeding with dirty hands or bits of cloth. Women wandered among the dead or wounded, looking for husbands or sons but then the enemy cannons started up again, scattering them as plumes of earth and stones erupted on the hillside, and balls linked by chains scythed through bushes.

Across the marsh, the enemy was forming up for another attack, the front line already wading thigh-deep through the water and the sucking earth beneath.

Saint-Ruhe and Sarsfield watched as their infantry commanders, Major Generals Dorrington and Hamilton, re-set the defences, moving the second line of men down to the first ditch among the wounded and dead of the first assault.

The enemy came on and the second assault followed the same pattern as the first, the Williamites forcing their way over the first line of ditches only to be thrown back by a counter-attack and chased across the marsh, leaving another layer of bodies behind.

'Good, good,' Saint-Ruhe muttered to himself, scanning the length of the front with his telescope. There was nothing happening over near the castle. The enemy who had moved forward earlier was still cowering behind a ditch. Straight ahead of him, he could see the enemy infantry preparing for another attack. At the other end of the battlefield, the enemy cavalry looked like it too was preparing for another onslaught.

'They're about to attack there again,' he said to Sarsfield, pointing towards his part of the battlefield.

Sarsfield took the information as an order and headed back to the next round of cavalry fighting. Saint-Ruhe turned his attention to the preparations below him to receive a third assault on the line of ditches, watching as some fresh men from near the castle were brought into the centre to strengthen the defences.

Mackay

'God-damn,' Mackay muttered as he watched the assault on the enemy's centre, causing his closest aide to raise his eyebrows in surprise at the first oath he had ever heard the major general utter.

The orders had been very clear: they were to advance to the solid ground at the bottom of the hill, take the first line of ditches, and stop there. Then they were all to move forward in a united line along the whole length of the front. But the attackers had kept going, crossing the ditch and chasing the papists, with the result that Mackay now watched in horror as they were pursued back across the marsh.

Talmash had raced away with a stream of explosive curses to rally them, to stop their flight, turn them around and get more men into the line to attack again.

Mackay was still in position near the castle where the enemy, encouraged by the success of their centre, had increased their rate of fire from cannon and musket. If they attack us here now with the centre in disarray, they could win the battle, he thought, blinking into the sun coming over the hill. A sudden memory of Killiecrankie caused him to shudder: that day, the day of his defeat, he had been blinded by the sun too as Bonnie Dundee's men had coming charging down the hill with the sun behind them, routing his lines.

He dismissed the uncomfortable memory. It was just a coincidence, didn't mean anything. The Irish aren't attacking, he told himself.

He moved back to Ruvigny and his force of Huguenot and English cavalry. 'We have to attack along the causeway,' he told Ruvigny and his senior officers.

Several of the officers shook their heads. 'There isn't room,' an English lieutenant colonel protested. 'We can't force our way through that narrow path.'

'You have to,' Mackay snapped back at him, fear of defeat causing his voice to rise in determination. 'Don't tell me you can't do it. Your honour, your religion, your liberty depends on it. You must and you will do it. You must give a lead to the infantry. Show them that we can and we will prevail.'

Everyone went silent and Ruvigny ordered them to mount up.

Mackay ordered the infantry forward as the first horsemen, only a few abreast, cantered along the causeway and the edge of the marsh to be met with musket fire from the castle. Then a squadron of dragoons appeared in front of them, firing their carbines, dismounting, and attacking on foot with swords, dodging in among the horsemen with greater manoeuvrability than the mounted riders. The first line of cavalry was forced back. Those coming up behind them surged forward and attacked again but they were also stopped in their tracks.

Mackay tried to keep an eye on what was happening elsewhere but the battlefield was now becoming clouded with gun smoke as the breeze dropped and the shadows lengthened. Talmash had got the infantry in the centre to attack again and there seemed to be fighting all along the front. But it was impossible to follow its progress elsewhere and he turned his attention back to the immediate fighting.

The cavalry was making no progress and Mackay decided they had to try and widen their attack. He ordered the English lieutenant colonel who had spoken up earlier to take a squadron forward closer to the castle.

'I will not,' the lieutenant colonel retorted.

'It's no more dangerous than for anyone else.'

'Then do it yourself.'

Mackay thought angrily of telling him he had more to do than lead every battalion or squadron but he didn't have time for an argument. He ordered the lieutenant colonel's men to follow him and he raced ahead to run the gauntlet by the castle, less than fifty yards from its defenders. He jumped a stream. His horse stumbled as it landed in the soft earth and Mackay was tossed to the ground. He thought at first he had been shot but then realized he hadn't been hit and neither had the horse. The soft ground had broken his fall and his right side was covered in muck. He struggled to his feet in the squelching ground, musket balls plopping around him.

His horse was trying to run away, going deeper into the marsh and struggling to lift its hooves. There was no sign of the squadron he had been attempting to lead. One of his aides jumped the stream on horseback, leading a spare horse. Mackay remounted quickly, crouching low in the saddle and bracing himself against the expected thud of a musket ball. But nothing hit him or the horse as he jumped back over the stream and out of harm's way.

Back on safer territory, he tried to take stock of what was happening. His infantry was moving forward towards the lower line of ditches, receiving less fire than he had expected. The enemy had withdrawn some of the defenders from there, he realized, probably to reinforce their centre. But the cavalry wasn't making much progress. They were getting more men along the causeway and onto the firm ground, keeping the enemy dragoons and cavalry occupied and away from the infantry.

A movement up the hillside caught his attention and he tried to focus his telescope on it. A troop of horsemen was trotting down from the hilltop, heading towards him. They faded away as a cloud of gun smoke drifted in front of the lens. Coming this way, he thought. Not in a great hurry. He tried to get a clear picture, moving the telescope back and forth but the smoke kept drifting between him and the horsemen, turning movements into shadows or disappearing them altogether. They're not in a hurry, he thought again.

A sudden sense of panic gripped Mackay.

They're waiting for more of our cavalry to cross the causeway, he thought, to destroy them in a pincer movement. Once enough, but not too many, have crossed. And that would leave them free to counterattack along the causeway with few to stop them.

The cavalry troop on the hillside came into sight again as the gun smoke cleared away to wisps and he tried to make out the pennants they were flying. White with something on it. Maybe the fleur-de-lis. French, in any event. Maybe the French general's personal troop. He watched it for a moment, trying to figure out how to deal with this threat. Should he pull back the cavalry? Or push as many forward as quickly as possible?

Then the troop stopped and lost its shape, turning from a purposeful unit moving forward into a group of individual horsemen wheeling about. Mackay shifted the telescope ahead of them and around them to see what had stopped them but he could see nothing obvious, hindered by bushes and other obstacles and by the drifting clouds of gun smoke.

He lowered the scope for a moment to focus on what was happening nearby. His infantry was being threatened by enemy dragoons while Ruvigny's cavalry tried to protect them and itself but it was under pressure. There's no choice, he decided. We have to send in more cavalry as quickly as possible. We cannot afford to pull back now, to show any weakness or lack of determination.

He raised the telescope again and couldn't find the troop of

223

enemy cavalry where it had been. He scanned closer to his own position, along the line it had been taking, fearing the worst, that they were joining in the cavalry fight here. But there was no sign of them. In desperation, he moved the scope right and left and up and down, trying to locate them. He found them where he least expected them. They were near the brow of the hill, riding away.

That makes no sense, he thought.

But there was no time to think too much about it. Ruvigny's cavalry was barely holding on and needed urgent reinforcements. He rounded up the remaining cavalry and led them along the causeway, holding back from the fighting to try and keep a clear picture of the overall situation.

Suddenly, he spotted men moving back up the hill and thought that the infantry in the centre had broken through but the fighting was still going on along the first ditches. Then the horsemen attacking there seemed to thin out and he realized that the enemy was indeed pulling back. His first suspicion was that it was another trap, like the one the infantry had raced into earlier. They're trying to entice us forward. To an ambush above? To the reinforcements the general feared were over the hill?

But there was no time to try and reach a considered conclusion. Ruvigny's cavalry was already seizing the opportunity of the enemy's indecision or hesitancy or whatever it was. It charged forward and then wheeled to the left to cut down the infantry defenders behind their ditches. To their right the defenders around the castle were still firing on those within range but they were fast becoming irrelevant, bypassed by the action, about to be isolated and surrounded.

Seeing the cavalry coming towards them from an unexpected direction, the Jacobite second line of infantry began to turn, then to move back, then to flee up the hill. They are breaking from the back, Mackay thought as he cantered after Ruvigny's cavalry, as they always do. It was always the men at the back who melted away first when things went wrong.

Sarsfield

This end of the battlefield was now in shadow. The intensity of the fighting had slowed and exhausted cavalry men were no longer able to swing their swords with the same energy. More than six hours of attacking, engaging, defending, disengaging, had left both sides in the same positions as they had begun the day. Bodies lay everywhere, moving and unmoving. Loose horses raced about. Horsemen everywhere were spattered with their own and other men's and horses' blood.

Sarsfield rode among some squadrons who had just disengaged from another clash with the foreigners, offering words of encouragement. Wounded men were sliding from their saddles, clutching bloodied arms, trying to balance on damaged legs. A young lieutenant raised his head from where he had rested it on his horse's neck and a smile crossed his strained face when he saw Sarsfield approach.

'We've shown them,' he said as he straightened up.

Sarsfield clapped him on the shoulder as he passed by. 'We have,' he said.

He rode back to his vantage point. Another cavalry engagement was going on but the exhaustion on both sides was evident. The noise was muted, voices no longer raised in war cries, the ringing of steel on steel a slower rhythm, even the howls of hurt now sounded more subdued. Both sides were mainly concerned to hold their ground, neither making any great effort to push the other back.

To his left, the latest Williamite infantry attack had gone down to hand-to-hand fighting over the first ditches under the cover of the cloud of gun smoke. It was difficult to tell one side from the other until the defenders began to move back, drawing the attackers into the same ambush they had already fallen into earlier. Sarsfield shook his head in wonder that the enemy was making the same mistake again.

He turned back to watch his own men's engagement. Another squadron of enemy cavalry was cantering up to join in and he hesitated about sending in one of his own exhausted squadrons to reinforce the men already there. But only for a moment. There was no choice but to match them. He gave the order and heard the trumpet sound it. Weary men raised themselves from the ground, mounted up, unsheathed their swords and cantered down the hill.

'Look,' one of his aides said in a shocked voice.

Sarsfield turned to look where he was pointing back up the hill. The general's bodyguard was riding towards the rath on its crest and he watched in confusion as they disappeared over it. Then he caught sight of a rider coming towards him fast.

'The Frenchman's dead,' the rider said as he pulled up his horse in a turning movement.

'What?' Sarsfield asked, seeking confirmation even as his thoughts struggled to come to terms with the shock.

'Cannonball,' the rider said, struggling for breath. He rode off again at speed.

Sarsfield looked back up the hill where some of the infantry were now running towards the crest.

Everything began to move quickly.

He turned back to his own field of operations and saw more enemy cavalry riding towards them at speed, their determination and surge of energy evident. Back towards the infantry battle, most of the defenders were still enmeshed in hand-to-hand fighting but individuals and then small groups were detaching themselves and running up the hill. And then from the far side of the hill horsemen appeared, cutting through the fleeing soldiers.

Sarsfield snapped a series of orders, sending a couple of his resting squadrons to try and stop the enemy cavalry charge across the hillside and ordering his men already fighting in their positions to pull back up the hill to avoid being surrounded. He joined the squadrons riding to block the attack across the hill, meeting their spearhead on the sloping ground among the fleeing infantry, now turning into a panicked rout. Men ran between the horses as their riders slashed, hacked and stabbed at one another and the triumphant attackers roared their war cries and friends as well as enemies were cut down and trampled in the mayhem of the moment.

There was no time to think, no time for anything but instinct, no time for any instinct but survival.

Sarsfield pulled back from the battle, breathing heavily, to get an overview of the situation. His squadrons were holding the attacking cavalry on the hillside but those on the wing were being pushed backwards up the hill. And further enemy horsemen were coming along the hillside. The enemy infantry was also coursing up the hill, pursuing the defenders and stabbing with their bayonets at horsemen and their mounts. It was only a matter of time before his men would be pushed back in both directions, fighting a rearguard action.

Defenders were falling everywhere, under the bayonets and pikes of their pursuers on foot and the swords of cavalry. The front line had collapsed and they were in full rout, racing for safety over the hill, desperate to find sanctuary from the pursuing horsemen, trying to huddle in the corners of ditches. Sarsfield consolidated his two forces into one in an attempt to hold back the enemy cavalry, an exhausted force against an enemy energised by the scent of victory, their blood up.

Under attack on two sides, the Jacobite horsemen tried to move backwards up the hill in a controlled fashion but it was next to impossible. The action became a fighting retreat, gathering speed, as they were chased over the hill, outpacing the running infantry, who were now being joined by the fleeing camp followers. Screams and shouts of terror blanked out appeals for mercy as the pursuing cavalry cut down everyone in its path. They gave up the chase after a few miles and turned back to finish off those they had missed.

A bank of grey cloud had moved up the sky from the west, dousing the setting sun, and a gentle mist began to settle, like an apology, on the blood-drenched hill.

Mackay

Mackay sat on the raised earth of the rath's circle, his elbows resting on his knees, his head bowed, scarcely aware of the soft mist drifting down. It was the will of God, he was thinking. Nothing was ever clearer. The King's army was on the point of defeat and Providence intervened. There was no other explanation.

The hill sloping below him was strewn with bodies among the holes ploughed by cannon shots. Mounds of bodies were gathered in the corners where they had sought refuge from the marauding cavalry and were now being pulled apart by men in search of plunder. Wounded papists were being shot or bayoneted to death. Those in the grey French *trucoats* were easily identified. The password was demanded of those in red uniforms who were conscious enough and able to discard the scraps of white paper from their caps and replace them with green sprigs. Wounded horses unable to raise themselves from the ground were also killed. Around the hilltop, the detritus of the enemy camp was everywhere: torn tents, abandoned standards, ransacked trunks, scattered papers. The remnants of a rout.

Mackay looked up as he heard angry shouts. A number of

infantrymen were squabbling over something one had found on a dead body, pushing and pulling at the finder who broke away from them and tried to run away. They chased him and fell on him. Talmash, riding by, stopped and began shouting and slapping at them with the flat of his sword. They disentangled themselves and sloped away, arguing in a language Mackay couldn't quite distinguish.

More infantrymen were streaming back over the hill from the pursuit, some pulling women with them, others carrying casks of beer and sides of beef looted from the enemy's sutlers. Men slumped on the damp ground in exhaustion, ignoring their comrades who were lighting fires and settling down to eat and drink. In the distance, a trumpet sounded the retreat, recalling cavalrymen who had not yet returned from the pursuit.

Off to the left, a large group of prisoners sat in a disconsolate circle near the crest of the hill. Beyond them, the baggage wagons were coming across the causeway, past the castle where the defenders had been surrounded and forced to surrender.

Mackay paid little attention to the activity around him. He felt tired now that the heightened emotions of the battle were seeping away like the daylight. It was a glorious victory, he knew, but he felt little sense of elation. That might come later but, for the moment, he could still smell the mixture of powder and blood and feel the visceral savagery of the killing, which always unsettled him. It was the will of God that took the heart and spirit out of the enemy, that made this victory, that proved the rightness of their cause. But was all the slaughter really necessary? If only people would see the error of their ways.

Württemberg rode over, dismounted, and sat down beside him on the damp earth. 'They're destroyed,' he said in a flat voice without any hint of his earlier belligerence or scorn for the enemy. 'Utterly destroyed.'

Mackay remained silent. The statement of the obvious didn't require any comment. It was evident from everything around them; the thousands of dead, the wounded and captured, the abandoned headquarters, the discarded weapons and cannons. The Jacobite army was in total disarray.

'Van Holtzsappel's dead,' Württemberg said after a moment of one of the Dutch major generals.

'What happened?'

'Don't know yet.'

They lapsed into silence, then Württemberg got up and walked away without a word.

Sometime later, Talmash appeared with a bottle of red wine and sat down beside Mackay, handing him the open bottle. Mackay took a drink and passed it back.

'You were right.' Talmash raised the bottle to him in a toast. 'To wait until the whole line attacked.'

Mackay accepted the apology for their earlier disagreement with a nod.

'It made all the difference,' Talmash continued. 'We mightn't have succeeded if we had moved forward by the castle when I wanted to. You saved the day.'

'It was the will of God,' Mackay said in what he hoped was a light tone.

Talmash smiled as he took another drink. Mackay being Mackay, he thought. 'But He needed some assistance at the right time.'

'I think the rumour's true, that their general was killed.'

Talmash restrained himself from saying, 'smitten by the hand of God'. 'Even so,' he said instead. 'That doesn't explain their sudden collapse. Where was his second in command?'

'We think he was killed too. We shot a French officer in their last charge as we broke through.'

'Ah,' Talmash nodded, 'that makes sense.'

It made sense of what I saw, Mackay thought. Their general's bodyguard riding away, undermining their confidence, a moment of indecision, causing them to falter and run. Then a last-minute charge by Ruvigny's cavalry, in which the French officer was shot and their panic was uncontrollable. 'It gave us the opportunity to break through,' he said.

'Just as well you did. Things were not going well in the centre. Or anywhere else.'

'It was all a close-run thing.'

'Victory is all the sweeter for that.'

Mackay reached for the bottle and took another drink of wine, feeling the alcohol go to his head. A whiff of meat roasting on a spit nearby made him realise that he hadn't eaten all day. It was dark now, a translucent summer darkness, making the campfires along the hillside glow brighter. The rain still drizzled down in a soft mist.

'You heard about Colonel Earle?' Talmash asked.

Mackay shook his head and handed him back the bottle.

'He was captured during the first attack in the centre. He escaped but he was captured again during the second attack. Nevertheless, we managed to rescue him at the end of the day.'

'Lucky man.'

'Luckier than Colonel Herbert, who was also captured. They killed him when we were overrunning their position.'

'A lot of men met their maker today.' Mackay felt a sudden desire to close his eyes, curl up on the rath and go to sleep.

'You talked to the prisoners?'

Mackay glanced over to where they were gathered, hundreds, maybe a thousand, on the side of the hill and shook his head.

'Most of their infantry commanders were killed, as far as I can tell,' Talmash said, following his gaze. 'Couple of generals, more brigadiers, colonels and downwards. God knows how many.'

'This has to be the end of it,' Mackay said. 'They can't go on fighting.'

'Not if they have any sense,' Talmash said with an

undercurrent of regret.

They fell silent for a time, passing the bottle back and forth. Then Mackay asked: 'What was that row about earlier? The one you broke up?'

Talmash laughed. 'Fortune smiled on one of the Danes. He found a *louis d'or* on a body and wasn't inclined to share it.'

'On a French body?'

'No. A local papist by the looks of him.'

'Wonder what he'd done to earn that?'

'Probably stole it from a Frenchman.'

Later, Ginckel summoned all his generals to his tent, newly erected beyond the hill, out of sight of the battlefield. This area, too, was strewn with bodies, of combatants and camp followers who had got in the way of the pursuit. An aide poured glasses of brandy and they toasted King William and Queen Mary.

'To the end of this campaign,' Ginckel added and they raised their glasses again.

'Is it over?' someone dared to ask.

Ginckel pursed his lips, reluctant to say it was. He, like everyone else there, recognised the scale of their victory, the scale of the enemy's defeat. It was rare in all of their experiences to witness such a decisive outcome to a pitched battle. 'Perhaps,' he said. 'But we still have to take their ports.'

'Is it true their French commander was killed?' Talmash asked.

'That's what some of the prisoners say. Hit by a cannon shot.'

'So there is some justice in this world,' Ruvigny murmured, remembering General Saint-Ruhe's role in persecuting Protestants in France. '*Le missionaire botté* has received his just deserts.'

'Where's his body?' Mackay asked. 'Have we found it?'

Ginckel shook his head. 'One of the prisoners says his guard took it away.' He raised his glass again. 'Another toast. To the

Marquis de Ruvigny, who led the charge that won the day.'

They raised their glasses. Talmash gave Mackay an almost imperceptible shake of his head over the rim of his. They both knew that Ruvigny had merely been following Mackay's instructions. It was another example of the general favouring the continental commanders.

'How many men did you lose?' Ginckel was asking Ruvigny.

'Altogether in that action? Three hundred or so killed between mine and the English cavalry. It was fierce for a while. I don't know how many were wounded. Another couple of hundred at least.'

The mention of the heavy casualties brought a respectful silence as an aide went among them re-filling glasses. The conversation resumed with an exchange of news about the dead and injured among their officers, the acts of heroism, the lucky escapes, the quirks of fate that saw some die and others live.

'By the way,' Talmash said to Mackay. 'Your reverend friend's prophecy came true.'

'I don't think it was his prophecy.'

'He'll believe it now, even if his interpretation was wrong. Our men did indeed find their coats to be too heavy as they ran up this hill, in pursuit.'

Sarsfield

arsfield dropped his hat and wig on the grass, took a few steps into the lake at Loughrea, bent down, scooped up water and buried his face in it. The water was warm and silky and he did it again and again, washing away the grime and tension of the day. But not the desolation: nothing could wash that away.

He straightened up, shook the drops from his hands, rubbed his face with a sleeve and stepped back to the shore. The lake was dark, barely pocked by the mist dropping silently onto its surface. Along the shore, men sat or lay on the ground, in ones and twos and, here and there, small groups. No one was talking. The only sounds were of horses moving about in search of fodder, harnesses clinking, and the groans of some wounded men being attended by surgeons.

He knew he should walk around, rallying them, but he couldn't bring himself to do it just yet. He sat on a rock, staring at the lake in the gloom of the short night, images from the slaughter running out of control in his mind. Friends hacked from their horses; the men he had killed or disabled; infantrymen half-decapitated, their legs still trying to run while their heads were already partly severed; women screaming as they tried to flee from the thundering horses; children standing petrified in the midst of mayhem, abandoned.

And the catalogue of the lost, already long, seen or sensed during the fighting retreat and certain to get longer. The officers and troopers who had been with Sarsfield for the last two years and some he had known even longer, cut down in the last hour of chaos after such a gallant fight for the best part of a day. He had been so proud of their defence of the pass. And then it had all fallen apart and turned into the worst defeat he had ever witnessed. Worse, much worse, than the Boyne or any of the skirmishes in England against Monmouth or the prince of Orange.

He knew he should think of what to do now but he couldn't bring himself to do that yet, couldn't look beyond the day. He stared unseeing at the dark lake.

He became aware later of someone approaching him and he raised his gaze from the lake.

'Thank God,' Luttrell said, putting a hand on Sarsfield's shoulder. 'You survived.'

'You too.' Sarsfield patted Luttrell's hand.

Luttrell eased himself down on the grass beside Sarsfield's rock.

'What happened?' Sarsfield asked after a brief silence, bringing himself back to what needed to be done. First, he had to know exactly what had happened and if the defeat was as devastating as he feared.

'We couldn't hold them,' Luttrell sighed.

Sarsfield waited in silence for him to continue. As far as he understood it in the chaos of the moment, their left wing by the old castle had given way, causing the collapse all along the front.

Luttrell took a deep breath. 'The line near the castle had been weakened. Men and horse were moved from there to help out in

236

the centre. We were holding them but then the men saw the general's troop riding away and ...' he paused. '... a panic set in. There was no holding them then.'

Sarsfield thought about that, visualizing what had happened. 'Did you see what happened the general?'

'No. They say he was hit by a cannonball. And that he was on his way to reinforce us, replace the horse and men he had moved away earlier -- to help us push them back. But the reinforcements never arrived. And the enemy just kept coming.'

'And Tessé? Wasn't he over there too?'

Luttrell nodded. 'He tried to lead a counterattack but he was shot three times.'

'Dead, too?'

'No. He took a pistol shot in the face and two in the chest but he's in a house in the town with a surgeon.'

So Tessé is in command now, Sarsfield thought. That did not fill him with great confidence: Tessé hadn't shown any great leadership abilities as Saint-Ruhe's second in command. He had never offered any meaningful suggestions at the councils of war or shown any rapport with the men under his command. 'I should go and see him,' Sarsfield said.

'Yes. You might be in command now.'

Sarsfield gave him an inquiring look but he was already considering that possibility. 'And what do you think we should do?' he asked.

Luttrell gave a heavy sigh as if, for once, his heart wasn't in planning and plotting the way ahead. 'Go back to the original plan, before the Frenchman decided to stand and fight at Aughrim. What else can we do?'

That was the only option, Sarsfield knew, the option that should have been chosen in the first place: defend Galway and Limerick and use the cavalry to harry the prince of Orange's men, disrupt their supply lines, upset their control of the countryside, and force them backwards until the army could be reinforced by the Kings in France.

'You should probably go to Limerick,' Luttrell added. 'I don't think you'll be welcomed with open arms in Galway.'

'Probably not.'

'My lord Dillon is among the dead,' Luttrell added, thinking of the governor of Galway, Dillon's eldest son Henry, who was now the new viscount. His younger brother Arthur was already in France, leading part of the regiment raised by their father and sent abroad the previous year under Lord Mountcashel. 'I'll get a complete list of the casualties.'

Sarsfield felt a wave of exhaustion overwhelm him: he needed to sleep. 'We'll talk about it all tomorrow,' he added, although it was already the morrow.

Daylight seeped in slowly under unbroken cloud. The mist had done nothing to refresh the countryside and had faded away, leaving the air heavy and still. Exhausted stragglers were still arriving after hiding from their pursuers. The roll call of the missing lengthened as musters sought to bring some order to the fractured forces.

Sarsfield called to the house where Tessé lay on a bed of rushes, rough bandages around his head and chest. 'I'm all right,' he said, struggling to sit up. 'What's the state of affairs?'

'Major Generals Dorrington and Hamilton have not appeared, taken prisoner, we fear, possibly wounded or even killed. My lord Dillon is definitely dead. Also missing are scores of officers: Burkes, O'Neills, Butlers, Maginnises, Brownes, Dillons, Tuites, Fitzgeralds.'

The names meant nothing to Tessé but he could tell from Sarsfield's stricken face what they meant to him.

'Catholic Ireland's leaders have been decimated,' Sarsfield explained. The list was getting longer by the hour as more news came in and missing men failed to turn up.

Tessé lowered himself back onto the bed and closed his eyes.

'Did you see what happened the general?' Sarsfield asked, still trying to figure out what exactly had turned success into a rout.

'No. Only the result of his unfortunate death.'

'Where is his body?'

'In the friary graveyard here. The monks gave him a proper burial, I'm told.'

They could have waited, Sarsfield thought. Everything he had heard suggested that the hasty action of Saint-Ruhe's guard in taking his body away from the battlefield had contributed to the collapse, perhaps had even caused it.

'What do you propose we do?' Tessé tried without success to phrase the question as if he was merely seeking Sarsfield's opinion.

'Fall back on Limerick,' Sarsfield replied without hesitation.

'And Galway?'

'Galway can withstand a siege under d'Usson,' Sarsfield said, keeping his doubts about whether it had the will to do so to himself. He didn't know how much Tessé knew about his own past relations with the city's leaders, that he had jailed some of them the previous year for defeatism and trying to do a deal with the prince of Orange. His opinion of their likely intentions hadn't changed but now was not the time to go into lengthy explanations. 'Limerick is a better base of operations. It will allow the cavalry greater freedom of movement.'

'But Galway is a safer port?' Tessé sought reassurance against an opinion he had obviously heard someone express.

Sarsfield shrugged. 'More difficult to blockade, if that's what you mean. A wider bay. But Limerick is a better choice all round.'

Tessé nodded and sank back onto the bed, squeezing his eyes against a spasm of pain in his chest.

'We can't delay here,' Sarsfield said. 'We need to leave before they come.'

'They're on the march?' Tessé asked in surprise.

239

'Not yet, as far as we know. But if I was the Dutchman, I wouldn't waste any time. I'd want to press home my advantage.'

'Get everyone ready to move to Limerick,' Tessé ordered.

Sarsfield emerged from the gloom of the house, squinting into the brightness although the day was still overcast. Men wandered about, many dazed from the trauma of the battle, some staggering from hunger and exhaustion. More hungry mouths were coming over the hill above the town, stragglers from the battlefield and refugees from among the camp followers. But there was little food to be found. Loughrea had been the staging post for the army but all its supplies, except those in transit from Limerick, had been moved to the camp at Aughrim and were now in enemy hands. There was neither much food nor materiel left; no heavy guns, no weapons to replace those lost or thrown away in the rout, no ammunition except for what little they still carried individually after the battle.

Sarsfield made his way back to the house he had occupied, abandoned by its owners as word of the defeat and the oncoming victors had spread. One of his aides pointed to a chunk of bread and a pitcher of milk and water on the table. 'That's all I could find, my lord,' he said apologetically.

Sarsfield ate the dry bread and drank some of the diluted milk -- the normal ration of the infantry -- standing up. Then he made his way back to the lakeshore and saw Luttrell in the distance in what seemed to be an agitated argument with Colonel Charles O'Kelly, who was jabbing at him with a furious finger. O'Kelly walked away as Sarsfield approached and muttered something as he passed by.

'Colonel,' Sarsfield said to stop him but the old man continued on his way, shaking a fist in the air above his shoulder.

'What's wrong with him?' he asked Luttrell.

Luttrell sighed. 'He's very angry. Accusing us of abandoning the infantry.'

Sarsfield raised his eyebrows in a dismissive gesture. Tensions and bad feelings between the cavalry and infantry were nothing new.

'His son Denis was hurt. Had his horse shot from under him.'

Sarsfield nodded, as if that was a more likely explanation for O'Kelly's anger. 'Seeing him just reminded me,' he said, 'of Balldearg O'Donnell. We need him and his men more than ever now.'

'Too true.'

'Ask him to contact O'Donnell again. Get O'Donnell to support Galway.'

'I don't think he wants to talk to me. You'd better ask him yourself.'

'He doesn't seem to want to talk to me either.'

'Come over here.' Luttrell took him by the arm and led him towards a small group of ragged men sitting in a half-circle on the ground. 'There's someone who just told me some bad news.'

Sarsfield pulled back, forcing him to stop. 'What?'

'Honor's brother.'

'Killed?'

Luttrell nodded. 'Worse than that. Ulick was murdered.' He tugged at Sarsfield's arm again. 'This man saw it.'

One of the men stood up and stepped forward as they approached. He was gaunt-faced and had a bloodied piece of cloth wrapped around his upper right arm which he held tightly against his body with his other hand. *'Abair leis,'* Luttrell said to him.

'I saw my lord Galway being killed,' the man said in Irish. 'He was captured by some of the Vikings. They were bringing him up the hill where they were holding the prisoners when another foreigner came over and ran his bayonet through him. He fell on the ground and started coughing up blood and twisting about until he died.'

'You're sure it was him?' Sarsfield asked.

The man nodded several times. 'I grew up in Portumna like

241

himself and your ladyship.' He looked as if he was about the same age, early twenties, as Lord Galway, Honor's only full brother.

'Why did they kill him?'

'I don't know, my lord.'

'Did the man who did it say anything?'

'If he did, I didn't hear it. I was lying half in a shot hole, pretending to be dead and hoping they wouldn't come to strip me before I could crawl away in the dark.'

'What about Lord Bophin?' Luttrell asked. Bophin was Honor's half-brother from her father's first marriage. 'He hasn't turned up yet,' he explained to Sarsfield.

'I don't know, my lord,' the man said to Sarsfield. 'I didn't see him.'

Sarsfield walked away, then turned back and said: 'We're going to Limerick now. Do you think you can make it that far?'

The man looked at his companions and then shook his head as if he had received some imperceptible message. 'If we had something to eat.'

'I'll see what I can find,' Sarsfield said. 'Then perhaps you should head for Galway. It's only half the distance of Limerick, about twenty miles. They need good men like you there.'

Is there no end to it, he wondered as he left them. No end to the list of the lost?

Mackay

The piles of recovered weapons were growing higher and higher, the biggest the one of matchlock muskets, the smallest that of the newer flintlocks. Alongside were pikes, many with broken shafts, swords, bayonets, knives, and some sickles. A disgruntled English soldier examined the coin given to him in return for a matchlock and looked up in disgust at the artillery sergeant handing out the reward for each one recovered.

'What's this?' he demanded, the silver coin with a 2 at its centre on the flat of his hand.

'Tuppence.' The sergeant glared back him, stating the obvious in an aggressive tone that dismissed any further complaint.

'They said it was sixpence for every papist musket.'

'It's tuppence now. It's only because the general's in a generous mood that it's anything at all. He doesn't need any more of these,' the sergeant said, indicating the hundreds of muskets already collected.

Ginckel was indeed in a benevolent mood. He had declared a day of thanksgiving, ordered up extra food from Athlone and turned a blind eye to the wholesale drunkenness of his forces.

243

Beer, wine and even spirits were plentiful from the looted enemy sutlers: their own sutlers, arriving at haste from Ballinasloe, were doing a lively business, exchanging drink and meat for saddles, harnesses, uniforms, rings and even accepting, at a large discount, the brass money found on the dead. Lines of wagons continued to arrive along the causeway by the old castle, bringing tents and replenishing ammunition. Many trundled back the same way carrying the wounded to a field hospital in Ballinasloe and on to Athlone, and eventually, for those who survived the journey, to the Royal Hospital in Dublin.

On the hilltop, the land was cleared of bodies to make way for the spreading encampment. The army's workmen dug trenches to bury their own dead and those of the enemy who were in the way of the tents. The locals had all disappeared and the bodies of the Irish, stripped naked, were left like large white stones cast up by storm tides along the hillside.

Unlike most of the dead, buried with peremptory ceremony, Major General van Holtzsappel was interred with full military honours. A bugler sounded the Dutch taptoe and a volley of shots was fired over his grave in the presence of the army's senior commanders. Afterwards they gathered in the headquarters tent to discuss the next phase. First, Ginckel instructed 1,200 cavalry and dragoons to go to the River Shannon crossings south of Athlone and demand the surrender of the enemy garrisons at Meelick, Banagher and Portumna. Then the usual arguments began.

Talmash and Württemberg favoured a quick strike at Limerick. 'Cut the head off before they have time to organise their defences,' Talmash urged, opening his hands in a gesture that said the move was so obvious, it did not require debate.

Mackay shook his head, backing what he knew would be the general's view. 'Better seize Galway first. Cut their territory in half.'

'And seize their best port,' Ginckel added. His main fear was still that French reinforcements would land there and he was conscious that his numbers were being depleted by having to garrison more captured territory.

'But the campaign will be over if we take Limerick,' Württemberg interjected. 'We shouldn't waste any more time bringing it to a conclusion.'

Ginckel gave him a suspicious look, wondering if the German was reporting to the Danish king that his troops were being kept in Ireland unnecessarily. 'We may not have to waste much time seizing Galway,' he said. 'If what we hear is true, they will surrender without a siege.'

'But they shouldn't be offered unduly generous terms,' Mackay said, suddenly concerned about what the general might have in mind.

'The terms are as already offered.'

'I assumed, my lord, that those terms have lapsed,' Mackay retorted. 'That they were on offer for surrender after Athlone, before they rejected them by fighting a pitched battle here. And all the blood and effort that has cost us.'

'True,' Talmash added. 'There's no need to be as obliging now.'

'That's a matter for the lords justices,' Ginckel said, closing down the debate. 'Our job is to bring the campaign to a close as quickly and efficiently as possible and not to let it drag on into the winter and another season.'

'All the more reason to strike at Limerick,' Württemberg said, repeating his main point. 'Seize that and the campaign will be over.'

'It would be a mistake to change direction now,' Ginckel said. 'We are closer to Galway and there's every possibility it will capitulate. Captain Aylmer has been ordered to take his ships from Kinsale to Galway Bay to blockade the city and make sure the French can't land there.'

'The French aren't going to waste more men on a hopeless

cause,' Württemberg said, looking to Ruvigny for support as if the Huguenot could divine the thinking of King Louis XIV.

Ruvigny gave him a Gallic shrug that said maybe, maybe not.

A troop of seven riders approached from the west later, their trumpeter sounding the chamade, the signal that they wanted to talk. Their leader, a Jacobite cavalry officer named FitzGerald, was brought to the general's tent, seeking to change sides.

'King James's army is in disarray,' he told Ginckel and some of his assembled generals. 'What's left of them are going to Limerick but many won't make it that far.'

'What about Galway?'

'Galway has to fend for itself. There's a French general there, d'Usson. They're expecting help from Balldearg O'Donnell.'

'Where is he?'

'Nobody knows for certain. In Mayo, they think, on his way to Galway.'

'How many men?'

'They say he has seven thousand.'

'Have you seen them?'

FitzGerald shook his head.

'And Galway? How many men there?'

'They say it's well defended and well supplied. And with the help of Balldearg that it can hold out as long as in the last war.'

Württemberg gave a dismissive laugh but the prospect of a prolonged siege was Ginckel's other main worry. Cromwell's forces hadn't been able to take Galway for nine months forty years earlier, unable to surround it and cut it off from the wilderness to the west. It only agreed to surrender on terms after being afflicted by hunger and the bubonic plague. If it held out for nine weeks now, that would be long enough to push the campaign in Ireland into 1692, the last thing their Majesties wanted.

'He's spreading false information,' Württemberg suggested

after Ginckel had agreed to the surrender of FitzGerald and his men and dismissed him.

'Perhaps,' Ginckel agreed, sending them back to Athlone, away from the front as a precaution. But the worry lines that preceded every stage of this campaign were back on his face.

The next day, the Jacobite garrisons from Banagher and Portumna began to arrive after surrendering, on condition that they be allowed to rejoin their army at Limerick. But, first, they were brought to the camp at Aughrim to see the devastation wreaked on their comrades. Then they were offered the opportunity to lay down their arms and go home.

'Five shillings to every man who lays down his arms,' one of Ginckel's aides called out as sixty men who had been defending the Shannon crossing at Banagher were formed up before him. Most of them took up the offer.

'That'll encourage others,' Talmash said to Mackay as they watched. 'And not a shot fired.'

'Why can't they see the error of their ways?' Mackay said, shaking his head in wonder as about twenty of the garrisons marched off to Limerick.

'You mean the futility of their situation.'

'I mean both,' Mackay said. 'Why can't they accept God's will?'

Talmash gave a light laugh. 'We can't all see it as clearly as you.'

'How can you doubt it after what happened here?'

'The fortunes of war,' Talmash shrugged. 'A game of chance. Chance and luck.'

Mackay was about to respond with something sanctimonious about life not being a game of dice but he changed his mind. There was no point: Talmash was a heathen at heart.

On the fourth day after the battle they left the ravaged hill, leaving behind the decomposing bodies of men and horses, the detritus of

247

the defeated army and the celebratory camp. Swarms of flies and insects buzzed and feasted on the corpses as the smell of death thickened in the sultry air.

They followed the route taken by the fleeing Jacobites, their way marked by more bodies, some of women and children, as they moved south-westwards towards Loughrea. The town itself had been stripped and burned by the retreating army, leaving nothing of use to them. They rested there for the night, men washing off the sweat and grime of the previous days in the warm waters of Lough Rea.

The next day they moved on ten miles to Athenry and camped by an old castle. Most of the inhabitants of the town, including a community of monks had fled with their belongings. Those who remained pleaded for protection. Then, a small but steady number of emissaries began to arrive, sounding out what was on offer to those who swore allegiance to King William and Queen Mary. The generals watched as they came and went but Ginckel kept his counsel, not sharing their identities or whatever intelligence they provided. Whatever he was hearing lightened his mood and his habitual worry began to dissolve.

'I hope he knows something that we don't,' Ruvigny muttered to Mackay as they watched some of the comings and goings.

Mackay nodded. Ruvigny wasn't the only one to be growing concerned. There was plenty of fodder for the horses around the town, untouched so far by the war, but other supplies were being used up and not entirely replaced by the long journey from Athlone. And the siege guns, which were needed to reduce Galway's defences, were still resting there. It would take up to a week to bring them forward and put them into place.

'Why don't you ask him?' Ruvigny added.

'Me?'

'Yes,' Ruvigny said with a slight smile. 'You're always arguing with him.'

'I always give my opinion when it is requested.'

'And even when it's not.'

Mackay gave a harrumph and walked away, curbing his irritation at the Frenchman's insolence. Typical of that race, he thought, even those among them who followed the reformed church.

But the more Mackay thought about it, the more he realized that Ruvigny had a point. Everyone wanted to end this campaign as soon as possible and the general was putting that at risk. Furthermore, Mackay suspected that all the comings and goings were about the terms of a surrender. And he wasn't the only one worried about what was afoot: some of the Ulstermen were already muttering that the general was too anxious to persuade the papists to surrender. And that he would agree to let them keep their lands, their priests, and their superstitions. Better that the war should continue, Mackay agreed, than that the papists be allowed to continue their wickedness and simply await another opportunity to overturn the established monarchs and church.

It was time to have another talk with the general, he decided.

He timed his arrival at the general's tent just as a man in civilian clothes was riding away on horseback. 'A messenger from the city?' he asked.

Whatever Ginckel had heard had put him in a good humour. 'An emissary from an emissary,' he said with a short laugh. 'A messenger from a Mr Daly, who want us to send a detachment of troops to his country house to escort him here so that he is not seen to come to us of his own volition.'

'The Dalys whom Sarsfield arrested last year?' Mackay had heard the gossip about Galway's leaders and was still trying to piece together who was who and which faction was which among them.

'One of them. That was Judge Denis Daly, who has been in talks with us on and off for some time now.'

'He wants to negotiate Galway's surrender?'

Ginckel looked over Mackay's shoulder to make sure no one

249

else was in earshot. 'They say that he also represents my lord Tyrconnell.'

'So he may be ready to negotiate Limerick's surrender as well?' Mackay asked in surprise. No wonder Ginckel was in good humour and sanguine about the immediate future. But that also rang a warning note: the general was even more likely to offer easy terms if he thought he could bring the Irish campaign to an end at the stroke of a pen.

'I hope so.'

Mackay plunged in. 'There are a lot of worries in the camp,'

'Worries?' Ginckel raised a surprised eyebrow.

'Yes, my lord. That's what I wanted to talk to you about.' Mackay took a deep breath. 'For a start, some officers are concerned that we have left ourselves in a vulnerable position here.'

'I'm aware of that,' Ginckel said but there was no trace of anxiety in his voice. 'We'll send a trumpet to Galway in the morning and demand its surrender.'

'And you think they will?'

'We shall see.'

'People are concerned about the terms.'

'I've told you before.' Ginckel said irritably. 'The terms are those already offered by the lords justices.'

'So you've said,' Mackay began but Ginckel raised a hand to stop him.

'I know who's concerned about them,' he said. 'Tell them that those terms have been approved by their Majesties and if they're good enough for the King and Queen, they're good enough for them.'

Mackay left the tent trying to curb uncomfortable thoughts. Were the King and Queen really concerned about the reformed church? Or were their interests solely temporal, consolidating their control of England and Wales? And of Scotland and Ireland too, of course? That would be disappointing if it was true but he did not believe it was true. It could not be true. If the King was willing to show undue mercy to his rebellious Irish subjects, it was probably only for strategic reasons, to ensure that this campaign did not jeopardise the war over the fate of Continental Europe.

He was too deep in his thoughts to notice Talmash hurrying towards him on his way to the general's tent.

'Have you heard?' Talmash paused, his face flushed. 'The Spaniard and his bog-trotters have turned up.'

'Here?' Mackay felt a touch of panic. They were not in a good defensive position in Athenry, indeed had given scarcely any thought to the possibility of an attack.

'A place called Tuam,' Talmash said. 'Fifteen miles north of here. O'Donnell heard that the town was planning to surrender and he sacked it.'

So the semi-mythical Balldearg O'Donnell was real after all, Mackay thought. He had emerged from the miasma of rumour and myth. That would put an end to talk of terms of surrender.

D'Usson

L ieutenant General d'Usson stood on the middle rampart
where it jutted towards the east above Galway's main gate
and watched the enemy's trumpeter ride away between
the ruins of levelled cottages and past the new defensive works
on the hill overlooking the walls. Around him the gunners' shouts
of abuse died away as the rider disappeared over the brow of the
rise, taking back the uncompromising response to the demand
that the town surrender.

It was another beautiful Sunday morning, a fresh breeze from
the bay cooling the bright sunshine. The town's numerous
churches were full, the prayers for God's assistance given an
added urgency by the appearance that morning of the heretic
forces outside the town. Their arrival was not a surprise, though
it was unexpected in the sense that d'Usson had no cavalry or
dragoons to reconnoitre the surrounding countryside and warn of
enemy movements. He would have liked to have had more time
to prepare for the siege, especially to have strengthened the new
defensive works designed to deny the enemy the high ground
overlooking the town. But he was optimistic that he could make
up for the loss of Athlone here, if not fill the void left by the defeat

at Aughrim. The town was surrounded on three sides by water, the bay and its inlets to the south, the River Corrib and the large lake that fed it to the north and west. The enemy's only possible approach was along the ridge of high ground to the east, over which the trumpeter had disappeared.

The town's own walls were secure, its inhabitants well supplied with food, and its ships free to sail unhindered across the bay into friendly territory or make for Limerick and France. On the other hand it lacked sufficient arms for the couple of thousand soldiers now crowded within the walls, including several hundred exhausted and weaponless men who had made their way there after the disaster at Aughrim. The garrison also included the men who had panicked at Athlone and let the enemy grenadiers cross the river: d'Usson did not have much faith in them after that. But Balldearg O'Donnell and his considerable force was said to be approaching, expected to arrive very soon.

'So the die is cast,' a voice beside him said.

D'Usson hadn't heard anyone approach and he glanced up in surprise to see the earl of Clanricarde, Richard Burke, the commander of the Irish forces in the town, towering over him. He immediately regretted the sudden twist of his head. The headache that had afflicted him since he was knocked down in the rout at Athlone had faded into a dull pain, ignorable when he forgot about it, but any sudden movement brought it back.

'Yes,' he said, hoping that the die was indeed cast. The demand for surrender and its rejection were usually only the opening moves. But it was the point of no return on this occasion: he wanted to hold this town, to keep open this lifeline to France, and to prove his abilities to his King.

Clanricarde nodded slowly, as if he did not altogether welcome that news. He had remained silent earlier when the town's governor, the new Lord Dillon, had summoned its council and leading citizens to discuss General Ginckel's demand that they should surrender on the terms already on offer. D'Usson had

253

argued strongly against it and been pleasantly surprised at the unanimity of support he received. Maybe the rumours that some of them, even most of them, wanted to capitulate were not true after all. Likewise the rumours that numerous people were slipping out of the town to treat with the enemy.

Clanricarde, Sarsfield's wife's eldest half-brother, had remained silent during the discussion but that had been put down to him mourning his family's losses at Aughrim. His brother, Lord Bophin, was now a prisoner and his half-brother, Lord Galway, had been murdered after surrendering.

'The messengers from Limerick are arriving,' Clanricarde said, revealing the purpose of his presence.

They moved off to the right, towards Shoemaker's Tower where the ramparts turned westwards overlooking Lough Atalia, one of the bay's last inlets. The tide was out, far below the high-water mark along the blackened rocks. Puffy white clouds scudded across the bay from the Clare hills opposite, pushed by a breeze bearing an invigorating scent of salt and seaweed. One of d'Usson's aides came racing up the stone steps from Pludd Street and looked at Clanricarde before saying anything.

'Qu'est-ce que c'est?' d'Usson demanded with a hint of impatience.

'A message that someone tried to give to the enemy trumpeter,' the aide said in rapid French, casting a cautious eye again at Clanricarde as he handed d'Usson a folded sheet of paper.

D'Usson scanned the note, glossing over the nuances of some of the English phrases that were not altogether clear to him. But there was no mistaking the burden of the message. General Ginckel had no need to bring up his siege guns from Athlone. Galway had had enough of this war, which had devastated the country and destroyed its foreign trade and would agree to honourable terms.

'Who is Sir John Kirwan?' he demanded of Clanricarde,

reading the name from the end of the letter.

'One of our leading citizens,' Clanricarde said. 'Mayor a few years ago.'

D'Usson handed him the note and watched as he read it. Clanricarde handed it back to him, without expression.

'Arrest this Kirwan,' d'Usson ordered the aide, looking at Clanricarde.

Clanricarde said nothing.

'What does it mean?' d'Usson demanded as the aide went back down the steps and hurried away towards Skinner's Street.

'People are tired of the war,' Clanricarde said with a shrug.

'Nobody said that at the meeting this morning.' The room had been crowded, people trying to look in the doorway from the hall. The mood had appeared united as they accepted d'Usson's recommendation that they should resist to the last man. As the reply to Ginckel had said. 'Was this Kirwan there?'

'I didn't notice him.'

They walked on towards the harbour, passing the gardens of the Dominican priory below them. From the cloisters came the sound of Latin chants. A little farther on, the smell of rotting fish rose from the fish market in Earl Street, now closed for the sabbath.

'Do many people think like this Kirwan?' d'Usson asked.

'Some.'

'But nobody said that this morning.'

'Nobody did,' Clanricarde agreed.

D'Usson gave up with a sigh: Clanricarde clearly had no intention of confiding in him. The Frenchman really did not know what was going on, aware with certainty only of his own ignorance about the politics of the Irish factions; aware that what they called the 'new interest men' – the merchants and lawyers who had bought up a lot of land in the preceding decades – were keen to restore peace and get back the business which the war had destroyed. Aware, too, that he was suspect in some eyes because of his own past as a Protestant in France.

Was that why Clanricarde was being uncommunicative? Was he aware of the lies muttered behind his back in Athlone that he, d'Usson, had let in the heretics? Or was he among those who wanted peace and a return to this town's normality?

'Have you heard anything of your brother?' he asked, making small talk.

'They say he's being sent to England.'

That was not a good sign, d'Usson thought but he said nothing. From what he understood, only those accused of treason were sent to London and its infamous Tower.

'People remember the last siege,' Clanricarde added, as if he had at last found an appropriate response to d'Usson's earlier comments.

'But that was forty years ago.'

'Yes,' Clanricarde agreed, 'but it is well remembered.'

'The town held out bravely for almost a year.'

'At an enormous cost,' Clanricarde said with an air of finality. 'It took decades to recover.'

So that was it, d'Usson thought as they went down the steps to the new strand gate and through it to the quay where a small two-masted boat was coasting in, its dark brown sails flapping loosely in the breeze as its momentum took it to the stone landing. They had an unhappy memory of the last time. Still, their resolve to resist had not been tempered by any expressions of doubt this morning.

Two uniformed men, one French, the other Irish, jumped ashore as soon as the boat was close enough.

The French officer shook his head as he approached them. 'Limerick says they cannot send any assistance,' he said, addressing d'Usson in French.

'Colonel Luttrell was beaten back at Kilcolgan as he tried to come here,' the other man told Clanricarde in Irish. 'They say they don't have enough men to force their way through.'

Clanricarde translated for d'Usson. That was no surprise, the Frenchman thought. He hadn't really expected to get the 1,500 extra men he had requested from Limerick. Sarsfield appeared to have little time for him and even less for the most influential of Galway's citizens, if all he had been told was true. The new Lord Dillon was the Duchess of Tyrconnell's son-in-law; d'Usson had thought that might have counted for something but the viceroy seemed to have no real power as far as he could see.

'*Bon.*' He rubbed his hands together, as if the news had been a relief. 'We are on our own.'

The Williamites fanned out on the rise outside the town throughout the afternoon and evening, moving northwards towards the channels of the river. Cannon shots from the walls kept them at a distance and some musket fire was exchanged around the defensive works. A probe towards the river to make a crossing to the west was repulsed with ease by the small garrison at Menlo Castle. A small flotilla of tin rowing boats appeared from one of the bay's inlets but made little progress against the incoming tide. Defenders mocked them with musket shots that dropped as imperceptibly as pebbles into the implacable waves.

D'Usson patrolled the ramparts, watching the enemy's moves, issuing orders. He sent more men across the River Corrib to defend its western bank against any attempt to cross it and encircle the town. The officer in charge of the outworks was told to be ready to resist the inevitable attack there: the enemy needed to seize them as a first priority. Then, as the last light lingered late in the western sky, the Frenchman retired for the night.

It was still dark when he was woken by a crash of cannons. He stumbled out of bed as his door opened and an aide said, 'They have seized the outworks. And they've crossed the river.'

D'Usson struggled for a moment to accept the message. How could the two most important positions in defending the town have fallen so quickly? And at roughly the same time?

'They attacked just after three o'clock,' the aide said. 'And there was a brief exchange before they overran the outworks.'

'How could they do that?' d'Usson demanded as he dressed hurriedly. There had been enough men to hold up the enemy for days, at least until they brought up their heavy guns.

'My lord Clanricarde ordered his men to withdraw. Most of them were back inside the walls before the attack.'

D'Usson stopped pulling on a boot. This was treachery, sabotage. Clanricarde had deliberately left the outworks undermanned, had withdrawn defenders in contravention of his direct orders. 'And the river?' he asked, trying to control his temper as he pulled on his other boot.

'They overwhelmed the men at the castle they call Menlo and then came over the river in the little boats they had on the bay earlier. There was a brief skirmish but they are across in numbers.'

'Did the Irish run too?'

'No, my lord. They stood and fought but they were outnumbered. There were only fifty men there.'

'Fifty?' d'Usson shook his head in despair. More treachery: he had ordered that the likely river crossing should be defended by a regiment, four hundred at least.

He finished dressing and ran up the steps to the ramparts, trying to come to terms with what he had been told and what it meant. It was clear to him that he was not in control of the army here. His rank counted for nothing, he was ignored by his supposed subordinates, and dismissed by the country's leaders in Limerick. The town's intention was to capitulate in spite of all the assistance that King Louis and France had given Ireland.

It was beginning to get light and everything had gone silent. From the ramparts above the Great Gate nothing much could be seen or heard to the east, no sign of men moving or shots being fired. The gunners were on the alert but had ceased firing. He asked some of them what had happened but they spoke only Irish, or pretended not to have another language. D'Usson moved on, around the walls to the north and west.

There were signs of activity to the west, shadows moving along the far bank of the fast-flowing Corrib as it emptied its huge lake into the sea. There was no point shooting at them; they were beyond musket range. And there were no cannons on these walls; all were pointing to the east or south towards the bay.

The drawbridge at the middle gate on the bridge over the river was up, so there was no danger of an immediate assault on the town. That was not the enemy's intention anyway. By taking the western bank of the river, they had cut off the town from relief by sea from Limerick or France and had prevented Balldearg O'Donnell and his men from coming to their aid from the west. We truly are on our own now, D'Usson thought.

He made his way down to the quay, now empty of vessels. A couple of his men were standing there, watching the last of the ships making its way out towards Mutton Island, fleeing before daylight. The rest of the ships were distant shadows, already disappearing towards the mouth of the bay.

One of the men took a deep breath. 'The prisoner Kirwan has gone,' he said with the gravity of one bearing bad news. 'On his ship.'

'He escaped?'

The man looked at the ground.

'They let him go,' d'Usson nodded to himself.

It was all abundantly clear.

It had turned into another glorious morning, the sun warm and the wind fresh, which seemed to mock the mood in the town. The faces in the street were grey and strained. The markets were deserted, neither sellers nor buyers bothering to appear, except for two optimistic stalls in the general market on Cross Street offering farming implements. In the distance a crowd was on its

259

knees at the Augustinian's open-air altar at the junction of Pludd Street and New Tower Street.

D'Usson and his French officers came up from the quay towards the town's main street, Great Gate Street. Ahead of them the clock on the tower said it was just after half past ten. Townspeople stood in huddles on corners and outside the doors of the houses of the leading families, waiting for news. Mumbled conversations stopped and eyes were averted as the Frenchmen passed by, as if they were an occupying force.

'They hate us,' the engineer Lacombe said as they passed a group of men outside the high stone home of the Lynches. Lacombe had been in Galway since the start of the year, trying to build up the defences with workers who were often too weak from hunger to do much of the necessary heavy labour.

'Why?' Methelet, one of the commissary officers, asked with a sigh. 'We're here to help them.'

Lacombe gave him a pitying glance. 'They think we're here to continue the war.'

'Don't they care about the outcome? If the heretics win?'

'Heretics,' Lacombe snorted. 'They're all heretics here. Some kind of druids.'

Methelet pointed at the altar in the middle of the street. 'What's that?'

'Ah, don't talk to me about religion,' Lacombe retorted, adding, with a total disregard for logic, 'After all the effort we put into building up those defensive works, they handed them over with hardly a shot.'

'Maybe you didn't do much of a job,' Methelet said.

'I'd have had an easier job if your people had done your job properly and kept us all fed.'

D'Usson half-listened to their banter behind his back. He'd heard it all before: the mutual abuse of the different divisions of the army; the ingratitude of the Irish; the pointlessness of this war. All that was missing, in deference to his proximity, was the usual complaints about the stupidity of the generals.

A drumbeat sounded ahead of them at the entrance gate to the town. They stopped in unison, looking from one to the other, recognizing the signal immediately. D'Usson swore under his breath. So that's why everybody has disappeared this morning, why no one will talk to me, he thought. He had gone in search of Clanricarde but he was not to be found. The governor, Lord Dillon, also couldn't be found, nor the mayor, Arthur French.

But the drum, beating a parlay, confirmed his suspicion. They were surrendering without his agreement or even his prior knowledge.

Around them, people seemed to come alive, their mood lightening as they hurried towards the walls and crowded around the steps to the ramparts. The Frenchmen pushed their way through, clearing a passage for their general with elbows and shouts, and d'Usson emerged onto the ramparts.

Lord Dillon was there, watching his emissaries approach the enemy lines behind their drummer.

D'Usson marched over to him and said, 'What's the meaning of this?'.

Dillon turned his attention to the irate little Frenchman. 'We've decided to consider terms,' he said in a tone that suggested he had the upper hand in negotiations.

D'Usson gave a snort of derision. Then a sudden thought struck him: was this the result of a secret message from Limerick the day before? 'Does the viceroy know about this?'

Dillon looked surprised. He shook his head and lowered his voice, changing his tone. 'It's for the best,' he said. 'We all discussed it and everyone agreed: the council, the leading merchants, the archbishop and clergy, the military men.'

'Except me,' d'Usson shot back.

Dillon looked away. His emissaries had now disappeared over the hill to the enemy's camp.

'When was this decided?' d'Usson asked. 'Last night?'

261

'This morning. These walls' -- Dillon spread his arms out to indicate them -- 'won't last for twenty-four hours. We don't have enough men. There isn't enough lead in the magazines. We don't have enough artillery officers. The best men were all lost at Aughrim. We cannot win.'

D'Usson shook his head repeatedly, disputing each reason as it was enumerated. 'I can hold out here for weeks with five hundred men,' he said. 'We can keep –'

Dillon waved his hand, silencing him. 'People are fleeing the town,' he said. 'They remember the last siege. What their parents and grandparents went through. How long it took to recover. Everybody wants peace.'

The emissaries came back over the hill and down Bohermore towards the gate, moving quickly, a spring in their step. As they neared the gate, the drummer beat a marching tune and one of the group waved a hand. The crowd on the ramparts took it as a sign that the Williamites had agreed to talks and a great cheer went up.

I'm not going to be held responsible for this disaster, d'Usson thought.

Mackay

A chaplain stood by as the gravediggers lowered the bodies of half a dozen men and a woman into the hole they had dug beside Menlo Castle. Mackay gave them barely a glance as he stepped with care from the shallow boat that had brought him back across the Corrib after overseeing the deployment on the west bank. It had been a good night's work, with less resistance and fewer casualties than he had anticipated. Rumours that Balldearg O'Donnell was already closing in on Galway from the north and west had proved to be untrue. The mysterious Spaniard seemed to have disappeared again.

Everything was going according to Ginckel's plan: his faith in a quick surrender had been vindicated. He didn't have much strategic or leadership ability but Mackay had to admit that Providence certainly favoured the Dutchman.

A horse was waiting for Mackay and he rode towards the town's walls, anxious to examine them as closely as possibly in case the surrender talks came to nought. He followed the river down as far as he could but it stopped him well short of the defences as it opened into a wide pool and channels that protected the northern walls, making them almost impossible to attack.

As expected, he thought, we'll attack from the east, if we have to.

In the east the army had moved forward, among the ruins of the suburbs that the papists had burned as a precaution. They offered little cover but none was needed. Everyone was behaving as if the surrender had already been agreed. Some of the English and Scottish soldiers were having shouted conversations with men from the same kingdoms on the walls, asking about acquaintances and families. Civilians outnumbered soldiers on the ramparts, watching and listening to the exchanges as if attending a stage performance. The atmosphere was one of cautious relief on both sides but it was clear that neither expected a resumption of hostilities. As far as they were concerned, the siege was over. Mackay hoped they were right.

A troop of horsemen came over the rise to the east and down the road that he now knew the Irish called Bohermore. He recognized Talmash at their head. They halted less than a hundred yards short of the gate and Mackay trotted over towards them, assuming that this was the usual exchange of hostages to ensure each side's good faith during the negotiations.

The town's main gate opened and four horsemen approached them at a walk. Mackay recognized their leader, Robert Shaw, the town clerk who had already been to their camp on a secret mission on behalf of the mayor. He watched, too far away to hear the details, while Shaw introduced the three others to Talmash, who in turn pointed out three of his companions to Shaw. The exchange was concluded and three of the Williamites rode into the town with Shaw while the three Jacobite officers went with their escort to Ginckel's camp.

Talmash remained behind, also taking the opportunity to survey the walls up close.

'I hear you did it anyway last night,' Mackay said as he reached him. He had refused to let Talmash accompany the party he had led across the river. But Talmash had joined those attacking the outworks instead.

Talmash grinned. 'Ah, it wasn't much of a fight. A disappointment really.'

Mackay shook his head like a disapproving parent. 'You shouldn't tempt fate so irresponsibly.'

'What's the point of soldiering without seeing some action?'

To implement God's will, Mackay almost said but he saw the glint in Talmash's eyes and realized in time that the Englishman was trying to be provocative. 'Captain Burke's information was good?' he asked, changing the subject. Burke was a deserter from the town who had appeared in their camp the previous day, recommending an attack on the outworks as soon as possible. He had then guided the assault party to the defences' most vulnerable point.

'Very accurate,' Talmash nodded. 'He brought us right up to their walls before they realized it and the grenadiers had it very easy.'

'Let's hope the capitulation will be as quick,' Mackay said as they went over the crest of the rise and made for their headquarters.

'Why wouldn't it be?'

It didn't prove to be as quick as Mackay had hoped. Ginckel emerged from his tent in the late afternoon looking exhausted. Messengers had been going back and forth to the town all day, seeking new instructions and carrying proposals and counterproposals. Galway, it appeared, had not been prepared to fight but it was determined to drive a hard bargain. Rumours began to circulate that the papists were looking for much more generous terms than those on offer since the capture of Athlone.

'Have you heard?' one of the Irish Protestant officers demanded, barging into Mackay's tent where the general lay on his bunk reading. 'They want all their priests to be allowed to carry on with impunity. As if the Reformation and the Revolution had never happened.'

Mackay closed his book and sat up. That was what he had feared. The presumption in the camp that the enemy would quickly accept whatever was on offer was giving way to a growing realization that it was not going to be so straightforward.

'The town is full of churches, friaries and monasteries,' the officer continued, his voice rising in outrage. 'Do you know how many papist buildings there are? And how they treated God-fearing people after the Restoration?'

'I'm sure the general won't agree to anything inappropriate,' Mackay suggested with a certainty that he did not feel. Ginckel, in his eyes, was all too eager to make peace at almost any price.

'And they want to keep all their lands too. How can we trust them if they say they'll conform and we let them carry on as before? They'll just bide their time until they can murder us in our beds again.'

'I'll talk to the general.'

'Do that. Make him see what's at stake here.'

Mackay entered Ginckel's tent to find the general sitting at his makeshift desk in a pensive pose, his hands joined in a prayer-like gesture over his nose and mouth.

'Forgive this intrusion,' Mackay said.

Ginckel widened his hands and gestured towards a chair beside the desk. 'I know your concerns,' he said.

'Not just mine. Some of the Irish officers are angry about what's going on.'

'And what do they think is going on?'

'That you're allowing the papists too generous terms.'

'Too generous,' Ginckel repeated, pursing his lips. 'What do they think is too generous?'

'Terms that should not be allowed to an enemy defeated

266

decisively on the field of battle.'

Ginckel nodded as if he was considering that as a formula for negotiations. 'We can end this campaign here,' he said, 'with patience and the right terms.'

'Right for whom?' Mackay replied, his concern increasing at what sounded to him like the talk of lawyers, parliamentarians and courtiers, not the language of generals.

'Right for us. Bring this to an end and get the army back to Flanders where it is needed.'

'And will we leave behind a pacified kingdom?'

'This kingdom has been destroyed. You've seen it yourself. We've all seen it. God knows how long it will take to recover.'

'But we can't leave the recusants entrenched here, storing up trouble for the future.'

'Their cause will wither without the French to encourage it,' Ginckel said with a dismissive wave of his hand. 'And France is only encouraging it for her own reasons. She'll stop when she has nothing to gain from it.'

Talmash pulled back the tent flap and stood in the entrance. 'This is ridiculous,' he interrupted, without preamble. 'Why are we letting them prolong this nonsense? As if we can't seize this town now?'

Ginckel glared at him.

'We can move in now and put an end to it,' Talmash added.

'No,' Ginckel said in a voice that was heavy with restraint.

'Why not?'

'Because we agreed to a ceasefire and talks.'

'Break off the talks. End the ceasefire. Recall the hostages.' Talmash threw the tent flap back into place as if he was slamming a door on his way out.

'It's not just the Irish who are unhappy,' Mackay offered in a placatory tone.

'You think Talmash is also concerned about scriptural differences?'

267

'No,' Mackay raised his palms in a conciliatory gesture, 'but it appears that we are giving an unnecessary advantage to a defeated enemy.'

Ginckel took a deep breath, calming himself. 'Look,' he said, putting his palms flat on his desk as if he was outlining a plan of campaign. 'If we get the terms right here, Limerick might capitulate too without any more bloodshed. My lord Dillon, the governor of this place, is related to my lord Tyrconnell, or at least to my lady Tyrconnell. By all accounts, this town is full of Tyrconnell's supporters. They have no time for Sarsfield's hotheads. Fair terms here will encourage them to hand over Limerick as well. And the campaign will be concluded successfully.'

Mackay could see the logic of that in strategic terms but it begged one question, one very big question. 'What are we fighting for?'

Ginckel appeared taken aback by the question. 'What do you mean? We're fighting for the King and Queen.'

'For the Revolution,' Mackay corrected him. 'The Glorious Revolution that put an end to the great popish plot to enslave England.'

'And the King's alliance, whose victory will secure the future of the reformed church in Europe,' Ginckel added, not to be outdone in fealty to the greater cause.

They lapsed into silence. Then Mackay stood up and gave a small bow of departure.

'There is another element to this,' Ginckel said, ignoring Mackay's intention to leave. 'The Spaniard O'Donnell.'

Mackay waited, his obvious question hanging in the air as Ginckel paused for effect. 'He is seeking terms.'

Mackay sat down again. 'O'Donnell?' he asked, an expression of surprise rather than a query.

'You know the English officer Richards?'

Mackay nodded, trying to place him in a regiment.

'Don't ask me how but his brother has been with O'Donnell and has come to us as an emissary.'

'What does O'Donnell want?'

'Everything,' Ginckel gave a mirthless laugh. 'A pardon; pension for himself; employment in the King's army for all his men.; and his old family title, earl of Tyrconnell.'

Mackay laughed as well. 'Earl of Tyrconnell? Not duke?'

'It seems he will be happy with the earldom. A modest man,' Ginckel added, a hint of merriment in his eyes.

'And what have you replied?'

'That we shall consider all his reasonable requests.'

'Can you imagine what my lord Tyrconnell will make of this?'

'I would like to see his face when he hears of it. Can you imagine what the superstitious Irish will think when their saviour with the red mark joins us?'

Mackay remained, at Ginckel's invitation, when the talks resumed, aware that the general was keeping him there to involve him in whatever might be agreed and to defuse his objections. Most of the terms of the capitulation were already settled. All those in the town who surrendered would be pardoned, guaranteed their lands, and be allowed private practice of their religion. Gentlemen could carry pistols and a sword if they considered them necessary for their personal security. Those who wished could stay in Galway, go home if their home was elsewhere, or march off to join their army at Limerick.

'With flags flying, guns loaded, and all their equipment?' Clanricarde inquired, his pen poised over clause six of the draft agreement.

'Flags, muskets loaded, and match lighted,' Ginckel agreed. 'But only what each man can carry of weapons, ammunition and food.'

Clanricarde made a note on the agreement. 'And we can bring

all our cannon, field guns, powder and balls?'

'How much would that be?'

Clanricarde shrugged. 'I couldn't say.'

Ginckel gave a half-smile to show he understood Clanricarde's reticence, that he was tempted to hold back information that would be of use if the siege resumed. Just in case, unlikely though it was. 'And you have enough wagons and horses to take all those to Limerick?'

Clanricarde returned a similar smile. 'You could assist us with the transport.'

'How many horses and wagons?'

'Let's say horses for twenty guns and twenty wagons.'

Ginckel paused as if he was considering the proposal. 'We'll send some officers in to examine the guns and magazines and agree on a number.'

'I don't think that would be possible.'

'Aren't we talking in good faith here?'

'Yes, certainly,' Clanricarde replied, 'but I don't think it would be acceptable to the French.'

'They don't want an agreement?'

Clanricarde made a vague gesture with his hands, implying that the French were always awkward. As Ginckel himself knew.

Mackay watched the exchange impatiently. Ginckel's invitation for him to attend the discussions was having the opposite effect on him. This was a ritual being played out, he knew, but it was a ritual that was merely wasting time and increasing his disquiet. It surprised him that the general was prepared to give so much time to it – and, more importantly, concede so much -- even if he was aiming for a bigger prize than the capitulation of Galway alone.

The draft agreement already confirmed the fears of the Irish Protestants. All the papist priests in the town were to be guaranteed the safety of their persons and property and exempted from any penal laws against the private practice of their religion.

Nobody in the town, neither clergy nor laity, was required to swear allegiance to King William and Queen Mary. And it seemed that their soldiers were being promised immunity and pardons even if they went on to Limerick and continued fighting against their Majesties' forces. And now Ginckel was actually offering to give them horses to transport their field guns to Limerick.

'If we're not talking in good faith here,' Ginckel said sharply in a change of tone, as if pushed suddenly beyond a limit, 'then we need some further reassurances.'

'That's not necessary,' Clanricarde replied, backing off.

Ginckel gave an impression of calming down. 'Three guns and reasonable supplies for each,' he said.

'Ten.'

'Six.' Ginckel sliced the air with a horizontal hand, indicating that this part of the discussion was at an end. 'None of them more than twelve-pounders.'

Clanricarde studied him for a moment, then nodded.

'And when we've agreed these terms,' Ginckel added, pushing his advantage, 'I can send officers into the town to inspect the stores and magazines to ensure there is no embezzlement before the handover.'

'I will need the approval of the governor and town council.'

'Very well,' Ginckel sighed. 'We will continue the cessation until ten o'clock tomorrow morning.'

The formal atmosphere of the talks dissolved as they rose from their seats on either side of the table. The evening was beginning to draw in, shadows lengthening outside, and the light dimming inside the tent. Ginckel signalled to an aide and said, 'We will have a glass of wine before dinner.'

Mackay was about to seek a private word with the general but he was prevented by Clanricarde's approach. 'We are making good progress,' he said to Ginckel.

'Yes, but we have to conclude it by tomorrow morning,' Ginckel said, casting a pointed glance at Mackay. 'People are getting impatient.'

'On our side too. People are desirous of certainty,' Clanricarde said. 'There is one change that could remove some of the uncertainties.'

Ginckel raised an inquisitive eyebrow as he took a glass of wine from the silver tray offered by an orderly. Clanricarde took a glass too, raised it in a silent toast to Ginckel and sipped the wine. 'All the terms apply to people who are in the town,' he said. 'But there are some who would normally be here but who are not for one reason or another. If they were included, it would help to bring matters to a quick conclusion.'

'Like your brother,' Mackay interjected. 'The prisoner, my lord Bophin.'

Ginckel glared at him, unimpressed by his lack of diplomacy.

But Clanricarde didn't appear to take offence. 'And others too,' he said mildly, still addressing Ginckel. 'Like Sir John Kirwan, who was jailed for communicating with you but escaped and is now on the high seas, perhaps on his way to Spain. It would be unfair if he was to be attainted merely because he cannot be in the town when the articles are signed, though he would certainly agree to them.'

Ginckel drank some wine for a moment's thought. 'What do you suggest?'

'That we amend clauses seven and thirteen to include inhabitants of the town who are entitled to be here but are not. And officers of regiments in the town, even if they are not now present. That way we would cover individuals like Sir John without having to specify details or reasons for absences.'

'How many people does that include?' Mackay demanded, irritated by Clanricarde's tone and even more at Ginckel's calm consideration of his proposals, as if he was dealing with an equal, not a defeated enemy.

'Not many.' Clanricarde still addressed his answers to Ginckel.

'There would have to be a time limit on it,' Ginckel suggested.

272

'Of course.'

'A week,' Mackay said.

'That would not be adequate for someone like Sir John.'

'Or your brother,' Mackay said, making no attempt to hide his disgust at Clanricarde's shameless self-interest on behalf of his own family. It was said Clanricarde had adopted the reformed faith but, if he had, he still had the mentality of a typical papist, Mackay concluded. This was why they had to be treated like what they were: defeated enemies who stood in the way of peace and progress and the victory of the enlightened over darkness and superstition.

'We should talk about this later,' Ginckel said tactfully, moving away to detach the conversation physically from Mackay.

'It doesn't all have to be written down now,' Clanricarde said, moving with him.

Mackay finally got his opportunity to accost the general after dinner as the group broke up. All but him were in a mellow mood, a mixture of alcohol and the absence of tension. If anything, the little wine Mackay had drunk had only increased his unhappiness as the full implications sank in of the terms on offer to the town.

'It's outrageous,' he said to Ginckel.

The general sighed and sank back in his chair.

'You are granting them immunity and allowing them go on to Limerick to continue their resistance against the lawful King and Queen. So they can fight as long as they like and when we finally defeat them they can still have their pardons and their lands and their superstitions no matter what the terms of their final surrender.'

'I thought you were only concerned about the priests.'

'This is worse,' Mackay retorted. 'You are allowing them to continue their intransigence. Even encouraging them.'

'I'm trying to bring the war to an end.'

Mackay shook his head vigorously. 'You're doing the opposite.'

'I'm carrying out their Majesties' instructions. To end this campaign as soon as possible.'

Mackay stared at Ginckel. 'Does the King approve of these terms?'

'The King wants the war here over before the end of the summer. He knows the difficulty of doing that, of capturing Limerick. Which he failed to do himself last year.' Ginckel raised a finger to summon an orderly and pointed at his empty brandy glass. 'The lords justices in Dublin and London want the conflict over too before summer's end.'

'Not at any price.'

'You want to read their letters?'

Mackay suddenly felt deflated, watching the orderly pour a glass of brandy for him as well. What was this war about if it wasn't about the defeat of popery? In every place where it was still entrenched? And if we can't eradicate it in a small kingdom like this, how shall we ever eradicate it in a large kingdom like France?

'We will have the town by Sunday,' Ginckel was saying. 'Two weeks after the battle at Aughrim and in the time it would have taken us just to get the siege guns in place.'

'Why Sunday? Why not tomorrow?'

'They want to send a messenger to Limerick with the terms.'

'And what if they send back reinforcements? Or a French fleet arrives in the bay?'

'They don't have reinforcements to send. Not after Aughrim. With luck, they'll send a message seeking the same terms as Galway.'

Would that be a positive development? Not really, Mackay thought, but he kept the thought to himself. He was still taken aback by Ginckel's revelation that their masters just wanted this war ended on any terms. And the unsettling suggestion that King

William and even the parliament might not be fighting for what he himself was fighting. He found it difficult to believe that was so.

'What if a French fleet turns up in the bay instead?' he repeated, harking back to Ginckel's main fear since they had taken Athlone.

'What could they do? We have the town surrounded and its harbour is under our guns now, thanks to the success of your foray across the river last night.'

Ginckel finished his brandy and left Mackay staring into his glass as if it contained something noxious. He went back to his tent to write a report to the King which would have to be worded with care. He knew he was risking his displeasure and, even more, the displeasure of parliament by offering such generous terms. But how else was he to carry out their demands to bring the war to a swift conclusion? If Galway had resisted, it could have pushed the campaign into the winter and another year.

'You know what I've been told to do?' Talmash asked rhetorically the next morning, a day of darkening clouds. 'Go over the river and allow safe passage to some scoundrel who's been hiding in the mountains to the west, so he can cross the bridge into the town and avail himself of the articles of surrender. Can you believe that?'

'Unfortunately, I can,' Mackay replied. 'There are all sorts of chicanery afoot.'

Talmash gave a harrumph of disgust. They were standing on the rise above the town watching Clanricarde ride towards its main gate. Ginckel had agreed that Clanricarde should consult the mayor and town council and had set a deadline of 10 o'clock for agreement on the surrender terms. Or else the siege would be resumed.

'Fire a shot in the air when you want to start fighting again,'

Talmash called out to Clanricarde as he mounted his horse. 'A single shot will do it. Just one.'

Clanricarde glared back at him as he spurred his horse to move. 'The only shots you'll hear from us will be in response to yours.'

'Why do you think they're trying to drag it out?' Talmash asked now. 'Do they think the Spaniard is still going to come? The French?'

'I don't know,' Mackay muttered. Ginckel had told him to keep the negotiations with Balldearg O'Donnell secret until an agreement was signed and sealed. 'I think they're trying to look after themselves.'

'About time,' Talmash interrupted, referring to field guns and mortars being pulled into position on the brow of the hill to their left. Sappers began to arrange them into firing positions. 'Now we can get on with it.'

But the appearance of the guns was an unnecessary threat. Just ahead of Ginckel's deadline a large party of horsemen emerged from the gates, including Clanricarde and the governor, Lord Dillon. A ceremony was arranged and the surrender was signed by Dillon, Clanricarde and Lord Enniskillen on behalf of the town and Ginckel on behalf of the King. No French officers were present.

'You will despatch a messenger to Limerick,' Ginckel said to Clanricarde after toasts had been exchanged and promises of good faith repeated.

'Immediately, my lord.'

'You think they will respond positively?'

'I'm sure they will see the sense in avoiding further bloodshed.'

The days passed peacefully. Rain blew in from the bay, sometimes a barely perceptible spray on the wind, sometimes a drenching mist that came like curtains rippling across the landscape, smudging everything in shades of grey. Both sides stuck to the immediate terms of the agreement. Ginckel sent his deputy paymaster into the town to examine its stores of food, gunpowder and ammunition. The guns on the town's walls were dismantled.

The day after the signing an enemy trumpeter arrived from Limerick and was escorted to Ginckel's headquarters. Word spread quickly and all the generals in the vicinity hurried to hear the hoped-for news. Ginckel broke the seal on the message and his face betrayed his disappointment before he looked up with a hint of disbelief, even disgust. 'They want to exchange prisoners.'

Württemberg gave a loud laugh which had no humour in it. 'With whom? They have no prisoners.'

'They're really looking for information about who we're holding.' Ginckel crumpled up the paper and turned to the trumpeter. 'This does not deserve a response.'

The trumpeter departed empty-handed. But Ginckel had not given up hope that his strategy would work and Limerick would agree to surrender. 'They wouldn't have had time to consider the terms and come back with a proper reply yet,' he told them.

The town's messenger to Limerick had not returned by the time Sunday arrived and the handover of Galway was scheduled. D'Usson and his French staff finally emerged from the gates to exchange formalities with Ginckel at seven o'clock in the morning. Their escort to Limerick was drawn up, waiting, while garrons were provided to haul their wagons.

Mackay watched the small round Frenchman in conversation with his own French general, Ruvigny, and wondered idly what they were talking about. Probably about mutual acquaintances: both had been Protestant officers in the French army but had gone their different ways after their king had tried to extirpate their religion, Ruvigny into exile and d'Usson into the arms of Rome. I hope he regrets his mistake now, he thought.

After the French party had moved off, the Irish, English and

Scottish papists who had opted to leave for Limerick were led out with their drums beating and flags flying. There was a sudden loud explosion and a cloud of grey-black smoke rose above the town's skyline. Everybody stood still in a moment of stunned surprise, then Williamite soldiers reached for their weapons and dropped into defensive stances. The Jacobites responded in similar fashion, falling into fighting mode, one line kneeling, a second standing, muskets levelled. They were both in battle formations, hardly fifty yards apart. But the Jacobites had the advantage, their muskets already loaded, their match lit, ready to fire. The Williamites, not expecting any trouble, rammed balls down the barrels of their flintlocks as quickly as possible.

'Treachery,' Talmash shouted to Ginckel.

But the drummers on the other side had gone silent and no orders were sounded. Ginckel held his breath. The silence stretched into seconds that seemed like minutes. Nobody moved. Everybody waited for what was to happen next.

Then a horseman came riding out of the gate, shouting something they could not hear. The Jacobites visibly relaxed, the front line lowering their muskets and rising to their feet. Everybody breathed again.

The horseman turned out to be Clanricarde who pulled up in front of Ginckel. 'An accident,' he said in a breathless voice. 'Some powder blew up when it was being moved. A few men hurt. Blinded.'

The arrangements continued. Six cannons and their wagons were dragged manually out of the town's gate and Williamite garrons were hitched to them. Then the drums beat again and the column of some 2,000 men moved off, their wagon train and camp followers trundling in their wake.

Clanricarde remained with Ginckel, watching the troops move south around the inner fingers of the bay.

'Why no news from Limerick?' Ginckel asked, breaking the silence.

'I don't know, my lord.'

'It can't take this long for a messenger to get there and back again.'

'We have no assurance that he ever got there. He may have had an accident. Fallen foul of rapparees.'

Ginckel gave him a sceptical look. 'What do you think it means?'

Clanricarde paused to consider his answer. 'That they are undecided,' he offered.

'My lord Tyrconnell in favour, General Sarsfield opposed.'

Clanricarde nodded. 'My lord Tyrconnell is a pragmatic man.'

'And Sarsfield?'

Clanricarde hesitated.

'You know him well?'

'Well enough.' Clanricarde paused again, searching for suitable words. 'He can be impatient, impractical. Easily led.'

'But not by my lord Tyrconnell.'

'Indeed not. By people whom he thinks are his friends. Like Luttrell and Purcell. You know of these two colonels?'

'They're not his real friends, are they?' Ginckel asked, picking up on Clanricarde's phrase but unsure whether he correctly understood its nuances.

'He thinks they are but they don't really have his best interests at heart.' Clanricarde changed the subject, uneasy at the direction of the conversation about his half-sister's husband. 'The mayor and town council would like to welcome you at the Great Gate.'

Ginckel filed away the information about Sarsfield's friends. 'Not the Great Gate for long. We'll rename it William's Gate,' he replied, thinking that might be another mollifying line when writing to the King about the surrender terms.

As he prepared to go into the town, Mackay came to him with a report that the English fleet had finally arrived in the bay.

Ginckel grunted. 'Just when they're no longer needed.

AUGUST

Mackay

I t took them ten days to get little more than halfway to Limerick after they had crossed the Shannon at Banagher. The general had sent an advance party along the road to repair it for the heavy guns on their way from Athlone. But everything was moving at a snail's pace, covering only three miles a day through the sodden landscape. Progress was not helped by a shortage of horses for the guns and wagons. An appeal for more horses had even been sent to Dublin where the wealthier were asked to give up their carriage horses for their Majesties' cause. Reinforcements were also summoned from other parts of the country, rapparees being left to local Protestant militias to deal with in the small scale but bloody skirmishes that continued unabated all over

'Have you ever seen such a desolate land?' Ruvigny said, riding alongside Mackay. Their woollen uniforms were already soaked, the damp reaching through to the skin. Rain dripped relentlessly from the brims of their hats onto their backs.

'You're not used to the rain,' Mackay chuckled, thinking of the Highlands.

'I'm not surprised nobody lives here.'

'What do you mean?'

'There are no people.'

'They keep out of the way.'

Ruvigny grunted, not convinced.

'Who do you think owns all those cabins we pass?' Mackay added.

'Hovels, you mean. They're only temporary places. Used by nomads.'

'I don't think so. The people are here somewhere. Hiding in the bogs and woods.'

The infantry shuffled along, worn down by the incessant rain, the sucking mud, a shortage of bread, and the fading of the boost created by the battle at Aughrim. Drummers abandoned their efforts to beat a marching pace. An occasional effort to raise a verse of Lillibulero faded at the first refrain.

'They seem to think in London that our task is finished,' Ginckel said, tossing a letter in frustration onto his desk in his tent when they reached Nenagh. 'They're insisting that I send ten thousand men to the Continent.'

'That's ridiculous. Premature, at the very least,' Mackay said.

'I've told them,' Ginckel agreed, raising his hands in despair, 'but they're ignoring me.' 'They' were the lords justices in London representing King William, who was in the Netherlands where the war with the French was at a stalemate since his Grand Alliance had lost the city of Mons more than three months earlier.

'Can't we ignore them back?' Mackay suggested, giving the general a sly half-smile.

'We have to. We can't spare ten thousand men. We don't have enough to mount a proper siege at Limerick as it is. And the navy is still sitting in Galway Bay,' Ginckel added, waving another piece of paper in the air. 'Captain Cole says he's awaiting orders and won't go to Limerick until London instructs him to. And, of course, London is going to tell him to take our men to Holland.'

'You have to make it clear to them that it's not finished here yet.'

Ginckel nodded. 'We're victims of our own success. They think the battle of Aughrim decided it.'

'It did,' Mackay argued. 'The papists cannot recover from that. When has there ever been a more decisive engagement?'

Thomas Coningsby, the Irish lord justice, turned up with a detachment of reinforcements from Mullingar next day. Ginckel was not pleased to see him, expecting more political pressure. But he got his concerns in first; trying to get the naval ships moved to Limerick and to persuade Coningsby of the foolishness of London's demands.

'I understand,' Coningsby agreed. 'I'll see if Captain Cole can be ordered to the Shannon estuary. But' -- he raised a warning finger -- 'don't think of merely blockading Limerick, of only preventing the French from supplying or reinforcing it.'

Ginckel was taken aback: that was exactly what he had been thinking.

'You have to besiege it,' Coningsby added, seeing his surprise. 'A blockade is not enough. That would send the wrong message to the papists, encouraging them to hold out. They must be defeated by force of arms. That's what people expect.'

Protestants, Ginckel reinterpreted his words, attuned by now to the politics of this campaign. That's what the Protestants of Dublin, the new establishment, expected. 'Will they accept a treaty?' he asked.

Coningsby sighed and concentrated on tapping snuff from a silver box onto the back of his hand. 'Look,' he said, pausing to inhale a little of the snuff through his right nostril, 'this campaign must be concluded this year. You know that. The King needs this army on the Continent. And, you should know too, that there is no possibility of getting any more men here next year if, God forbid, it's not over by then.'

And someone else will be in command, Ginckel thought. 'All

the more reason why we need every man we have here right now,' he added.

Coningsby nodded and took another sniff and wiped his nose with his handkerchief. 'Finish it,' he said in a tone that suggested he could give Ginckel an order, 'with another devastating defeat for the papists such as you have achieved at Athlone and Aughrim. Put an end to their pretensions. Establish peace in this kingdom once and for all.'

After Coningsby had left, Ginckel sat down at his desk to draft another proclamation, extending for ten more days the surrender terms that had been on offer since Athlone. Anyone who came over to the King's side would be pardoned, have their estates restored, and receive a reward. There would be a similar or better position in the King's army for any officer who surrendered a castle or brought over a body of men. This was their last chance.

It is also my best chance, Ginckel thought as he signed the proclamation and summoned an aide to make copies and have infiltrators take them into Limerick. Then he sat back in his chair and sipped a glass of brandy, pondering how best to achieve the quick victory demanded of him. Force of arms alone wouldn't do it; neither would Mackay's prayers. The terms on offer should help but didn't seem to be enough by themselves. He was already out on a limb over the generosity of the Galway terms and could not go further. But more was required to sap the enemy's will. Another victory, as Coningsby demanded, would do it. But was that achievable with winter coming and a well-defended city, by all accounts, to be besieged?

He suddenly remembered something Ruvigny had told him about the aftermath of Galway, how one of his officers had had a conversation with the Irish Colonel Luttrell, who expressed an interest in settlement terms. And it was said that Luttrell was Sarsfield's confidant. Which might be a way to get to Sarsfield and present him with the offer the King had suggested that he, Ginckel, make to him. Give him anything he wants to come to

286

terms, the King had instructed.

Ginckel poured himself another glass of brandy and tried to think through how he might exploit this opportunity. He called out to an aide to find Ruvigny.

Sarsfield

Sarsfield rode across Baal's Bridge, linking the two parts of Limerick, English Town on King's Island with Irish Town. The right-hand side of the bridge was lined with workshops, carpenters, tanners and shoemakers spreading out of doors to reduce the already narrow roadway. On the other side, the brown water of the Abbey River, muddied and engorged by the torrential overnight rain, piled up to push through the arches and re-join the Shannon below the city. The sky was still heavy but it had exhausted itself for the moment and the morning was dry.

He continued up John Street through Irish Town and went out through John's Gate to where Tyrconnell was inspecting the muster with the French generals Tessé and d'Usson, in front of the newly completed slope of the glacis. At first sight, the massed ranks looked impressive; row upon row of men, albeit in a mixture of uniforms that ranged from the passable to the tattered. They included the stragglers from Aughrim, some still displaying open wounds or rough bandages. The newly arrived garrison from Galway bolstered their numbers, along with those rounded up from neighbouring areas by Tyrconnell's proclamation that all men between sixteen and sixty were to join in the defence of Limerick. There were some 18,000 in all but fewer than half were armed.

Sarsfield joined the line of major generals, halting his horse beside John Wauchope, recently promoted to fill one of the vacancies left by the loss of the two generals, Dorrington and Hamilton, at Aughrim. Tyrconnell was riding slowly by the front line of infantry, his huge bulk making his large charger appear overburdened. Sarsfield rubbed his eyes to ease the dull ache from the previous night's drinking session with Luttrell and Purcell as they tried to work out the meaning of the viceroy's transformation.

Tyrconnell was like a new man. The defeat at Aughrim had energised him, caused him to do an about-turn from defeatism to belligerence. He was outraged at Galway's easy capitulation and was determined to hold Limerick and take the war into another year. 'This is far from over' was his new slogan.

'They could have held out for a month,' Tyrconnell had declared in an angry outburst when the messenger from Galway had arrived with news of the planned surrender. 'or longer. But a month with ease. Forcing Ginckel to withdraw into winter quarters and putting an end to the prince of Orange's hopes of seeing us off this year. Taken the campaign into 1692. When the King and King Louis' – he bowed towards Tessé – 'will send us more men and supplies.'

'But will they?' Major General Sheldon blurted out. The recriminations after Aughrim had raised suspicions of bad faith between all the factions: between the French and the Irish; the English and Scottish Jacobites and the Irish; the Old Irish and the Old English; the 'new interest' men of all backgrounds and everyone else.

'They will,' Tyrconnell declared in a tone that defied dispute. 'They have said so. And I believe the word of the King of France. He is already dispatching supplies from Brest but cannot spare any men until next year.'

No one argued. Sarsfield forbore from pointing out that the 'new interest' men of Galway who had surrendered were those whom Tyrconnell had supported the previous year when he himself was willing to seek terms with the prince of Orange and was only prevented from doing so only by his, Sarsfield's, opposition.

'What message do we send back to Galway, my lord?' one of Tyrconnell's aides asked.

'Haven't I made myself clear?' Tyrconnell retorted.

But the message never got back to Galway, as Luttrell had told Sarsfield when he returned to Limerick the previous day after escorting the French and Irish columns from Galway into the city. 'It wasn't that they got the message and decided to ignore it,' he had reported.

They were in the lord mayor's old tower house, Sarsfield's quarters, in the dining hall on the first floor. They had discussed the current situation over dinner and, now over drinks, had got to the stage where everything had become repetitive. 'At least, that's what they say,' Luttrell added. 'They never got the message from Limerick.'

Sarsfield sighed. 'What happened the messenger?'

'God knows. He could have met with some mishap. Or joined the rapparees. Or be hiding somewhere. Even in Galway. Hidden by people who didn't want to hear the message. Or didn't want other people to hear the message. Or maybe he was never meant to deliver the message at all.'

Sarsfield topped up his glass of port. The rain was beating down outside, driven by an angry wind. Gusts from the spiral staircase made the candlelight dance and lifted the edges of the faded tapestries of religious scenes on two walls. Purcell was at the table too, asleep on his folded arms.

'That doesn't make any sense.' Sarsfield heard himself slur slightly.

'What?'

'That he was never meant to deliver the message at all.'

Luttrell gave him his patient look, the one that asked how often do I have to educate you in the devious ways of the world?

'You heard him,' Sarsfield said. 'They shouldn't surrender. The message was clear.'

'But did he mean it?' Luttrell leaned forward over the table as if he was about to deliver a conclusive point and wagged a finger in Sarsfield's face. 'Has Lying Dick really changed his tune?'

'You don't think so?'

'I don't know.' Luttrell leaned back in his chair. 'It seems he has. Probably. And for this reason. Because he thinks he's in charge now that Saint-Ruhe is dead and the King hasn't appointed anyone in his place. Tessé and d'Usson are no match for him, neither as generals nor courtiers. So he's prepared to fight now that he's in control.'

'But,' Sarsfield said, trying to get his thoughts in order, 'he was in control last year when he wanted to capitulate.'

'It's different now. He thinks he's really in charge this time because you and he are on the same side.'

That made sense, Sarsfield thought, but this conversation was hovering on the verge of incoherence. Luttrell, he knew, was as drunk as himself, even if he did not show it. 'We'll talk about it tomorrow,' he said.

'We will. But we can't assume that he's really on the same side just because he pretends to be.'

Sarsfield shook his head and drained his glass. 'Tomorrow,' he repeated.

'You had a skinful last night,' Wauchope said under his breath to Sarsfield now as they watched the muster.

Sarsfield groaned in confirmation. He had woken up unusually late this morning with a sore head and a dry mouth but he was thinking of something else, something prompted by the previous night's discussion about Tyrconnell's change of heart.

291

Honor had stopped asking if she could go to France, making no mention of it since his return from Aughrim as she lapsed into formal mourning for the loss of her two brothers in that battle. But he knew that she still wanted to go and maybe it was time she did. The mourning period would give her some protection from the many predators at the court in Saint-Germain.

Luttrell had previously used the duchess's failure to return from Paris with Lying Dick at the start of the year as further evidence of his defeatism. But now that Tyrconnell wanted war, that couldn't be used against him. Sarsfield couldn't be accused of defeatism either if Honor was to go to Paris now. And he wouldn't have to worry about her when the siege started.

The muster ended and the ranks of men broke up, making their way back within the walls. 'They've done a good job,' Wauchope said, inclining his head towards the long embankment leading up to the walls that would protect them from cannon fire and make it impossible for an enemy to get near without exposing himself to deadly fire. The glacis was covered by new bastions, giving defenders a clear field of fire and greatly improving the city's defences.

'If they couldn't take it last year, they have no chance of taking it this year,' Sarsfield said.

The bridge onto King's Island was clogged with men and it took Sarsfield a while to make his way across. At St Mary's cathedral he turned down to the harbour. A couple of small square-masted ships were tied up, their cargoes being unloaded onto carts at the quayside while other supplies waited to be brought on board.

'*Quand ces navires vont revenir à Brest?*' he asked a French sailor lounging by the gangway.

'You'll have to ask the captain.'

Sarsfield dismounted and handed the reins to the sailor who took them with a hostile glower. He found the captain on board and repeated his question.

'When the wind permits.' The captain gesticulated downriver where a strong wind was blowing straight up the estuary making it almost impossible to tack out to sea.

'Can you take a passenger?'

'You'll have to arrange that with Monsieur Fumeron.' Jean-François de Fumeron was the civilian commissary in charge of supplies and logistics.

Sarsfield went back down the gangway. The French sailor had passed his horse to an Irishman who had been helping to unload the vessel.

'*Cathain a'mbeidh siad ag seol*?' he asked the local.

'It'll be a good few days before the wind changes and lets them out.'

'What are they bringing back?'

'Bits and pieces. Lot of broken equipment.' He pointed to a chest on the quay. 'The French general's things -- the one who was killed. They're bringing his horse too.'

Sarsfield wondered idly what was in the chest. There were rumours that it contained thousands of gold *pistoles* but Fumeron and the French officers had opened it away from any Irish eyes. News that they were sending back the chest, with its possible cache of gold coins, would not help allay suspicions about the French.

'Any passengers?'

'I wouldn't know about that, my lord.'

Sarsfield went home to his quarters in the mayor's house. Honor was on the second floor, reading a book beside the light from the small window in the east wall. She was dressed in mourning black, her veil folded back from her pale face, making her look even younger than her seventeen years. Sarsfield slumped down in an armchair and she placed a marker in her book and gave him a worried look.

'I think you should go to Paris after all,' he said without

293

preamble.

A flash of youthful delight, mixed with surprise, lit up her face and then changed to worry. 'Why? What's happened?'

'Nothing. But it'll be better for you, in all the circumstances.'

'You think they'll take the town?'

'No, I don't. There's even less chance than last year. But they will bombard it and I would be happier if you weren't in the way of harm.'

She searched his eyes, trying to discern any other meaning behind his words.

The longcase clock with a single hand ticked away the moments.

'When?' she asked with suppressed eagerness.

'In a few days. A couple of small ships are preparing to sail. I'll talk to the French commissary to arrange it.'

He stood up to leave.

'Is there any more news of John and Richard?' she asked, referring to her captured brother and half-brother.

'Nothing more about John,' he replied. 'Richard stayed in Galway, accepted the terms there and signed them.'

'He's safe then?'

'Yes. There wasn't any fighting. He has secured the lands under the terms. So the family will be all right. I'll ask Henry to talk to you,' he said, meaning Luttrell.

'There's no need.' She returned to her book.

'You don't want to talk to Henry?' He was aware that she didn't like Luttrell but did not really know why. He assumed it had to do with their late-night drinking sessions and Luttrell's reputation as a womaniser. 'He escorted the column from Galway yesterday. He might have heard more news of Richard. Maybe even of John.'

'I'm sure Richard's all right. We'd have heard by now if he wasn't, wouldn't we?'

'Of course we would.' He paused at the doorway. 'I'll ask

Henry anyway.'

'Thank you,' she said, giving him a wan smile.

All was quiet in the headquarters in the Citadel beside John's Gate in Irish Town. There was no sign of Tyrconnell and the French lieutenants general were out inspecting the defences, Tessé showing d'Usson what had been completed since he was last in Limerick shortly after their arrival from France. Wauchope was there, writing a report on the latest known movements of the Williamites.

'Colonel O'Kelly was looking for you,' he told Sarsfield.

'What for?'

'He didn't tell me.' Wauchope gave a half-smile. 'I'm a foreigner. But he's angry about something.'

Something to do with Balldearg O'Donnell, Sarsfield thought, and his failure to come to Galway's aid.

He found O'Kelly at the corner of the ramparts by the rebuilt Black Battery, looking northwards as if he expected to see the enemy come into view at any moment.

'They won't be here for a week,' Sarsfield assured him in Irish as a greeting.

'Have you heard?' O'Kelly demanded, his rheumy old eyes glowering.

'Heard what?'

'Balldearg has gone over to the invaders.' He spat out the words as if he was clearing his mouth of a venomous taste. 'The real lords of Tyrconnell must be turning in their graves. Having Lying Dick steal their title and now this.'

Sarsfield leaned on the cold stone and bowed his head. Balldearg had been no help during the past year but switching sides was a different matter. The news came at the worst possible time as people were beginning to question the future, the point of fighting on.

'Who can you trust these days when we can't trust one of our own?' O'Kelly continued, paying Sarsfield a sideways compliment by including him among the true Gaels, although he was only half one of them through his mother.

'Where is Balldearg?'

'In Mayo. Heading for Sligo to help the English take the garrison there.'

They won't need much help, Sarsfield thought. Sligo had no chance of holding out on its own and they had no means of going to its assistance. It was too far away through enemy-held territory now even if they had the men and the means to get them there by land or by sea.

'I talked to him myself,' O'Kelly said. 'Pleaded with him. Begged him not to betray his own ancestors, his family, his country, his religion. Even urged him to go back to Spain, forget all about us. But it was no use. He's after their money. He's nothing but an adventurer, a heathen opportunist.'

Sarsfield patted him on the shoulder, feeling his obvious anguish at O'Donnell's betrayal. 'You did your best,' he said. 'We never relied on him for anything anyway. *Ná bac leis.*'

O'Kelly shook his head; he could not forget about O'Donnell. 'There's treachery and traitors everywhere,' he said. 'Do you believe Lying Dick's road to Damascus conversion? He's only biding his time to hand us over to them at the right moment. Mark my words.'

Life went on in a desultory fashion as the city awaited the inevitable. People carried on with their day-to-day activities, bartering, baking and brewing, tanning and weaving. Farmers in the surrounding area harvested their crops, unsure if it was worth the effort and ready to flee at first sight of the enemy. The same question was on everyone's mind. To stay or to leave? Stay within the walls that everyone said were invincible and wait for the

French to rescue the city, or leave and roam the uncertain and inhospitable land outside? Everybody knew the war was coming back to Limerick. Nobody knew what would happen.

Doubts about continuing the fight were beginning to emerge from mutterings behind hands into open discussions, developing a momentum that gathered pace with every conversation. Tyrconnell tried to stop the debate spreading among the officers by requiring them to sign a pledge that they would remain united, stick together to the last, and do only whatever received the approval of King James.

'No, no, no,' Luttrell shook his head when he heard about it.

'Why not?' Sarsfield retorted. It made sense to him, a means of stopping the growing levels of mutual suspicion about each other's motives, of uniting everybody behind a clear position.

'Because,' Luttrell adopted his explanatory tone, 'he's just trying to consolidate his position. He effectively wants everyone to swear loyalty to himself. He will tell us what the King has approved, speaking as the King's representative. Which means he will decide what to do with us all.'

'And what will that be?'

'Who knows? He could do anything. Sell us to the prince of Orange or to the French. But,' he pointed a finger at Sarsfield, 'whatever he does, you can be sure of one thing -- that it will be to his own benefit. Come what may, he'll be all right. As always.'

'You agree with Colonel O'Kelly.' Sarsfield gave Luttrell a sceptical glance, knowing that he and O'Kelly had no time for each other.

'So be it,' Luttrell shrugged. 'The old fumbler is right this time.'

Sarsfield changed the subject and told Luttrell that Honor wanted to know if he had any news of her brothers.

'Clanricarde was one of the negotiators of the terms in Galway,' Luttrell said while he searched his mind for anything else. 'And he managed to get my lord Bophin included in them. So he should be released, able to go home to Portumna if he

297

doesn't join us here.'

'I doubt he'll do that,' Sarsfield said. 'He's probably had enough of warfare.'

'Hard to blame him. I hear you've decided to send Honor to Saint-Germain.'

Sarsfield nodded. 'It's best for her.'

'That it is.'

Sarsfield turned away and strolled down to the bank of the river, thinking about Tyrconnell's pledge. They were at the cavalry camp at Cratloe, outside the town and in County Clare, a scene of rural languor. The sun had broken through, the wind from the west was warm, horses grazed the plentiful grass and men lazed about. The river was full, pushed up high on its banks by the incoming tide from the distant ocean and the swell from the recent rain.

Maybe Luttrell was right, he thought: it was just an attempt by Tyrconnell to seize control of the army. The French were also unhappy about this pledge: d'Usson had told him that he thought it was a bad idea, that it would create divisions rather than heal them.

Sarsfield rode back alone towards the city and crossed Thomond Bridge into English Town, his horse's hooves sounding hollow on the wooden drawbridge over its central arch. An officer at the gate of King John's Castle halted him as he went by. 'His grace would like to see you,' he told Sarsfield, indicating the gate behind him.

To sign his pledge, Sarsfield thought. Which I should do: unity is the most important thing now. The last thing we need, as we try to build up the army's confidence, is to add to our divisions. I'll sign it, he decided; no matter what Luttrell and Purcell think.

Tyrconnell was in a room beneath the ramparts overlooking the bridge. 'Hungry?' he asked. He had clearly been waiting for Sarsfield's return and had probably seen him cross the river. The table in the centre of the room had plates of cold meats, bread, and fruit. A bottle of red wine was open with two glasses alongside, one already half-empty.

Tyrconnell filled the second glass for Sarsfield and lowered his bulk onto the chair with care, breathing heavily. Sarsfield took the chair opposite him.

'*Le commissaire* Fumeron tells me you're sending Lady Honor to Saint-Germain,' Tyrconnell said after they had helped themselves to some slices of meat.

'She'll be safer there.'

'Yes, indeed. I'm sure she's very upset about her brothers. It's a relief to me that Frances stayed at the court when I returned. I'll ask her to look after Honor, make introductions and see that she settles in well.'

'Thank you.' Sarsfield gave a small bow. 'How is Mark?' Colonel Mark Talbot, Tyrconnell's son by one of his mistresses, had been badly wounded at Aughrim. Several of his relations were also killed on Kilcommodan hill but they were distant enough that Tyrconnell did not feel obliged to wear a black armband.

'Recovering well. He's young and he'll get over it. Like we did in our day.'

They ate in silence for a little while. Sarsfield wondered what was coming next. Tyrconnell wasn't in one of his usual modes, neither persuading nor browbeating. He appeared to be unusually subdued.

'Of course, you're still in your prime.' Tyrconnell said. 'But I'm too old for war. I've seen enough of it. And if I had a choice, I wouldn't see any more of it. But we don't have a choice, do we?'

Sarsfield assumed this was a rhetorical question and bit off a chunk of bread. Tyrconnell stared at him, waiting for a reply. 'No,' he said, when he had finished chewing. 'We don't have a choice. But our situation is far from critical.'

'Agreed, agreed,' Tyrconnell nodded. 'Very far from critical. We can break out with French reinforcements in the spring and retrieve a lot of Connacht. The enemy can't afford to bring more men here from the Continent. And' -- he raised his fork to emphasise the point -- 'don't forget: they lost a lot of men at Aughrim too.'

'They did,' Sarsfield agreed. 'Any news from Brest?'

'They haven't sailed yet as far as I know. But they will. There's no doubt about that.'

They lapsed into silence again, Sarsfield becoming impatient. If Tyrconnell wouldn't get to the point, he'd have to do it himself. 'The pledge,' he said.

Tyrconnell waved his fork, dismissing the subject. 'I fear it's too late for that.' He put down his knife and fork and dabbed at his mouth with his napkin. 'I've received some distressing information, from General d'Usson.'

Sarsfield put down his knife and fork too.

'He has received a message from one of the French renegades, the Marquis de Ruvigny, whom he met at the capitulation of Galway.' Tyrconnell paused to catch his breath. 'Which says that Colonel Luttrell is in communication with the enemy.'

Sarsfield felt his stomach churn but shook his head in an unconscious denial.

'I'm sorry to have to tell you this,' Tyrconnell added in a neutral tone. 'It's not the kind of information I wanted to hear either.'

'I don't believe it,' Sarsfield said. Was this another of the devious ploys that had earned Tyrconnell his nickname?

'You know my view of Colonel Luttrell and, no doubt, his view of me,' Tyrconnell added, 'but, believe me, it gives me no pleasure to tell you this.'

'It's a lie,' Sarsfield said. 'An enemy lie. They're trying to create divisions in our ranks.'

'That is possible,' Tyrconnell agreed. 'But we have a way of testing the truth of it. Ruvigny's message to d'Usson says they are sending a trumpet this afternoon with a message for the French commander. And he will be carrying a secret message for Colonel Luttrell as well.'

Sarsfield felt his heart sink.

'I think you should be present to receive the trumpet,' Tyrconnell added.

Sarsfield pushed his unfinished plate away, his brain reeling, unable to say anything.

They waited in silence at the Citadel in Irish Town for the messenger, each lost in his own thoughts. D'Usson had joined them and Sarsfield quizzed him about the letter he had received from Ruvigny. D'Usson handed it to him without a word. Sarsfield read through it quickly. After the usual salutations and references to their conversation at Galway, it said that General Ginckel would be sending a response to the questions Colonel Luttrell had put to Colonel Pierre de la Bastide Saint-Sebastian during their conversation a few days earlier. It ended with the hope that they would renew their acquaintance at greater length in more peaceful times in the near future.

'Who is this Bastide Saint-Sebastian?' Sarsfield demanded.

'The officer commanding the escort they gave us from Galway,' d'Usson said.

'You spoke to him too?'

'Only to exchange formalities.'

'And Colonel Luttrell? How long did he speak to Saint-Sebastian?'

D'Usson shrugged. 'Not very long. The handover from one escort to the other was not drawn out.'

Sarsfield looked to Tyrconnell, whose poker face was fixed on d'Usson.

'Why has Ruvigny sent you this letter?' Sarsfield asked.

'I don't know,' the Frenchman replied. 'I am not in correspondence with him.'

'It's suspicious, don't you think?' Sarsfield looked from d'Usson to Tyrconnell and back again. Was this some French plot, he wondered? Involving d'Usson, Ruvigny and this French heretic colonel?

Tyrconnell maintained his poker face and gave no inkling of what he was thinking.

The Frenchman reddened and his left hand clasped the hilt of his sword with enough strength to whiten his knuckles. 'Are you questioning my loyalty to my King?' he demanded.

Sarsfield closed his eyes and ordered himself to calm down. 'No,' he said, although he had just been remembering that d'Usson was a Huguenot before he converted to Catholicism. But d'Usson had had no part in the surrender of Galway. On the contrary, by all accounts he had wanted to fight on but had been overruled. 'My apologies,' he said, taking a deep breath. 'This is very upsetting news.'

General John Wauchope entered and was about to say something but the obvious tension in the room stopped him. 'We're awaiting the arrival of a messenger,' Tyrconnell told him blandly.

Sarsfield paced the room, trying to contain his anger, alternatively aimed at Tyrconnell and Luttrell. Was it one of the viceroy's ploys to destroy Luttrell? Remove him from a position of influence? Or was it true that Luttrell was secretly negotiating with the enemy? He could not countenance the thought that Luttrell had betrayed their friendship after all they had been through together. But if it was ---.

Tyrconnell's bland face gave nothing away. D'Usson now appeared to be lost in his own thoughts. Wauchope watched them all, bemused.

They didn't have long to wait. A shout from a lookout on the walls alerted them and, shortly after, they heard the trumpeter ensuring his safe passage with the repeated notes of a parley. He was escorted in through the open John's Gate: a short, square

302

youth of about 14 wearing the gold uniform of his position. 'Message from General Ginckel, my lord,' he said, picking out Tyrconnell for a bow as the most senior man in the room. He handed over a sealed letter from his satchel.

Tyrconnell broke the seal, scanned the letter and handed it to Sarsfield without a word. It requested details of the Williamites who were being held prisoner in Limerick and suggested an exchange with some of the Jacobites captured at Aughrim. In effect it was a response to the letter sent to Ginckel in Galway two weeks earlier and a change from Ginckel's dismissive refusal to consider a prisoner exchange then.

Sarsfield handed the letter back to Tyrconnell. 'Do you have any other messages?' Sarsfield asked the trumpeter.

'No, my lord.'

'I will ask you again and then I will have you searched. If you are lying, you will be treated as a spy and hanged immediately.'

The youth's gaze flickered from one to another of the implacable faces watching him.

'Do you have any other messages?'

The trumpeter's eyes flickered faster and turned into a look of consternation but he said nothing.

Sarsfield nodded to the officers who had escorted the trumpeter into the room. They moved forward and the messenger took a step backwards. He opened a button, reached inside his tunic and took out another sealed message.

Sarsfield snatched it from him, saw it was addressed to Luttrell, and broke it open. He took in its brief contents in a single block, not reading the individual words or sentences, just absorbing their meaning as a stomach-hollowing whole. A second sheet fluttered to the ground. He ignored it and turned to Wauchope and said, 'Arrest Colonel Luttrell.'

'What?' Wauchope said in shock.

'Now,' Sarsfield shouted, releasing some of his anger.

Wauchope nodded to one of the officers to follow him and left.

'Do you have any other messages?' Sarsfield asked the trumpeter, as if he was repeating the earlier question and hoping for a different answer.

'No, my lord.' The young man bowed his head.

'Search him,' Sarsfield ordered.

An officer took the messenger's satchel while two others stripped him roughly. Nobody said anything. When the youth was naked Sarsfield nodded at him and he began to dress himself again, his hands shaking as he buttoned his tunic.

Tyrconnell held out his hand and Sarsfield gave him the message. Tyrconnell scanned it and sighed heavily before passing it to D'Usson. As Ruvigny's letter had predicted, it was from Colonel Bastide Saint-Sebastian and assured Luttrell, following their recent conversation, that General Ginckel had complete power conferred on him by King William and Queen Mary and their lords justices in Ireland to reach a settlement with the opposing army in Ireland.

Tyrconnell pointed at the page that had fallen on the floor. An aide picked it up and handed it to him. It was Ginckel's latest proclamation offering surrender terms. 'A court martial,' Tyrconnell said, handing the document to D'Usson.

'No,' d'Usson said after scanning it. 'Hang him now. Immediately. Make an example of him.'

Tyrconnell glanced at Sarsfield. He was white-faced and didn't appear to have heard the Frenchman.

'No,' Tyrconnell said. 'We'll convene a court martial.'

'This is a military matter.' d'Usson waved the letter and the proclamation, asserting that it was a decision for himself and Tessé. 'We have to put an immediate stop to any treasonous action.'

'It's more than a military matter,' Tyrconnell retorted in a tone that asserted his vice-regal authority. 'We shall court martial him.'

Sarsfield headed for the door.

'What'll we do with him?' one of the officers in the room asked him, pointing at the messenger.

Sarsfield ignored the question as he went out.

Mackay

They moved on from Nenagh in sunshine and a warm wind, which sent large white clouds smoothly across the blue sky and cast leisurely shadows over the benign-looking slopes of the Silvermines mountains on their left. But they knew those hills were anything but benign. Ginckel ordered a detachment of horsemen to patrol the rising ground, aware that it was a natural home for rapparees and even for forays by enemy cavalry, although all reports made it clear that the Jacobite cavalry was on the other side of the Shannon.

'He's not taking any chances,' Mackay said in reply to Talmash who had been complaining about their slow progress.

'Giving them every opportunity to prepare for our arrival,' Talmash retorted.

They were riding near the end of the column, just before the wagon train, the sutlers and the straggling camp followers. There was no sign yet of the siege guns from Athlone which were making even slower progress, frustrating the cavalry and dragoons that had been assigned to protect them.

'At this rate it will be Christmas before we get there,' Talmash muttered.

'Patience is a virtue,' Mackay said with a sweet smile.

Ginckel summoned his generals to a council of war that evening to discuss the strategy for taking Limerick, anxious to quell the grumblings of the impatient ones by letting them debate a plan of action.

An aide rolled out the map of Limerick and the surrounding countryside. As it neared the city, the River Shannon switched from north-south to east-west and continued in that direction to the distant Atlantic.

'A siege or a blockade?' Ginckel asked, throwing open the discussion.

'No question,' Württemberg shot back. 'A siege and a quick assault. Take the Irish Town first.'

'I agree,' Talmash said. 'We have to maintain the momentum. Don't let them think for a moment that they can avoid defeat.'

'Why not go for their stronger position first?' Ruvigny said, pointing to the English Town and running his finger across the Abbey River towards the town. 'Attack across here where it looks narrow.'

Mackay cleared his throat, prompting one or two sniggers that said: here he goes again, at odds with everyone as usual. 'I'm not so sure that we can take either town so easily,' he said. 'By all accounts, they have as many men inside as we have. And you need superior numbers to take a defended city.'

'That doesn't apply,' Talmash said. 'They're badly armed and their spirit is broken.'

'The rules of war still apply,' Mackay insisted. 'They don't all need to be armed behind good defences. And we're told those defences have been improved greatly. It is still impossible to take a well-defended city without superior forces.'

'What about Athlone?' Württemberg asked. 'We didn't have a superior force.'

'That was different,' Mackay said. 'Their main force was not in the town. Would we have taken it if it was?'

Württemberg gave a dismissive shrug. 'What are you suggesting? That we withdraw to winter quarters and wait for another year?' he asked, his voice heavy with sarcasm.

'A blockade,' Mackay said. 'We can block the river and surround the town, cutting off their supplies from the hinterland and from France. Make it clear they're on their own, with no prospect of relief.'

'No,' Ruvigny said, with an emphatic shake of his head. 'We can't conduct a blockade over the winter in this climate. We'll lose more men to the flux than at Aughrim. Like the winter before last at that awful place –' He looked around for someone to prompt him the name of the place where they had lost a large section of their army to disease before the battle at the Boyne river.

'Dundalk,' Ginckel said, his first intervention in the debate.

'Yes, Dundalk,' Ruvigny said.

'And,' Talmash added, 'we'd weaken our force by dividing it on opposite sides of the river. With their cavalry all over there.' He stabbed at the map, pointing to County Clare on the western side of the divide.

'Their cavalry is not a problem,' Ruvigny said, sensing a slight against horsemen by an infantry commander.

Mackay looked at Ginckel, surprised that he had not come to the defence of his argument. It was his natural inclination to avoid risky operations and a siege was very risky. 'What if we besiege it and fail?' he asked. 'Their confidence will recover very quickly. And then they can wait for relief from France over the winter.'

'We won't fail.' Württemberg sliced the air with his hand, as if putting an end to the discussion. 'They'll capitulate once they see our determination.'

'They didn't at Aughrim,' Mackay said.

'So why did we win then?'

'Because it was the …'

'All right, gentlemen,' Ginckel said. 'We don't need to debate that. We'll besiege Limerick and trust you are right,' he added, looking at Württemberg.

As they approached Limerick, a trickle of enemy deserters began to arrive, seeking the pardons and promises on offer, and bringing with them news of divisions within the city.

'How much of that can you believe?' Ginckel asked after he and Mackay had interviewed a dragoon captain who had come over the river with half-a-dozen troopers. 'That my lord Tyrconnell wants to hold out?'

'It's not what we expected,' Mackay agreed.

'No, and it can hardly be what this captain thought we wanted to hear.'

'So it must be true.'

'Yes. A surprise. But can it mean that Sarsfield is for surrendering?' Maybe we have miscalculated, Ginckel was thinking. Perhaps we should have used Luttrell to make a direct offer to Sarsfield, rather than this scheme of Ruvigny's to cause division in their ranks by alerting their French generals to a secret message to Luttrell.

'These papists are an unreliable lot,' Mackay said. 'They call each other liars, even their own viceroy.'

'Lying Dick,' Ginckel nodded. 'Have you ever met him?'

'Never had the pleasure,' Mackay said, making it clear that it would have been anything but a pleasure. 'But his reputation as a scourge of our religionists is all we need to know. He would have been as big a persecutor of Protestants in this kingdom as the king of France in his if he had had his way.'

'He was prepared to discuss terms last year but now he's become more intransigent when they're in a weaker position,' Ginckel said with an air of wonder. 'I don't understand it.'

Mackay shrugged. You couldn't expect popery to make sense in his view; it was just a collection of corruptions and irrational superstitions.

'It's a pity we have nobody in the camp at present who knows him well,' Ginckel mused. 'My lord Marlborough is on the continent again. He and his lady might be able to throw some light on what the Tyrconnells are thinking.'

'You think my lady Marlborough is in contact with my lady Tyrconnell?' Mackay asked in a shocked tone.

'They are sisters.'

'Yes, but they hardly share secrets of state.'

Ginckel shrugged. To him this campaign was really a civil war between people -- English, Irish and Scottish -- who were all somehow related or had known one another for years. Like the former king, James, whose mistress and mother of his bastards was Marlborough's sister and the kings themselves, all related in one way or another.

'This is idle talk.' He stood up from behind his desk, took a sheet of paper and held it out to Mackay. 'Mundane matters. Have somebody copy this, send it to the sutlers and post it around the camp.'

The proclamation set maximum prices for drink and food in an attempt to stop a rise in prices which was leading to grumbling among the ranks. Ale was to be sold at between fourpence and sixpence a quart, depending on how far it had come: that from Dublin and Wicklow was the most expensive, the more local the brew the cheaper. Claret was to cost no more than two shillings and sixpence a quart and brandy three shillings. White bread was limited to three pence a pound weight, brown bread to two pence.

'Perhaps it would be better to let the liquor prices rise,' Mackay suggested, knowing there was no use proposing his ideal solution of a total ban. 'It would lead to less drunkenness.'

'And more thieving,' Ginckel replied. 'We have to put a stop to that and the sutlers profiteering too much. It's not good for the men's spirit.'

The other part of the document warned sutlers against buying cattle from officers and soldiers who had seized them on raids or patrols. Any sutler found doing so would be prosecuted for dealing in stolen goods. And any soldier who reported such activity would receive half the sold cattle as a reward.

An aide pulled back the tent flap and told Ginckel, 'The trumpet's coming back from Limerick, my lord.'

Ginckel stood up as if this was a significant development. 'Inform my lord Ruvigny immediately,' he ordered, as he strode outside.

Mackay followed him, wondering why this trumpeter was so important. They watched as the rider came up the hill and Ruvigny hurried over. Is the general in negotiation with the enemy again? Mackay wondered, or is Ruvigny dealing directly with the French papists?

The young messenger brought his horse to a halt, slid from its back and bowed. 'There is no reply,' he stuttered with nerves.

'No reply?' Ginckel remonstrated.

'The secret letter,' Ruvigny interrupted. 'What happened to the secret letter?' Did they find it?

The trumpeter told them how Sarsfield had threatened to hang him if he didn't hand it over. 'I had to give it to him,' he said in a quiet voice, his head lowered, expecting punishment.

Ruvigny clapped his hands with a broad smile. Mackay looked on, confused by Ruvigny's response.

'What did Sarsfield say?' Ginckel demanded.

'Nothing, my lord.' The boy kept his eyes lowered. 'The Frenchman said they should hang Colonel Luttrell immediately.'

Ruvigny gave a short laugh of delight. 'Which Frenchman?'

'I don't know, my lord.'

'Describe him.'

The messenger did so. '*Le marquis d'Usson*,' Ruvigny nodded. 'And who else was there?'

The messenger described Tyrconnell and another officer whom they couldn't identify from the youth's vague outline.

'My lord Tyrconnell said they would have a court martial,' the messenger added.

Ruvigny clapped his hands again and gave a barking laugh. *'Magnifique!'*

Ginckel allowed himself a smile but did not seem as enthused by the story as Ruvigny. The messenger kept his hands clasped tightly together, trying to stop his body from shaking, still expecting punishment. Ginckel seemed to notice his distress for the first time and said, 'You did well.'

The youth looked up in surprise and was ushered away by one of the general's aides.

'What's all this about?' Mackay asked. 'A court martial for Colonel Luttrell?'

'In a minute,' Ginckel replied, summoning an aide with a raised finger. 'Send them back a message,' he instructed him. 'Tell them I will execute prisoners of the same rank if they hang anyone who is in discussion with us about their Majesties' most generous terms.'

'We can't have them hanging people who want to talk to us,' he added to Mackay as he went back into his tent.

Mackay turned to Ruvigny. 'What was all that about?' he inquired again.

Ruvigny gave him a broad smile and a wink. 'We have played a little trick on them,' he said.

'What?' Mackay demanded as Ruvigny walked away.

Ruvigny told him. 'I think it is working,' he concluded with a delighted laugh.

Sarsfield

Colonel Nicholas Purcell came out of King John's Castle, asking everyone he met if they had seen Sarsfield. No one had. He asked the guard at Thomond Gate but Sarsfield had not ridden out of the town to the cavalry camp at Cratloe since they had come on duty at dawn. Purcell went back through the English Town, checking at the mayor's house, the Exchange, the tholsel, the harbour, but no one knew where Sarsfield was.

He crossed into Irish Town and asked at East Watergate but Sarsfield hadn't left through there either. But someone on John's Street said he had seen the general walking towards the Citadel earlier. There, he was told that Sarsfield had been and gone but no one knew where.

'Is it urgent?' General Wauchope asked him.

Purcell looked at him as if that was too ridiculous a question to require an answer. Of course it was urgent. Luttrell was facing a court martial for his life that morning and Sarsfield had disappeared.

'What's the matter?' Wauchope added.

'I must talk to him.'

As he left, a cornet who had overheard the exchange said, 'He's at the Black Battery.'

Purcell climbed the stone steps to the rampart and saw Sarsfield standing at the battery, the eastern corner of the town's defences and the farthest point within the city walls from King John's Castle where Luttrell was incarcerated. He couldn't have put a greater physical distance between himself and Luttrell and still remain within the walls. Standing stock still, almost posing, his hand on the hilt of his sword, the plume of his hat nodding forward in the westerly breeze, he looked out at the surrounding land as if he was willing the enemy to appear at any moment.

Sarsfield gave no indication of being aware of Purcell's presence as the colonel went up to him and stood beside him in silence. 'Henry wants to talk to you,' Purcell said.

Sarsfield did not respond.

'Please,' Purcell added. 'He can explain what happened. He's not a traitor. He met one of their officers, a French renegade called Saint-Sebastian, who asked him why we couldn't end this war, seeing how devastated the country was and how much blood had been shed. And Henry asked him if General Ginckel really had full powers to reach a settlement or was it up to their lords justices. The enemy officer said he thought the general had the power but he would let him know for sure. That's what the message was about.'

Sarsfield gave no indication that he had heard him.

'It was polite talk,' Purcell pleaded. 'That is all. Nothing more. Henry's not a traitor. You know that.'

Sarsfield turned to him. 'Did you know about it?'

'Me? No.'

'So he betrayed you too.'

'No, he didn't,' Purcell said, shocked at the idea. 'He never expected anything to come of it. It was a casual conversation, which has been exaggerated out of all proportion.'

'No, it wasn't,' Sarsfield retorted. 'That's not how the enemy saw it. And that's clearly not how it was.'

Purcell closed his eyes, wishing he had Luttrell's persuasive powers. 'You know Henry,' he said; 'he will talk to anybody about anything. That's what he does. He loves bargaining.'

'So he was bargaining,' Sarsfield said with satisfaction. 'Negotiating.'

Purcell shook his head in frustration at having his words twisted. 'No, he wasn't. He was asked a question, answered with another one. He never expected a reply and wasn't waiting for one.'

Sarsfield shook his head and walked away.

'So you're going to let Lying Dick hang him today,' Purcell shouted at his back, his voice rising in anger and bitterness. 'He's packed the court martial with his bastard and his men. Tyrconnell is getting his own back on you now by hanging Henry. And you're going to let him.'

Sarsfield turned around. 'He shouldn't have consorted with the enemy, especially at a time like this.'

'The heretics will hang some of our prisoners too if Henry is hanged.'

'That's their concern.'

'You really think he should hang?' Purcell's voice rose in disbelief. 'He who has always looked out for you? Who has worked tirelessly in your cause? Your best friend?'

Sarsfield shook his head, a short, sharp movement, his face lined with anguish.

'At least go to the court martial,' Purcell pleaded. 'Show him some support. And let Lying Dick know you're watching him.'

Sarsfield turned away again and disappeared down the steps.

'Who sent him off to meet the enemy escort anyway?' Purcell called after him, a final rhetorical thrust but Sarsfield was gone.

Purcell leaned his arms on the battlements and his shoulders slumped in defeat.

***

315

Sarsfield summoned a squadron of cavalry and led them out of St John's Gate. They headed south eastwards at a canter, his officers glancing at one another, wondering at the pace and where they were going. Was he going back to Ballyneety where he had destroyed the cannons the previous year? They all knew the court martial was taking place back in the city but nobody mentioned it, still trying to come to terms with the shock of the news. The silence was broken only by the jangling of harnesses, the thud of hooves, and the breathing of horses.

The day was sunny and warm, a parting reminder of the dying summer. The countryside was green, the trees heavy with foliage, and they splashed through hollows where the rain of the previous days was slow to seep away. They threaded their way with care through an oak wood, bending down under the low branches, and then speeded up again.

After a couple of miles Sarsfield told his trumpeter to sound a walk and left wheel and their horses, as attuned to the signals as the riders, turned northwards without human direction. Sarsfield rode alone at the head of the column, accompanied only by his young companion, paying little attention to where they were and where they were going. Purcell's accusations had hurt but not as much as Luttrell's betrayal of their friendship and of their cause. How can I see it any other way? he asked himself. Luttrell had kept his dealing with the enemy secret. Not just from me but from Purcell too, which suggested that he wasn't just bargaining as Purcell had put it. He was thinking of abandoning the cause.

But that was difficult to believe too. Luttrell had fought as hard as anyone in this war. Had been as bitterly opposed as himself to Tyrconnell's desire to make peace the year before. Had gone to Paris to argue against that policy, narrowly avoided imprisonment in the Bastille for his efforts.

Why didn't he tell me, Sarsfield wondered again. There was only one answer to that: because he was looking out for himself, thinking of changing sides.

Luttrell's actions had left Sarsfield in a difficult position. Many assumed that, as usual, Luttrell was acting on his behalf and that therefore he, Sarsfield, was in favour of negotiations and lying about his intentions to defend the city. And perhaps that both he and Tyrconnell had come to a secret agreement to capitulate. He was conscious of receiving suspicious glances already since word of Luttrell's treachery spread.

'My lord!' the frightened young voice of his trumpeter broke through his thoughts.

He looked up and saw they were moving towards a party of enemy horsemen on a rise about three hundred yards away. His first instinct was to sound the charge but he reined in his horse to a standstill instead and beckoned forward a captain behind him.

'How many?' Sarsfield asked him, scanning the hillside and the surrounding countryside. There was nobody else in sight but they were on low ground, small hills and woods dotted around them. He realized he had been moving towards the enemy for a while without noticing them, prompting the trumpeter's evident alarm.

'Less than a squadron,' the captain said. 'Should we engage them?'

Yes, Sarsfield thought. What he wanted now more than anything was action, a swift engagement where instinct and survival would take over and he wouldn't need to think, to clarify the confusion of thoughts and emotions created by Luttrell's betrayal. But it was risky. 'What do you think?' he asked.

The captain hesitated, unused to being asked a tactical question by a general. 'There might be more of them, my lord,' he said, voicing a fear that he hoped would not be held against him. 'Beyond the hill.'

The shadow of a cloud drifted across the open ground between the two patrols. Neither made a move.

Yes, Sarsfield agreed silently, there could well be more of them -- an ambush. He ordered a left wheel and they moved westwards at a walk. After a moment the enemy patrol followed suit, turning right and tracking them. They kept their distance for almost a mile, watching each other, neither making an aggressive move. The enemy's hill gradually eased down to level ground and then another wood came between them and they lost sight of each other. When they had passed the trees there was no longer any sign of the enemy.

We should have attacked, Sarsfield thought. They didn't have any reserves. Am I losing my nerve?

The enemy did not reappear and they carried on, stopping after midday on a small hill to eat cold meat and bread and drink wine and ale. The afternoon wore on and they criss-crossed the deserted land. Corn was ripening in makeshift fields marked out by fences of sticks but there were no inhabitants to be seen: they had gone to the higher hills with any animals they still had. Those without animals to protect had made their way to Irish Town, pleading to be admitted through the closed gates.

It was evident by now to most of the squadron that the purpose of this foray was simply to allow Sarsfield to remain out of the city while Henry Luttrell's court martial and execution took place. Eventually, in the late afternoon, Sarsfield turned them for home and they headed towards the lowering sun. The wind had died and the shadows were lengthening under a blue sky fringed to the west by a line of white cloud waiting to smother the sun before it reached the horizon.

Wauchope emerged from the Citadel as they entered through St John's Gate. 'Good news,' he said, his lean face aglow. 'He's not guilty.'

'Not guilty?' Sarsfield's horse shied backwards from Wauchope as if it, too, was astonished by the news.

'Aye. My lord Tyrconnell's own men decided it wasn't a hanging matter. They accepted Henry's account of what happened.'

Sarsfield dismounted, his feelings a jumble. How could this

be? Luttrell was dealing with the enemy and was clearly guilty. But he was relieved too that he didn't have to cope with Luttrell's death. The hurt of his betrayal and the light it cast on himself was still there, still dominant.

'Where is he now?' he asked as he handed his reins to an aide.

'Ah, there's the rub,' Wauchope replied. 'Tyrconnell won't release him. He's still locked up in the Castle. You had better talk to him.'

'To whom?'

'His grace. Get him to release Luttrell.'

Sarsfield said nothing. Should he talk to Luttrell too? Hear his excuses from his own lips? Let him talk his way out of the difficulties he had created? As he had heard him talk his way out of so many other situations?

'There is no reason to keep him locked up if he's not guilty,' Wauchope added, giving him an odd look, wondering why he was being obtuse.

'The enemy's coming close,' Sarsfield said. 'We encountered an advance party.'

He strode away, down John's Street. Wauchope watched him go, confused by his evident lack of delight at the good news.

Word of Luttrell's unexpected reprieve had spread and Sarsfield was greeted by smiling faces as he went through Irish Town and across the bridge into English Town. Most presumed he was happy about the news: few took note of his stony expression. He went up Mary Street and Nicholas Street to King John's Castle and sought out Tyrconnell in one of the offices he used in the decaying building.

'He talked his way off the gallows,' Tyrconnell said, barely disguising his disgust, as soon as Sarsfield entered.

'What happened?'

'He spun a tale about meeting this enemy officer when he took over the escort for General d'Usson at Sixmilebridge. He convinced a majority of the court martial panel that there wasn't enough evidence against him. But,' he pointed a warning finger at Sarsfield, 'I will not release him.'

'I haven't asked you to.'

Tyrconnell showed no surprise but gave Sarsfield a more searching look and nodded a couple of times. 'He's a traitor,' he said in a calmer voice. 'People say he sold the pass at Aughrim. That he let the enemy through.'

Sarsfield dismissed the charge with a wave of his hand, feeling his anger rise at what he saw as one of Tyrconnell's typical tricks. 'If that's why you're holding him, you should detain your friend Sheldon too,' he retorted. '*He* was in command on that wing.'

Tyrconnell made a soothing motion with his left hand, his lace cuff fluttering. 'There's no point talking about the "could have been's and the should have been's." That's for coffee house generals and pot valiant soldiers.'

Sarsfield almost laughed at his about-turn but Tyrconnell fixed him with a stare as he leaned on his desk to help himself raise his bulk from the chair. 'We . . .' he said, breathing heavily as he moved to a side table and poured two glasses of wine, 'we have to play the cards we're dealt.'

He held a glass out to Sarsfield like a peace offering. Sarsfield hesitated but took it.

'Who knows what happens in men's heads in the heat of battle?' Tyrconnell added, raising his own glass in a toast.

Sarsfield did not reciprocate. Tyrconnell drank some wine and shuffled back to his desk again.

'No,' he said, as he eased himself back into his chair. 'That's not why I won't release him. I won't release him because we can't trust him.' He looked up at Sarsfield, daring him to challenge him again. 'Neither of us can after this episode. You even less than me.'

Sarsfield hesitated and sipped at his wine. He shook his head.

Tyrconnell finished his wine, eyeing Sarsfield over the rim of the glass. 'The message they sent to D'Usson about the letter to Luttrell is suspicious,' he said, as if he was making a concession in return for Sarsfield's confirmation that Luttrell had kept him in the dark. 'Clearly they wanted to make sure we found it. They saw an opportunity to discredit him. Sow dissension among us.'

'That's what Luttrell says?'

Tyrconnell raised his shoulders in what might have been a shrug and continued to haul himself out of his chair. He poured himself another glass of wine, ignoring the question.

'We have to remain united,' he said. 'Now more than ever. Which is the point of the pledge.' He settled himself back at his desk. 'We can't allow anyone make private deals with the enemy. Or even appear to. That's why we can't release him.'

Sarsfield held Tyrconnell's stare, noting how he had not so subtly turned 'I will not release him' into 'we can't release him'. But he couldn't argue with Tyrconnell's logic. He put down his unfinished glass on the desk, nodded, and walked out without a word.

Tyrconnell permitted himself a fleeting smile. He had finally lanced the Luttrell boil.

Sarsfield spent the following days out of the city, preferring the open countryside to the claustrophobia of the crowded streets where unspoken questions challenged him in every look. He rode up and down the western bank of the Shannon, checking on its defences, and spending nights at the cavalry camp at Cratloe.

Some troopers were unhappy about Luttrell's treatment after his acquittal, especially those of his own regiment. Why was he still imprisoned if he was innocent? Purcell had stopped talking to Sarsfield, had given up pleading with him and was now pointedly ignoring him when their paths crossed. Others conveyed their disapproval with looks and side-of-the-mouth comments but the subject was closed in Sarsfield's mind: he could no longer trust Luttrell. Tyrconnell was right. They had to make an example of him; they must stick together.

Fears and suspicions built on each other and multiplied by the day as the enemy approached. Mutual distrust of one another's intentions and motives corroded the army's cohesion. Anti-French feeling rose because there was no sign of the promised supplies from Brest. Men disappeared in the night, gone over to the enemy, gone home or gone to the hills and wastelands to take their chances as rapparees.

Charles O'Kelly kept Sarsfield abreast of the depressing news about Balldearg O'Donnell. He had apparently switched sides again at Sligo. 'But it was only a cynical ploy,' O'Kelly said a couple of days later. 'He came back to our side only to pressure the heretics to accede to his demands. And it worked. They've promised him everything he wanted.'

'Forget about him,' Sarsfield advised.

'How can I forget the dishonour he has brought upon a noble family?' O'Kelly retorted.

They were riding southwards along the riverbank, heading back towards Cratloe after visiting Brigadier Robert Clifford's cavalry unit. It was camped near an island in the Shannon where the river looped around a short distance upstream.

'You can't trust Clifford either,' O'Kelly said. 'You should replace him.'

'Just because he wasn't promoted a major general?' Sarsfield asked in a weary voice. Clifford had been hoping, even expecting, to fill one of the vacant generalships left after Aughrim.

O'Kelly answered with another question. 'Is he Irish at all?'

'Yes. He was born here.'

'But he spent a lot of time in England.'

'As did I,' Sarsfield said. 'In the same regiment.'

'That's not the same thing at all,' O'Kelly replied, adding pointedly, 'You have to pick your friends with great care these days. Treachery is on the march all around us.'

Sarsfield kicked his horse into a canter, away from O'Kelly, tired of all the suspicion and the talk of conspiracies. It's the waiting, he told himself; people's nerves are always strained by the waiting. It will be different when the siege is joined. We're well placed to receive them. But he knew in his heart that it was not just the waiting this time. It was also the delayed effects of Athlone, of Aughrim, and the surrender at Galway. Especially of Aughrim.

The daylight was fading and he could pick out the lights of the campfires of Cratloe ahead of him. As he came closer, he realized that something had happened. The camp was in a state of excitement, energised by something unusual. Nobody was preparing for action. Men stood around the fires in animated groups, their faces aglow with more than the heat of flickering flames. A group of officers hurried towards him as he reined in his horse.

'The duke has had a seizure,' said one.

'They say Tyrconnell's been poisoned,' another blurted.

'Where is he?' Sarsfield demanded.

Nobody seemed to know.

'Is he alive?'

'Some say he is but he can't talk,' his first informant said.

Sarsfield spurred on his horse and rode at speed towards Limerick, crossing the drawbridge into English Town over the dark river. A group was gathered in silence outside Tyrconnell's quarters in the bishop's former house across from the castle.

Sarsfield dismounted and pushed his way through. Inside, the Archbishop of Armagh, Dominick Maguire, was disappearing up the stairs, presumably to Tyrconnell's bedroom. The French generals D'Usson and Tessé were waiting in a room off the hallway, along with Wauchope and the other generals.

'D'Usson will tell you what happened,' Wauchope said in a low voice in reply to Sarsfield's unspoken query. 'They had dinner together.'

'He was in very good humour,' d'Usson told Sarsfield with the air of a man retelling a story that had already become repetitious. 'No indication of any problems. He was telling me about his younger exploits, of trying to assassinate Oliver Cromwell. How he held his nerve when he was interrogated by the tyrant himself in the Tower of London. And he was very positive about the future. That we will push back the prince of Orange next year.'

'Is he still alive?' Sarsfield asked impatiently, noting D'Usson's use of the past tense.

'*Mais oui*,' D'Usson replied in surprise. 'The surgeon is with him.'

And the archbishop, Sarsfield thought. Which was not a good sign.

They stood around, waiting, each immersed in private speculation about what Tyrconnell's death would mean, no one voicing his thoughts aloud. The surgeon came downstairs eventually, a lugubrious-looking man carrying his bag of implements, vials and poultices. 'He's very feeble,' he said, shaking his head. 'Very, very feeble.'

The city seemed to hold its breath over the next days as Tyrconnell hovered between life and death. It was awash with rumours and fears for the future. The undoubted leader of Catholic Ireland since the King had ascended the throne six years earlier was in danger of departing this life at a critical time and leaving the country to an uncertain fate. His opponents were in as much disarray as his friends were distraught.

The story was repeated and reinterpreted over and over. Tyrconnell had drunk a lot of ratafia cordial with D'Usson at their last dinner. Had someone dropped poison into the crushed apricot stones before they were added to the brandy? If so, who? Was it the French because they didn't want to fight on as Tyrconnell wanted? Or was it Sarsfield, in retaliation for the court martial and Luttrell's trial? Or one of Luttrell's friends in the army? Or because Tyrconnell was secretly negotiating with the rebels? Or a rebel spy who had managed to infiltrate D'Usson's quarters?

Everyone had a theory of what had happened and what it meant for the future. On the second day after his dinner with D'Usson, a Wednesday, Tyrconnell was given the last sacraments by the archbishop. Word went around that he had put his worldly affairs in order. On the Thursday he lapsed into unconsciousness. On Friday, August 14th, at two in the afternoon, he died.

The bell of St Mary's Cathedral, usually rung only at the start and the end of the day, tolled the news around the city with single peals interspersed with silences. Sarsfield was in his quarters in the tower house on Mary Street when he heard it, waiting to escort Honor and her maid to the French ship in the harbour. She stopped, a worried look on her young face, and asked, 'What does it mean?'

'Tyrconnell's dead.'

'I mean what does that mean?'

'We'll have to wait and see.' But Sarsfield knew that he was now the leader of Catholic Ireland, no longer the 'real' leader of just the army. The French generals outranked him in name only; they could do nothing without his approval. Neither could anyone else. Nobody on the civilian side of the administration had anything approaching Tyrconnell's authority.

He walked with Honor down the hill and along by the Abbey River to the harbour, the bell from St Mary's tolling all the time as if their progress was a funeral march. Her maid walked behind them with two servants carrying Honor's travelling trunk. The few people on the streets bowed their heads as they passed and it occurred to Sarsfield that this was unfortunate timing. That he should be seen sending his wife to safety in France at such an uncertain moment. But it couldn't be helped; the wind had come around, the tide was about to turn, the ships had to leave now.

D'Usson was at the quay, talking to the commander of the small flotilla. 'They can't sail now,' he said to Sarsfield. 'They'll have to wait.'

The commander shrugged. 'But the wind won't wait.'

'It will have to,' D'Usson snapped. 'You'll sail when I order you to.' He told the commander, stepping away and bringing Sarsfield with him. 'We have to wait to report to Versailles and Saint-Germain on the viceroy's death,' he explained. 'We have to open your King's commission. Decide what we do now.'

Sarsfield nodded: he could see the point of waiting. It was surely a good idea to confirm the plans for resisting the coming siege and to be able to report to Paris on the transition to the post-Tyrconnell era.

He explained the delay to Honor and her servants and sent them back home again. It was just as well, he thought, as he watched them retrace their steps, that she was not seen to be leaving within hours of Tyrconnell's death. Then he joined d'Usson to walk up the hill to King John's Castle where the attorney general was about to open the King's sealed instructions for the continuation of power in the event of his viceroy's death.

'You know, if the worst happens, you can bring the army to France,' d'Usson said. 'Rather than accept defeat. Rather than surrender.'

'We're not going to surrender or be defeated,' Sarsfield retorted, mentally cursing Luttrell again, blaming him for creating doubts about the future. Doubts that had now spread to the French generals. 'We're in a strong position, much stronger than last year. You know that.'

'Yes, yes,' d'Usson nodded. 'The defences will hold. But will the army?'

'Yes, it will. If your king fulfils his promises.'

'His Majesty always abides by his word,' d'Usson sniffed, ending the discussion.

***

The civil leaders were gathered in the castle, their faces as sombre as their mourning clothes. The attorney general, Sir Richard Nagle, who had been Tyrconnell's adviser throughout his years in control, looked around as Sarsfield and d'Usson entered. 'We are all here now,' he said, eager to get on with the formalities. Tessé and the other generals were already in the room.

There was silence while Nagle opened a carved box with a key and took out a sealed scroll. He broke the seal with an ornamental dagger and a look of surprise crossed his face. He took a deep breath and said, 'His Majesty has appointed three lord justices to represent him in his kingdom of Ireland. My lord Gawsworth, Francis Plowden, and myself.' There was a spattering of applause and handshakes for Gawsworth, the lord chancellor, and Plowden, the commissioner of revenue, who had recently returned from France. Nagle himself looked awestruck, surprised at his elevation. He waited for silence and added, from the scroll, 'And His Majesty appoints Lieutenant General the Marquis d'Usson commander of his forces in Ireland.'

There was another spattering of polite applause and Sarsfield gave d'Usson a short bow, acknowledging his promotion but they both knew it was a mere formality, lacking in substance.

'The King knows nothing of what is really happening here,' Wauchope said under his breath to Sarsfield as they left the castle.

Sarsfield didn't disagree. He knew, as everyone knew, that he was now in charge.

Tyrconnell's funeral took place late on the Sunday night in St Mary's Cathedral. It was dark and windy outside. Draughts blew through the high arches of the cathedral's interior and sent the shadows cast by the flickering candles in constant motion across the stone walls, like a restless crowd of silhouetted onlookers.

Archbishop Maguire celebrated the requiem Mass, assisted by bishops and priests, all draped in heavy black vestments edged with gold braid. The cathedral was full, the new lords justices in the front row with the French generals: the majors general, Irish, English and Scottish, in the row behind them. Tyrconnell's son Mark, his face still pale from his wounds, held himself stiffly in the front row on the other side of the centre aisle alongside the viceroy's daughter Charlotte, who was shrouded in black.

The Latin chant of the celebrants and a choir of monks reverberated off the stone walls, mingling with the smell of melting wax from the scores of candles on the altar and the chandeliers. The choir sang the *Dies Irae*, predicting the day of wrath when heaven and earth would end in ashes, the chilling words rising and falling in their beautiful chant. In moments of silence, the wind whistled through gaps in the doors and windows and banged the loose boards of a confessional.

'The day of judgement,' the archbishop intoned from the high pulpit, 'has come for the duke of Tyrconnell. As it will for us all. His worldly treasures are of no use to him now. As ours will be of no use to us. He cannot hide from God's judgement behind his possessions. Or plead the high opinion of other men of his character. Or dissemble with fine words and brilliant argument. There is no avoiding the righteousness of God's judgement.'

Sarsfield's attention wandered as the archbishop sketched a picture of the last judgement familiar to him from many funerals, the joy of the saved, the terror of the damned, the eternity of Hell's fires, the bliss of everlasting happiness. There had been so many deaths -- two generals, dozens of colonels, hundreds of lower officers, thousands of men – in the ten weeks since the French generals had arrived. And now the day of temporal, and perhaps divine, judgement was approaching for them all.

It was clear to Sarsfield what needed to be done: how to do it was a different matter. They needed to be united, confident of success, and in good spirits. But they were far from any of these things. The French had lost their authority. The lords justices had little or none. Two of them were Englishmen, more or less. The third, Nagle, was a bureaucrat at heart, an able adviser but not a leader. Nobody had the standing of Tyrconnell, who had restored his co-religionists to power, and around whom everything had revolved, whether you were for him or against him.

And I am expected to step into his shoes? Sarsfield thought. With the French distrusting us and we distrusting them. With the old Gaelic families trusting no one. With the old English wary of everyone. With the English and Scottish Jacobites doubting our allegiance to the King. And with Luttrell deserting me when I need him most. And not just deserting me but casting doubt over my resolve. What to do with him?

For the first time he was aware of the loneliness of power. Of all the fates resting on his shoulders and on his alone.

'God has punished us for our sins,' the archbishop was saying. 'For our lack of devotion. For the evil of our ways. He has allowed our enemies to prevail as a warning. For straying from the path of truth and righteousness, for putting our faith in our own strength rather than in Him, for taking pleasure in the carnal, rather than looking after our souls, for being distracted by the ways of the flesh from His word. But,' he paused for effect, raising a halting hand, 'but He will not allow His enemies, our enemies, to be victorious. He will not allow His people to be vanquished. He has given us a warning, time to repent our sins, an opportunity to change our ways. And He will come to our aid now. He will lead us to victory if we do His will.'

The interment took place after the Mass in a side chapel where a vault had been opened in the thick outer wall of the cathedral. The prayers of the burial rite were mixed with the sprinkling of holy water and the clicking of a thurible as it spread the heavy scent of incense around them. They waited in silence while the vault was closed up again, the only sound the scraping of masons' tools as they put stones in position.

Then they filed out into the dark of the city, everyone alone with their thoughts.

Mackay

G inkel pursed his lips and said in a doubtful tone, 'I'm not
so sure.'

Thomas Coningsby, the lord justice, looked around
the circle of military faces staring back at him in the half-light of
the tent, not caring that they were treating him with the usual
scepticism of soldiers for courtiers. 'Tyrconnell's death is the end
of them,' Coningsby repeated slowly, as if they needed educating.
'They can't survive it. He's the only one who could hold together
the Os and Macs, the English degenerates and the French.
Without him they'll be at each other's throats.'

'I thought they were at each other's throats with him,' Ruvigny
responded, earning a few laughs.

They really are stupid, Coningsby thought. They think the
world is all about sieges and swords, understanding little or
nothing about power. Of how Tyrconnell had kept all the papists
together by absorbing their disputes, advancing and withdrawing
when necessary, and steering them along the path he favoured.
Which was the path of popery, with the aim of recovering the
three kingdoms for the Stuarts and overturning the Revolution.
He had been all too successful and now that he was gone the

situation was changed.

'They say he was poisoned,' someone remarked.

'I hope he was,' Coningsby replied with a mirthless smile. 'And I hope even more that they believe he was, whether it is true or not.'

'What about General Sarsfield?' Mackay asked.

'What about him?'

'It appears he's effectively in command now, if what the deserters say about the Irish attitude to the French is true.'

'He's merely a cavalry officer,' Coningsby shrugged, staring at Ginckel, daring him to challenge the dismissive statement. He could hear Ruvigny's intake of breath but the Frenchman restrained himself from coming to the defence of cavalry officers.

'All right.' Ginckel raised his palms to bring this pointless discussion to an end. 'We shall advance on Limerick in the morning as planned. We will do it quietly at first light. No drums.'

'Yes,' Coningsby nodded with approval. 'Let's hurry up and get this campaign over. The King and Queen are getting impatient.'

Coningsby turned and left the tent, aware that he had insulted most if not all of them. But they were testing his patience. Ginckel was too cautious by far but he, Coningsby, couldn't complain about him too vociferously to London or the King. The Dutch tended to stick together and all the continental soldiers considered themselves to be superior to the English. Which would be infuriating enough if they had reason for their viewpoint but was even more infuriating considering their slow progress against an army of bogtrotters. All they were doing here was wasting time and, more importantly, money.

'Such impertinence!' Ruvigny exploded into a torrent of outraged French as soon as Coningsby was out of earshot, prompting an outbreak of laughter which lightened the atmosphere in the tent.

'Is it true what they say?' Württemberg asked in a

disingenuous tone. 'That the lord justice has been helping himself to the army's funds?'

'That's a matter for another day,' Ginckel said, confirming the rumours. 'His Majesty is well aware of the situation.'

'I hope he will receive his pound of flesh,' Talmash muttered. 'The lord justice can spare it.'

They were ready to move before dawn, the army divided into two columns half a mile apart. Each was led by an advance guard of a thousand infantry, six hundred cavalry, three hundred dragoons, and two hundred grenadiers whose job was to clear any enemy positions or ambushes from their path. They met with little resistance, scouting parties falling back before them, lightly manned outposts firing shots and withdrawing without any serious engagement.

Ginckel and Mackay followed the advance guards at the head of the left-hand column of the main body. The day was bright and dry, a pleasant breeze from the south-west clearing the clouds from the tops of the Silvermines, opening up the smooth hills to visibility after all the mist. But the land was still soggy and progress was slow. They marched in silence, as the general had ordered, no drums beating the time, although their advance would be no surprise to the enemy.

'What do the latest deserters say?' Mackay asked about the half-dozen papist dragoons who had turned up at their camp overnight.

'The usual,' Ginckel grunted. He seemed out of sorts this morning, not like a confident general eager for the coming conflict; more like a man carrying out a reluctant duty. 'What we want to hear. That the Jacobites are in a state of confusion.'

'Maybe it's the truth.' Mackay glanced at him, hoping that his dour Dutch face wouldn't undermine the confidence of the men. 'They can't be in good shape after all that's happened.'

A flurry of musket shots ahead made them pause and the column behind halted. They couldn't see anything. The wind carried the sound of a few further scattered shots and then the advance column began to move forward again.

'You heard the lord justice last night,' Ginckel said as if he was replying to Mackay's earlier remark. 'Our masters think our work here is already done.'

'The lord justice should know better.'

'These people think they can make things happen just by willing them, by making speeches. With strokes of their pens.

'They don't appreciate the risks. Maybe you should reconsider the decision to invest the town.'

Ginckel gave him a sharp look. 'We've been through all that.'

They rode on in silence. Mackay realized that Ginckel's heart wasn't in the plan to try and take Limerick. Which didn't surprise him: it was certainly contrary to Ginckel's usual caution. It was risky to try to force an entry when the number of attackers was scarcely greater than the number of defenders, even if those defenders were badly armed and their spirits were low. A failed attack would revive their confidence and set back the successful conclusion of the entire campaign. Ginckel had to know in his heart that it made more sense, as he, Mackay, had argued, to simply surround and starve the city. Let the hopelessness of the papists' situation sink ever deeper into their thoughts.

It was afternoon before they came within sight of the city and began to spread out in an encircling line around the Irish Town, the right flank branching off towards the Shannon above the town, the left continuing on towards the river below the town. Ginckel established his headquarters to the south-west, well back from cannon range. He spread out his maps on the table in his tent and directed the first moves in the siege, the enemy outposts to be seized before establishing the lines of circumvallation, the trenches that would seal off the town and protect the besiegers from sallies by the defenders.

Mackay was ordered to seize an old fort from the Cromwellian siege of the town forty years earlier, strategically placed beside Singland Hill which overlooked the city. He didn't know how strong the garrison was, or how much resistance they were likely to mount but he took no chances. He ordered up a regiment of infantry, reinforced by horsemen, and they approached the fort slowly in a line across the rising ground. A spattering of musket fire greeted them when they came within range. They charged forward and the firing died out. The grenadiers swarmed into the earthen fort and it was empty, its defenders already falling back to another defensive position closer to the town.

Mackay rode up to the top of Singland Hill and got his first proper view of the city, laid out in the hollow before the low line of the hills of Clare on the far side of the Shannon. The river wasn't visible from here but he knew from the maps that it was there, curling around the English Town, a channel they called the Abbey River turning it into the King's Island, before stretching off towards the distant ocean. The square tower of St Mary's Cathedral stood up from the jumble of buildings on the island, old tower houses protruding like teeth among the slated roofs. Closer, the walls of the Irish Town appeared deceptively squat, an impression helped by the earthen glacis banked up against them.

The shadow of a cloud passed over the town and crossed the new no-man's land between it and Mackay's vantage point. Ginckel rode up beside him and surveyed the scene through his telescope. He gave a heavy sigh as he handed the glass to Mackay. 'They've made it more difficult,' he said. 'Even more difficult than last year.'

Through the telescope Mackay could see the signs of the new works, the new stones unweathered in the walls and the earthen bulwarks still raw before the lower reaches. It would take a lot of time and ordnance to break them down, probably more than they had of either. And the walls were too thick to try and collapse them by tunnelling underneath.

'That's where we broke through the outer wall last year,' Ginckel said, pointing to the eastern side of the wall around from St John's Gate but they repulsed our attack with an unexpected ferocity.'

Mackay looked again at the area Ginckel had mentioned. It appeared to be impregnable.

'We'll have to find another point of attack,' Ginckel added. He gestured to the land between them and the Irish Town where the sun glistened on scattered pools of water. 'We can't even get the siege guns down there this time. They'd just sink into the mire.'

He wheeled his horse around to head back towards his headquarters as if he had already abandoned the siege as an impossible task. Mackay, taken aback, followed suit a moment later, spurring his horse to catch up with the general.

'We can't let the enemy suspect our difficulties,' he said, still worried by Ginckel's lack of enthusiasm, even the tone of defeatism.

'Of course not,' Ginckel said. 'We'll get the mortars into position first on that hill and rain down fire on them. Make clear our intent to lay waste the city.'

By the next morning's dawn, the mortars and field guns were in position on Singland Hill, sending a steady stream of explosive carcasses and small cannonballs over the walls into the Irish Town. The sounds of the explosions in the city were covered by new blasts from the mortars and guns. Thin plumes of smoke began to rise from among the buildings, dispersed quickly by the warm breeze.

Mackay watched from the earthen rampart of the fort, now named after him, by Singland Hill, thinking that the onslaught looked puny from this distance, although he knew that it was otherwise on the receiving end. But it would not help them directly to take the city: it was designed solely to terrorise the inhabitants, to undermine the will of the defenders to continue their resistance.

Away to his left he could see sappers preparing a battery near the bank of the river to target Thomond bridge, the city's only supply line from the land beyond the Shannon. If they could break that, they would divide the papists' cavalry in the countryside from their infantry inside the walls and cut off the city's easy access to food. To his right, another group of workmen and artillery men were manhandling guns into positions from which they could fire across the river at the English Town on the King's Island.

Talmash climbed up to him, the pipe drooping in his mouth making him breathe heavily as he inhaled tobacco smoke. He took the pipe from his mouth, sniffed at the acrid air, and cast an eye over the scene before them.

'So he's decided not to batter down those walls,' he said, pointing the stem of the pipe at the Irish Town. 'A mistake.'

'I don't think so,' Mackay retorted. 'It would take longer than we have.'

'The one thing we've learned in this campaign is that they'll buckle under a direct assault. Run straight at them and they'll fold.'

'They didn't at Aughrim.'

'They did at Athlone.'

Talmash turned his attention to the party preparing the siege guns to attack the English Town on the island. 'That's better,' he said. 'That'll take down the wall, open up the city.'

'We'll still have to cross the river. Cover a lot of open ground to attack a breach.'

Talmash gave Mackay a stern look. 'This is no time for defeatism.'

'That's realism, not defeatism,' Mackay said. 'We can't afford any false steps that give the papists hope now.'

'They've no hope,' Talmash shrugged. He gave a short laugh.

'They're in such a state, they're hanging each other as spies.'

'What do you mean?'

'One of our men who went into the city to distribute proclamations saw them hang one of their own they found with a leaflet. They thought he was distributing them.'

From the town a cloud of leaden-coloured smoke began to billow upwards as a fire took hold. As if in response, there was a flash from a cannon on the walls by St John's Gate but the shot fell short with a splatter at the bottom of their hill.

'One determined assault,' Talmash said as he turned away. 'That'll do it.'

'Good news,' Ginckel told his assembled generals. 'Captain Cole has got his ships from Galway into the estuary at last.'

'That'll decide it,' Württemberg exclaimed. 'No more help from France.'

'I hope not,' Ginckel nodded. 'Meanwhile, we've taken all the forts and castles on this side of the river. They have all surrendered.'

'What are we doing with the prisoners?' Ruvigny asked.

'Sending them off to the Continent to fight the Turks,' Ginckel said. He looked around and asked if there was anything else to discuss.

'Yes,' Mackay said, taking the opportunity to raise some information he had received from one of the northern Irish officers who now saw him as their champion. 'I've been told that the papists are holding some Protestants prisoners on an island in the river. Is that true?'

'Yes.' Ginckel looked to one of his aides, who nodded. 'Information from a deserter. Some of the city's leading Protestants are on the island, he said.'

'Shouldn't we release them?' Mackay asked.

'Yes, we will. In due course.'

337

'Why not now?' Mackay insisted, looking around the table for support. Württemberg gave him a 'why not?' shrug but nobody offered further encouragement.

Ginckel noted the consensus view that it was not a priority but said to Mackay, 'Look into it.'

As the meeting broke up Ginckel called over his aide and told him to bring the deserter to Mackay. 'Don't spend too much time on it,' he warned Mackay.

'It will be good for the men's enthusiasm,' Mackay suggested.

Ginckel shrugged, knowing what he meant, that it would encourage the Irish in their ranks but it would make little or no difference to the rest. 'Just remember, our task is to win this campaign, not settle all the affairs of this country.'

'I'm well aware of the larger canvas,' Mackay replied.

'We don't want to become involved in local rows,' Ginckel added as he sank into his chair and picked a sheet of paper from his desk. 'Trouble in Galway already,' he said with a sigh, holding up the paper. 'The Protestants there want the papist gentlemen to be disarmed. Our governor has agreed.'

'Breaking the terms of surrender?'

Ginckel let the sheet of paper drop to his desk. 'He says he has no choice. Otherwise, there will be trouble.'

'What did you tell him?'

'To consult the lord justices.'

Mackay shook his head in disapproval. 'That's the problem with offering the papists generous terms. This country won't be settled by half-measures.'

'Our task is to end this campaign with victory as soon as possible. The larger canvas. As you said yourself.'

Mackay bowed and left to see about rescuing the Protestants held captive on one of the river's islands.

Sarsfield

Sarsfield covered his mouth and nose with his hand and hurried through a cloud of smoke coming from the burning thatch of a house on John's Street. Two women were pulling rough furniture and other possessions out of the building and passing them to a group of children to pile on the street. One of the women put out an appealing hand for help as he veered around the heap but he was in a hurry. He passed by a straggle of people carrying bedding tied up into sacks as they crossed Baal's bridge into King's Island. Behind them in the Irish Town another carcass exploded, followed in the silent aftermath by a series of shrieks and screams.

He turned down to the harbour where the last of the convoy was coming in between the piers, its square mainsail holed in several places. Nearby another was anchored to one side of the harbour, black smoke rising from its hold as its crew emptied buckets of water into it. The other ships were already tying up at the quay, two deep in places. Sarsfield threaded his way through the onlookers, disembarking sailors and passengers crowding the quayside, trying to identify the vessel on which Honor had left.

He spotted her at last, sitting on her trunk while her maid

made her way down the gangway carrying a small wooden case. She rose to greet him and he put his arms around her and hugged her for a moment before stepping back and examining her pale face. 'Are you hurt?'

She shook her head and attempted a reassuring smile.

'You're sure?'

'Yes. Our boat wasn't hit.' She pointed at the ship as if to prove it was intact.

The captain was coming down the gangplank. 'She is not hurt, my lord,' he reassured Sarsfield in French.

'*Que s'est-il passé?*'

'We were attacked by English ships near the mouth of the estuary. They sank two of our pinks and scattered some others. I think they landed on the southern coast.'

'How many English ships?'

'About twenty.'

'Are they blockading the estuary?'

The captain swept an arm towards the ships in the harbour. 'Against unarmed pinks, yes,' he said. 'Against our warships, no.'

That was a relief if true, Sarsfield thought. And not just an excessive French belief in their naval superiority.

He accompanied Honor back from the harbour, passing St Mary's Cathedral where the barrel of a small field gun now protruded from the top of its square tower. As they went by, it fired a ball at the enemy sappers who were building a battery on the far bank of the Abbey River.

'The ship with the French general's horse was sunk,' Honor said as the sound of the cannon shot faded. 'And all his possessions lost.'

It seemed to Sarsfield like a long time since Saint-Ruhe had arrived but it was only three months since he had stepped ashore in Ireland at this very spot. 'Were there any passengers on that ship?'

'No.'

'And the sailors?'

'They said they were rescued. Most of them anyway.'

Smoke drifted out of a laneway where a line of cabins was on fire. A body lay on the ground, stepped over by people rushing about with pails of water to stop the flames from engulfing the dwellings.

Sarsfield paused at the door of the lord mayor's house and glanced at Honor's travelling trunk carried by two French sailors. 'Don't unpack too much,' he said. 'The lords justices and the other ladies are across the river in Clare. In a safe place. My lady Dillon has been killed in her house.'

'Which Lady Dillon?'

'The old one,' he said, meaning the recently widowed wife of the viscount killed at Aughrim and mother of the new Lord Dillon, the governor of Galway. 'It's best you move to Clare as well.'

'When?'

'Soon. I'm sorry you had to go through that frightening experience. I should have sent you to France long before now.'

'It wasn't too frightening.' She gave Sarsfield a grateful smile. 'Our ship was near the end of the convoy and we turned back quickly, before we reached the English ones. I didn't see much.'

Sarsfield made his way up John's Street the next morning. It was deserted, most of the buildings abandoned by their occupants, ruins appearing overnight with the randomness of a rash. Smoke rose from burned out houses and another carcass exploded off to his right but he was barely aware of it. In the Citadel Wauchope was leaning over a table reading something. He looked up as Sarsfield entered and pointed to what he had been reading. 'Have you seen this?'

'What is it?'

'It's supposed to be the duke's last testament. A blatant

341

forgery.'

Sarsfield glanced at the document. The first sentence said that if the Irish were ever capable of thinking, they should do so now because they were on the brink of ruin. He spotted his own and Luttrell's names farther down the page and read it more carefully. French help was only an illusion, it said, and he, Tyrconnell, sought the pledge to await the King's decision only because of the efforts of Lord Lucan and Luttrell to ruin his reputation.

Sarsfield gave a bark of disbelief. 'Are there many copies of this around?'

'Quite a few.'

He read through the rest of the document which warned the Irish against going to France, denied that the war was about religion and declared that whoever urged the defence of Limerick until French help arrived would be guilty of murder. 'God damn this.' Sarsfield pounded the table with his fist. 'Why can't we put a stop to these things?'

'I've ordered that anyone found with more than one copy is to be hanged on the spot,' Wauchope said. 'But ---.' He spread his hands in a gesture of helplessness. He looked around to check there was nobody within earshot but dropped his voice anyway. 'It's telling some people what they want to hear. You'll find them saying that Tyrconnell told them not to trust the French.'

Sarsfield nodded. It was true that Tyrconnell distrusted the French but then he distrusted everybody, even his own henchmen at times. 'Have the Frenchmen seen this?'

Wauchope raised his eyebrows. 'They're outraged,' he said. 'As usual.'

'Where's d'Usson?'

Wauchope pointed a finger upwards to indicate the wall above them.

Sarsfield turned to go but stopped. 'Many deserters last night?'

'Most of another squadron of dragoons.'

'Luttrell's?'

Wauchope shook his head.

Sarsfield sighed. It was impossible to stop this exodus, which was sapping the army's spirit, creating a corrosive defeatism, and encouraging others to follow suit. Hanging anyone caught sneaking out of Irish Town made little or no difference to the nightly departures. Especially to the horsemen in Clare who could easily slip across the river at several points in the dark.

Sarsfield climbed the steps to find d'Usson standing by the rampart near a field gun which was pointed towards the sky to try and cover the distance to Singland Hill and its greater elevation. It fired as Sarsfield arrived, blasting a spearhead of flame and sparks from the barrel amid a cloud of acrid grey smoke.

D'Usson lowered his telescope and both men waited for the ringing in their ears to die away. 'It's a waste of time,' d'Usson said, waving his hand towards Singland. 'That fell short again.'

Sarsfield was about to mention the forged will but the battery on the hill opposite flashed and an explosive canister whistled overhead moments later and dropped onto the town behind them. It was followed by a cannonball, visible as it slowed and dropped down from the apex of its flight. 'And that's a waste of time too,' d'Usson shrugged as the shot dropped through the roof of a building, damaging only what was in its path. He appeared to be more interested in what was happening up here in the open than in the gloomy rooms below.

'They're waiting for their siege guns,' Sarsfield suggested.

'Perhaps. But they are not serious about a siege.' d'Usson pointed over the wall to show off his improved defences. 'It would take weeks to break through here. If it is possible for them at all. And to do that, they would have to bring the siege guns much closer, within range of ours.'

'It looks like they're going to try the walls of the English Town instead.'

D'Usson made a 'poof' sound. 'That's a nonsense,' he said.

'Yes, they can breach the wall there but then they will have to cross the river and cover a lot of ground under fire from our fort before they get to the breach. The idea is ridiculous.'

Sarsfield said nothing, deferring to d'Usson's greater experience of sieges.

'It's all a pretence,' d'Usson added. 'A pretend siege.'

There was another burst of fire and smoke from the hill opposite and seconds later a carcass flew overhead and dropped into the town. They waited for the explosion but there was none. 'You see,' d'Usson said as if the dud proved his point. 'They are just waiting for you to surrender.'

'We are not going to surrender,' Sarsfield said, noting the Frenchman's use of 'you' instead of 'us'.

'That's good,' d'Usson said. 'Then we can defeat them. They will have to withdraw when our convoy arrives. They can't sit out there all winter.' He looked up at the grey sky. 'Not in the Irish rain.'

The rain held off for another few days, days of scattered sunshine and a warm wind from the south-west which brought the English warships close to the town, firing into the cavalry camp at Cratloe as they passed by, killing a few horses and wounding two troopers. Two ships docked on the south bank of the river near the town and could be seen unloading cannons before tacking back with the ebbing tide into their blockading position nearer the mouth of the estuary. That they had to borrow naval cannons was another sign that the enemy did not have enough guns in place for a serious siege.

The Williamites finished their battery downriver of the town and began lobbing mortars into English Town and targeting Thomond Bridge with the naval cannons. In response, two field guns were dragged to the opposite bank of the Shannon and opened fire, forcing the enemy to move back and reducing their chances of cutting the city's lifeline into Clare. On the other side of English Town, the enemy's siege guns fired across the Abbey River, battering at a stretch of the vulnerable walls near Baal's Bridge.

'It's time to leave,' Sarsfield told Honor as English Town came under more sustained bombardment.

They left in a convoy of coaches, waiting at Thomond Gate until there was a pause in the firing at the bridge. The cannonade had done little damage so far; few shots had hit the structure and they had caused only minor damage. The cannons on the castle walls fired repeatedly, trying to force the enemy gunners to retreat, creating a great din.

The coaches raced across the bridge, barely wide enough for them. They all crossed safely and went by the fort on the Clare side and on for a few miles to a house where the lords justices were already installed. Sir Richard Nagle took Sarsfield aside as soon as he arrived and before he had seen Honor settle in. 'Well?' he demanded when they were alone in the garden.

'It seems that they are going to try an assault across the Abbey River on English Town,' Sarsfield said.

'And?'

'It won't succeed.'

Nagle didn't look very reassured. 'You know what people are saying? That the French are not coming at all.'

'They *are* coming,' Sarsfield said. 'It's just a question of when.'

'What's delaying them?'

'We don't know. But they're not going to leave their generals here.'

'Why not? What are a couple of generals and their staffs to them?'

'What did his grace think?' Sarsfield batted the question back at Nagle who also avoided it.

'His so-called testament is causing confusion.'

'Which is what it's intended to do.'

'But how do we counteract it?'

'Assure everyone that it's a lie. You knew him better than anybody. You can reassure them that it doesn't reflect his views of the French. That it is a forgery.'

Nagle gave a half-nod but it lacked conviction. 'They always have their own interests at heart. He knew that.'

'For God's sake,' Sarsfield exclaimed, 'now is not the time for raising doubts.'

'I'd be laughed at if I said the duke never doubted the French,' Nagle said, straightening his already straight wig. 'It's your job to maintain confidence in the army.'

'That's what I'm trying to do,' Sarsfield said wearily, realising he wasn't going to get any assistance from the lords justices.

At the cavalry camp at Cratloe the tents had been moved back from the river after the attack by the English ships. Sarsfield rode by Luttrell's regiment, noting the men turning away when they recognised him. Nicholas Purcell emerged from a tent and watched him approach, stony-faced. Sarsfield was about to ignore him but he changed his mind and reined his horse in. The two men stared at each other in silence for a moment.

'It's not possible to release him right now,' Sarsfield said, trying to strike a conciliatory note.

'You're making a big mistake.' Purcell pointed back towards Luttrell's dragoons. 'His men are very unhappy. You can see for yourself.'

'They should be very unhappy with him. He betrayed them too.'

'No! he didn't! He hasn't betrayed anybody and you know it. Even Lying Dick couldn't convict him with his rigged court.'

Sarsfield sighed. He thought of explaining that the French were also insisting on keeping Luttrell under lock and key. If they'd had their way, they would have hanged him immediately without a court martial. Releasing him now would be a sign of weakness, d'Usson had insisted, a sign that everyone could pursue their own interests, decide what was best for them, negotiate with the heretics if they felt like it. It would destroy the army, fatally weaken the Kings' cause, d'Usson had argued.

'It's not personal,' Sarsfield said. 'It's in the interest of the army as a whole.'

Purcell gave a bitter laugh. 'Of course it's personal. You always resented him. Because without Henry you'd never know what to do.'

Sarsfield felt his jaw clench, his hand going unconsciously to the hilt of his sword. He had tried to meet Purcell halfway but Purcell clearly had become even more intransigent. He forced himself to remain calm.

Purcell looked away, realizing he might have articulated one truth too many. He turned back to Sarsfield and said in as emollient a tone as he could summon, 'You need him now more than ever. We all need him now more than ever.'

'We need to stand together now more than ever,' Sarsfield said, matching the other's tone. 'We can't have people making decisions in their own interest alone.'

Purcell dug the toe of his boot into the soft earth and drew it back as if he was drawing a line. 'He wasn't doing that,' he said. 'You know it. He walked into a trap, that's all.'

Sarsfield resisted the instant response that he wouldn't have been trapped if he hadn't been underhand but he had no desire to continue this dispute with Purcell. He sighed and changed the subject to neutral ground. 'Did the English ships do much damage?'

'Not much. But how could they even come up the river and fire on us here? Where are the French ships?'

'On their way.'

'Nobody believes that.'

'It's true.'

347

Purcell shrugged.

'You don't believe that Tyrconnell forgery, do you.' Sarsfield gave a short laugh in an attempt at incredulity.

'That doesn't matter. People believe what they see and what they don't see. They see English ships in the estuary where they've never seen them before. And they don't see any of the French ships that are supposed to be commanding the seas.'

Sarsfield rode on, trying to shake off the sense of weariness that had descended on him. He seemed to be spending most of his time defending the French to the Irish while reassuring d'Usson and Tessé that their fears of the Irish capitulating were groundless. There was a vacuum now in their leadership, he knew. Something missing that Tyrconnell had provided, even if he had only united everyone in opposition to himself. The lords justices certainly didn't fulfil that missing leadership. And as for himself ---.

There was a kernel of truth in what Purcell had said. He had relied on Luttrell's advice, on his understanding of Tyrconnell's intrigues, on his ability to detect the intents amid the feints, to sift the hard facts from the covering fictions. I need his advice now, he thought. But what would it be? That we discuss terms with the Dutchman?

But even to ask for Luttrell's advice would be a sign of weakness. A sign that he too was prepared to talk to the enemy. And how could he trust Luttrell anymore? And if he did would anyone else trust him, Sarsfield? He wondered if he was ever right to trust Luttrell. Was he always playing his own games?

It was difficult, even impossible, to know. Especially now that everything was in such a state of uncertainty. People changed their minds by the day; prepared to negotiate yesterday; to fight to the death today; to surrender tomorrow. What to do? To accept the terms offered to Galway; to recognise the usurper as the new king; to stand by the Stuarts; to trust Louis XIV and the French; to say a pox on them all, we need our own Irish king? A Catholic

Irish king. But there was no prospect of that. Even if the old Gaelic chieftains and the old Norman-English could agree on it.

So what was the best choice? And how could it be achieved?

Meanwhile, the only obvious choice was to fight on. To believe that Archbishop Maguire was right: that God might have punished his people but he would not see them destroyed.

It's time we struck back, Sarsfield decided.

SEPTEMBER

Mackay

The flash from the cannon lit up the countryside, throwing the group of men carrying tin boats to the bank of the river into sudden relief. They froze in their positions as the darkness hid them again, waiting for shouts of alarm to come from the island in front of them. None came.

Their major muttered a curse and signalled to his militiamen to move forward to the riverbank from the trees that hid them. Mackay told him to wait and ordered a trumpeter on his own staff to ride back to the battery beside the river and tell them to stop firing at the walls of English Town until further notice.

The night was almost over but there was no sign yet of the dawn. Out of the trees the dark was translucent, the sheen on the Shannon showing the water moving fast, displaying no movements on the island. There were one or two abandoned houses there and the ruins of an old church, according to a deserter, but it wasn't possible to tell them apart from the trees that stood against the stars in the western sky. They didn't know where the Protestant townspeople were being held prisoner but Mackay expected it would be in the church ruins. Their jailers would have taken the better buildings for themselves.

The major drummed his palm against his thigh, demonstrating an impatience that he was not prepared to put into words in front of this baby-faced Scotsman. Mackay glowered back at him but his expression was lost in the darkness. He didn't have a high opinion of this group of militia and their leader, all Protestants from County Cork, but Ginckel wouldn't let him have any of the regular army for this operation. 'I can't spare them,' he had said in response to Mackay's request. 'You saw yourself last night how stretched we are.'

Mackay couldn't argue with that. A sally from the walls of Irish Town had exposed just how vulnerable the line of circumvallation was: had the enemy realized it and pressed the attack it could have been overrun, which would have been a serious setback. But they had been driven back by a determined volley.

'You can have one of the militias,' Ginckel had said before ordering cavalry units to man some of the trenches. They had gone in grumbling, on foot and without banners, so that the Irish and their French commanders wouldn't realize how weak the besiegers were.

The trumpeter returned and Mackay gave the major the go-ahead. The militiamen moved down to the bank, pushed the boats into the current, and rowed diagonally across to the island. The boats came back for a second wave. There was a volley of shots on the island, some indecipherable shouting and then a silence. Mackay commandeered a boat and was rowed across.

He made his way through the belt of trees at the edge of the island and into a clearing where there were two crumbling walls of an old church. The other walls had been demolished to build two cabins nearby. The militiamen were in a circle around the jailers, now squatting on the ground. Two of them were lying flat, dead or wounded.

'They gave in as usual,' the major said in a tone that implied that Mackay had suggested otherwise. 'Didn't fire a shot. A few ran away.'

'Where are their prisoners?'

The major nodded at the ruin.

The prisoners, all men, were huddled by the walls, covered with ragged coats and blankets. Some were getting to their feet, their faces gaunt and pale, their hair and beards long and straggling.

'Everyone well?' Mackay asked, the words sounding ridiculous to him as soon as he uttered them.

'We're hungry,' one tall man said. 'We've had nothing to eat.'

Mackay told the major to start moving the prisoners back to their side of the river before the dawn came up.

'What'll we do with them?' the major said, nodding at the prisoners' guards.

'They didn't resist, you said.'

'Well ---,' the major mumbled.

'Did they or did they not?'

The major shook his head.

'Did they ask for protection?'

'They might have,' the major conceded. 'I couldn't understand them.'

Mackay stepped closer to the guards and counted them with a pointed finger. 'Bring them back too. All of them.'

The battery at the Abbey River opened up again on English Town as Mackay rode back towards his headquarters. The eastern sky ahead of him began to lighten.

The batteries were now at full force -- some sixty siege guns, field guns and mortars, all bombarding the city from three directions. Smoke from numerous fires in English Town and Irish Town drifted inland and the nights were broken by the glows of continuous fires and the flashes of the guns. The 24-pound and 16-pound cannon across the Abbey River steadily battered the wall of English Town across a few hundred yards of open ground on the King's Island. The breach on the wall widened steadily up to about forty yards.

The defenders fired back from the walls and, most effectively, from the tower of St Mary's Cathedral, the highest point in English Town. Ginckel ordered his gunners to target the tower and it was slowly smashed to pieces.

'We can leave the church alone now,' he told a morning council of war.

'But,' Württemberg protested, 'one of the deserters says that's where they're storing their ammunition.'

'Another says it's here.' Ginckel put his finger on a spot in the centre of his map of the English Town. 'Concentrate our fire there.'

'We could concentrate on both,' Talmash suggested.

'Leave the church alone for the moment,' Ginckel ordered. 'We need to send reinforcements back upriver to Killaloe. There are reports that General Sarsfield is planning a crossing there to cause us some trouble.'

'How reliable is that information?' Mackay asked.

'As reliable as anything else we've heard.'

'May I lead it, my lord?' Ruvigny asked. 'I'd like to come to grips with this Sarsfield.'

Ginckel shook his head. 'I need you here.'

'But,' Talmash said with a grin, 'it might be a good idea to put my lord Ruvigny's men out of the way of temptation.'

Everyone laughed except Ginckel who was not amused at the reference to the recent hanging of a woman who had tried to entice Huguenot soldiers to desert and join their fellow countrymen in the city.

'My men have no need to resort to papist temptresses,' Ruvigny countered.

'Gentlemen,' Ginckel interceded as several others made to say something. 'This is not a matter for levity. It's a reminder that the enemy is not defeated and will try in every way to thwart our endeavours.'

'Then let us put an end to it by assaulting the breach in their walls,' Württemberg said.

'It's too soon,' Ginckel declared, looking around to see if anyone else disagreed with him.

No one did.

On his way back to his tent afterwards, Mackay was accosted by a tall gaunt man in rags. It took him a moment to recognize him as the prisoner he had spoken to on the island some nights earlier.

'My lord,' the man was saying. 'Can you help us in the name of God?'

'What is it?'

The man motioned with his head for Mackay to follow him and they went down the hill from the camp to where stacks of fascines and woolsacks had been gathered in preparation for the assault on the city. The man led him in among the bundles of sticks to where a lean-to had been created with woolsacks for beddings. Men lay around in various degrees of lethargy.

356

'They took everything from us,' the man said.

'Who did?'

'The militia who brought us here. They stole what little we had left. Anything the papists hadn't taken.'

Some of the men on the woolsacks caught Mackay's eye as he looked around. Most were too listless to pay him any heed.

'We helped your men who were prisoners in the city before we were put out,' the man was saying. 'We brought them food and things.'

'Have you had any food?'

'No, my lord.'

'I'll see what I can do.'

Mackay went back to Ginckel's tent and told him what he had seen and heard. 'These men should be disciplined,' he said of the Cork militiamen.

Ginckel gave him a patient sigh. 'We could spend all our time trying to discipline the militias.'

'We should make an example of some of them. Like this lot. Their major at least.'

Ginckel shook his head. 'They can't stay here,' he added of the prisoners. 'Order the next sutlers going back to Dublin to take them with them.'

A cheer went up from the battery by the Abbey River and a great cloud of smoke rose from the centre of English Town.

'What is it? Their ammunition?' Mackay asked Talmash, who had a telescope to his eye.

'Hard to tell. More like a big fire than an explosion.'

They were standing on Singland Hill. Beside them, the field guns and mortars were lobbing balls and carcasses into Irish Town: those that overshot fell conveniently on English Town, including the one that had created the cloud of smoke. Off to their left, the field guns near the Shannon were still trying without success to make Thomond Bridge impassable and firing at random at King John's Castle and the harbour. To their right, the heavy siege guns beside the Abbey River were blasting away at the wall of English Town, continuing to widen the breach.

Mortars from the batteries on the left and right also tossed their large explosive balls into both towns, targeting their occupants' will to resist.

Mackay took Talmash's telescope and scanned the towns. The new cloud of smoke indicated a much bigger fire than any they had caused hitherto. Smoke was also rising from numerous other locations, blowing towards them on the breeze, smelling mostly of wood fires. Flames could be seen on the roofs of some buildings; others were already blackened by old fires and the tower of the cathedral was gone, no longer a focal point of English Town.

Talmash said something but his words were lost in the blast of a nearby field gun, replacing the sweet smell of wood smoke with a cloud of mephitic gun smoke. He repeated himself. 'It's time to go to the next stage. Attack the breach.'

Mackay lowered the telescope. 'You've heard the latest deserter. There's a deep moat in front of that wall.'

'That fellow should be questioned more closely. I think he's a spy. Nobody else has said anything about a moat.'

'We'd want to be sure it doesn't exist before trying anything.'

Talmash gave a dismissive grunt. Mackay was becoming even more cautious than the general. Talmash decided to talk to Württemberg and convince the German to try and persuade the general to take the next step. Otherwise, he could foresee being here all winter.

Württemberg took up the cause at their next council of war. 'There are no other signs of a moat,' he said. 'We can't see it. None of the other deserters know anything about it.'

'They've come from the other side of the river,' Ginckel pointed out. 'They haven't been in the city.'

'Some of them have,' Talmash said.

'But not recently. Not since the recent rain. Not even since the French arrived in May. And we can see how they improved the defences of Irish Town. They could have done the same at English Town too.'

'Can't we send some men across to have a look?' Mackay suggested. Ginckel nodded.

'And hang that deserter if he's been lying to us,' Talmash added.

Ginckel tapped his finger on the map of the city. 'All right,' he said.

'Gather all the empty casks in the camp and bring them down to the Abbey River and prepare rafts for an assault.' He paused and then added with a smile: 'Meanwhile, there is some good news. The Turks have been defeated in Hungary. I think we should celebrate it.'

Nobody, except Mackay, who had previously fought the Turks in Crete, looked excited by the news from far-off battlefields. 'That is good news,' he said.

'Hand out extra rations tonight,' Ginckel continued. 'Give everyone the evening off.'

'Is there any news of the French fleet?' Mackay asked, knowing that the information about the Turks' defeat must have come with a messenger from England.

'It's still at Brest. Or at least it was when the messenger left London.'

Which meant, Mackay calculated, that it would be at least two weeks before the Irish got any relief from France, probably more. Plenty of time to tighten the screw.

Sarsfield

Sarsfield and Wauchope stood on the wall by St John's Gate trying to deduce what was happening. The Williamite guns had all gone silent and bonfires were blazing in the darkness on Singland Hill and at points along the circumvallation line. A faint sound of music came from the enemy camp when the breeze died away. Smoke drifted over them from the fires still smouldering in the city behind them.

'Could the English navy have defeated the French fleet?' Wauchope wondered, voicing their unspoken fears.

There was no news from their people in County Clare who were keeping an eye on the English ships in the estuary and watching for the expected French fleet.

'We'll just have to wait till our men get back,' Sarsfield replied. They had sent several spies across the Shannon upriver to try and find out what was happening.

'There's no reason why we should let them celebrate in peace,' Wauchope muttered, turning to go back down to the Citadel.

Sarsfield stayed where he was, wondering what would happen if the rebels had defeated the French fleet. Would it make the Jacobites' situation untenable? No, he decided. It would make it more difficult but not impossible. They could still hold out for longer than the Williamites could continue the siege. They had enough food and access to more in County Clare. The cold and wet would weaken the enemy in their trenches. Disease would doubtless set in, diminish their numbers. And then his cavalry would attack them in the rear, cutting off their supplies. They would have to withdraw, if they could, or suffer an even greater defeat at Limerick than the prince of Orange had suffered the year before.

The cannon nearby began firing again but it was unable to hit any of the bonfires: the ones at the trenches were too low down and too close and the one on Singland Hill was too high and too far away. Wauchope's order was more a symbolic gesture of defiance than a real threat.

Sarsfield left the wall and walked back through Irish Town. The streets were strewn with stones and rubble and an occasional unexploded mortar ball. The stench of death seeped up from bodies broken under piles of debris and mixed with the stink of human waste where blocked channels had created ever-widening pools of urine and faeces. In the silence, people wandered around, drawn out of their shelters beneath the town's walls by the unexpected ceasefire after so many days and nights of incessant bombing.

'What's happening?' an elderly man asked Sarsfield.

'Nothing.'

'Is it over?' the woman with him asked.

'No. It's not over.'

Wauchope caught up with Sarsfield as he crossed Baal's Bridge and they walked into English Town. A screen of rough material strung across the river above the bridge hid it from the enemy gunners and the structure had escaped any serious damage.

'That was a waste of ammunition,' Sarsfield said.

'Let them know their celebrations are premature,' Wauchope snorted. 'Whatever they're about.'

They went by the building where scores of casks of brandy had been stored. They had gone up in an inferno when hit by an exploding carcass. The fire had taken a row of houses with it; embers still glowed among the blackened stones and the wood had been reduced to ash as grey as the original colour of the stones.

'Now would be a good time to go across the river and burn their fascines and woolsacks,' Wauchope said.

'That's a much better idea,' Sarsfield replied, clapping him on the

361

shoulder.

They turned right and made their way down to the breach in the city walls. Sappers were at work, taking advantage of the ceasefire to build another low wall a short distance behind the damaged outer wall in order to turn the breach into a killing ground for anyone who was able to storm through. D'Usson was standing on a pile of rubble, inspecting their progress.

Sarsfield told him of Wauchope's plan to destroy the fascines and woolsacks the enemy had gathered across the Abbey River in preparation for storming the breach. D'Usson nodded his approval, aware that they were informing him, not seeking his permission as titular commander.

Sarsfield and Wauchope made their way through the covered passageway leading from English Town to the star fort on the northern end of King's Island which protected the city walls from attackers. Wauchope called for volunteers and gathered thirty grenadiers and musketeers, all eager to do something other than hunkering down under the rain of cannonballs and mortars. They filed out through a sally port into the darkness and made for a couple of flat-bottomed boats drawn up on the riverbank.

The two generals waited in silence on the battlements, trying to detect real movements amid the tricks and shadows of the night light. 'There,' Sarsfield said at last, pointing to a small flicker of light by the opposite bank of the river, well forward of the nearest bonfire. As soon as he pointed, the light disappeared but a moment later another appeared nearby and soon a string of flickering lights along the waterline on the far bank began to grow into small flames. Shouts carried across the water followed by musket pops.

The raiding party filtered back into the fort, untouched. 'We even brought back someone,' their captain said, pulling forward one of their spies who had crossed over earlier in the night.

'What's going on over there?' Sarsfield asked.

'They're celebrating a victory over the Turks.'

'The Turks!' Wauchope echoed with a laugh.

'This deserves a celebration of our own,' Sarsfield said.

'Has all the brandy gone up in smoke?' the captain asked with an innocent smirk.

'Not at all,' Sarsfield said. 'Come with me.'

'It's not poisoned, is it?' someone else inquired with a grin, slyly suggesting that Sarsfield might have had Tyrconnell killed and indicating his approval if that was the case.

The dawn brought a drenching grey drizzle blowing like an airborne tide in waves up the estuary. Sarsfield woke with a heavy head, drank a tankard of ale for breakfast and was halfway to the headquarters when the silence struck him. The bombardment had not resumed.

D'Usson and Tessé were at a table in the Citadel drinking coffee and d'Usson signalled to Sarsfield to join them. An orderly brought him a mug and poured coffee into it from a jug. 'Are they quitting?' Sarsfield asked.

Tessé glanced at d'Usson as though they had been just discussing that and had reached an agreed conclusion.

'You don't think our little attack last night will frighten them off?' Tessé asked.

'No. But why haven't they resumed the cannonade?'

'Perhaps all their gunners have sore heads from their celebrations,' d'Usson said.

Sarsfield nodded and winced as a pain flared in his head. 'I can understand that.'

'Last night was good for our spirits,' d'Usson went on. 'We need to do everything we can to keep them high.'

Ah, Sarsfield thought, breaking a chunk of bread off a loaf and dipping it in his coffee, that's what they were talking about. Their worry that we'll surrender is becoming a constant obsession with them.

'Your Irish rain has come to our aid at last,' Tessé said. 'That was what beat them last year.'

'And their defeat at the wall beside us,' Sarsfield corrected him. 'When they breached the wall and assaulted it and were beaten back by the people of Limerick. And the prince of Orange himself was left with nowhere to go but to flee the country and return to England.'

The Frenchmen exchanged glances, surprised by the vehemence of Sarsfield's response. But he was tired of their suspicions that the Irish had lost the will to fight and were waiting for an excuse to surrender. He dipped some more bread in his coffee, chewed it and drained his cup.

'More coffee?' d'Usson urged in a conciliatory tone, raising a finger to his orderly.

They waited in silence while more coffee was poured.

'What can we do to keep the men feeling positive?' d'Usson asked.

'It would help if your promised supplies arrived.'

'I agree but there's nothing we can do to hurry them up. Paris knows how urgently we want them.'

'So what's the delay then?' Sarsfield demanded. He knew they knew no more than he did. 'You could open the King's coffers,' he suggested. 'Give the men a bonus. Show you believe in them.'

Tessé gave d'Usson a sharp glance that looked to Sarsfield like a warning. D'Usson stirred a small spoon of sugar into his coffee. 'You think it will help?'

'Yes. A demonstration of good faith.'

'Very well,' d'Usson said, avoiding Tessé's eye. 'I'll talk to Fumeron. But,' he added, 'you know what commissaries are like. They hoard the money as if it's their own.'

The rain eased later in the day and Sarsfield rode across Thomond Bridge into Clare under a sullen sky to visit the positions protecting the Shannon crossings. All reported that their sections of the river were quiet; there were no signs of enemy activity apart from irregular patrols and lookouts placed at strategic points. Be vigilant, he told them all. Especially for spies and the spreaders of lies. Anyone caught carrying enemy proclamations or other documents was to be executed on the spot.

'Is the siege over?' Brigadier Robert Clifford asked Sarsfield as his troop dismounted for a break at Clifford's camp at Parteen, a few miles upriver.

'What?' Sarsfield responded in surprise.

'We haven't heard their guns since yesterday.'

'No, it's not over,' Sarsfield snapped. 'And don't let anyone think it is.'

Clifford bristled at his tone, knowing that their one-time friendship was now a long time in the past and something neither had any desire to rekindle. 'So why their silence?'

'I don't know. But I do know they're still there and have made no move to withdraw.'

'They say they don't have enough men to take the city,' Clifford said, unwilling to let Sarsfield have the last word.

'Who says?'

'People,' Clifford said with a vague gesture. A circle of junior officers had formed around them, watching the clash of wills and relishing the prospect of telling their colleagues about it later.

'People who know more than I do then,' Sarsfield said.

'You think they have enough men to cross the river and encircle the city?'

'What I think is none of your business. Your business is to carry out your orders and make sure the enemy doesn't cross the river in your area.'

Clifford started to move away but Sarsfield halted him, demanding that he take him on a tour of this stretch of the river to review their defences. Clifford went to get his horse with bad grace, aware that Sarsfield was trying to humiliate him in front of his own men. They set out along the bank of the river and Clifford pointed out where he had posted lookouts.

'And where are the horses?' Sarsfield demanded churlishly.

Clifford turned away from the river and led them back several hundred yards from the camp to where his dragoons' horses were grazing.

'They're too far from the camp and the river here,' Sarsfield said.

'There's no forage left on the riverbank.'

Sarsfield had to accept that the grass there had been grazed down to the earth.

'Anyway,' Clifford added, 'there are no fords on this stretch of the river.'

That's it, Sarsfield thought: he's not just angry at being passed over

365

for promotion to major general but at being posted here, out of the way.

Back at the camp, Charles O'Kelly was waiting for them on his horse. 'I heard you were here,' he said to Sarsfield, ignoring Clifford, who dismounted and strode away without a word. O'Kelly watched him go with a half-smile and then shook his head at Sarsfield. 'I warned you about him,' he said in a low voice.

'What are you doing here?' Sarsfield asked, not wanting to hear another of O'Kelly's complaints.

'On my way back from Killaloe. It looked as if the English were going to try something in the last few days. They moved a good body of men up there but then they saw that we were ready for them and they've pulled out.'

'Is that an opportunity for us?' Sarsfield asked with sudden interest as they rode back towards the city.

'Ballyneety again.' The old man gave him a crooked smile. 'That's the spirit.'

'If we had information,' Sarsfield said, relishing the prospect, but they didn't have enough intelligence on a specific target. They could raid across the river at random but waste a lot of time and energy and put themselves at considerable risk without solid information. And another disaster could have consequences out of all proportion to what might actually be lost.

'Surely the rapparees can help,' O'Kelly said.

'Most of the action is south of the estuary. In Kerry. But we can't get around there. And anyway we don't know exactly what's happening other than that the heretics are trying to clear the area of our people.'

The drizzle began to drift down again, barely perceptible at first but growing in intensity as they neared Thomond Bridge.

'How are our French friends?' O'Kelly asked with an emphasis on 'friends' that suggested they were anything but.

'Nervous.'

'What have they got to be nervous about? We're the ones who have a right to be nervous. About their intentions.'

Sarsfield regretted saying anything as O'Kelly launched into a litany of complaints about everything the French had done, or rather not done, since they had come to Ireland the previous year. 'Except for that General Saint-Ruhe, God rest him, who came near to pulling off a great victory if it wasn't for Luttrell and his ilk.'

Sarsfield didn't interrupt O'Kelly, letting him vent all his frustrations and complaints. In the past he would have come to Luttrell's defence but not any more. As they reached the bridge, however, he grew weary of O'Kelly's tirade. 'You're sounding like Lying Dick's testament,' he snapped. 'The forgery.'

'There's often a lot of truth in a lie,' O'Kelly shot back.

Mackay

'God-damn it,' Ginckel slapped the table. 'What does he mean nobody gave him the order to fire?'

Mackay shrugged in agreement. The sergeant's excuse for not opening fire sooner on the raiding party across the Abbey River was ridiculous.

'What did he think he was there for?' Ginckel paused. 'Is he a closet papist?'

'I don't think so.'

'Court martial him. For treason.'

None of the general staff questioned the order, though they all knew it was excessive in the circumstances. The guard on the fascines had been drinking, taking part in the celebrations, although they weren't supposed to, and were slow to react to the raiding party. But they also knew that Ginckel's order was an expression of his frustration, treating a minor enemy success as if it was a serious setback.

The siege was making no progress. The Williamites were no closer to storming the city now than when they had arrived. The approaching winter and the worsening weather were against them. Some of the gunners were already warning that they would have to withdraw to higher ground if the heavy cannons were not to become bogged down near the rivers. And impossible to move should they have to withdraw later. Already one of the ships had come back upriver to retrieve its cannons.

'I was talking to one of their officers last night,' Talmash said into the silence that followed Ginckel's outburst. 'A cavalryman. And he said that the thing they feared most was having their link to Clare severed. If we could cut the link between their horse outside and their infantry inside the walls they would collapse.'

Ginckel looked around the table, inviting comments.

'The gunners can't get close enough to destroy the bridge,' Mackay said.

'But we could cross the river and send a force around to blockade it,' Talmash said, putting forward his proposal now that they had taken the initial bait.

'Too dangerous,' Mackay retorted. 'We don't have enough men to surround the city.'

'It's a risk,' Talmash conceded, half-regretting that he hadn't discussed this plan with Mackay beforehand to secure his agreement. But that would never have been forthcoming, he knew: Mackay always wanted to do things by the book -- if not The Book -- and the book said besiegers must outnumber defenders several times over. 'But it's a risk worth taking.'

'And what happens when half our men are on the other side of the river and they break out on this side? We've scarcely enough as it is to beat them back if they make a determined sally against our circumvallation line.'

'The cavalry and dragoons will deal with them.'

'And their cavalry and dragoons on the other side of the river will deal with us there.'

Talmash looked to Ginckel and the others who had let him and Mackay set out the arguments without interruption. 'We have to do something,' he pleaded.

'Is there a place to cross?' Württemberg asked.

Talmash gave a half-smile of victory and moved his finger along the curve of the Shannon on the map. 'There,' he said, pointing to a string of three little islands or sandbanks in the river.

'Is it a ford?' Ginckel asked in a sceptical tone as they gathered around the table.

'Not exactly,' Talmash said. 'But that's the point. That's why it might be perfect.' He looked around to confirm that he had everybody's attention. 'You can walk across to the first and second islands and from the third island to the other bank. But the channel between the second and third is deep. So it's almost a ford but not quite. Not somewhere they'll expect us to cross.'

'How narrow is this channel?'

'We need to find out exactly. And how many pontoons we'll need to bridge it.'

Mackay shook his head in disbelief. 'And what will the papists do while we're building our bridge?'

'With luck, they won't see it. They're not on the third island, I think.'

'You think?'

'Let's find out,' Ginckel interrupted. 'Tonight. Send some scouts and engineers to see if it's feasible.'

'I'll lead them myself,' Talmash said.

'No,' Ginckel ordered, fearing Talmash's enthusiasm might get the better of him if he saw a way over. 'You stay here.'

The scouts and engineers reported back the next morning. Yes, it was feasible. It would take about twenty-five pontoons to bridge the channel between the second and third islands. There was no sign of enemy forces on any of the islands and no sign of an encampment nearby on the other bank.

Ginckel questioned the scouts closely. What was the land like on this side of the river? Uncultivated, overgrown with reeds and bushes, a flood plain in winter. And on the other side? Rising up to hills. Can we get into position without alerting them? Yes, with care, in the dark. Could the placing of the pontoons be kept secret? With care again: the noise of the fast-flowing river will cover them.

'All right,' he said at last to Talmash. 'We'll go tonight if it's dark enough. Meanwhile, nobody is go near that area today other than our normal patrol.'

The meeting broke up with a renewed sense of energy after the lassitude of the last few days. The siege guns had opened fire again, although at a reduced rate, an unspoken acknowledgement that they were achieving little. The breach in the wall of English Town was getting wider although there was a growing acceptance that it could not be stormed. On that score, at least, most of the senior officers agreed with Mackay.

'You'll come with us tonight,' Talmash said to Mackay after the council of war.

'To what purpose?'

To see that I'm right, Talmash almost said. 'In case I need your assistance.'

'Why would you need my assistance?'

'In case I'm felled. You're a brave and resourceful man in a fight.'

Mackay was surprised. Flattery, he thought. What's the purpose of this? Intimations of mortality? Unlikely. Consolation for his victory at the council? He had no particular desire to go along, not sharing Talmash's love of action for its own sake. But it would be ungenerous to reject this offer. Although in many respects he disapproved of Talmash, he liked him, if only because they had been thrown together as the only Britons on the general staff of this polyglot army.

'All right. But just as an observer.'

'Unless you're needed.'

'Unless I'm needed.'

Daylight dimmed and disappeared even earlier than usual into a murky mist, making the darkness more dense.

'Perfect,' Talmash said to Mackay, rubbing his hands in delight. 'Victory weather. Your prayers have been answered.'

He had assembled a column of almost two thousand men, cavalry, dragoons, grenadiers, labourers, and fifteen of the lighter field guns, careful to do so out of sight of the city's walls. They moved out, led by scouts, as soon as the darkness was absolute. Visibility was down to yards; each group followed the one immediately in front of it. The silence was broken only by the splashing of hooves into puddles, the muted jangle of equipment, and an occasional horse neighing.

371

Talmash was in the vanguard behind the scouts. Mackay stayed back, riding at the head of the horsemen, behind the infantry and labourers carrying the pontoons. He assumed they were nearing the river as the ground became softer and the mist closed in, reducing visibility even more.

The column halted for what seemed an age. Mackay could see nothing and hear nothing other than a faint hissing of water but whether it was the rain or the river or both he couldn't tell. Horses near him shook themselves and stamped on the sodden ground but the sounds were deadened and subsumed in the mist. At last a soldier emerged out of the murk at the head of his horse.

'The general says you're to come forward,' he said, grabbing hold of the horse's bridle and leading Mackay forward.

Mackay had no idea how his guide could see where he was going or, indeed, how he had found him in the first place.

They passed by the field pieces being hauled by men over the soft ground and were then splashing through water, the first of the fords. Then they were on drier land for a short distance and then through the second ford and onto the second island. Mackay could hear the heavy breathing of labourers manhandling the guns into position, although he could see nothing more than ephemeral shapes in the constantly shifting mist.

Talmash appeared beside him and Mackay slid from his horse.

'All's well,' Talmash whispered into his ear, his breath hot against Mackay's cheek. 'We've checked the third island and it's clear. The pontoons are nearly in place.'

Now that he knew they were lashing the pontoons together to create a bridge, Mackay thought he could hear dulls bangs as the tin boats collided or grated off each other. But everything was muffled by the mist, the sound of running water and the occasional splash of a bird or fish.

The night wore on, all sense of time lost. Around Mackay, men moved forward, riders dismounted and led their horses, the occasional curse was muttered as someone stepped on something, and the column was slowly filtered across the pontoon bridge onto the third island.

The dawn came up at a hesitant pace, the black dissolving slowly into a slightly less impenetrable gauze before lightening into a translucent grey. Shapes began to take form. Mackay could see the field guns lined up, their crews moving about, stacking ammunition, ramming wadding and the first balls down the barrels as silently as possible.

'Come on.' Talmash grabbed Mackay's sleeve and they made their way through scores of grenadiers and fusiliers and a few dozen dragoons to the edge of the island. The light was beginning to break down the darkness and they could see the black river flowing past with a smoothness that indicated its depth. They stepped carefully on to the moving pontoons and crossed to the third island. It was already crowded with scores of grenadiers, hunkered down amid the bushes and waist-high reeds. A squadron of dragoons waited behind them, dismounted, soothing their horses.

Talmash led the way to the edge of the island and the two men squatted down behind bushes, still heavy with their summer foliage. The opposite bank was taking shape, covered in similar bushes. There was no sign of life but the cover could have hidden a host of armed men.

'Time to go,' Talmash whispered and added an order to one of his staff, who disappeared behind them.

Moments later twenty horsemen, pistols drawn, came past them, splashed into the water and began to cross the narrow ford.

Mackay held his breath. Now they would find out if they had surprise on their side or if the enemy had seen their manoeuvres and was prepared for them.

The dragoons were halfway across, the horses up to their knees in the water, when the first flash appeared from a bush opposite. It was followed by a couple of others but no sustained volley of shots. Mackay let out his breath: there were only a few musketeers there.

The dragoons opened fire, pushed forward their horses and had their swords drawn as they went through the bushes opposite. A horde of grenadiers and fusiliers were already in the water following them. Talmash had disappeared among them. More and more came filing by, splashing through the water, and disappearing up the opposite bank until all were across.

Scattered shots and grenade explosions sounded from the other side but nothing like a sustained engagement.

Mackay got up from his position and stepped into the river. The water lapped at the top of his boots, sending splashes into them. He was almost across when a trumpeter on horseback came in from the other side. Mackay caught his horse's rein to halt him and asked the youth what was happening.

'They're running away, my lord,' he said, excitement lighting up his boyish face. 'We're chasing them.'

Mackay's relief at the apparent success of the crossing turned back to worry. Was Talmash getting carried away? Literally going too far and leading everyone into trouble?

'My lord,' the trumpeter interrupted. 'I have an urgent message for the artillery captain. To bring the guns over.'

Mackay realized he was still holding the horse's reins and released them. 'Get on with it,' he ordered.

He climbed up the low bank and went inland among the bushes and reeds. The first body, already stripped, was a few yards back from the bank, its head half severed. There were a couple of others nearby but it was clear that there had been only a few men posted here, a lookout.

The day was bright now, as bright as it would get under such a weighty sky, and the mist had softened into a light grey haze. Mackay turned to look back at where they had come from and was surprised at how close the islands were. It was a miracle that they had managed to get so many men, boats and guns this close without being spotted.

The surprise had been total, the operation a success.

Sarsfield

B rigadier Robert Clifford stood in the middle of the group of senior officers, pale-faced, dishevelled, his tunic half-unbuttoned. It was an informal enquiry, not yet a court martial but there was no mistaking the hostility of his interrogators. Or their belief that he was guilty of negligence at least and probably of treachery.

'Why didn't you heed the warning?' d'Usson demanded again. One of the lookouts had seen movement in the bushes on the islands and run back to Clifford's headquarters at Parteen to awaken him.

'There was nothing definite,' Clifford repeated. 'One man thought he saw something. A patrol that rode by at about the same time saw nothing.'

'And that man was right.'

'Lookouts are always seeing things in the dark,' Clifford said in a weary voice, knowing there was nothing he could offer as a successful defence. This jury was rigged: there was nobody here likely to defend him, a Tyrconnell man. Besides, he knew he had to take the blame for what had happened.

'And why didn't you counterattack?' Sarsfield demanded. 'Drive them back into the river?'

'The situation was confused and we didn't have enough men ready quickly enough. There were too many of them. Thousands.'

'Thousands!', Wauchope exploded with incredulity. 'How could thousands cross the river without you noticing a thing and come right up to your camp?'

'No one ever thought they could cross there.'

'And you let them come right up to your camp?' Wauchope repeated.

'They were there before anyone knew it.'

'People knew it but you didn't believe them.'

'Treachery,' O'Kelly hissed over Wauchope's shoulder. 'You arranged it with the heretics.'

'No.' Clifford blessed himself. 'I swear before God I didn't.'

'Your dragoons have been going back and forth to the enemy, negotiating secret deals,' O'Kelly persisted. Everyone knew that most of the deserters slipping away had gone from among the horsemen outside the city, in Clare.

'If I'd done that, would I be here now?' Clifford retorted, spurred into an unexpected show of spirit by O'Kelly's accusations and the realization that he would be lucky to get out of this with his life. 'I'd be feasting in the Dutchman's tent.'

'Liar,' O'Kelly threw back, caught off-guard. 'You're staying here to do more of his dirty work.'

'All right.' d'Usson caught Sarsfield's eye and Sarsfield gave a slight nod. 'You'll face a court martial,' he told Clifford, as he and Sarsfield had agreed earlier. 'Lock him up,' he ordered.

'I told you so,' O'Kelly turned on Sarsfield after Clifford had been taken away to King John's Castle. 'Didn't I warn you? You should have been up there yourself. You or General Wauchope.'

'Thank you, Colonel,' d'Usson said with a noticeable lack of gratitude. 'Please leave us now.' He waved at all the senior officers, Irish and French, who had crowded into the room. 'We need to consider the situation.'

'And Major General Sheldon?' d'Usson said once the room had cleared, leaving Tessé, Sarsfield, Wauchope and himself. 'Where is he now?'

'At Sixmilebridge, as far as I know,' Sarsfield said.

'Why didn't *he* counterattack?' Tessé chimed in. 'He had enough men and cavalry, more than enough. And he was even closer than ---' he waved a finger at the door as though he had already forgotten Clifford's name --- 'than this useless officer, this traitor.'

'You'll have to ask him yourself,' Sarsfield snapped back, in no mood to defend the Englishman or to pander to the Frenchman's tone which implied that everyone else was to blame for this disaster. His nerves, like everyone's else's, were frayed by the setback, the divisions, the indecision, the uncertainty.

Sarsfield, Wauchope and their escort waited for the drawbridge on Thomond Bridge to be lowered, revealing the crowd of refugees from Clare trying to get into the city. Some pushed narrow handcarts carrying crates of chickens and ducks: most had their possessions wrapped in blankets or shawls. All began to move forward as the wooden bridge came down. Soldiers pushed back to keep them at bay and clear a passage for the cavalrymen to leave in single file. The drizzle swept up the river from the Atlantic, drenching everyone. A shot from the enemy field gun on the south side of the river fell with a splash into the full tide, almost unnoticed. Occasional mortars and blazing carcasses, lighting up the gloomy sky, fell on both parts of the city. The crowd kept trying to move forward, crushing those at the front, desperate to get back into the city which some had fled when the bombardment had begun.

'*Fag an bealach*!' Sarsfield shouted to little effect and spurred his horse to keep it forcing its way forward. We'll have to get the lords justices and the ladies, including Honor, back into the city, he thought.

Progress was slow but they eventually burst through the crowd and cantered along the river towards Parteen. Another body of horsemen came towards them, led by Colonel Purcell.

'Where are they?' Sarsfield asked him.

'Stopped at Parteen. Looting Clifford's camp as far as we can see.'

'Is it just a foray?' Sarsfield asked in surprise. Maybe this was not as bad as he had feared.

Purcell shook his head. 'They've brought field guns over.'

'And more men?' Sarsfield's brief optimism disappeared.

'Some. But not a great body. As far as we can tell.'

'What do you make of it?' Wauchope asked.

'What do I make of it?' Purcell repeated, staring at Sarsfield. 'What I make of it is that this was the action of a real traitor.'

'That's not your concern, Colonel,' Wauchope retorted.

Purcell turned to Wauchope. 'I think the brigadier left the way open for them to cross. How else could a thousand men or more sneak up on us like that with field pieces and horsemen and build a bridge?'

'That's no help,' Wauchope said. 'What we need to know now their intentions.'

'You're the general,' Purcell said, glaring at Sarsfield and riding off.

Wauchope turned his horse as if he was about to pursue him but then he thought better of it. He wheeled back alongside Sarsfield and muttered something about the lack of discipline creeping into the army. Sarsfield shrugged, tired of Purcell's relentless hostility.

They rode on until they came within sight of the Williamites now occupying Clifford's camp, their flags listless in the damp. It had much the same air as Clifford's camp previously, a place into which its occupants had settled as though they were going to be there for a time. There did not appear to be much activity, no sign of urgency or that they were planning a further expansion.

'They might be surprised at their success,' Wauchope mused. 'Maybe they didn't trust Clifford. Feared he was luring them into a trap.'

'Would they risk that many if they feared a trap?'

'Enough to fight their way out of it.'

'Perhaps.'

A group of horsemen appeared in front of the Williamite camp and stood there, watching them observing it from a half a mile away. Sarsfield had been about to ride off but he changed his mind, unwilling to let them think their presence had intimidated him.

'Are they trying to entice us to draw enough infantry out of the city to push them back?' he wondered.

'And weaken English Town's defences in preparation for an assault across the Abbey river?' Wauchope finished the thought.

'Or are they thinking of surrounding the city?'

'But have they enough men for that? Enough left on the other side to stop us if we break out from Irish Town?'

'That would be a good plan,' Sarsfield brightened up. 'We should do nothing and let them bring more men over, commit themselves to this side of the river as well. And then attack out of Irish Town. Overrun their circumvallation line.'

'And they'd be cut off here, isolated.'

'Yes,' Sarsfield said, turning his horse back towards the city.

The breeze from the estuary was replaced the next day by a wind from the north-west which cleared the sky of cloud and brought a foretaste of what was to come with a drop in temperature. The rain had put out the fires and made the firing of carcasses into the city pointless: everything was too wet to catch fire. Refugees huddled in ruins and raised shelters from half-charred wood. Rocks from mortars and balls from cannons continued to kill and maim at random.

There was still no sign of the French fleet.

'They're not coming,' Lord Dillon said.

He was among a group of mostly younger Irish officers closeted with Sarsfield in a room at the top of the Citadel.

'Don't give up yet,' Colonel Mark Talbot offered. He had recovered from his Aughrim wounds but still wore the black armband of bereavement for his father. Like him and Dillon, many of them wore armbands in memory of fallen relatives, most of whom had perished at Aughrim. 'They'll come. My father was sure of it.'

There was a snort of derision from one of them at the reference to Tyrconnell but the others ignored it. It was in bad taste to blame the son for the father's sins, especially a grieving and wounded son.

'Even if they do come, what'll they bring?' someone else demanded. 'More arrogant fops to give orders and do nothing.'

That got a murmur of approval.

'So what do we do?' Sarsfield prompted. He hadn't taken any part in the conversation, being there simply to listen to what the sons of most of the main families in the country thought. Besides, his own thoughts held more questions than answers.

There was silence. Men shifted and avoided one another's eyes. Finally, Piers Butler, Lord Galmoy, the largest landowner there and probably the oldest, though only in his late thirties, put into a word what no one had wanted to say aloud. 'Negotiate.'

It was an attractive proposition and they all knew it. They would be allowed to go home after years of devastating warfare, major battles, endless minor clashes, sudden death and injury, hunger, disease, the loss of fathers, brothers, sons, and friends. They were all tired of it. After Aughrim their spirit had gone. They were reduced to their last stronghold and the trap was closing on it.

'The same terms as Galway,' Dillon said. Pardons for everyone, permission to go home and keep their lands, practise their religion.

'If they'll keep to them,' someone said. 'They're breaking them in Galway already. Disarming Catholics. The town's heretics are intent on revenge.'

'We would have to get stronger guarantees.'

'What's the word of a heretic worth?'

'Nothing. Their whole so-called religion is whatever you want it to mean.'

'We've lived under a Protestant king before.'

'That wasn't a great time.'

'Was it worse than this?'

'We can survive the winter here better than they can. Wait for better terms.'

'Do we have enough food now, with all the extra people in the town?'

'Yes, we do.'

'And if the French come, there'll be no shortage. And we can break the blockade.'

'And then what?'

'Wait for more French troops in the spring.'

There were a few guffaws at that. What had the French troops done the previous year when there were thousands of them in Ireland? Nothing other than lord it over the Irish with their superior rations, real gold and silver coins, and evident disdain for the country and its inhabitants.

The debate was interrupted by the door opening. General Wauchope stepped in and stopped when he saw the gathering, immediately aware of what it was -- a meeting of the Norman Irish or the Old English families. Another of the examples of the break-up of the army into its constituent parts, everyone cleaving to their own group as long-festering mutual suspicions were forced to the surface by the pressures of their predicament.

He muttered an apology and was backing out when Sarsfield beckoned him in. 'It can wait,' Wauchope said.

'What is it?' Sarsfield asked.

'These are appearing on walls.' Wauchope handed him a sheet of paper, its corners torn from where it had been ripped from nails.

It was another proclamation from Ginckel giving the garrison and inhabitants of Limerick a final chance to take advantage of the generous terms on offer since the fall of Athlone. They had eight days to comply or suffer the consequences.

'Thank you all,' Sarsfield said, dismissing the officers. He waited until they had left and Wauchope had closed the door. 'You're having them taken down?'

'As quickly as possible.'

'How can they spread this poison with such ease?' It was a rhetorical question: the enemy had no difficulty infiltrating the city at will. Sarsfield read through the last few sentences again: 'But if they shall still continue obstinate, and neglect to lay hold of this favour, which is the last that will be offered to them, they must be answerable for the blood and destruction they draw upon themselves; for I hereby acquit myself before God and the world, and wash my hands of it.'

'A regular little Pontius Pilate,' Wauchope said.

Sarsfield nodded absent-mindedly. Wauchope didn't have to be told to know what he was thinking. They were in the classic quandary of the besieged in an uncertain position: hold out too long and be shown no mercy if and when finally overcome, or negotiate at the optimum time and extract the best possible terms. And live to fight another day.

'We're not beaten,' Wauchope offered after a few moments.

'I agree. But,' Sarsfield paused before putting into direct words what he hadn't said to anyone yet either, the essential question, 'can we win the war?'

Wauchope shook his head several times slowly. 'Not here. Not now.'

Yes, they could hold out for the winter, with or without supplies from France. And then what? Break out and recapture Connacht? It was doubtful that could be done, even if the French sent more troops in the spring. It wasn't the same as a year earlier when they had held all Connacht and Munster, from Sligo down the line of the Shannon to Limerick and on to Cork and the convenient port of Kinsale. Now they would have to retake Athlone and Galway. As for Sligo nobody knew for certain what was happening there although it was rumoured to have fallen with the help of the treacherous Balldearg O'Donnell.

'What was the feeling among your people?' Wauchope asked about the meeting he had interrupted.

'Most want it to be over. To go home.'

'You want to go home?'

'Me?' Sarsfield gave a humourless laugh. 'Go home and do what? Be a farmer? I'm a soldier.'

'Me too.'

'Which leaves us one option.'

Wauchope nodded, knowing what he meant.

Sarsfield tore up the proclamation into smaller and smaller pieces and tossed them into the air.

But they didn't have eight days' grace. The crossing of the river and Ginckel's ultimatum prompted more open debate about the future and more talk of terms. Men were disappearing across the river every night, leaving those left behind wondering if they should go too, before it was too late. Verbal abuse of some of the French officers threatened to become physical.

'This is intolerable,' d'Usson complained to Sarsfield. 'One of my officers was spat upon in the street. Another had a bayonet put to his face when he stopped a man from robbing his quarters.'

'I'm sorry,' Sarsfield sighed. 'Everyone is upset.'

'*Bouleversé!*' d'Usson repeated back at him as if the word was another insult. 'We are here to help you and this is how we are treated.'

'Everyone's worried that we're being abandoned. Where are your ships?'

D'Usson stepped backwards to glare up at him. 'They will come.'

'I know,' Sarsfield agreed to appease him, 'but people don't know what to think anymore. They need to see the ships with their own eyes.'

D'Usson turned away for a moment and then faced Sarsfield again. 'I no longer believe the Irish want to fight. We are wasting our time and our King's money here.'

'It's our lives and our families' lives and our futures that are at stake. You and your staff will go home to France, safe. We have nowhere to go.'

'You will come to France with us,' d'Usson said with the air of one stating the obvious.

'You think the prince of Orange will let us go like that? To continue fighting him in the Spanish Netherlands?'

'Why not?' d'Usson shrugged. 'That's where the war will be decided -- not here.'

The war, Sarsfield thought. Whose war? A wave of weariness swept over him. This is where he needed the advice of someone like Luttrell, even Tyrconnell, someone who could unknot the twisted political issues, who could detect and strike the right balance of advantage amid the contradictions and complexities.

Is the war on the continent our war too? Yes and no. Pope Innocent XI had been against France, supporting the heretics, which made no sense to people fighting for Catholicism here. As to the new Pope, another Innocent, his position is unknown. The only hope of maintaining our lands is through the restoration of the rightful King, James, and the overthrow of the usurper. Or a French victory. But do the French care about what happens to Ireland or even to England? Meanwhile, the here and now is more important. How to keep the army together, to avoid defeat, to plot a course for the winter and the next campaigning season and beyond.

'Has Monsieur Fumeron agreed to pay the men?' Sarsfield asked.

'Yes. He will do so at the appropriate moment.'

'The appropriate moment?' Sarsfield shot back. 'He needs to do it now.'

D'Usson raised his palms to calm him down. 'I'll talk to him.'

'Do it now. Stop the talk of negotiations.'

'Yes.'

The distribution of French gold and silver worked like a balm, soothing suspicions and stopping some men who had been on the point of deserting. It was helped, too, by stories filtering out of Galway of tensions there and the impositions of the new governor on Catholics. Could the Dutchman's terms be trusted? Rumours that some who had gone over to the Williamites had been treated badly suggested not; they had been robbed blind by Ulstermen, Vikings or the English and cast out into the countryside with nothing. On the other hand, men were said to have been allowed go home with real money in their pockets from selling their horses and arms to the rebels.

There was no way of knowing for sure which rumours were true and which were false.

Mackay

Mackay rode out from his fort by Singland Hill to summon Ruvigny back for a final council of war. They could have sent a trumpeter but Mackay had offered to go himself because he wanted to see the new river crossing-point. It was downriver from the islands where they had crossed a few nights before, closer to the city and probably within sight of its walls. The decision to send a substantial force across the Shannon had been made earlier at a council where those who favoured more aggressive tactics had finally won the day. Ginckel had agreed to what appeared to Mackay to be more an act of desperation than of common sense.

Body parts of rapparees quartered after they were hanged were stuck in the bushes by the roadside for several hundred yards: they had been captured when they attacked soldiers who were digging potatoes in a farmer's enclosure. Legs, arms and torsos were spread at random on hawthorns and amid the blackberries and hazelnuts, as if an angry god had tossed them out of a heaven onto the early morning earth. The long-haired head of one sat on top of a pike, its dead eyes staring.

'A welcome sight,' a voice said as a rider caught up with him.

Mackay turned to see one of the artillery officers, an Englishman called Richards.

'I hear the general wanted to put them on the wheel,' the officer went on. 'But he was told that wasn't allowed under English law. More's the

385

pity. The continentals have the right idea.'

'You don't think hanging, drawing and quartering is enough for them?'

'They're the curse of this country. Murderous highwaymen.'

'You lost some men to them?'

The officer shook his head. 'If they want to join the papist army, that's one thing. But they're just out for robbery and murder.'

'Most of them are deserters from the papist army.'

'My point exactly.'

Mackay wasn't sure he followed Richards's logic but he had no interest in seeking clarification. Rapparees were merely a pest, symbols of the state of lawlessness and even, paradoxically, of the victories over the Irish. They would be dealt with easily once the war was concluded and order restored.

'By the way, what is the general up to?' Richards asked.

'What do you mean?'

'He keeps changing his mind. We're moving guns from one battery to another. From the right flank to the left flank and back again. On and off the ships. Up to your fort. Down to the river crossing. Back again.'

'Keeping the enemy on its toes,' Mackay said although he believed the real answer had more to do with Ginckel's indecision. 'Not knowing where the assault's going to come from.'

'They know where it's going to come. At the breach of the English Town's walls.'

No, it's not, Mackay thought. Richards might have an artillery man's pride in the fact that his gunners had demolished a long section of the town's wall but it was largely a waste of time. It was obvious to all the general staff now that that section was an easy target for a reason. The French hadn't bothered improving its defences because any assaulting force had to cross the Abbey River and some four hundred paces under fire before they even reached the breach and, depending on which deserter you believed, may or may not then have to cross a moat. The siege guns had made little impression on the improved defences of Irish Town which was the obvious place to storm.

Instead, Ginckel had finally agreed that they had to surround the city, cut off its access to Clare since the gunners were unable to do so by destroying Thomond Bridge. It was a risk but something had to be done to break the stalemate. Time was pressing.

As they approached the river, they passed hundreds of mounted cavalrymen and dragoons who were letting their mounts wander around a tight area in search of the sparse grass. Thousands of infantrymen and sappers were waiting by the bank, mostly sitting on the damp ground. Pontoon boats were lined up but the new bridge had not yet been put in place.

The river was wide and slow here, barely contained by its low banks as the tide pushed in from the ocean and the heavy rainfall of recent days flowed down from Lough Derg. On the other bank, the flags and banners of the men who had crossed by the islands streamed towards them in the brisk breeze.

Ruvigny glowered at the scene of inactivity from a small hillock near the river's edge. Richards and Mackay rode over to him, Mackay deferring to Richards while Ruvigny gave instructions about where to place the guns to protect the bridgehead across the river.

'What's the delay?' Mackay asked when Ruvigny had finished and Richards had ridden away, raising his eyes to Mackay as he left. This was more of it, he seemed to indicate -- more of the chopping and changing.

'Not enough boats to bridge the river since it has risen,' Ruvigny said. 'They're bringing up carts and old barrels to help.'

'How long will it take?'

'A few hours. We'll get across by midday.'

'The general wants a final council.'

'Now?'

Mackay nodded.

'Is he changing his mind again?'

'I don't know.'

Ginckel surprised the sceptics when they had all gathered. 'I will lead the attack across the river myself,' he announced.

He realises how important this operation is, Mackay thought immediately. He knows what's at stake.

387

'Is that wise, my lord?' Talmash couldn't resist interjecting, disappointed that he hadn't been chosen for the task.

'Why not?' Ginckel demanded with the air of someone ready to take offence.

'Wouldn't it be better for your lordship to remain at the headquarters and have an overview of developments?'

'You and Major General Mackay will remain on this side of the river,' Ginckel instructed. 'Your task is to prevent the enemy from using the opportunity to break out of Irish Town when he sees our forces being divided in two. Should that happen, you will signal to us immediately.'

Ginckel ran through the details of the plan again, who was to go where and do what. It was straightforward: they would cross the river in force, join up with the men on the other side, and seize the fort protecting Thomond Bridge. He concluded with a rhetorical 'All clear?' which invited only one response.

The council broke up, one of the shortest they had had. The general is being pushed to take a chance he's not comfortable with, Mackay thought but he has run out of options. All their efforts so far had produced no progress. Deserters gave conflicting reports of supplies in the city: they were extensive or they had mostly been destroyed by the bombardment. Their spirits were terrible, disputes grew by the day. But the arrival of a French fleet would change all that. Something had to be done to force the issue to a head, or at least to position themselves for a long blockade. Which meant isolating the city from its hinterland.

'So we have to stay at home and mind the fort,' Talmash muttered in disgust to Mackay, 'while the foreigners have all the fun.'

It hadn't escaped Mackay's notice that Ginckel had pointedly left his two British generals behind but he was more used than Talmash to finding himself overruled. 'We have to do a lot more than mind the fort,' he replied, aware of the dangers inherent in Ginckel's venture. 'There's a real possibility they will try a sally here at the very least. A full-scale break-out at worst.'

'Let them come. They'll pay through the nose.'

Mackay ordered the siege guns facing Irish Town to strike the walls with everything they had. All available men were sent to the

388

circumvallation trench and fascines brought up to the front line as sappers pushed forward the attack trenches. Everything was to be done to indicate an imminent attack even if, logically, it was impossible because there was no breach in the walls.

'A waste of time,' Talmash said, still in a sulk. 'None of that's going to fool them.'

'We don't have to fool them,' Mackay said. 'We just need to keep them guessing. Stop them from attacking us.'

'Hmm,' Talmash muttered, glancing almost longingly at the pike on top of the hill with a large torch on top of it. It was to be lit as a signal for Ginckel if the papists attacked from Irish Town. 'Perhaps we shall see some action here.'

Nearby, two men loaded a large explosive ball into a mortar, unlit fuse downwards, a safer way of firing than the previous practice of lighting the fuse first which sometimes caused it to ignite the propellant and explode the mortar barrel. A gunner touched the match to the breach and the ball went off with a deafening bang and a huge cloud of smoke.

A young trumpeter came riding up the hill from the river and slid from his horse in front of Mackay and Talmash. 'The general wants a report, my lords,' he said with a bow.

'All is quiet. There's no sign of enemy activity yet.'

The trumpeter sprang back on his horse, adrenaline fuelling his excitement.

'What's happening across the river?' Mackay asked him.

'The papists are putting up a fight,' the trumpeter said, wheeling his horse around and riding off.

Talmash gave a snort of disbelief. Mackay watched the trumpeter go, trying to suppress his pessimistic thoughts but there was no point ignoring the fact that this could all go terribly wrong. If Ginckel became bogged down on the other side of the river they were in real trouble.

Sarsfield

From the top of the tower on King John's Castle Sarsfield watched the attack on the fort protecting the far end of Thomond Bridge. It was almost four hours since the enemy had crossed the river on their new pontoon bridge, four hours during which they had deployed thousands of men and pushed towards the bridge. They had been halted for a time by Colonel Stapleton's infantry but then Stapleton had been forced back to the fort by superior numbers.

The constant boom of enemy field guns firing at the fort was drowned out by the return fire of the cannons on the castle walls. But the distance, firing over their own fort in the general direction of the attackers, meant there was little accuracy. Clouds of grey smoke drifted eastwards in the sullen air under a sky of equally dirty clouds but the rain held off. Between the smoke and the noise of the guns, it was difficult to work out what was happening but the general situation was clear. The enemy was trying to cut the city off from County Clare.

Sarsfield lowered his telescope as Wauchope emerged from the stairs. 'They're throwing everything at Irish Town,' he said.

'What? Planning an assault?'

Wauchope shook his head. 'Targeting the sally ports to stop an excursion. Trying to dissuade us from counter-attacking.'

'Could we?' Sarsfield shouted as a cannon fired near them. It could be an opportunity, he thought, depending on how many of their men

390

had crossed the river into County Clare. It was a substantial force, certainly more than a raiding party, which would have depleted their numbers around Irish Town.

'It will take some time to get organised,' Wauchope shouted back, a hand behind his ear to try and deflect the din. 'Especially under fire.'

'What does the Frenchman say?'

'He wants to know where the cavalry is. Why it hasn't moved against the enemy forces, attacked their rear.'

'As far as we know,' Sarsfield said, coming to the defence of the cavalry. He had dispatched a rider to alert them as soon as word had come through that the enemy was crossing the river. There was no sign that the cavalry had left their camp at Sixmilebridge but, for all they knew, they could be attacking the enemy even now.

Wauchope said nothing. They watched in silence the clouds of smoke rising from the enemy artillery firing at the fort. There were 800 men there, more now that reinforcements had gone out of the town, enough to hold it against the attack, especially if the cavalry harried the enemy from behind. The threat of a cavalry attack might even be enough to force the Williamites to pull back.

Colonel Charles O'Kelly shouldered his way in between them and faced Sarsfield, his eyes blazing with anger. '*Cá bhfuil siad?*' he stabbed Sarsfield's chest with his finger. 'Where's the horse?'

Sarsfield stepped backwards, taken by surprise.

'This is their doing.' O'Kelly said, still stabbing Sarsfield, his finger emphasising each short sentence. 'They've done a deal. Let them cross the river. Clifford and your friend Luttrell.'

Sarsfield raised his palms in a placatory gesture. 'Calm yourself.'

'I will not,' Kelly shouted, his face going a deeper shade of red as he gulped for air. 'Good men are dying out there. All their fault. Luttrell, Clifford and the rest.'

Wauchope took hold of Kelly's arms from behind and gently drew him back from Sarsfield's face, understanding enough of the Irish from his own knowledge of Gallic to know what he had been saying. The old man allowed himself to be moved and his shoulders dropped as his anger deflated.

'Wait and see how this develops,' Sarsfield tried to reassure him. 'They're not making much headway.'

Wauchope swore into a sudden gap in the cannon fire and Sarsfield and O'Kelly turned their attention to the fort. Men were emerging from its gate, a few dropping from its walls, running towards Thomond Bridge. The numbers turned quickly from tens into hundreds and they bunched up as they reached the narrow bridge. Moments later enemy soldiers appeared on its walls, firing their fusils and hurling grenades after the fleeing group. Then they too were dropping from the walls and emerging from the gate in pursuit, slashing with swords and bayonets, clubbing with the stocks of flintlocks.

The pursuers and the pursued turned into a melee of hand-to-hand fighting in the bottleneck of the narrow bridge. Shouts and clangs of steel could be heard by the watchers on the castle walls as waves of their comrades were mown down. The big guns had gone silent, unable to fire on the attackers without hitting their own men.

'Ochón is ochón ó,' O'Kelly gasped in a choking voice as the drawbridge two-thirds of the way across the bridge began to rise, blocking the escape route into the city. Those nearest jumped at it, a few hanging on as it rose. One of them fell, hit by a musket ball. Others jumped at the edge of the bridge as it rose ever higher. Most failed to grab hold and fell into the deep river.

'What's he doing?' O'Kelly cried in horror at the action of the commander of the gatehouse, who controlled the drawbridge.

Men lining the castle's walls were shouting and screaming as they looked on, impotently. Some fired futile shots in frustration. The enemy had stopped pursuing the men now trapped on the bridge, drawn back and was pouring a continuous rain of lead shot and tossing grenades at the helpless men. Those already near the rising drawbridge were forced into the river by the press of bodies behind them. Some jumped into the gap and others clambered over the parapet and tried to swim to safety. Bodies were beginning to bob against the narrow arches of the bridge where the incoming tide pushed against the seaward drift of the river, creating small whirlpools.

Those trapped in the middle of the bridge, unable to move, tried to surrender, raising their hands, waving handkerchiefs. There was no mercy to be had. The musket fire continued to thud into the already dead and the dying. An occasional grenade exploded, tossing spatters of blood and bits of flesh into the air.

O'Kelly was sobbing, mumbling an alternating litany of curses and prayers. Wauchope wiped away a tear with the cuff of his tunic. Sarsfield was numb.

It ended at last, the popping of shots dying away like the last drops of a cloudburst on a tin roof. There was no more movement among the bodies piled on the bridge and around its entry. Survivors were helped from the water on the city's shore or were pulled over the bridge's parapet from where they had managed to cling to the stonework. The enemy withdrew into the cover of the fort, expecting retaliatory fire from the castle's cannons but none came.

A silence settled over the walls and the scene of the massacre.

Sarsfield made his way through the men on the bridge. Some were stunned, others angry. The wounded groaned and writhed on the ground. A man who was fished out of the river at the end of a long pike flopped on the stones, apparently lifeless. The castle's cannons started up again, hurling furious volleys of red-hot shot overhead at the captured fort.

Angry men were hammering at the door of the gatehouse, barred against them. 'It was the French,' one of them shouted at Sarsfield as he shouldered his way through them. He was aware that the commander of the gatehouse was a French officer.

He got to the front of the crowd, turned and ordered them back. They resisted for a moment. 'Give us the Frenchman,' one shouted, to a chorus of approval.

'Leave this to me,' Sarsfield replied. 'Move back.'

They did, with a reluctant shuffle, and Sarsfield hammered on the door and shouted his own name. He heard a plank being lifted and the door opened a crack and then some more to let him in. Two pale-faced soldiers slammed it shut and dropped the plank back into place to bar it behind him.

'Where is he?'

One of them pointed to a corner where the French officer was propped against the wall, a dark patch of blood seeping through his grey uniform. His face was white and his dark eyes stared straight ahead, unseeing. His chest was rising and falling in uneven jerks with the effort of breathing.

Sarsfield turned his attention back to the soldiers.

'He was hit by an enemy ball while the bridge was going up,' one said quickly.

The other nodded. 'He ordered it. We told him it was wrong but he did it himself.'

'He said the heretics would overrun the town if he didn't,' the first one added.

Sarsfield looked from one to the other. He didn't believe them about the Frenchman's wound but it hardly mattered. The damage was done. The horror of what had happened was imprinted on everyone's memory. And these two would be telling everyone later that they shot the madman but couldn't stop him. There would be no stopping the rise of anti-French feeling either now.

He went back outside and announced that the French officer was dead. 'Save your anger for the people who killed your comrades,' he added. 'For the enemy who refused to accept surrender and shot down trapped men in cold blood. You all saw what happened.'

'That we did,' one man retorted. 'Why did he raise the drawbridge?'

'He was afraid they would storm the town.'

There was a chorus of derision. It would have been suicidal for the enemy to have tried to storm English Town over the bridge. It was too narrow to allow anything more than a trickle of men across, a trickle that the garrison would have dealt with easily. For the same reason they couldn't use the bridge to counterattack, even if it wasn't now blocked by the bodies of their dead.

'Get back to your positions,' Sarsfield said. 'We will have our revenge on those who did this.'

The order was met with grumbles but the heat had gone out of the immediate situation. The cohesive force of the group's anger seeped away. The cannonballs continued to roar overhead but they were nothing other than an emotional response to what all had witnessed.

Cannonballs, mortars and carcasses continued to rain down on both English and Irish Towns throughout the night, even though the fine rain, persistent and wetting, dampened their effects. Infantrymen huddled in their lean-tos under the walls that sheltered them from the bombardment, drinking and playing ever more reckless rounds of cards. Discipline was close to breaking point. In their better quarters, senior officers also had sleepless nights. All knew that a moment of decision had arrived.

The officers gathered just after daybreak in the Citadel for a council of war, all chalk-faced. They avoided one another's eyes, buried in their own thoughts, while deferring to d'Usson's seniority to get the discussion underway.

'It's intolerable,' he began, 'that my officers are being insulted and threatened with violence in the streets.'

No one said anything. Intolerable maybe but, most thought, understandable. Hadn't he seen what had happened the day before?

'The man responsible has died of his wounds,' he continued, knowing what they were thinking. 'That should be an end to this unfortunate incident. He has paid the price for his mistake. We must look beyond it.'

The silence that greeted his half-hearted apology was broken by a hostile voice demanding, 'Where's the French fleet?'

'I know no more than you do,' d'Usson replied. 'Have no doubt, it will come.'

'Where's the cavalry?' Tessé threw back, coming to his colleague's aid. 'Where were they yesterday? Where are they today?'

'Ask Clifford,' a bitter voice suggested.

'We wouldn't have seen what happened yesterday if he hadn't sold the pass,' another added.

A chorus of complaints broke out, about traitors, false friends and enemies within. D'Usson let it go on for a few moments, then held up his hand. 'That is all very well. What do we do now?'

'Get the cavalry to cut the heretics' pontoon bridges,' someone suggested.

'And attack from Irish Town. We can overrun their trenches.'

'And then?' d'Usson asked.

'Push them back to Dublin,' the enthusiast for a counterattack said, raising a muted cheer. But they all knew that was a fantasy. For one thing, the campaigning season was all but over. For another, they didn't have the strength to push back the Williamites, to recapture all that had been lost in the past year. To think of retaking Dublin was an impossible dream.

The reality behind the bravado brought a glum silence.

Sarsfield took a deep breath: it was time to put into practice the plan he had been trying to resist for weeks. 'It is time to negotiate terms,' he said aloud.

The silence turned from glum to shocked. To all but Sarsfield's closest associates, it was a total surprise that the man who had always resisted negotiations, even when the likes of the wily Tyrconnell favoured them, had now changed his mind.

'Now is the time,' he went on, into the silence, 'while we still hold some cards. Wait too long, until we run out of food, until we are weakened further and we will have no hand to play.'

'Are we running out of food?' a sceptical voice asked.

'In less than a month,' Wauchope interjected. 'Now that we're surrounded and can't get into Clare. And,' he cast a sideways glance at the French generals, 'even if the French fleet arrives there's no guarantee it will be able to come through through the English blockade.'

D'Usson bridled and appeared about to argue the latter point but thought better of it.

'We can't continue the war here,' Sarsfield went on quickly, to head off any dissent. 'Even if we can hold out for the winter, what then? Face defeat in the spring? Will France send us enough men and supplies to take back the country?' He paused and looked around at the tired faces. 'No. The war in Ireland is over.'

There was a sharp intake of breath in the room. A few shook their heads in denial.

'But the war *for* Ireland isn't over,' he added. 'The only way we can protect our religion and our lands is by defeating the usurper, the prince of Orange. We can't defeat him in Ireland any more but he can be defeated elsewhere. And we can help to do that.'

'Fight for France!' a derisive voice interrupted.

'Fight for Ireland wherever we can,' Sarsfield shot back. 'In France, the Spanish Netherlands, in England. Wherever we can overthrow this usurper and get back our rights and our rightful King.'

'And what does that King say? What about Tyrconnell's oath?'

'We don't know the King's wishes but I'm sure he does not wish us to share the fate of our comrades yesterday. We all saw what the rebels will do to men who are no longer in a position to fight back.'

'Is that what you want?' Wauchope intervened again, glaring at those who had been raising objections. 'To wait until they storm the city and put everyone to the sword?'

'If you come to France ---' d'Usson began.

Sarsfield cut him short. 'If we go to France, it will be to lead an invasion of England, to remove the usurper from that kingdom and this kingdom.'

'And the kingdom of Scotland,' Wauchope added, prompting a titter of laughter which lightened the atmosphere for a fleeting moment.

'We have to strike while the iron is still hot,' Sarsfield said. 'While we have some power to negotiate favourable terms.'

'And you think they'll be willing to give us favourable terms?' The questioner managed to inject some hope into the query.

'If not, we *will* fight on. We are not defeated yet.'

The prospect of continuing the war hung in the air, drawing out the weariness in everyone's bones, except for those who were the most bellicose. The prospect of reasonable terms looked enticing compared to a future that offered only more of the setbacks of the last couple of years, more of the deaths, misery and hunger that had engulfed the country, destroying livelihoods, crops, animals and even the land itself.

'We will not surrender,' Sarsfield assured them. 'We will talk as equals or we will not talk at all.'

The grumbles died away. He knew that he hadn't persuaded them all but, clearly, no one had a better plan.

The cannons stopped firing from the walls of both towns at the appointed time and the noise and smoke drifted away with the rain on the wind. Into the silence, drummers beat the chamade from the castle and the Citadel and white flags were raised over both. After a short pause, they received the answering confirmation signal from both Williamite camps. Wauchope called out in Dutch from the castle's walls that they wanted a parley while a brigadier did the same from the Citadel.

Wauchope was invited to cross the river under a safe conduct and he and Sarsfield got into a rowing boat beneath the castle walls. The tide was ebbing and the oarsman struggled against the torrent of water heading for the sea. Dead bodies bobbed in sheltered pools among the rocks as they came close to the far shore. Nobody said anything.

A detachment of horsemen moved along the Clare bank, tracking their progress to the point where they finally came ashore. Once the boat was grounded, Sarsfield and Wauchope stepped out and Ruvigny dismounted and came forward. They introduced themselves in French, following Ruvigny's lead, three generals who had in their time shared armies as well as enmities. Sarsfield and Ruvigny had once been in the army of King Louis of France; Wauchope, in the English army of King James, had been seconded to Holland to fight the French; and now Ruvigny was in the army of the Dutch King William, fighting the armies of Kings Louis and James.

'General Ginckel?' Sarsfield inquired.

'He is not available at present. You wish to speak to him?'

'Yes.'

'To what purpose?'

'To discuss terms.'

If he was surprised or pleased Ruvigny gave no sign of it. 'I will inform him.'

'Only if he is prepared to consider our army going abroad, to wherever it wishes.'

'I will inform him,' Ruvigny repeated, acknowledging the condition with a small bow. 'Meanwhile, a twenty-four-hour ceasefire?'

'Yes,' Sarsfield agreed.

They shook hands and Sarsfield and Wauchope got back into the boat.

The oarsman pulled it out into the stream and let the flood water and tide carry it downriver as he steered it with one oar towards the safety of the harbour beyond the castle.

The die was cast.

Mackay

T he unexpected beat of the drum was still sounding in his head as Mackay rode quickly from Singland Hill back to Ginckel's headquarters.

'You've heard?' he asked as soon as he dismounted and strode into the general's tent.

'What?'

'They've beaten a parley.'

Ginckel was at his desk writing letters and sat back in surprise. 'You've accepted?'

'Yes.'

'Interesting.'

Ginckel leaned forward again and dropped the lid on his ink-holder. 'What do you make of it?'

'They probably want a ceasefire to bury their dead,' Mackay suggested. He had heard the reports of the slaughter at the bridge and was surprised later to find Ginckel in a downbeat mood when the general had returned to his headquarters from the river crossing.

Even though the operation had been a total success, the general was not happy. Indeed, earlier that morning, he had despatched a report to the lords justices admitting that he could not assault the city and that he would have to settle into a long blockade over the winter. As he told them, he had been taken aback at the papists' determined resistance to his approach to the bridge. I'm listening too much to people like Talmash, who think the Irish will always run, he had told himself.

He stood up and blotted the paper on which he had been writing. It was another appeal to the Admiralty to send more warships to seal the mouth of the Shannon: Captain Cole was badgering him daily for reinforcements, fearful that he could not withstand an attack from a French fleet. And the word from the spies at Brest was that the French had assembled a large fleet destined for Limerick. It was probably already on its way.

They rode back together to Singland Hill where a trumpeter had arrived to say that the papists were sending a boat across the river and Ruvigny was awaiting their emissary.

Ginckel stood on the hill, looking down over the two towns, noting the unusual silence as he waited. There was no sign of life on Irish Town's walls. Beyond, in English Town, the broken tower of St Mary's Cathedral jutted up among the other jagged ruins of tower houses. Thin spirals of smoke rose here and there, barely discernible from the drifting mist. Nearby, his men were huddled in their waterlogged trenches. He imagined he could almost see his batteries sinking deeper into the soft ground, one of his nightmares coming true. A winter blockade was going to be very unpleasant but, if it had to be done, it would be done.

A trumpeter arrived at last from Ruvigny. 'They have agreed a twenty-four-hour ceasefire, my lord,' he said. 'And they want to discuss terms.'

Ginckel felt an enormous weight lift off his shoulders.

'My lord Ruvigny said they're trying to impose a condition,' the messenger added. 'They want to be allowed leave Ireland, to go abroad.'

Ginckel nodded to himself. That was not an insurmountable problem. Certainly not if it was up to him.

'Who insisted on this condition?' Mackay intervened in a suspicious voice. 'The French?'

'General Sarsfield and General Wauchope.'

Better and better, Ginckel thought. By all accounts Sarsfield was the most important papist leader now that Tyrconnell was dead and the one most opposed to negotiating an end to the war. And it seemed he might be ignoring the French or, at the very least, they were going along with the decision to seek terms. This was very good news.

'Where do they want to go?' Mackay demanded, still suspicious. He didn't like the sound of this. What would have been the point of all this fighting if we are to let them go off to continue fighting against us elsewhere? It was normal to let a garrison of a town surrendered under terms to leave and re-join their army but this was different. This was not just about the surrender of a town. This was about ending the war in Ireland, ending the revolt against the new order in the three kingdoms of the British Isles.

'I don't know, my lord,' the messenger replied. 'My lord Ruvigny didn't say.'

Ginckel dismissed him and turned to Mackay, finally allowing himself a smile. 'The war in Ireland may be over,' he said. And he would have achieved what the King wished, ending it in 1691. Ending it, indeed, at the very spot the King himself had failed to do so the year before.

Mackay returned a sour look. 'They're in no position to impose conditions,' he said, waving a hand that took in Irish Town and English Town. 'It's impertinent to even try and do so.'

'We'll see how strong their resolve is,' Ginckel reassured him, unperturbed. He certainly had the upper hand now that they were suing for terms.

Word spread quickly through the camp, lifting most people's spirits as the prospect of going into winter quarters somewhere drier replaced that of severe discomfort, sickness and death in this sodden place. But not everyone was happy.

Two of the Ulster officers accosted Mackay, their religious ally among all the foreigners on the general staff. 'That can't be allowed,' one of them said. 'They can't just pick up their camp and move it someplace else after they've been defeated.'

'And continue their revolt against the lawful order,' the other added. 'And against the Revolution and the Reformation.'

'It's a matter for the general,' Mackay said. He agreed with them. but there was no point raising their expectations. He had seen Ginckel's reaction and knew that he would be of a mind to agree generous terms, as at Galway, or even worse. Anything to put an end to this war before the winter.

'Surely it's not just a matter for the Dutchman. The lords justices must have a say in it too.'

'You should talk to them,' Mackay suggested.

'Are they coming back?' Sir Thomas Coningsby had left Limerick shortly after the siege had settled into stalemate.

'I imagine they will. They'll have to approve the terms before they're agreed.'

'They didn't at Galway,' one pointed out.

'We should make sure they do this time.' Mackay felt a twinge of guilt at the fact that he was fomenting dissent behind the general's back but he excused himself on the grounds that there were more important matters at stake on this occasion.

The Ulster officers nodded to each other. 'Aye, that's what we'll do,' one said. 'And you'll talk to them too?'

'I'm always prepared to make my views known,' Mackay said.

'Good. Good.' The officers went away content that they had a plan of action to stop the papists getting favourable terms.

Mackay watched them go, knowing that they would have their work cut out to overcome the pressure for a deal from the Dutch and Danes, perhaps even from the King himself, who all wanted an end to this war as quickly as possible. He himself would like to go home to Clara in Holland but there were bigger issues at stake than the convenience of any one man. Like the fate of the whole continent, whether it was to return to obscurantist superstition or continue to turn towards Godliness.

Mackay turned his attention back to the scene before him. The mist had dwindled away, almost imperceptibly, the sky was a lighter grey but the air was still damp. Men had emerged from the trenches and a few had ventured over towards the walls of Irish Town and were shouting up to papists on the battlements from the foot of the steep glacis. He couldn't make out what they were saying, not even what language they were speaking, but it was probably the usual: complaining about their fool officers and their tight-fisted commissaries who carried on as if all food and money was coming out of their own mouths and pockets.

Wauchope, he thought, now a papist general. He remembered him as a mid-ranking officer in the former king's army in Holland. Indeed, Wauchope had taken over from him as colonel of one of the regiments in the Dutch brigade before siding with King James and returning to England. Gossip at the time hinted that the real reason he had to leave Holland was because he had had an affair with the prince of Orange's English mistress, Betty Villiers.

Talmash interrupted his reminiscences. 'I wouldn't have given them a ceasefire,' he said. 'There was no need.'

'The general is keen on terms.'

'Hah,' Talmash snorted. 'Not as keen as the papists. They know they're beaten. There's no need to do anything but accept their surrender.'

'Don't you want to go home?' Mackay asked him with a sideways smile.

'Home!' Talmash retorted, providing the expected answer. 'Home is where the action is.'

'You'd like to go back to Tangier?'

'I wouldn't mind a spell in a warmer climate again.' Talmash sounded wistful about the campaign against the Moors in north Africa.

The fighting here really is over, Mackay thought, realizing that everyone, including himself, was already thinking of a future somewhere else. Even the enemy with their wish to go abroad. There was probably a lot of talking to come. But that was politics, not warfare, and there were certainly reasons for disquiet about where that would lead.

The general's desire for a quick end to the campaign had already led him down a dangerous path. The terms he had given to Galway were ridiculous, encouraging the papists to continue with their misguided beliefs. Indeed, he had been offering unnecessarily and unwisely generous terms ever since they had taken Athlone. And, Mackay knew, it would be difficult for Ginckel to go back on those terms now even if he wanted to. Which he didn't.

'My lord,' a messenger interrupted his thoughts, 'the general wishes you to accompany him across the river to meet the enemy.'

Mackay glanced back to see Ginckel's entourage approaching Singland Hill from his headquarters. He hurried away to his horse.

'Don't worry,' Talmash called after him. 'I'll be here if they try any tricks.'

OCTOBER

Sarsfield and Mackay

Colonel Charles O'Kelly finally managed to waylay Sarsfield as he made his way through King John's Castle towards the gate where the rowing boat was waiting. Sarsfield, he suspected, had been avoiding him since the decision to seek terms, knowing that he opposed it.

'You're going to extend the ceasefire,' he said, an admission to himself more than a question. He cast a glance over Sarsfield's shoulder at the crate of claret in the arms of the orderly behind him.

Sarsfield nodded. The ceasefire was due to expire later in the day but nobody doubted that it would be extended. The mood in the city had shifted already, publicly accepting that the war was over: a flood gate had been opened by the previous day's agreement.

O'Kelly shook his head in sadness. 'After all this time,' he said. 'You were so steadfast for so long.'

'There's no choice now,' Sarsfield said with a roughness that he regretted immediately. 'You know it too,' he added in a softer voice. 'We cannot win here.'

'The French might still come.' O'Kelly knew he was clutching at straws even as he said it: he had little time for, or belief in, the French, who cared nothing about Ireland.

'Even if they do ---.' Sarsfield shook his head.

Wauchope came back from the boat where he had been waiting. 'The oarsman wants to go before the tide turns,' he said.

O'Kelly stood aside to let Sarsfield and the orderly pass. Sarsfield touched the old man's shoulder as he went by.

The tide was still coming in, easing the pressure of the flood waters pouring downstream. The oarsman managed to keep the boat on a more or less straight course, close to the bridge and the gaping arch where the drawbridge was still pointing to the heavens.

Ruvigny was waiting for them on the far bank and led them to a newly erected tent nearby. One of Sarsfield's bottles of claret was opened, glasses poured. The Frenchman sniffed at his and gave an appreciative nod. Sarsfield wondered if he was aware that 'claret' was also slang for blood in English. Probably not.

'We would like to extend the ceasefire,' he said in French, 'while we consider whether there is a basis for an agreement.'

Ruvigny took another sip of the wine to give the impression of considering the proposal, although it was what had been expected and their response agreed. 'Three days?' he suggested.

'That should be adequate.'

'And you may send a party across the bridge to bury your dead.'

'Thank you,' Sarsfield said.

'And in return, perhaps, we may have something?' Ruvigny said, adding with a slight smile, 'as well as this excellent wine.'

'We shall release all our prisoners of war.'

'How many?'

'Two hundred and ten,' Wauchope said. 'Unfortunately, thirty were killed by your bombardment.'

'That is regrettable,' Ruvigny said as a matter of course, without any noticeable regret.

'And our condition?' Sarsfield prompted, getting to the nub of the conversation.

'That's a matter for our general,' Ruvigny said. 'I will take you to meet him now.'

Sarsfield breathed an inward sigh of relief. Presumably, Ginckel didn't want to meet the delegation in order to reject the condition.

Horses and an escort were provided for Sarsfield and Wauchope, and Ruvigny led them back towards Ginckel's tent along the road to Cratloe. Sarsfield had travelled the road and area numerous times in the previous weeks but it had already taken on an indefinable air of enemy territory. A squad of pikemen stepped aside to watch them pass.

Ginckel's tent was well back from the front lines, behind a hill and a copse of trees that sheltered it from the cannons' spotters on the castle walls. He and Mackay were standing behind a trestle table, cleared of its maps, awaiting their visitors. Chairs were lined up on both sides of the table.

Ginckel and Sarsfield bowed briefly, both interested in their first sight of each other; one with a reputation for caution, the other for daring; the heavy-set Dutchman a decade or more older than the taller and leaner Irishman; one with all the cards, the other with few.

'My lord Lucan,' Ginckel said, making a point of recognising Sarsfield's Jacobite title as a gesture of respect.

Mackay and Wauchope nodded to each other, former commander to former subordinate, both Scots. Each decided the other looked older than the few years since they had been in the one army. But then a lot had happened in less than five years. From their respective viewpoints, King James had either abdicated or been overthrown, both were rebels or traitors, one to the old regime, one to the new. The defining line was their religion, one Protestant, the other Catholic.

Ginckel indicated that they should all sit. 'I have heard a lot about you,' he said in Dutch to Sarsfield.

After a moment's hesitation, Wauchope translated for Sarsfield.

'And I about you,' Sarsfield replied in English.

Mackay translated it into Dutch.

Ginckel gave a wan smile. 'It will be simpler if we all speak English,' he suggested.

'Thank you, my lord,' Sarsfield acknowledged the concession. The omens look good, he thought: Ginckel doesn't want these talks to fail.

'You are setting a condition for discussions,' Ginckel prompted.

'Yes, my lord. We are prepared to discuss terms if our army is free to go abroad, wherever it chooses.'

'But not to Scotland,' Mackay interjected, his vehemence bringing a surprised laugh from the others. That possibility had not occurred to anyone else but Mackay was acutely aware that there were still troublesome pockets of Jacobite support in the Highlands.

'Not to Scotland,' Sarsfield confirmed. 'To France.'

'That is not permissible under the generous terms their majesties have approved,' Ginckel said. 'They will grant your men pardons, guarantee their lands and religion, and give them the option of joining their Majesties' army at a similar or better rank. You would obviously be very welcome as senior generals,' he waved his hands to include Wauchope.

Mackay gave Wauchope a sour look, indicating that he did not relish the prospect of having a former subordinate and a papist as an equal or, worse, a superior in the King's forces.

'These are all points worthy of discussion, my lord,' Sarsfield said, 'but only if we are allowed to go to France.'

'All of you?'

'Yes.'

'You will not give your men a choice?'

Sarsfield hesitated. He hadn't really been prepared for this level of discussion. A momentary wish that Luttrell was by his side came into his mind but he suppressed it. 'That and all the details can be discussed once we begin negotiations.'

'Very well,' Ginckel said. 'I agree in principle that the Irish army may go abroad. To France. Subject to a final agreement on all the terms, of course.'

Mackay gave Ginckel a sharp look, surprised at his ready agreement. He must have given some thought to this in advance, he realised. Must have known that this condition was coming.

'Of course,' Sarsfield nodded. He had got the only concession he really wanted. The details should be easy enough to work out. 'There is one other thing,' he added. 'It is necessary that we include some cavalry officers in our preparations for negotiations.'

'Yes, certainly,' Ginckel grasped his point immediately and looked to Mackay. 'Arrange for them to pass through our lines into the city.'

Ginckel and Mackay stood outside their tent, watching the enemy generals ride away with their escort. Large drops of rain began to fall, slowly and individually at first and then rapidly, churning up the muddied ground. They stepped back inside.

'A good day's work,' Ginckel said in Dutch, clearly very pleased. 'It's excellent that Sarsfield himself is leading the delegation.'

Mackay nodded his agreement to the latter circumstance. A concern had been that the French would surrender the city but that Sarsfield would lead a breakaway Irish group who would join forces with rapparees and wage an endless campaign of small-scale strikes and counter-strikes, leaving the country in a state of neither war nor peace and tying up the King's army here indefinitely. 'But I don't think the lord justices will be so happy with your concession,' Mackay ventured.

'It's none of their business,' Ginckel shot back. 'It's a military matter. My domain.'

'But there are wider consequences than the purely military.'

'Our job is to end the war here. Their Majesties have been very clear about wanting us back on the main battlefields on the Continent.'

'And having to fight them all over again if we let them go there?' Mackay raised a thumb over his shoulder to point back at the way Sarsfield and Wauchope had gone. 'When we've already defeated them here.'

The rain hammering on the roof had found a weak spot in the canvas and water began to run along the tent's frame and plop down like a slow drumbeat onto the seat of the chair Sarsfield had vacated.

'It's no different from allowing the garrison at Galway to come to Limerick to fight us here,' Ginckel said.

'It *is* different,' Mackay insisted. 'That was a matter of taking a town, seizing their territory, narrowing their options. This is different.'

'This is also a matter of seizing their territory,' Ginckel pointed out. 'The whole island.'

'Exactly,' Mackay agreed. 'But what will it do to Ireland? The papists will believe they have not been defeated. It will encourage their intransigence, to hold on to their superstitions, and dissuade them from accepting reformed religion, which is the point of this campaign. It's not just a part of the wider war.'

Ginckel gave him a look that said he didn't need a religious sermon right now. 'Wouldn't it be worse for Ireland to have an army of defeated and disgruntled men remain here? How many rapparees would there be then? Maybe with Sarsfield and some of the others to lead them?'

That was a good point, Mackay had to concede. And he had to accept that Ginckel was right: what became of Ireland wasn't their immediate problem. Ending the campaign was.

'Besides,' Ginckel added, 'how many of them will actually go to France? I'll insist that they are given a choice. And not that many will go if the Irish and French dislike each other as much as we've been told.'

The rain stopped as it had begun, petering out to single drops and then ending altogether. The drumbeat on the chair slowed and ceased. The flap was pulled back and a drenched messenger entered. 'My lord,' he said, bowing to Ginckel, 'the pontoon bridge has broken. The river is so swollen, it swept away the barrels at one end.'

Ginckel and Mackay exchanged glances, both thinking the same thing. They were isolated on this side of the river, their army really split in two now. Extremely vulnerable to an attack on either side but for the ceasefire. It couldn't have come at a better moment. Providence, Mackay thought. Providence has favoured our cause once more. And coincidentally favoured this general in spite of his shortcomings.

'Tell Württemberg to get it repaired,' Ginckel ordered, 'without delay.'

'Might they seize the opportunity?' Mackay wondered as the messenger hurried away. He didn't think so. Honourable men wouldn't break their word but the enemy were all papists and their priests were all Jesuits at heart, adept at finding weaselly ways to make the end justify the means.

Ginckel raised his hands in a 'don't know' gesture. 'Issue passes for their cavalry officers to go into the city and send them out with a trumpeter immediately.'

Mackay nodded. In other words, proceed with the ceasefire agreement as quickly as possible.

'And invite them to dine with us on their way into the city,' Ginckel added. 'It would be useful to gauge their thinking.'

In the city questions began to accumulate. What exactly would an agreement mean? For those who went to France? For those who remained at home? For their families? For their lands and religion? The few copies available of the terms accepted by Galway and tattered copies of Ginckel's last proclamation were passed from hand to hand and scrutinised closely, every man reading the sections most relevant to himself, trying to divine an unknowable future.

'Never mind that!' Colonel Charles O'Kelly snatched a copy of the Galway treaty from the hands of a young captain. 'Don't you know they've broken it already?'

'What have they done?'

'Tried to disarm the Catholics there.'

The captain didn't look too upset at the information. He tried to take back the papers but O'Kelly held onto them and the young man was forced to walk away empty-handed. O'Kelly stalked off through the city streets in search of Sarsfield.

Now that the bombardment was over, people were no longer hiding under the shelter of the main walls but were moving openly, picking through debris, salvaging whatever there was worth saving. Rough lean-tos were springing up in the ruins of houses as their occupants made a semblance of moving home and securing their property. Drains were repaired to sluice away the build-up of sewage in blocked streets. Decomposing bodies were uncovered amid the ruins and buried quickly outside the walls on King's Island.

O'Kelly found Wauchope in the Citadel and asked him where the general was, not needing to specify which of the four generals in the city he meant. 'I don't know,' Wauchope lied. 'I was looking for him myself.'

O'Kelly waved the copy of the Galway treaty at him. 'Let this be a warning to you all. They have broken it already. Their word is worthless.'

Wauchope gave him a weary nod. 'Sir Toby Butler is coming from Galway today,' he said. 'He can tell us all about it. By all accounts he's the best lawyer in the country.'

'Not if he's sober,' O'Kelly retorted, repeating the general belief that

Butler, the solicitor general, was an excellent advocate but only at his best after copious quantities of brandy.

'We can make sure he won't be,' Wauchope gave him a wry grin.

O'Kelly continued his search for Sarsfield. He went back through Irish Town, pausing to stop two young boys in tattered clothes rolling an unexploded mortar ball down the hill. They ignored him and continued pushing it with their bare feet to keep it rolling every time its handles brought it to a halt. He crossed Baal's Bridge, where the torn screen partially closed off the sight of the Abbey river and the enemy battery beyond, and climbed up Great Street to the mayor's house.

'Is the general in?' he asked a sentry outside the door. Loose stones knocked by cannonballs from the top floor of the tower house were piled nearby.

The sentry shook his head, under orders to deny Sarsfield's presence to any but a handful of his confidants.

Sarsfield was upstairs, in a drawing room, watching Honor working on some lace on a small circular frame. She was sitting by the narrow window, where the light was strongest, her head bowed intently over her work. The tower house's roof and top floor were gone This room was still intact but rain had coursed down one of the walls. Its tapestry had been rolled up and now lay across a table which was pushed with other furniture into the dry corner.

Sarsfield sat on an armchair, its back jammed against the table, the tapestry protruding by his arm. He felt trapped. Not just trapped in the city like everyone else but also imprisoned by the accumulating demands on him from all quarters -- from the army, the archbishops, the merchants, the local lawyers; all wanting to know what would happen to them and demanding that he protect their interests. What he wanted more than anything now was to go for a fast ride in the country to clear his head. But that was impossible. He was no longer a free man.

'You're making me nervous,' Honor said without looking up, 'watching me like that.' She and the other ladies and the lords justices who had sought refuge in County Clare had returned to the city as soon as the enemy had crossed the river and before the massacre at the bridge.

'Like what?'

'Like one of the nuns.' She turned to him, half her face in shadow. 'The old one who taught me embroidery.'

He gave a short laugh. 'You think I look like an old nun.'

'Not exactly.'

'Sorry. I'm not really examining your work.'

'You can if you wish.' She gave him a sly smile and turned back to her needlework.

But his mind was elsewhere. The opening negotiations had been simple. He'd had only one thing on his mind: the right to take the army to France and continue the fight from there. But now there were these other questions: how they were to get there; what would happen to their families and relatives who remained behind; and, of course, their lands? Then there were questions about those who would remain behind. What rights would they have, to their lands, and to their religion?

The archbishop of Armagh, Dominic Maguire, had given him a lengthy lecture earlier in the day and a list of demands required to guarantee the rights of Catholics. They must be equal in every way with those of heretics. There must be a priest in every parish. Landowners wanted security and those who had already lost property in earlier settlements must have it returned now. 'New interest' men who had bought land from previous settlers were determined not to forfeit what they had paid for. Those who had seized the houses of Protestants in Limerick insisted on holding onto them. Merchants wanted to continue their rights to trade freely with France, even if it remained illegal under English law. Lawyers demanded that they be accorded equal recognition with Protestant members of the bar.

The lords justices were not happy that Sarsfield had effectively seized the initiative. 'We should have waited for the King's decision,' Sir Richard Nagle had told him.

'How could we?' Sarsfield had retorted.

'Surely it is not impossible to send an emissary to Saint-Germain,' Nagle replied, neatly implying that the responsibility for keeping open the lines of communication with France rested on the military. Which meant on him, Sarsfield. 'Any agreement reached will have to be approved by the King before it is signed.'

'How is that possible?' Sarsfield said, his anger rising. 'You haven't noticed that we are besieged, surrounded?'

'Nevertheless, you and the others signed the duke's oath not to capitulate or surrender without the King's consent.'

Sarsfield bridled at the word 'surrender' but thought better of continuing to argue with the lawyer. Going to France was not a surrender but a way of avoiding surrender. 'You are the King's representatives here,' he said instead. 'You can approve it.'

Nagle turned and walked away, making it clear from his demeanour that neither he nor his fellow lords justices had any desire to take on that responsibility.

At least the French are happy, Sarsfield thought. D'Usson and Tessé had congratulated him on making the right decision and agreed that everything look favourable for an invasion of England from France in 1692. But the French, still nominally in command of the army, were no longer a factor in Limerick; they were all housed together now for their protection after the massacre at the bridge. It had all come to rest on Sarsfield's shoulders.

'When will we leave for France?' Honor interrupted his thoughts, still intent on her embroidery.

'Soon,' he said without thinking. 'The sooner the better.' The crossing was unlikely to be pleasant at this time of year, never mind later, with every possibility of Atlantic storms causing delay and possibly worse. But, first, it had to be organised. Would the prince of Orange provide ships? Or allow transport to come from France. Which could mean that the departure, if agreed, would not take place for months. And what would happen in the meantime? With a demoralised army cooped up in the destroyed city?

Colonel Mark Talbot emerged from the spiral staircase. He was now one of Sarsfield's confidants, to the surprise of his other close associates. But both seemed to be carrying on the late alliance between his natural father, Tyrconnell, and Sarsfield. 'The cavalrymen are coming across the river now,' he said. 'I thought you'd want to know.'

Sarsfield nodded but remained seated. Talbot bowed and murmured 'my lady' to Honor as he left.

418

Wauchope had already brought the cavalry officers up to date with events when Sarsfield joined them in King John's Castle. 'I was just telling Wauchope about our dinner with Ginckel and his staff,' Major General Dominic Sheldon, their English commander said, as Sarsfield entered. 'They certainly don't want for anything.'

Sarsfield shrugged, unimpressed. Of course they would have made an effort to show how well supplied they were, as he had done with his gift of the case of claret. He noted that Purcell was among the new arrivals, wearing a black mourning armband. 'Did you learn anything of interest?' he asked Sheldon.

'He expressed astonishment that we have managed to hold out for so long after Aughrim. In his experience, he said, any other army would have sued for terms the day after.' Sheldon paused. Nobody said anything. 'And he said he had never seen a land so ravaged and devastated by war. No crops growing anywhere. No animals to be seen. People living in hedges and ditches, surviving on he knew not what.'

'So he is prepared to offer reasonable terms?'

'He said the usurper had already offered very generous terms. And he had exceeded them in Galway on his own authority. For which he has been criticised by his own side.'

Was Ginckel now signalling that Galway was beyond the limit of his generosity. 'And what did you tell him about what *we* want?'

'What could I tell him?' Sheldon opened his arms wide. 'I didn't know what you had decided here until Wauchope just informed us.'

'And you think it's the right decision? To go to France?'

'Yes. It's the best possible decision in the circumstances.'

Sarsfield nodded, relieved that the cavalry officers were on his side, although he had never doubted that the troopers would follow wherever he led.

As they moved off to find accommodation somewhere in the city, Sarsfield waited for Purcell to approach him. 'I'm very sorry about Tom,' he said. Purcell's young brother, a major, had been among those who had died at the bridge.

Purcell acknowledged his condolences with a small bow. 'We stopped at the grave on our way here,' he said. 'They've nearly finished filling it in.'

'He was a good man,' Sarsfield said. 'There are a lot of good men in that grave.'

'How many?'

'I don't know for sure. Maybe five hundred.'

Purcell sighed, unwilling to talk any more about his bereavement and the slaughter at the bridge. 'Have you released him?' he asked instead, not needing to specify whom he meant.

Sarsfield shook his head. He had been thinking of it. He needed Luttrell's help now more than ever. And he would release Luttrell in a heartbeat if he could trust him. But he couldn't. Besides, to release him now could give the wrong impression -- that Luttrell had been acting on his behalf all along and that he, Sarsfield, had merely been biding his time for an excuse to open negotiations with the rebels.

'Why not?'

'Because he was treating with the enemy behind our backs.'

'And what are you doing now?'

Sarsfield ignored that as not worthy of a reply.

'Sending the enemy presents,' Purcell continued, his tone dripping with disgust. 'The Dutchman gave us a glass of your claret last night. He had to admit, he said, that it was better than any wine they had.'

'Why did the cavalry pull back?' Sarsfield went on the offensive. 'Take no action when they crossed the river?'

'To avoid being trapped. Like the men on the bridge.' Purcell closed his eyes and his body slumped. He nodded to himself, an acknowledgement of his grief and an acceptance of why Sarsfield was negotiating. 'Can I see Henry?' he asked in a more emollient tone.

Sarsfield nodded.

Purcell stopped at the door and turned back. 'You need him now more than ever.'

Sarsfield gave no sign that he had heard him.

Mackay began to splutter with outrage as he read the proposals. 'These are preposterous. As if they are the victors. As if a century and a half of reform has meant nothing to them.'

It had been formally agreed by both sides to enter negotiations; the ceasefire had been extended indefinitely. Four men of position on each side had been exchanged as hostages. The Irish side had made the opening move, sending a seven-point proposal to Ginckel as the basis for an agreement.

'Are they trying to insult us?' Mackay concluded, raising his hand to let the sheet of paper fall to the table as if it was soiled.

Ginckel nodded. It did indeed appear from the papists' suggested terms that they were not serious about reaching an agreement. Were they simply playing for time, hoping that relief would still arrive from France?

Mackay picked up the list again and began quoting phrases from it, stoking his outrage and trying to transmit it to Ginckel. Pardons for all crimes. Papists to get back all their estates. Liberty of worship. A priest in every parish. Equality with Protestants in the army, politics, professions, business, trade. He shook his head and let the paper float back to the table.

'It's not from Sarsfield,' Ginckel said, putting his finger on clause five. It proposed that the Irish army continue in being and be paid the same as King William's forces if it decided to fight with him against France.

'The pope talking,' Mackay said flatly. 'It's from their priests. We're not talking terms with them, are we?'

Ginckel shook his head. This had to be a distraction, nothing to do with what Sarsfield clearly wanted -- to take his army to France. He sat down at his desk and opened his ink container. Mackay went to leave but Ginckel told him to wait.

The Dutchman wrote a short note saying that he knew enough of the laws of England to know that these terms were so contradictory to them as to amount to an insult to himself. He would not grant them. He signed it, blotted the page and handed it to Mackay for his approval.

'And order a new battery to be erected to the left of your fort,' Ginckel added. 'And stop any fraternising with the enemy. Everyone is to get back to their positions. Be ready to resume the bombardment.'

'Yes, my lord,' Mackay gave a small bow, happy with the decisions.

The preparations for resuming the siege quickly became apparent to the

Jacobite headquarters in the Citadel. Williamite officers were seen ordering their men back into the trenches: the work on the new battery by Singland Hill was noted: and ammunition carts could be seen replenishing supplies of powder, cannonballs and mortars to the other batteries.

Sarsfield resisted the urge to say I told you so as a conference was called to discuss Ginckel's curt dismissal of their proposals. Archbishop Dominic Maguire appeared to be taken aback by it. 'The insult is to us,' he retorted after reading the note. He turned to Sarsfield: 'I thought you said he was prepared to discuss everything.'

'About our departure to France,' Sarsfield pointed out.

Sir Toby Butler, the solicitor general, who had just arrived from Galway, cleared his throat as a way of creating speaking space for himself. 'If I may,' he began before clearing his throat again to secure the maximum attention, 'I think the general and the primate may be at cross-purposes here. I suggest that two separate agreements are required. One to cover the army's move to France. The other to cover the position of those of us who remain behind. As civilians.'

There were nods of approval all around: that made sense.

'We cannot accept anything less than the Galway terms,' the archbishop said, implicitly agreeing with Butler's proposal. 'Indeed, we should receive better terms since what is at stake now is much more than the control of one city.'

'A good point, your grace,' Butler said. 'And one that should be made forcefully to General Ginckel.'

'They say they've broken the terms at Galway,' a voice intervened.

Butler made a non-committal gesture with his hands. 'There have been difficulties. Some of the heretics have been impatient, trying to reassert their former dominance.'

'Have the Catholics been disarmed?' the voice persisted. 'Contrary to the treaty there?'

'There have been difficulties,' Butler repeated in a soothing tone, 'but I hope they can be resolved.'

'All right,' Sarsfield tried to cut the discussion short. 'How do we respond to the Dutchman's message?'

There was silence. Butler broke it after a moment: 'The obvious option is to ask him what terms he proposes and then we can proceed from there.'

'Agreed?' Sarsfield asked.

There were no dissenters and the meeting broke up, people dissolving into their own groups. Sarsfield braced himself for the inevitable confrontation with Purcell but Butler got to him first. 'Your impressions of the Dutchman,' he said – half-question, half-statement. 'It would be useful to have a measure of him before we talk.'

'Straightforward. Careful. Appears to be a man of his word.'

Butler waited for him to continue as if he knew there was more to come.

'He wants to end the war here as quickly as possible,' Sarsfield added. 'Before the winter really sets in. So he may be willing to make concessions.'

'What type of concessions?'

Sarsfield realised he didn't know. The one major concession that Ginckel was certainly prepared to make -- indeed, had made -- was to allow the army go to France. Other than that, he didn't know what he might or might not agree. 'My impressions are superficial,' he said. 'Based on one meeting. Talk to General Wauchope. He has more experience of Dutchmen. He also knows General Mackay, who was with General Ginckel when we met.'

Butler pursed his lips as if that was useful information. A whiff of brandy came from his breath as he thanked Sarsfield.

'We need to concentrate on the arrangements for going to France,' Sarsfield dropped his voice in case the archbishop or his colleagues would hear and misunderstand him. 'To make sure all the arrangements are as secure as possible.'

Butler raised a quizzical eyebrow.

'We shall invade England from France next year,' Sarsfield said, 'restore the rightful King and drive out the usurper from there and from Ireland as well.'

'You think it's possible?'

'Yes, perfectly possible. We will have a large army from here, resupplied and reinforced by France. The French navy controls the English Channel and we can seize London, overturn their so-called revolution, and rout the rebels.'

Butler nodded to himself several times, thinking it through. It was achievable.

'So it's imperative that the arrangements for going to France are watertight,' Sarsfield pressed home his argument. 'And not undermined by impossible demands, which will be only of a temporary nature in any event. Until our victory next year.'

'I take your point,' Butler said, also in a low voice. It was more than a point, he knew: it was an instruction. Concentrate on getting the army to France. Do not be overly concerned with what will be left behind since it will be only for a short time until a victorious return.

Purcell moved forward as soon as Butler stepped away. 'I've seen Henry,' he said.

Sarsfield resisted the natural impulse to ask how Luttrell was faring. 'And?' he asked in a weary tone.

'He can't understand why he is still locked up.'

'I hope you explained it to him.'

'It was a ploy by the French heretics,' Purcell said. 'To act as if he was negotiating with them, alert d'Usson and divide us. You fell for it.'

Sarsfield gave him a cold look. 'I don't have time for complicated conspiracies.' He turned away, irritated.

'Don't you want to know what he thinks of the situation?' Purcell shouted after him.

'No.' Sarsfield lied without looking back. More opinions and court conspiracies are not what he wanted now. What he wanted was a quick agreement so that the army could move on to prepare for the next stage of the war.

Ginckel drafted his counterproposals quickly; he was so accustomed to the terms of the many proclamations that it took little time. They offered pardons to all who took an oath of allegiance to King William and Queen Mary, restoration of lands that had been seized, the rights of Catholics to be as they were in the time of the previous king's brother, Charles II, and passage to anyone in the army who wished to go to France.

'And release of all the prisoners we have here,' he added to Mackay and Talmash.

'That's hardly necessary,' Mackay said, reading the terms. Some were more generous than he would have wished but he accepted they had already been on offer since Athlone and could scarcely be withdrawn now.

'Perhaps not but it will maintain the momentum towards an agreement.'

'And,' Talmash continued with a cynical grin, 'require them to feed some more mouths from their vast stocks of food.'

Ginckel need not have worried about the momentum for an agreement; it was now effectively unstoppable. The stage was set for formal negotiations.

Sarsfield led his delegation of about a dozen men out of St John's Gate in Irish Town early the next morning, a raw day of cold winds from the east which threatened rain. They included two archbishops and two cavalry officers, Nicholas Purcell and Lord Galmoy, and three lawyers, two of whom were also colonels. The French generals were absent: Wauchope was the only non-Irishman among the delegation. They rode by Singland Hill and the half-finished new battery, its construction halted, towards Ginckel's headquarters.

Ginckel noted without surprise the absence of the French generals. They are indisposed, Sarsfield told him, a fiction that covered their irrelevance, although they were still nominally the army's commanders.

Ginckel had gathered all his generals on his side, along with the civilian secretary for war in Ireland, George Clarke. Neither delegation included its lords justices, representing their respective kings. Introductions were made and formal politenesses exchanged.

Ginckel's headquarters tent had been expanded to take the extra numbers, a long trestle table in its centre, chairs ranked on either side. On the table were bottles of wine and brandy and a few pitchers of ale. Orderlies produced jugs of coffee as they all took their places, Ginckel and Sarsfield facing each other at the centre. Beside Sarsfield, Sir Toby

Butler reached for a brandy bottle and poured himself a generous helping.

Ginckel began proceedings with a formal welcome, to which Sarsfield responded in kind and they got down to business. Butler had carried out his instructions well, thinking through the logistics of moving the army to France and trying to ensure that there were no loopholes in any agreement.

'We have prepared proposals that we suggest should form the basis for our discussions,' Sarsfield said, handing a copy across the table to Ginckel. Further copies were distributed to all the Williamite participants.

Ginckel glanced at the proposals, content to see that they were mostly practical. He agreed and read out the first proposed article: 'That all persons without any exception, of what quality or condition soever, shall have free liberty to go to any country beyond the seas, where they think fit, with their families, household-stuff, plate and jewels.' He looked up. 'Except England and Scotland,' he said.

A ripple of general laughter lightened the formality of the occasion.

'Except England and Scotland,' Sarsfield agreed. The lawyers on both sides amended their notes and prepared to take over the negotiations.

The terms proceeded from there to specifics and the details of how the army would be transported. The Williamites would provide fifty 200-ton ships at Cork and a further twenty if required, to carry the Jacobite army to Brest or Nantes. The Jacobite army, including the French, would remain under the control of their officers and march to Cork with loaded muskets and banners flying, to be transported at the expense of the Williamites. The ships carrying them would be provided by the Williamites with forage for 900 horses and provisions for all their passengers, the cost to be reimbursed by the Jacobites when they reached France. If anything was robbed or taken from them on the way to the ships, the Williamites would compensate them.

'And this will include all outlying garrisons? They too will be included in the move to France?' Butler asked, referring to the few outposts in counties Kerry and Cork still in Jacobite hands.

'If they are under the command of your army,' Ginckel said. 'And choose to go to France.'

'Yes,' Butler said. 'And volunteers as well.'

'Volunteers?' George Clarke interjected. 'You mean bandits and brigands?'

'Volunteers,' Butler repeated in a calm tone, as if surprised by the other's reaction. 'Occasionally referred to as rapparees.'

'Cut-throats and murderers,' Clarke nodded. He turned to Sarsfield. 'You're not suggesting that such cut-throats and criminals are under the command of honourable men?'

'Many are members of the army who have become detached from the main body,' Butler said on Sarsfield's behalf. 'Merely seeking ways to return to their own lines.'

'By murdering Protestants and pillaging at random!'

'I'm not talking about such men,' Butler said with a dismissive wave of his hand, 'but of men forced to live off the land by the exigencies of unfortunate circumstances. As a result of the unsettled state of the country and shifts in front lines.'

'Define them how you will,' Clarke shook his head decisively. 'Bandits and criminals cannot be included in an honourable agreement.'

'But I have defined them,' Butler said with an air of strained patience.

Clarke gave a sardonic laugh. 'I fear no agreement is possible with rapparees included.' He sat back in his chair and tossed his pen on the table.

Both sides contemplated the breakdown of the talks, presenting a stony-faced obduracy at each other across the table. They all knew that Butler and Clarke were both right: the rapparees included Jacobite soldiers who had been left behind, as well as deserters, dispossessed men who saw themselves as part of the war, willing to assist the army and take orders from it, and bandits who robbed and murdered for personal gain, not caring whether their victims were military or civilian.

'Let me be clear,' Butler said at last, signalling an attempt at compromise. 'I am not talking about bandits and criminals but of men who were under our command and of volunteers who wished to come under our permanent command but were separated from us by circumstances. It is only such people I have in mind.'

'Volunteers is a very broad term,' Clarke noted, still reclining in his chair to show that he wasn't yet convinced.

'If you can suggest a better one ---.' Butler invited him to come back into the discussion.

'I think it is for you to propose rather than for me.' Clarke gave Butler a faint smile that said I know what you're trying to do but you'll have to try harder.

Butler took another sip of his brandy, pursed his lips and studied the document in front of him with raised pen. '"And also those called rapparees or volunteers",' he said, looking up. 'I think that 'or' makes it clear that what we are not talking about criminals but about people of the type I mentioned.'

Clarke sat forward and studied the clause with the amendment. He was about to say something when Ginckel leaned over and whispered in his ear. 'Very well,' Clarke said. 'We can move on to the next article.'

This is really outrageous, Mackay thought. Not just this insupportable nonsense about rapparees but the whole thrust of this agreement. We are providing our arch enemy and the enemy of all progress in Europe, Louis XIV of France, with a ready-made army and, astonishingly, we are paying for the privilege. The general is overreaching himself. The lords justices would have to put a stop to this, bring matters back to reality.

Sarsfield studied the bland faces opposite him as Butler and Clarke haggled over who would pay for provisions if there was not enough shipping ready for the infantry after the cavalry had gone and they were obliged to wait for new ships to arrive. They don't like it, he thought to himself with a quiet satisfaction. Neither would I if I was in their shoes, seeing the army you think you have defeated getting away scot-free. Although it had nothing to do with Scots, the phrase prompted him to glance at Wauchope, who had a small smile on his face as he noted the glower on Mackay's.

The morning wore on, with the lawyers warming to their task and Butler imbibing brandy at a greater pace than anyone else. Sarsfield was content to leave the negotiations to him, accepting that he knew what he was doing. Ginckel tried to follow the nuances of the different English words and phrases Clarke and Butler tossed back and forth across the table. Most of the military men found their attention wandering, bored as the lawyers parried. This was all largely irrelevant to the archbishops.

The agreement slowly took shape. The Williamites would occupy Irish Town, the Jacobites English Town until the ships were ready. Those who wanted to go to France would make their decision at a muster across the river in County Clare the following week, the infantry on Tuesday and the cavalry on Wednesday. Outlying garrisons, including that on its way from Sligo, would decide a week later. Once the path was chosen, changes of mind would not be permitted; those who tried to switch sides thereafter would be returned by the other side. Prisoners of war on both sides would be released.

'And members of the Irish army who are prisoners in England and Flanders,' Butler observed, as if this was just a minor detail.

Clarke shook his head. 'We're dealing with the situation *here*. The General cannot bind those in authority elsewhere.'

Butler shrugged. That was not his problem. He reached again for the brandy bottle.

Clarke looked at Ginckel. 'The General will use his best endeavours to have them released as well.'

Ginckel gave a weary nod and Butler smiled. Another small victory, though they both knew it did not necessarily mean much -- Ginckel's authority elsewhere was doubtful -- but it included the captured Jacobites now held abroad under the authority of the agreement. 'Article 18,' Butler said. 'The sick and wounded prisoners in your hands. They'll have the right to go to France too once they've recovered?'

'Yes,' Ginckel said.

It continued for another eleven clauses, culminating in the final one which made it clear that if Ginckel was replaced as commander of the Williamite army, his successor would 'observe and execute what is specified in these articles, or cause it to be executed punctually, and shall not act contrary to any account.'

Butler sank back in his chair and closed his eyes, satisfied he had made it as watertight as he could. Ginckel suggested they take a break and everyone moved outside with relief.

'Lawyers,' Talmash muttered to Mackay as they left the tent. 'I'd run them all through.'

The day had freshened, the sun breaking through the thin haze of cloud but its waning heat was whipped away by the cold breeze. Wauchope sought out Mackay and they began a neutral conversation about the fate of officers they had served with in earlier times. Butler, swaying gently on his feet, and Clarke began a similar reminiscence and were quickly trading stories about people they knew at the bar.

'A word, my lord,' Ginckel said to Sarsfield, drawing him away. They walked around the tent in silence and stopped behind it. 'That should meet all the requirements of those who want to go to France.'

'Yes, I think so,' Sarsfield agreed. 'Thank you for seeing it through.'

'At some cost to my reputation.'

'Surely not, my lord. Your reputation can only be enhanced by bringing the war in Ireland to an end.'

'Some think it's at too high a price.' Ginckel stopped and looked up into Sarsfield's face, like a father addressing a son who has outgrown him. 'You should think about the future. Reputations can be a fickle business.'

'I have,' Sarsfield said, thinking the future was all he was concerned with. Reputations could look after themselves.

'As fickle as warfare in some respects. Often a matter of chance.'

Sarsfield looked at the Dutchman more closely, wondering what had prompted this observation, and why he had made it. Ginckel certainly did not sound like a victorious general.

Ginckel glanced around to make sure there was nobody within earshot. 'His Majesty has authorised me to offer you an estate,' he said.

Sarsfield stared at him in surprise.

'Of course it would require you to stay in Ireland while some others go to France,' Ginckel said. There was no need to tell him that the King's proposal had been couched in the form of a bribe. Offer him an estate if he comes to terms. But they had already come to terms.

Sarsfield shook his head, not sure what to say. 'I'm a cavalryman,' he said after a moment. 'The army is my life.'

'Yes,' Ginckel concurred. 'Mine too. But you need to think about the future. Not just your own. Your family's. Your heirs'.'

'I have no heirs.'

'Not yet. You're a young man. With a young wife.'

The future lay in the restoration of the rightful King, Sarsfield thought. Which would result in the restoration of his own estate and secure all his family's and any future heirs' rights. He didn't need any promises from the usurper, who, God willing, would be ousted from England and Ireland by this time next year. 'I see a different future than your king,' he said.

'Well, consider what I have said,' Ginckel urged. 'And the excellent future you would have as well in their Majesties' army.'

The talks resumed on the civil articles, with most of the officers on both sides sighing inwardly when Sir Toby Butler asked what the proposed title meant. This was going to be another long session.

'It means what it says.' Clarke affected a puzzled air and paraphrased the heading of the document. 'Articles granted by General Ginckel to all persons now in Limerick and in the Irish army in counties Clare, Kerry, Cork and Mayo and any other garrisons in their possession. It's perfectly clear.'

'Outside Limerick, only the people in the army?' Butler queried.

'Yes. Only the people who are in a position to resist and are ceasing to do so under these articles.'

'So not the civilian population of these counties.'

Sarsfield shook his head vigorously. 'I'd rather die here than not take care of all those who have stood by us for so long,' he interjected, bringing a note of passion into what had become a dry legal process.

His outburst took the others by surprise. Butler was the first to recover, his pen hovering over the document to find a suitable place to carry out Sarsfield's wishes. 'In article 2,' he said, 'we could add the phrase, "and all such as are under their protection in the said counties", to include the rights of civilians, as well as the army, to their properties.'

Clarke held a brief whispered conversation with Ginckel and then straightened up and nodded. 'Agreed,' he said. 'Can we go to the first article now?'

'Certainly,' Butler nodded.

The first article had already been debated by Butler and Archbishop Maguire, who was far from happy with its assurance that Catholic rights to exercise their religion would be the same as they had enjoyed under Charles II. Which was ambiguous enough in itself without the qualifications now added that those rights had to be consistent with the laws of Ireland. King William and Queen Mary promised to summon a parliament in Ireland and endeavour to make sure its Catholics would not suffer 'any disturbance' on account of their religion.

'Is that even worth the paper on which it's written?' Maguire had protested when shown the draft agreement Ginckel had put forward. 'You know the parliament will be a Protestant one.'

Butler gave him a sympathetic sigh. 'Unfortunately, the rights of kings are not what they used to be since the revolution. Queen Mary may have once been the legitimate heir of King James but she and William rule now only on parliament's sufferance.'

'So their promises are worthless,' Maguire said.

'I wouldn't say they're entirely worthless,' Butler replied. 'They must be accorded some weight and must be taken into consideration.'

'And how much consideration do you think a Protestant parliament in Ireland will give to our rights?'

'I know,' Butler said in a soothing voice, conscious of Sarsfield's instructions and seeing this part of the agreement as merely temporary, until the rightful King was restored. 'But we can only do the best we can in the circumstances.'

Despite the slow start over the title, it didn't take long for the thirteen articles to be agreed. Most of them the Jacobites had already accepted, if reluctantly, including the oath of allegiance to the usurpers to be taken in order to retain lands. Others were uncontentious, like a provision giving Irish officers abroad on official business, including Henry Luttrell's older brother Simon, eight months to return if they wished to stay in Ireland and take advantage of the treaty's terms.

Both sides toasted each other when they had finished and it was agreed that the treaty would be signed as soon as the Williamite lords justices arrived in the city. There was no mention of the Jacobite lords justices being asked to sign.

'And the French generals will sign then as well?' Ginckel sought reassurance from Sarsfield as they were about to part. One of his worries was that the failure of d'Usson, the titular commander of the Jacobite army, to sign might leave it open to future assertions that the agreement was null and void. If, for example, the threatened French fleet arrived.

'Yes, they will sign it. They are very happy for us to return to France with them.'

'After all I heard about your bad relations with them.'

'And you've never had your disagreements with the English?'

Ginckel gave him a knowing smile. 'By the way,' he added as Sarsfield mounted his horse, 'think some more about what I said to you earlier.'

Waiting for the formal signing of the articles in the days that followed, the Jacobite cavalry moved in from County Clare to King's Island and the Williamite cavalry moved across to where they had been, beyond Sixmilebridge, in search of forage. Townspeople also moved to the open land of the island to get away from the stench and destruction of the battered towns. The weather cleared up, an early St Luke's summer of suddenly sunny and warm days, making it more pleasant to live outdoors and under scant shelters than in the fetid city.

'A bad day's work,' Colonel Charles O'Kelly told Sarsfield the next day as details of the agreement percolated throughout the city. 'Is this what all those good men died for at Aughrim?'

'Yes,' Sarsfield said, holding his patience in the face of such rhetoric. 'They died trying to win a battle to decide a war. And this allows us to keep the war going to achieve ultimate victory.'

'In a foreign field.'

'It doesn't matter where the field is. What matters is the ultimate victory.'

'A bad day's work,' O'Kelly repeated. 'You're leaving us to the mercy of the heretics without an army to protect us.'

'A defeated army here wouldn't protect anyone,' Sarsfield pointed out. This is why I excluded O'Kelly from the negotiations, he thought. 'Is that what you want? To hold out here until we are destroyed? And then what? Who will protect you then?'

'You could join the rapparees.'

'You think they can protect you? Is that what you want to do? Join the rapparees?'

'Not me. I'm too old for that life. But there are lots of young men who could.'

'And you'd condemn them to that life?' Sarsfield shook his head in dismay. 'Living in bogs and wildernesses. Being hunted like animals. And for what? For no prospect of victory.'

O'Kelly dropped his head, knowing that Sarsfield was right. Most of the rapparees ended up with their heads on pikes, having achieved nothing more than survival for a few months.

'An undefeated army going abroad can return,' Sarsfield continued. 'Come with us. And I promise you we'll be back within the year.'

'I hope you're right,' O'Kelly said without conviction, 'but my foreign journeying is long over. I'm too old to be going anywhere but home.'

'To Galway? Then the terms will protect you and your lands.'

O'Kelly gave him a look that said he was a foolish young man. 'You believe that?'

'Yes. They will protect you until we return.'

It was the kind of debate repeated over and over as officers sought out one another's intentions. Go to France and lose their estates or stay at home and lose their careers. Go to France and hope to win the war from there or stay at home under a hostile regime. Either way, the future was uncertain, the decision one that would affect their lands and children for generations to come. Few saw any attraction in Ginckel's offer of a comparable rank in the Williamite army.

The more land they had, the more difficult the decision. For the foot soldiers without land, the decision was simpler. Most had nothing to go back to, little to lose by going abroad. And if Sarsfield was right, they would come back as victors with all the benefits and spoils that that implied.

But was Sarsfield right? Or was he, as some who disliked him said, trying to further his own career by bringing a large force to the French king? Doing what Tyrconnell had been doing: selling men to the French for his own gain and aggrandisement? And would those men want to be at the mercy of the French after all their experiences of them? Their arrogance. Disdain. Willing to fight to the last drop of Irish blood but careful of their own blood and comforts.

'There's a lot of talk going on,' Wauchope told Sarsfield. 'We have to persuade people to come with us.'

'They'll come.'

'We can't take it for granted. There are mutterings in some of the ranks.'

'Who?' Sarsfield shrugged. 'O'Kelly? Purcell?'

Wauchope nodded. 'And others.'

'Let them mutter. When it's time to decide, they'll come around.'

The French generals and their staff kept to themselves, hosting dinners for senior officers at which the conversation remained uncontentious and the hospitality ostentatious, not so subtly signalling the benefits awaiting their guests in France.

Now that the war was over in all but name, groups of soldiers from both sides began to cross the lines, seeking out old colleagues or further information. But it didn't take long for complaints to come back to Sarsfield that some who had ventured out in small numbers or alone had found themselves robbed and stripped before being sent back. Sarsfield sent a complaint to Ginckel and they both ordered an end to all fraternisation.

Purcell pursued him daily with a single word, 'Today?'

'No,' Sarsfield replied. 'When the articles are signed.'

'This is ridiculous. There is no justification for keeping him locked up now.'

Yes, there is, Sarsfield thought but he kept his counsel. The last thing he needed now was someone like Luttrell, with his love of politics, trying to reopen negotiations on some of the terms and, if Wauchope was correct, fomenting the opposition to him. He knew from experience how good Luttrell was at negotiating, how successful he had been in undermining Tyrconnell's authority.

'He said to tell you that he's impressed,' Purcell added. 'You've got a very good deal in the circumstances.'

'You're coming to France, I presume. Bringing your dragoons with you.'

Purcell hesitated.

Sarsfield turned and walked away without a word. So, he thought, Luttrell is at it already from his cell: undermining me.

Mackay accosted Sir Thomas Coningsby as he and the other lord justice, Sir Charles Porter, emerged from a long conversation with Ginckel. 'People are appalled at these terms,' he said, falling into step beside them.

'Which people?'

'The foreign generals, the loyal Irish. Nobody has ever heard of such an arrangement where you defeat the enemy and then pay to put him back on his feet.'

'You exaggerate,' Coningsby said, opening the flap of his tent and reluctantly holding it back to invite Mackay inside. Porter continued on his way to his own tent with a smirk, happy to leave Coningsby to deal with these complaints.

Coningsby poured two glasses of wine and handed one to Mackay. They sat at opposite sides of the desk. Coningsby opened a silver snuff box and offered it to Mackay, who declined. He took a pinch for himself and inhaled it into his right nostril.

Outside, the sun was sinking among some lines of cloud, streaking them red, and the blue of the sky, reminiscent of summer, was darkening to indigo from the east. The light in the tent was dim and the air still heavy with the unexpected warmth of the day.

'You saw the inclusion of the rapparees?' Mackay exclaimed.

'That is going a little too far,' Coningsby conceded, rubbing his nose with the back of his hand and sniffing heavily, 'but the general is adamant that the articles stay in the form agreed. And it'll rid us of a lot of troublemakers. Let them murder the French in their beds.'

'Surely you can stop him. He is exceeding his powers.'

'Ah, there's the rub. He says he is within his powers and produces letters from his Majesty to prove it. Unfortunately, he seems to be correct.' And then he added with a shrug, as if it explained everything: 'Dutchmen.'

'But their Majesties can't have approved these terms.'

'Obviously they haven't seen them. But they have given Ginckel exceptional latitude to conclude the war here before the winter is upon us.'

Mackay sipped at his wine. 'Can you not make any changes?'

'We will try when it comes to the final discussion with the papists. But the general will not allow any major changes. He is in a hurry to get the papers signed. Afraid the French fleet will arrive and the papists will change their minds.'

That would be a disaster, Mackay conceded. Our army split in two and a resurgent enemy – there would be no choice but to withdraw. 'What about the civil articles?'

'What about them? There is nothing there to cause us concern. Papist rights are a matter for parliament when it comes down to it.' Coningsby smiled. 'Which is the way we want it, isn't it? Parliament can be relied upon to do the right thing.'

Ginckel was tired of the quibbling, most of it behind his back. 'We have turned a possible disaster into a success,' he said to Mackay, one of the few to put their grievances to him face to face. 'You know that as well as I do. You know how vulnerable we are here; what risks we have taken to achieve this success.'

'But the cost?'

'The cost has to be balanced against the alternative. We will now have an army to bring to the King's assistance in Flanders next year which could be the decisive year of the war. And the cost, if you are talking about money, is nothing compared to the cost of another season of warfare here.'

'We may end up fighting against them all over again in Flanders.' They were sitting in the Sunday morning sunshine outside the general's tent, waiting for the formal signing of the treaties in the afternoon.

'So be it. If we do, it will be without the disadvantages we are under here.'

437

The general and the lord justice had answers for everything, Mackay thought. A treaty was going to be signed within hours but none of their answers could shake his gut feeling that this wasn't right. It was wrong to allow a defeated enemy to walk away, fully armed and with banners flying. To fight again for their obscurantist cause which threatened the future of the whole of Europe. And to bring with them any cut-throats and brigands who wanted to pretend to belong to a king's army. Then there was the fact that the Williamites were paying for this in actual cash. At least the enemy were to pay for the on-board provisions but in arrears, once they got to France. Or so they said.

'What guarantee do we have that they'll even pay for the provisions once we've taken them to France?' Mackay asked.

Ginckel gave him a weary look.

'We could at least insist that the French pay up now,' Mackay added. 'According to the deserters, they have hoards of gold here.'

'According to the deserters,' Ginckel repeated in a dismissive mutter. 'You know what everyone always thinks of commissaries? They're always hoarding money.'

Talmash came by and pulled over a chair for himself. Ginckel switched from Dutch to English for his benefit and used his arrival to steer the conversation onto a different path. 'We must try to persuade as many of them as possible to join us or at least to give up soldiering and go home,' he said, conscious that he would be judged to an extent on how many of the papists decided to go to France. If few followed Sarsfield abroad, it would be easier to present the treaty as a great success. Less so if they all went. 'Talk to their Scottish and English leaders. Point out to them that the terms give them pardons and their lands in their own kingdoms. A last opportunity to go home with such generous conditions.'

'I'll try,' Mackay said, 'but I don't think Wauchope will easily change his mind. He had plenty of opportunity before.'

'He might have had his fill of warfare by now.'

'He may well have but I'm afraid he is an out-and-out papist.'

'And their cavalry general, Sheldon,' Ginckel said to Talmash. 'You've had words with him?'

'Only of a cursory kind but I'll broach the subject when I get an opportunity.'

'He doesn't appear to be very committed to their cause,' Ginckel observed. 'Offering no resistance when we crossed the river.'

Their conversation was interrupted by the arrival of the Jacobite delegation, including the French generals for the first time. They were greeted by the Duke of Württemberg, who was hosting lunch for them before the final talks and the signing of the treaty got under way.

'That's good,' Ginckel muttered, noting the presence of the Frenchmen. That meant they were prepared to sign the treaty. There would be no last-minute difficulties.

He turned to Talmash. 'You are ready to take over Irish Town?' he asked. Article 23 of the military treaty specified that the Williamites would occupy the area on the day the agreement was signed.

'Before the ink is dry, my lord,' Talmash replied with an over-dramatic bow.

In the event, the signing was a long-drawn-out process, stretching from the afternoon into the evening and late into the night. The agreements were gone through line by line by the Williamite lords justices. Phrases were amended, words argued over, breaks taken for consultation. Almost all the haggling had to do with the terms of the move to France: less attention was paid to the civil terms. Sir Toby Butler successfully defended his wording, including rapparees, in the agreement.

At the end of it all, nothing of great significance had changed. Everyone was exhausted, the atmosphere in the crowded tent heavy with tobacco smoke and the greasy tang of wax from the candles on the table. Most of the generals were bored beyond belief. Even the lawyers were bleary-eyed and finding it difficult to concentrate on what had degenerated into repetitious and pedantic arguments over minor points. Sir Toby Butler was finding it difficult to stay awake as a result of a day's intake of brandy.

It was near midnight when space was cleared and two sets of the final documents were placed on the table. Ginckel signed the military terms on his own authority. Across the table d'Usson and Tessé signed their names beside each other. Beneath them on a second line a third Frenchman, Latour Monfort, signed. Sarsfield dipped his pen in ink and wrote 'Lucan' heavily beside it. Wauchope added his name in small cramped letters beside Sarsfield's. A third line was signed by Mark Talbot and Lord Galmoy: Nicholas Purcell put his name beneath theirs.

Then the civil articles were presented and signed by Ginckel and the lords justices, Coningsby and Porter: Mackay and Talmash were invited to sign as witnesses. Across the table, all the seven signatories were Irish, headed by Sarsfield, Galmoy and Purcell and including Butler and the other two colonel-lawyers who had taken part in the negotiations, Garrett Dillon and John Browne.

There was a sense of anti-climax as tired men exchanged ritual politenesses. The atmosphere was sombre, not celebratory. Nearly three years of warfare in Ireland were at an end. Those who had endured them were conscious of the comrades who were no longer with them. No one knew how many had been killed and maimed in battle and how many were dead from disease, hunger and lawlessness. But everyone had comrades, friends, or family members who had lost their lives and others who were disabled and disfigured.

Ginckel was the first to break the mood. 'We will occupy Irish Town now,' he informed Sarsfield, beckoning Talmash with a raised hand.

'Now?' Sarsfield echoed. 'At this hour?'

'That's what the treaty says.'

'Very well. I will order the gates to be opened.'

'Perhaps it would be enough to simply occupy the outworks tonight, my lord,' Talmash suggested to Ginckel, finding himself in the unaccustomed position of being the diplomatic one.

Ginckel look at him in surprise. 'As long as there is no back-sliding,' he said to Sarsfield.

'Of course not.' Sarsfield sounded insulted. 'I will make the arrangements for the outworks and your entry into the town at first light,' he told Talmash.

Talmash bowed to them both, happy to have put off the occupation until morning. He had no desire to move into the wrecked town in the dark of a moonless night. You could already smell its stench from

440

Singland Hill when the wind blew from the Atlantic.

Irish Town was deserted when Talmash led his men through St John's Gate as the sun rose the next morning, heralding another fine day as it tinted the sky blue. The troops fanned out along the walls and occupied the Citadel where everything that couldn't be taken away had been destroyed by the departing garrison.

'We were never going to breach these walls,' Mackay observed, seeing their depth from the inside. He had accepted Talmash's ritual invitation to accompany him, curious to see the damage caused by their bombardment.

It was every bit as bad as they had imagined. They walked down John Street, stepping over stones, zig-zagging around piles of rubble, and avoiding foul-smelling pools. Infantrymen moved ahead of them, some with fusils at the ready. There appeared to be nobody left in the town but as the first lines passed by, a few people emerged from makeshift shelters beneath the walls.

The lines halted at the bottom of the street at Baal's Bridge and Talmash and Mackay could hear shouting as they approached. Some of their men were standing at the bridge, arms wide, chests thrown forward, shouting at three field guns drawn up at the far side of the bridge, daring their gunners to fire. The gunners at the other side shouted back, pretending to lower their lit match to the pans of their guns. The bridge itself was empty, its workshops abandoned.

'Stop that!' Talmash shouted at his own men over the cacophony of derision being traded back and forth across the bridge. All it would take would be a slip of someone's hand for all hell to break loose.

'We could rush them now,' one of his men said, as their shouts subsided.

'Come on, step onto the bridge,' a voice from the far side roared.

'You lot,' Talmash included them in a sweep of his hand, 'pull up some field guns and put them in position here.'

Muttered curses met his order: hauling field guns down that littered street would be no easy task.

'That's not our job,' one shot back.

'It is now.' Talmash glared at him.

The situation settled down quickly. People began to move across the bridge with white flags aloft at first but the flags were soon dispensed with. It was obvious that no one had any desire to restart the war, despite the initial outburst of bellicose rhetoric. The real battle now was over how many Jacobite troops would depart for France.

Ginckel circulated a document in English Town countering some of the rumours that he had heard were being spread. Anyone who joined King William's army would be paid immediately and would not be forced to serve in Hungary or other remote areas against their will, he declared. If they wanted to go home, they would be free to do so and could sell their horses, arms and equipment to the Williamite army. And if they went to France, they should know that they would never be allowed to return to Ireland.

'We have to do more to counteract this,' Wauchope said, showing Sarsfield a copy of the document.

Sarsfield shrugged. He wasn't unduly concerned, but many officers with lands to lose were agonising over their decisions. It was an easy choice for him but he realized that it wasn't as straightforward for others, especially for those who were not truly military men at heart but who had been caught up in the necessities of the time.

'What do you suggest?'

'Talk to as many as you can. Get my Lord Galmoy to do so as well, as an example to them,' Wauchope said. Galmoy, Piers Butler, was the biggest landowner with 15,000 acres in counties Kilkenny and Wexford and had the most to lose; he was committed to going to France. 'I will ask the archbishops to get the priests to help.'

'And the French,' Sarsfield said. 'I'll see if Fumeron will loosen their purse strings again.'

'What about Colonel O'Kelly? Is he encouraging men to become rapparees?'

Sarsfield thought about O'Kelly. Had he persuaded him against that? 'I don't think so,' he said. Surely O'Kelly could see the pointlessness of that course of action.

The food and drink supplies were opened up and more generous rations distributed now that they weren't required to last indefinitely. Fumeron paid overdue wages and priests circulated among the men, warning them that their decision was not purely a temporal one: their immortal souls would face eternal damnation if they assisted the heretics in the campaign against the one true church.

A messenger from Irish Town told Sarsfield that Ginckel wanted to see him as a matter of urgency, so Sarsfield followed the trumpeter back across Baal's Bridge, through the town where sappers were clearing the streets and on out through St John's Gate. More sappers, supplemented by infantrymen, were dismantling the batteries and beginning to fill in the circumvallation trenches.

Ginckel dispensed with the usual civilities when Sarsfield arrived at his tent. 'What's the meaning of this?' he demanded in a voice quivering with anger as he held out a letter to Sarsfield. 'This is totally unacceptable. An outrageous example of bad faith.'

Taken aback, Sarsfield read the letter. It was from a Jacobite lieutenant colonel who claimed to have been locked up in English Town because he wanted to join King William's army rather than fight for the king of France. He scanned to the bottom of the page and felt a wave of relief as he saw the signature.

'This is untrue,' he declared. 'This man,' he tapped the letter with a finger of his other hand, 'was imprisoned for insulting superior officers and refusing to accept orders.'

'And that order was that he must go to France?'

'No, my lord,' Sarsfield said. 'This affair predated the treaty and had nothing to do with the decision to go to France or not.'

Ginckel waited for him to elaborate. Sarsfield said nothing more, not wishing to explain that it was the officer's anti-French rants that had caused him to be locked up. They stared at each other, both knowing that this was a matter of trust. Ginckel gave in first: 'I have your word that this is so?'

'You do.'

'Very well,' Ginckel held out his hand to take back the letter, although his suspicions were not entirely allayed. He tore it up and dropped the pieces on his table. They had to trust each other: each was in the other's hands to a certain extent now. A breakdown of the treaty's terms could only lead to disaster for both, destroying their authority and reputations.

'This man and all our other prisoners of state are being released today,' Sarsfield added, 'even though the treaty does not require it. And they will all then be free to make their decision about whether or not they sail to France.'

'And have full freedom to do so?'

'Yes.'

Ginckel poured two glasses of wine, indicating that this dispute was over. 'There is another issue on which I need some clarity,' he said, gesturing towards two comfortable chairs away from his desk. They sat down. 'The payment for provisions on our ships taking you to France.'

Sarsfield nodded. He had been expecting that and had already discussed it with d'Usson: the terms specified that payment would be made when the army arrived in France. 'We propose to send back cargoes on your ships which can be sold here and the proceeds used to pay you back.'

Ginckel pursed his lips and exhaled. 'It would be simpler to send back gold coins.'

'It would,' Sarsfield agreed. 'but you have to know that the King has few resources of his own. He's dependent on his cousin, King Louis.'

'And his cousin,' Ginckel raised a quizzical eyebrow, 'will no longer assist him?'

'I imagine King James does not wish to impose on his cousin's hospitality any more than is necessary.'

Ginckel gave him a wintry smile and sipped some wine. 'It's not for us to determine such things. But you know your proposal could cause difficulties? It's against the law in Ireland to trade with France, to trade with the enemy.'

'But the civil terms allow our people here to continue doing so,' Sarsfield pointed out.

Ginckel nodded, a less than convinced confirmation that this was so. He had his own doubts about how the civil terms would be interpreted in practice but that was not his concern. 'It would be simpler if you could send back gold,' he repeated.

'I'll see what I can do but I am not hopeful.'

They lapsed into silence and Ginckel rose to retrieve the flagon of wine from the table. He refilled their glasses and asked when he had settled down again: 'Have you thought some more about his Majesty's offer?'

Sarsfield nodded, twisting his glass around to make the wine swirl. He wasn't comfortable talking about this but he had decided that he needed to make some provision for the future, for Honor and the heirs they would have. 'I will go to France. My mind is clear on that. But you were right about the future.'

Ginckel sipped his wine and waited for Sarsfield to go on but he was still staring into his swirling glass. 'Nobody can tell what the future holds,' Ginckel said to break the silence and encourage him.

'I would like to send back some goods to Ireland,' Sarsfield said. 'As part of those shipments we were talking about'

'What kind of goods?'

'Wine, obviously,' Sarsfield said with a laugh. 'Brandy. Cheese. Other foods. Clothes perhaps. I don't yet know precisely what.'

'I don't see any difficulty with that.'

'And that they be exempt from any taxes or impositions.'

'Of course,' Ginckel agreed. Otherwise their value would be diminished.

They finished their wine in silence. 'That's a wise decision,' Ginckel said when they got up. 'A man must provide for the future of his family.'

Henry Luttrell emerged grey-faced and thinner after almost two months of confinement. He climbed up to the castle's walls and stood in the sunshine, feeling the warmth on his heavily bearded face and breathing in the fresh air coming up the estuary from the distant Atlantic. Across the Shannon, enemy soldiers sat on the bank, playing cards. Beyond them, other Williamites lazed on the ground or wandered about without hurry or apparent purpose. The scene had all the air of a peacetime camp.

Luttrell wandered down through the city, observing the destruction. There were few people about, some of whom stared after him with belated recognition as he went by. He was walking past the Tholsel on

445

Mary Street when he saw Sarsfield emerge from his quarters in the lord mayor's house opposite. He stopped and waited.

It took Sarsfield a moment to notice the unkempt figure in the filthy uniform and then another moment to recognise him. He stopped.

They stared at each other.

Luttrell broke the silence. 'There was no need for any of that.'

'You consorted with the enemy behind my back.'

'I merely asked an obvious question. To which we all needed to know the answer.'

Sarsfield shook his head. 'You put me in an impossible position. Made it seem that I was thinking of seeking terms.'

'The question you should still be asking yourself,' Luttrell continued as if he had not been interrupted. 'Does the Dutchman have the power to make an agreement stick?'

'What do you mean?'

'Just that. Can the Dutchman ensure that all the terms of an agreement are implemented? And the answer is "no".'

'He will keep the agreement.'

'He'll let you go to France, yes. But he can't guarantee the other part.'

'He's not in a position to,' Sarsfield said.

'Exactly,' Luttrell said with a weary sigh. 'So the answer to the question you locked me up for asking was really "no". He can't guarantee it. Not all of it.' He paused. 'You could have done better.'

'You would have done better?' Sarsfield asked with heavy sarcasm.

Luttrell shrugged and moved off. He stopped after a few paces, turned back and examined the damage to the building from which Sarsfield had emerged. 'Is Honor all right?' he asked.

Sarsfield nodded.

'Good.' Luttrell turned away again and walked off towards Baal's Bridge.

Sarsfield watched him go, vaguely unsettled. So he wasn't impressed with the treaty in spite of what Purcell had said. Maybe Purcell had told him what he thought he wanted to hear. Or maybe Luttrell was just being vindictive. He shrugged and turned in the other direction, glad to be rid of such political talk, of trying to decipher the true meaning behind

446

others' words. It was a relief to deal with Ginckel in spite of the recurring disputes about the actions or complaints of someone or other. Thankfully, he too seemed to have no time for word games.

Luttrell crossed the bridge, his empty hands raised a little to signal his peaceful intent. He continued through Irish Town and up towards Singland Hill where he was stopped by a sentry near Mackay's tent. 'Colonel Luttrell to see General Ginckel,' he said.

Mackay emerged from his tent, surprised at the state of the figure before him. 'You are Colonel Henry Luttrell?' he asked with more than a hint of doubt. He had never met Luttrell before but this figure did not look like the influential person, Sarsfield's former right-hand man, of whom they had heard so much, the man who was sometimes said to be a match in deviousness for Tyrconnell himself.

'Yes. I apologise for my dishevelled state but I have been living in restricted quarters for some time.'

'General Ginckel is a busy man.'

'And one running out of time to dissuade the Irish army from going to France,' Luttrell said in a calm voice. 'I would like to talk to him about my regiment's decision.'

'Which is?'

'Unclear. Until certain matters are clarified.'

'You've seen the terms? They are very clear.'

'Up to a point. But there's always a need for clarification in relation to specific details.'

'Clarification of what?'

'That's what I wish to discuss with General Ginckel.'

Mackay beckoned to an orderly to get his horse and one for Luttrell and they rode in silence back to the headquarters tent. Mackay had a quick word with Ginckel before introducing Luttrell.

'You've had a difficult time,' Ginckel said, looking Luttrell up and down.

'Thanks to you,' Luttrell said with a hint of a smile to show he didn't hold any grudges. Ginckel went to say something but Luttrell raised a hand to stop him. 'I'm not one to complain about underhand dealings,

447

my lord,' he added. 'Even when their success was at my own expense. I'm more concerned now about the future.'

'You'll join us, I hope?'

'We're considering it but we would like certain guarantees.'

'You and your officers will maintain your ranks. Indeed, with your experience you may well become a brigadier. And you won't be sent to serve anywhere you don't want to go in Europe.'

'And after the continental war?' Luttrell asked.

'After the war?' Ginckel repeated as if that prospect had not entered his head. When in his lifetime had there not been a war?

'When your king has no need of my officers, men or me. What then?'

Ginckel glanced at Mackay and considered his response. 'You would receive a pension, I presume.'

'Presume.' Luttrell repeated the word to make clear what this conversation was all about. 'How much?'

'I couldn't say,' Ginckel looked to Mackay for confirmation. 'It's not for me to decide. Probably a matter for parliament.'

Luttrell shook his head with an air of regret. 'Vague promises. One needs as much certainty as possible in uncertain times.'

Ginckel exhaled noisily, an unconscious signal that he knew Luttrell had him in a corner. He needed to stop as many men as possible from going to France and Luttrell was trying to extract the maximum price for switching sides. He was probably bluffing; could he go back to Sarsfield's side after what they had done to him? 'How much of a pension?' Ginckel asked at last.

'Five hundred pounds a year. If my regiment is disbanded. Or I am replaced at its head.'

Ginckel nodded. That was a lot of money but it would only have to be paid in the distant future, if ever. And not by him.

'In writing,' Luttrell prompted with a thin smile. 'Since we're both aware of how much importance can be attached to a simple letter.'

Ginckel sat down at his desk but Luttrell interrupted before he began writing. 'There is also the matter of land,' he said.

'You owned land?' Ginckel asked, not knowing anything about Luttrell's previous circumstances.

448

'My family. My brother Simon.'

'Ah, yes,' Ginckel remembered. 'We made provision for him and others like him. He can return from France within eight months.'

'But if he doesn't return, I would like to keep the land in the family. Ensure that it is not attainted.'

'I'm not familiar with your situation. Your brother may return and he'll have the benefit of the terms then.'

'And he may not. I don't know his plans. But, with all due respect to the prince of Orange, I would hate to see my family lands being given to some, probably English, lackey.'

Ginckel could see his point: the general had already been through several of these kinds of decisions, especially in Galway. Special pleading from people with arguments that sometimes seemed valid, sometimes specious. He was not a lawyer; these things would all have to be resolved at law at some time in the future. Meantime, he needed all the Jacobites he could persuade to switch sides.

'Very well,' he said. 'I'll recommend that you have the lands if your brother is attainted.'

'A recommendation ---.' Luttrell spread his hands -- an indication that it was so open-ended as to be meaningless.

'A promise then,' Ginckel said. 'On condition that you encourage others to bring their regiments over to us as well as bringing your own regiment.'

'I will use whatever influence you have left me.'

Luttrell watched Ginckel draft the letter confirming the agreement, read it through and put it inside his tunic. He gave a small bow, said goodbye, and left.

'Such insolence,' Mackay muttered to Ginckel as they watched him gallop away, realising that he was also stealing one of their horses. 'Do we really want someone like that in their Majesties' army?'

Tuesday morning marked the end of St Luke's summer. The wind had shifted, now coming from the north, bringing cold air and piling up grey clouds, but the rain kept off for the time being. The infantry, some 14,000 of them, marched out of the King's Island across Thomond Bridge and formed up by the banks of the river across from St John's Castle. The generals from both sides gathered on horseback in two separate groups to observe the procedure.

It had been agreed that it would be overseen by two men: the French commissary Fumeron for the Jacobites and the English adjutant-general Withers for the Williamites. They would make one final address to the ranks and then each regiment would march by them, return to English Town over the bridge if they were going to France or turn left if they were staying in Ireland. Those who wanted to go home would leave their weapons and receive written pardons: those who chose to join the Williamite army would be taken into the ranks immediately.

The flags snapped in the stiffening breeze as first Withers and then Fumeron made last-minute appeals to the men, riding along in front of them. Withers told them they be would abandoning their kith and kin in Britain and Ireland to fight for a foreign king who had no interest in their future and whose grandiose plans to occupy the Continent of Europe were opposed by the Pope himself. Fumeron's French was translated by a cavalry colonel riding beside him as he told the ranks to remember the exhortation of their priests and leaders, the certain damnation of their souls if they joined the heretics, and the equally certain victory of an Irish army backed by the might of France overthrowing the usurper in England and returning to take control of their own lands in Ireland the following year.

Those that heard them were unlikely to be swayed: they had been exposed to the arguments numerous times in the previous days. But most did not hear them now because the wind whipped away the voices and they waited, minds mostly already made up, many in near rags, to be allowed to return to their shelters.

The moment of decision came at last. Drummers beat the order to march and the columns began to file past Withers and Fumeron, to turn onto the bridge and back into the city if they were for France, to turn left if they were for going home or joining the Williamites. The Jacobites had carefully placed one of the most loyal regiments nearest the bridge, to be the first to march past and so set an example for everyone to follow. Its 1,400 men turned right towards the bridge. Only seven of them broke ranks and turned left. A cheer went up among the men coming behind them as the solid group crossed the bridge.

Mackay glanced at Ginckel. He was looking straight ahead, stony-faced.

Matters subsequently improved a little from Ginckel's perspective. Lord Iveagh's regiment of Ulstermen turned left, as did several others. In the aftermath, Ginckel's staff reported that about 3,000 men had deserted the Jacobites and about 1,000 of them had joined his army. The rest were going home with their pardons and promises of keeping any land they had.

Sarsfield returned to the city in good humour. 'You see,' he told Wauchope as they rode across the bridge and into King John's Castle, 'there was nothing to worry about.'

'Tomorrow might tell another tale,' Wauchope said in a gloomy voice. On Wednesday the cavalry would decide and he and Sarsfield already knew that a good number of the landed officers had decided to go home. Few blamed them for opting to look after their families and their families' futures.

The two generals dismounted in the castle's courtyard and Sarsfield saw out of the corner of his eye Sir Toby Butler coming towards him, looking very pale. Hungover, he thought. But then he remembered that Butler never showed any visible after-effects of his drinking.

'We must talk,' Butler said. 'Something serious has occurred.'

'What?'

'Come with me.'

Sarsfield followed him, motioning to Wauchope to accompany them, but Butler stopped the Scot with an apologetic 'Just yourself' to Sarsfield. They went up the winding stone staircase into a room where Butler had the signed copies of the treaties laid out on the table. He put his finger on the second article of the civil treaty. 'The words are missing,' he said.

'What words?' Sarsfield read through it and realized immediately what Butler meant. The words that had guaranteed the civilian population of areas under their control the same rights as members of the army were no longer there.

'"And all such as are under their protection in the said counties",' Butler quoted the missing clause.

Sarsfield looked up in horror and then turned it over to the signatories' page. All their names were there as they had signed them. 'This is outrageous,' he said, letting his anger rise. 'They changed the terms and fooled us into signing them?'

Butler shifted uncomfortably and lowered his head. 'I should have read this copy in its entirety before we signed,' he admitted in a flat voice, acknowledging the acute embarrassment of such a rudimentary mistake. 'But it was so late and ---.'

Sarsfield read through the document again, half-expecting to find the words there, misplaced perhaps, but they weren't. 'And I made a particular point of this,' he said, slapping the table with his hand. It was difficult to believe that Ginckel and the others had played such a reprehensible trick. Their clerk had drafted the articles as they were agreed and someone must have signalled to him to leave out this particular phrase.

'I know,' Butler said meekly. He went to a cupboard and poured himself a glass of brandy, holding up the bottle to Sarsfield as an afterthought. Sarsfield shook his head, his mind preoccupied with the consequences of this discovery.

'It will have to be signed again,' he declared. 'With the full article. Or we'll tear up the whole thing.'

Butler sighed and took a long drink of the brandy. Colour was beginning to return to his face. 'We shouldn't be too hasty,' he said.

'This was done deliberately to deceive us,' Sarsfield retorted. 'To exclude the people who have supported us from the benefits of the treaty. It's intolerable.'

Butler sighed heavily again, drained his glass, and poured himself another. 'Are you sure?' he raised the bottle to Sarsfield again.

Sarsfield waved it away with an impatient sweep of his hand.

'I accept full responsibility,' Butler said. 'I should have read it.'

'That's not the issue! We should all have read it. But we thought we were dealing with honourable men. I have never heard of such an instance of bad faith, such underhand behaviour. Worse than anything even Lying Dick would do.'

Butler was about to reply but he thought better of it. Sarsfield strode over to the slit window and looked down on the courtyard. Purcell and Galmoy were talking, Galmoy ticking off points with his forefinger against his other palm, trying to get Purcell to change his mind.

'The danger is that if we reopen the treaty, we'll have to renegotiate it all over again,' Butler said in a quiet voice.

'Nonsense,' Sarsfield shot back over his shoulder. 'We just want the agreed terms signed again.'

'But will men put their signatures to it again without attempting to change any of terms?'

'Why not?'

'If the omission was deliberate, in bad faith, they won't agree to sign it with the clause there,' Butler said. 'We can cry foul and they can say caveat emptor, you've already signed it.' He bowed his head again, accepting that this was his fault. 'If it was not deliberate, they can use it as an excuse to reopen the negotiations. From what I hear, some of them are not happy about the terms under which you go to France. And we'll have to negotiate with Coningsby and Porter, their lords justices, this time, and probably involve out own lords justices too.'

And Ginckel might be even less happy today after they have seen how many are going to France, Sarsfield thought. He swore under his breath. What a mess. 'What do we do?'

'Talk to General Ginckel as a first step. You think he's an honourable man?'

'I thought so up to now. Can I be so sure anymore?'

'That's one of the things we need to know.'

Ginckel sounded genuinely surprised when they told him what had happened and asked to see his copy of the signed document. 'That's not possible,' he replied. 'It's on its way to England.'

'And is this clause in it?' Butler inquired.

'I don't remember,' Ginckel admitted. 'Genuinely,' he added, looking from Sarsfield to Butler and back to Sarsfield. He's either telling the truth or a very good dissembler, Sarsfield decided.

453

Ginckel summoned his war secretary, George Clarke, and asked him for an explanation. Clarke, too, appeared surprised and went off to question his clerk who had written out the two copies that were signed. He came back looking flushed and slightly breathless. 'Mr Payzant is acutely embarrassed. He said it must have been a regrettable oversight on his part. There was so much talk and so much debate back and forth and it was getting so late that his concentration must have lapsed.'

'And is it missing from both copies?' Butler demanded, recovering some of his lawyerly demeanour.

'Apparently so. He is certain your copy is a faithful copy of our copy, the original.'

'So there is nothing written down which confirms what was agreed?' Sarsfield exploded. 'Unbelievable!'

'Yes,' Ginckel agreed. He had no desire to reopen negotiations, given the mutterings about his undue generosity. Besides, messages had gone to their Majesties congratulating them on successfully ending the war in this kingdom, and the lords justices were preparing to depart for Dublin today. He glared at Clarke, expecting him to come up with a solution.

'We could consider a codicil,' Clarke said after a moment.

Butler gave him an inquiring look.

'Perhaps in their Majesties' confirmation of the articles,' Clarke suggested, thinking aloud. 'They could include the missing phrase and make it clear that it had been left out accidentally and was part of article two.'

Sarsfield glanced at Butler. 'Yes,' Butler said, dragging out the word almost to the point where it became a negative. 'This might not be for eight months, the period allowed to the king and queen to ratify the agreement.'

'Perhaps we could have it ratified sooner.' Clarke said, looking to Ginckel who gave a nod of confirmation.

'But you can't guarantee that,' Butler said.

'The general will use his good offices with his Majesty.' Clarke looked to Ginckel again, about to point out that the general had a close rapport with the King.

'Yes,' Ginckel agreed and turned to Sarsfield. 'You have my word. I will make sure it happens. And sooner.'

Sarsfield turned to Butler, who said, after a moment's hesitation: 'It may be the best solution.'

Sarsfield nodded, not entirely happy but grateful for a way out of the impasse.

'Draft a memo on this,' Ginckel ordered Clarke. 'Setting out what has happened, its accidental nature, and our agreed remedy. And I will send it to their Majesties with my strongest possible recommendation.'

The next morning it was the cavalry men's turn to make their decisions known. Before riding out of the King's Island, there were emotional scenes as men said goodbye to one another, men who had fought together for two years and more. Those who were going home assured those who were sailing to France that they'd be ready and willing to re-join them if needed when the King's army returned. Those who were about to switch sides were noticeable by their absence, especially Henry Luttrell and Robert Clifford. Half of the 4,000 cavalrymen were going home, accepting the pardons of the treaty and the guarantees of their lands. About a thousand were committed to going to France and the remainder were expected to join the Williamites.

The same procedure as the previous day was then acted out across the river, those going to France riding back across Thomond Bridge, those staying in Ireland or joining the enemy riding off to the left. Trumpeters sounded the order to move forward, then right wheel or left wheel as they came to the point of decision.

Luttrell rode by the reviewing generals, looking neither to the left or right, his trumpeter by his side. Sarsfield watched him go by with mixed feelings, remembering all the good times in each other's company, the battles they had come through unscathed, the scheming against Tyrconnell, Luttrell's delight in their little victories, and his role in burnishing Sarsfield's reputation. All gone now, their friendship another casualty of the war.

He heard the trumpeter sound Luttrell's unheard instruction to wheel left and Luttrell rode off to join the enemy.

Colonel Nicholas Purcell held Sarsfield's stare as he rode past, as if to remind him one last time that this was all his fault. His regiment wheeled left too and rode off to return to their homes. Clifford raised an ambiguous half-closed fist as he passed by, something between a challenge and a farewell. Sarsfield did not respond: this old friendship had been dead for a long time.

Ginckel was happy with the outcome, at least happier than on the previous day. 'He almost smiled there,' Talmash muttered out of the side of his mouth to Mackay as a large number of another regiment wheeled left in contravention of their trumpeter's order to wheel right. Mackay grunted in reply, undecided whether this was good or bad. Good that we won't have to fight them again somewhere else, bad that some of this kingdom's leading papists were staying in Ireland with their lands and religious rights guaranteed, a recipe for future trouble as far as he could see. And made him wonder what all the bloodshed had really achieved.

In the days that followed, the cavalry going to France rode off to Cork, led by Major General Dominic Sheldon, to board English ships. Back on King's Island, some infantrymen had second thoughts and sought to change their minds. Guards on Baal's and Thomond bridges were ordered to stop any deserters but those who were determined to go swam the Abbey river. Some who had gone to the other side had had second thoughts too and had returned. Both armies ignored the article of the military treaty that said deserters would be returned to the force they had left.

Ginckel continued to try to persuade men to change their minds and issued another proclamation offering amnesty to rapparees, volunteers or armed stragglers who gave themselves up to local justices. Württemberg came to him to say that his Danes were restless and wanted to go into winter quarters. Ginckel agreed and began to send other regiments back to established garrisons.

More queries about the terms were raised as people on both sides became better acquainted with them. 'What about the guarantee that our ships will be allowed to leave France after transporting papists there,' Mackay said to Ginckel, relaying a point that had been put to him by a colonel with a legalistic mind who had spotted the article requiring that the Jacobites provide hostages to ensure the ships' safe return. 'They haven't given us the hostages yet.'

Ginckel sighed and sought another meeting with Sarsfield, who agreed to give him a document promising that they would be allowed to leave or else he and Wauchope, his co-signatory, would present themselves as prisoners of war at Whitehall in London within three months.

Sarsfield himself was accosted by some landowners among the refugees leaving Limerick to return home who had heard about a missing clause. It will be all right, he assured them. Others wanted to know if their wives and children were included in the passage to France. Yes, Wauchope said, with more confidence than he felt.

'There could be a problem,' he told Sarsfield afterwards. 'There might not be enough room for everyone if they all turn up with extended families.'

'There are problems everywhere,' Sarsfield snapped back, fed up with the questions that came at him day after day. Men who wanted to change their minds. Men who wanted to know if their particular circumstance was covered by the terms. Would the fact that they had sought protection from the Dutchman in the past and then returned to the army be held against them? Did the terms cover prisoners as the Galway terms did? Would they get French or English pay rates in France? Why not invade Ireland rather than England the following year?

And then, Colonel O'Kelly shaking his head sadly at him, as if he was the village fool, saying: 'The missing clause. That's the way it's going to be. You can never trust them.' Implying, without saying, that he Sarsfield shouldn't have signed the treaty; that perhaps he was no better than Tyrconnell after all.

Everyone was restless. The King's Island had inadvertently turned into a prison camp, the absence of immediate purpose replaced with rumours and uncertainty about the future, creating an uneasy atmosphere that threatened to get worse as time went on and nothing happened.

Sarsfield just wanted this stage to be over, to complete the move to France as soon as possible and to get on with planning next year's campaign. 'I'm going to Cork,' Sarsfield announced to Wauchope a week

457

later. 'I'll take the first infantry battalions there and hurry developments along. You stay here for the moment.'

'And the French?'

'They can wait here too.' D'Usson and Tessé were still adamant that the French fleet would arrive. Rumours said they were already in Bantry Bay but they had heard such stories before and nothing had come of them.

'And if they don't arrive?'

'Then you can bring everyone else to Cork.'

'Including the French?' Wauchope asked with a grin.

'They can do what they like,' Sarsfield said. 'But they'll have no choice if they want to get back to France.'

Ginckel was preparing to leave Limerick for Dublin en route to England. Most of his army had already left the area for winter quarters in Kilkenny, Clonmel and Cork. The siege works had been dismantled. Irish Town was still being cleared of its rubble and the streets were beginning to take shape again.

'You will be in command,' he told Talmash. 'Take over English Town as soon as they leave.'

The Dutchman too was being pestered with questions and complaints about the treaty. 'What is this about a so-called 'missing clause'?' Coningsby wrote to him, demanding an explanation. Who is supposed to pay for the provisions for the papists' wives and children on our ships, the Admiralty wanted to know. Surely not us. Bad enough that we have to pay to transport their army abroad without having to pay for their offspring as well.

Ginckel and Sarsfield had a final meeting at which each recognised the other's impatience at all the complaints and uncertainties with which they were expected to deal. Neither gave voice to their frustrations.

Almost two weeks after the signing of the treaty, Sarsfield led the first infantry contingent to leave the King's Island across Baal's Bridge into Irish Town and up Broad Street to St John's Gate. They carried the

Jacobite banner declaring *Un Dieu Un Roi Une Foi* and regimental banners half-furled, parts of harps and legends visible. Drummers beat time and thin wisps of smoke rose from the lighted match of those who were armed. Williamites clearing the rubble stood back as they went by, some calling on the soldiers to stay after their officers had passed in the hope that Ginckel might pay them for any they persuaded. A few took the opportunity to change their minds about France, dodged into the ruins and were hurried away by their new friends anxious to claim a bounty.

Sarsfield kept his eyes to the fore, not looking up at the walls or the Citadel as they went by at a walking pace. Behind him and his party, the carriages of their ladies rumbled over the rough roadway, forced to circle around the remaining piles of rubble. A collection of unexploded mortars and used cannonballs was piled against the inner wall of a building whose outer wall no longer existed.

We'll be back, he thought with grim determination. And, God willing, we will not have to besiege these walls, but simply ride through the open gates after the usurper has been sent back to Holland.

Talmash and Mackay looked down in silence from the walls as the parade went by. 'The next time we'll see them will be through the smoke of another battlefield,' Mackay said in a surly tone. Nothing the general or anyone else had said to him had convinced him that this treaty was not a mistake, both unnecessary and unwise.

'Not me,' Talmash replied.

Mackay looked at him in surprise. 'What do you mean?'

'I'm giving up this life.'

'I don't believe you.' Mackay shook his head. How could someone with Talmash's love of action settle for any other life?

'What's the point?' Talmash said with a melodramatic air. 'You've heard about their Majesties' announcements?'

'The ennoblements,' Mackay nodded. Ginckel had been appointed Baron Aughrim and Earl of Athlone; Ruvigny Earl of Galway, the title previously held by Sarsfield's wife's family. Pointedly, after this latest round of honours, Mackay and Talmash were still the only generals in William and Mary's army in Ireland without titles.

'Bloody continentals,' Talmash muttered. 'Looking after themselves and one another. Only the British have been left out. Even you and you're half a Dutchman.'

The last of the infantry men passed through the gates, followed by supply and sutlers' wagons and then the camp followers, wives and children and among them the women whose yellow hair advertised their occupation.

'It's only proper the general should be recognised. But Monsieur Ruvigny?' Talmash added in an aggrieved tone, deliberately ignoring Ruvigny's old French title of marquis. 'What did either of them have to do with the victories at Athlone or Aughrim -- the real victories which led to this. And did Monsieur Ruvigny do anything at all at Galway that you can remember?'

Mackay avoided the invitation to grouse but it had not escaped his attention. He and Talmash might have expected some reward for their efforts during the campaign. But the King's distrust, even dislike, of Britons was no surprise to him: he had been aware of it for some time but he had bitten back his disappointment in favour of the greater cause of Protestanism.

'It makes you wonder if you're in the wrong army,' Talmash said.

'Don't be ridiculous. You're not going to join the papists.'

'Bastard son of the Lord Protector turns to Holy Father,' Talmash laughed, claiming Cromwell as his father once again. 'That would be a story to cheer the papists.'

Mackay scowled back at him. Such things were not a matter of amusement. The drumbeats of the marching men had faded away and the last of the camp followers made their way beneath the gates, their few belongings wrapped in shawls, their bare feet squelching in the churned-up ground at the gate.

'Ah, no,' Talmash sighed. 'I might just give it all up altogether. You're going home? To Scotland or Holland?'

'Holland,' Mackay said. That's where home was now. 'Tomorrow.'

Four days later the French fleet arrived, scattering the English ships in the estuary with ease, sinking one and capturing two of their frigates as it ignored the English protestations that the war was over. Admiral

460

Châteaurenault was too old to fall for that hoary old trick. He came up the river on one of his smaller vessels to find out for himself what was happening.

'Didn't I tell you so?' a beaming d'Usson said to Wauchope as they waited on the harbour wall for the ship to arrive with the high tide. The harbour mouth had been blocked by sunken boats during the siege to stop the English from coming in and it was still inaccessible. 'The King's word is as reliable as the gospel.'

Pity it hadn't been more timely, Wauchope thought but he said nothing, not wanting to upset d'Usson's delight.

The admiral was welcomed ashore by d'Usson and Tessé as if they were all old friends. 'So it is true,' the admiral said with a disappointed air. He would now have to hand back his captives. 'You have capitulated.'

D'Usson filled him in on what had happened as he led him and his party up the ruined city to King John's Castle. Wauchope spotted Simon Luttrell among the party, pleasantly surprised to see that he had returned, and he made his way over to him as they walked by the damaged cathedral, now missing its tower, and its roof holed by cannon shot and falling masonry.

'How long were you at sea?' Wauchope asked.

'Seven days,' Luttrell said, noting the inexpressive faces of the small groups of people who had gathered to watch the arrivals. They stood in silence, trying to determine what this meant. Would the French restart the war? Not exactly a warm welcome, Luttrell thought. Certainly not the welcome he had expected to receive. Or, presumably, would have received a few weeks earlier.

'You didn't know,' Wauchope calculated quickly, 'that we'd agreed terms ten days ago?'

There was no need to answer that. Clearly they didn't know, and, in any event. Luttrell's attention was now on the burned-out ruins of a row of small houses, their thatched roofs a mess of muck within blackened walls. A filthy child looked out with large eyes from a rough lean-to propped against one wall.

'Why the delay?' Wauchope asked. 'You were supposed to have left

461

Brest a month ago.'

'There was a lot of confusion,' Luttrell sighed. It had been a very frustrating month for him, trying to chivvy along various bureaucrats who had been engaged in their own obscure power struggles. 'It was difficult for the admiral to get clear orders from Paris. The ministers of war and the navy were arguing about things, which had nothing to do with us. Where is Sarsfield?'

'Gone to Cork. To organise the move to France.'

'And Henry?'

Wauchope coughed, not knowing where to start. 'You heard what happened?'

'That Tyrconnell tried to have him hanged on some spurious charge? Yes.'

Wauchope took a deep breath and told him the whole story. Luttrell made no comment as Wauchope concluded with his brother's decision to join the enemy. 'The terms include a provision for you and the other officers abroad to avail of them too, if you wish,' he added as an afterthought.

They had reached the castle by the time he had finished and everyone sat down to eat. After the preliminary pleasantries, they got down to business, deciding what to do now. Châteaurenault had 18 warships, four fire-ships and 20 merchant ships carrying food, money, ammunition and an assortment of other supplies for the army. Clearly they were not going to unload it and leave it to the enemy.

'At least,' the admiral said, 'we can bring it all back to France with many of your men.'

'How many can you take?' d'Usson asked.

Châteaurenault consulted one of his officers and then said, 'Perhaps five thousand. The King had been hoping to receive more recruits from Ireland under his agreement with the duke of Tyrconnell. So I had been told to make allowance to return with many men. But,' he added, 'His Majesty will not be happy about the capitulation. These are not the men he expected me to bring back.'

Wauchope, following the discussion in his less fluent French, noted d'Usson and Tessé exchanging nervous glances. This did not bode well

462

for their futures.

As the meal was concluding with glasses of brandy, an aide came to Wauchope with a message from Talmash, demanding an immediate meeting at his headquarters in the Citadel in Irish Town.

'May I come with you?' Luttrell asked.

Wauchope agreed, knowing why.

'Are we going to take back Irish Town now?' an aide holding his horse in the courtyard asked as Wauchope mounted.

Simon Luttrell listened for Wauchope's answer. But Wauchope did not reply. That was the question he expected Talmash, too, wanted answered. It would be very easy to take Irish Town, he thought. We have many more men than they do now and enough supplies to last the winter. We could force them out of Limerick with ease. He had dispatched a messenger to Cork to tell Sarsfield of the fleet's arrival and seek instructions. But he didn't expect any change of heart. Sarsfield was intent on going to France and continuing the war from there.

When they met in the Citadel, Talmash hid his fears about Irish intentions behind a screen of aggression. 'This is an outrageous breach of the terms by the French navy,' he said, striking the table with the flat of his hand. 'A most dishonourable action.'

'A misunderstanding,' Wauchope replied. 'Your frigates will be released.'

'And the ship that was sunk?' Talmash relaxed inwardly but maintained his aggressive tone. 'What about that? We will require compensation and suitable apologies.'

'You'll have to discuss that with the French.'

Talmash gave a harrumph and was about to protest that that was not satisfactory -- they had no direct dealings with the French. But he decided to let it go, relieved that the situation hadn't gone into reverse. 'What are your plans now?'

'To send as many of the infantry as possible away on the French ships. Your ships in the estuary could sail with them in convoy to Brest. Bring some more men away.'

That's a good idea, Talmash thought. Get as many of them as possible out of the King's Island and let me take over English Town and finish my

463

job here. 'I may have difficulty persuading Captain Cole of that after the unwarranted French attack on his vessels. But I'll do my best.'

'And you'll stop trying to bribe our men into joining you?' Wauchope added.

'We don't bribe anybody,' Talmash sniffed, as if that was an insult to his senses, 'but if men want to change their minds ---.'

'Then the terms require that they be returned.'

'Of course.' Talmash smiled with patent insincerity.

As the meeting ended, Luttrell asked to see his brother.

'Certainly,' Talmash said. 'I'll take you back to his camp myself. Colonel Luttrell is a great addition to our officer corps. Very popular with everyone.'

It was left to Wauchope to arrange the departure of as many men as possible on board the French and English ships. D'Usson, Tessé and all their officers left the city as soon as they could to take up cabins on the French ships and co-ordinate their reports for their masters in Paris on why the Irish had capitulated and upset the King's desire to keep the prince of Orange's army occupied in Ireland for another year. It was left to Wauchope to negotiate with Admiral Châteaurenault and an English naval officer about the number they could take to France. They set a limit of some six thousand between the two fleets, about two-thirds of the men still on the King's Island.

A major problem soon manifested itself: the men's relatives. More and more of them were arriving as word of the cessation of hostilities and rumours of the terms spread throughout the countryside. Families who had heard nothing from their fighting sons or fathers for a year or more turned up, fleeing destitution at home, in the hope of finding them and maybe travelling abroad together. Some found them, many didn't and had to assume that their menfolk were among the unburied at Aughrim or in mass graves elsewhere or, if they were still optimistic, fighting somewhere alongside rapparees.

'We're supposed to be transporting an army, not a rabble,' Châteaurenault complained at one of Wauchope's many meetings with him.

'The terms allow the men to bring their families,' Wauchope pointed out.

'They're not my terms.'

'They were signed by your generals.'

Châteaurenault gave him an expressive Gallic shrug. Neither the terms nor the generals were his concern. He hadn't agreed the terms and the French generals who had signed them, prematurely in his opinion, would have to answer for that in Paris in due course.

Wauchope gave up, realizing that the problem was being left to him to resolve. The terms had not defined what a family was, so men were insisting that parents, siblings and other relatives should be allowed travel with them. Some were trying to include women who were not properly related to them at all.

Wauchope settled on a figure and ordered the remaining battalions to march to Cork to join Sarsfield and the English fleet. Then the process began of loading the remainder onto the ships in Limerick. They had to be transported from the harbour wall by the smaller ships to the main fleet moored off Scattery Island near the mouth of the Shannon estuary. He ordered that the men be embarked first, anxious to get them committed to the journey as the English made another flurry of attempts to dissuade them from going.

The procedures went smoothly at first but panic began to set in as the ships in the estuary filled up. Crowds of women and children tried to push their way onto the harbour wall, fearing that they would be left behind as rumours spread that the last ships were leaving. Soldiers were ordered to hold them back but they too got caught up in the panic, dashing for the ships themselves.

On the bridge of one of the last two ships to leave, Wauchope closed his eyes against the unfolding horror as his plans disintegrated into chaos. Women left behind were screaming and wailing, children crying, old people on their knees pleading or praying. Some women and boys clung to the sides of the vessel and to its mooring ropes as it eased away from the wall and the wind grabbed its sails. A few were hauled on board. Impatient sailors prised the fingers of others from the sides of the ship and they dropped into the water.

465

Soon the only sign of them was the billowing of their heavy clothes on the ebbing tide, bearing their drowned bodies slowly seaward in the wake of the already distant ships.

Sarsfield heard about the disaster at Limerick a couple of days later when a messenger from Wauchope reached him in Cork. Paradoxically the news helped him with Count Nassau, the prince of Orange's cousin, who had been haggling for days over the numbers of relatives that would be allowed onto the English ships. Even the Williamites appeared to be shocked by what had happened: there were no more arguments about the numbers travelling. Both sides were weary of the verbal wrangling and anxious to get the move to France over with.

Back in Limerick, Talmash occupied English Town and the King's Island, completing the takeover of the last enemy stronghold in Ireland. The drownings had prompted last-minute changes of heart, men going over to the other side, mostly to return home, sick and tired of the death and destruction. Could the peace be any worse than the war?

The first infantry battalions that Sarsfield led to Cork had also lost hundreds of men along the way as soldiers changed their minds and disappeared into the countryside. But they were more or less replaced in the ranks by rapparees and deserters, some of them scattered since Aughrim.

Simon Luttrell turned up in Cork, to Sarsfield's surprise. He had heard that Luttrell had returned on the French fleet but nobody had told him that he was coming to Cork.

'I spoke to Henry,' Luttrell said.

Sarsfield looked at him in expectation, knowing he had more to say. They were standing on the quayside as men and their families were boarding one of the English frigates in an orderly manner. Nassau and some of his officers stood a little farther off, observing the embarkation. It was a grey day, the cloud pressing down on the hills behind them, the damp cold penetrating uniforms as a foretaste of more to come. Thin ice coated the puddles among the rough stones underfoot.

'He blames you,' Luttrell said.

'For his traitorous act in joining the enemy?'

466

'For leaving him no choice,' Luttrell sighed. 'For siding with Tyrconnell against him, falling into an enemy trap, allowing him to be dragged in front of a court martial.'

'I was the one without a choice after what he did.'

'Was it so bad -- asking a question of an enemy officer?'

'You don't think so?'

'You know Henry,' Luttrell said, side-stepping the question. 'He'll talk to anybody. Negotiate with anyone.'

'But he didn't tell me about it beforehand, nor afterwards. He told no one. He was treating with the enemy on his own behalf. I had to distance myself from him, lest anyone think he was acting on my behalf and that I was seeking terms.'

Luttrell forbore from pointing out that that was in fact what Sarsfield had done; that Henry Luttrell had simply been a few steps ahead of him and not for the first time. Simon could see both sides of it, caught in the middle between the needs of the cause and brotherly solidarity. 'You know Henry,' he repeated. 'He's headstrong.'

'That he is.'

'He said to tell you that he'll be ready to re-join the colours when you return.'

Sarsfield gave a non-committal grunt. He didn't believe it and, even if it was true, he no longer wanted Henry Luttrell on his side.

The last of the women had gone on board and the gangplank was slid onto the deck after them. The mooring ropes were loosened and the sails unfurled, flapping in the listless breeze until they were hauled into position and set.

'And you?' Sarsfield asked. 'What have you decided?'

'I'm coming with you,' Luttrell said, affronted. 'Did you doubt that?'

'Of course not,' Sarsfield lied. He wasn't sure whom to trust any more. He shivered in the chill air, bone-weary of it all.

DECEMBER

Sarsfield

It was three days before Christmas. People could scarcely remember when they had last seen the sun. The year's shortest days were darkened further into a gloomy half-light by the angry clouds which sped across the sky, driven by a cold north-westerly wind that sent stinging showers of hard rain and sleet ahead of it.

Patrick Sarsfield stood beside the English helmsman on the bridge as the ship cleared the harbour. He was wrapped up well but the cold still seeped through his coats and made him shiver. Honor was in their cabin, feeling queasy long before the full force of the Atlantic would hit. Behind them the last convoy for France was strung out in a long line and the land disappeared quickly into the gloom.

He didn't look back. There was no need to. This was just another stage in the war. Getting into position for next year's campaign. He would be back in Ireland soon enough. And back doing what he did best. Fighting.

The ship rose and fell as the full force of the Atlantic's long swells raised it and then dropped it into the troughs, the wind bulging its sails and driving it faster and faster towards the future as it cleared the shelter of the land.

AFTERMATH

The war went on for another six years on the Continent, killing five of the generals mentioned here among countless thousands of others.

Hugh Mackay was the first to die, killed at Steenkirk in August 1692 trying to stop a French cavalry advance whose members included *maréchal de camp* Patrick Sarsfield. Sarsfield himself was shot in the chest the following year at the battle of Landen (29 July 1693) and died days later at the nearby town of Huy. Three months afterwards, John Wauchope was killed at the battle of Marsaglia near Turin: he and fellow Scot Thomas Maxwell (whose loyalty had been wrongly called into question after the fall of Athlone) were shot dead at the head of Irish soldiers fighting for France against Savoy. Thomas Talmash fought at Steenkirk and Landen and died from a wound received when leading a disastrous English attack on Brest in June 1694.

Godard de Ginckel also fought at Steenkirk and Landen where he almost drowned. He and Sarsfield were still corresponding with each other after Steenkirk: Ginckel sent him a gift of two horses and Sarsfield offered Honor's services to send Ginckel's wife and daughters anything they wished from Paris.

The Marquis de Ruvigny was wounded slightly at Landen and captured by the French but apparently persuaded them to let him go because he was French too. Both he and Ginckel received from King

William large estates in Ireland which were later taken back from them by the English parliament but not before Ruvigny had settled many Huguenots in the Portarlington area. Both men survived their many wars: Ginckel died at home in Utrecht and Ruvigny in retirement in England.

Also captured at Landen was the Duke of Berwick, James FitzJames, the eldest of King James II's five children with his mistress Arabella Churchill and a friend and close associate of Sarsfield in Ireland in 1690. He married Sarsfield's widow, Honor, in 1695 and became stepfather to Sarsfield's then two-year-old son, James Francis Edward (named after King James's heir). The couple had another son, also named James Francis, and Honor died of tuberculosis in Languedoc in 1698 in her twenty-fourth year. Sarsfield's son served in the French and Spanish armies and died aged twenty-six at St Omer.

The two senior French generals in Ireland at the end of 1691 held their ranks and continued their careers in the French army but both died of disease, the Chevalier de Tessé of dysentery in Cremona in 1701, the Marquis d'Usson of pneumonia in Marseilles in 1705.

Colonel Charles O'Kelly retired to his estate near Aughrim and wrote, in Latin, one of the contemporary accounts of the war in Ireland, *Macariæ Excidium* (The Destruction of Cyprus) as an allegorical tale, giving Greek pseudonyms to the participants.

Henry Luttrell has gone down in Irish history as a traitor, blamed for the defeat at Aughrim although he was not held to account for it at the time and whatever blame existed also attached to his commander Dominic Sheldon. (Sheldon appears to have been exempted from blame at Aughrim and subsequently at Limerick because he went to France with Sarsfield.) Luttrell and his regiment were never used by the Williamite army but he received a pension of £500 a year. He kept his older brother's lands at Lutrellstown, initially refusing Simon's widow a share in them after her return from France. He was shot dead in Stafford Street, now Wolfe Tone Street, Dublin in 1717, aged sixty-three. His killer, variously rumoured to be a survivor of Aughrim, an irate husband, a distant relative with an eye on Luttrell's property, or someone hired by his mistress, was never caught.

In May 1692 King James's army of some 20,000 men -- those who had come from Ireland augmented by 7,000 French troops and artillery, all under the command of a French general -- gathered on the Contentin peninsula in Normandy for the invasion of England. Ready to board 300 ships, their French naval escort, still awaiting reinforcements from the Mediterranean, tried to clear a superior Anglo-Dutch fleet from the English Channel but was routed off La Hougue. The invasion plan was abandoned and the Jacobite forces from Limerick were absorbed into the French army. They became *les brigades irlandais* and existed as a separate unit for a century until they were disbanded during the French Revolution because of their royalist sympathies.

The Stuart cause rumbled on for more than 50 years until eventually it was extinguished by the defeat of James's grandson, Bonny Prince Charlie, at Culloden in 1746.

Back in Ireland, the Treaty of Limerick was abrogated in 1697 by the newly established all-Protestant Irish parliament, most of whom bitterly opposed the terms relating to Catholic rights to lands and religion. Many of those covered by the treaty's terms did manage to hold on to their lands but had to spend years in litigation and appeals. The steady introduction of draconian anti-Catholic penal laws gathered pace after the Treaty of Ryswick ended the Nine Years' War the same year, forcing descendants of those who had successfully used the treaty terms to switch to the established church to hold on to their inheritances.

The battle of Aughrim may not have left the 'noise in history' that the Williamite chronicler of the war in Ireland, the Reverend George Story, had in mind but its reverberations are still with us today.

ACKNOWLEDGEMENTS

I am deeply indebted to several people for their invaluable help in writing this novel. My friend Colman Morrissey, who has had a lifelong interest in the battle of Aughrim, encouraged me to tackle the subject as a novel. He allowed me access to his collection of contemporary works on the battle which is now under the stewardship of John Cox in the library of NUI Galway. Dr Padraig Lenihan of the history department in NUIG and author of the biography of the Duke of Tyrconnell, *The Last Cavalier*, answered innumerable questions and made many invaluable suggestions on the first draft, as did Piers Wauchope QC, a descendant of General John Wauchope and author of *Patrick Sarsfield and the Williamite War*. Dr Harman Murtagh, the president of the Military History Society of Ireland and an authority on the period, was also generous with his help about the siege of Athlone. Their assistance should not be taken to imply that they agree with all my interpretation of events. Mistakes are all mine, mitigated by the eagle-eyed proof reading and other astute editorial suggestions of Jonathan Williams.